About the Authors

__ordon loves to write about the fascinating ____ n of medicine and romance from her home ___re village. She is active in local affairs and __lled upon to write the script for the annual __tomime! Her eldest son is a hospital manager ___ with all her medical research. As part of a ___ family she treasures having two of her sons __se by, and the third one not too far away. This __ her the added pleasure of being able to watch __htful grandchildren growing up.

__inning author **Karen Rose Smith** lives in __ania and has sold over eighty novels since __r romances have made both the *USA Today* list __ Amazon Contemporary Romance Bestseller __eving in the power of love, she envisions __riting relationship novels and mysteries for __me to come! Readers can e-mail Karen at __enrosesmith.com or follow her on Twitter __sesmith and on Facebook.

__Thayer was born in Muncie, Indiana, the __' eight children. She attended Ball State __ before heading to California. A longtime ____ RWA, Patricia has authored fifty books. She ____ ominated for the Prestige RITA™ award and ___ of the RT Reviewer's Choice award. She loves travelling with her husband, Steve, calling it research. When she wants some time with her guy, they escape to their mountain cabin and sit on the deck and let the world

A Christmas Wedding

ABIGAIL GORDON

KAREN ROSE SMITH

PATRICIA THAYER

MILLS & BOON

First Published in Great Britain 2020
By Mills & Boon, an imprint of HarperCollins*Publishers*
1 London Bridge Street, London, SE1 9GF

A CHRISTMAS WEDDING © 2020 Harlequin Books S.A.

Swallowbrook's Winter Bride © 2011 Abigail Gordon
Once Upon a Groom © 2011 Karen Rose Smith
Proposal at the Lazy S Ranch © 2013 Patricia Wright

ISBN: 978-0-263-29837-6

SWALLOWBROOK'S WINTER BRIDE

ABIGAIL GORDON

For my nephew Shaun Murray and his son
Andrew, far away from me in Texas

CHAPTER ONE

SPENDING two weeks in Spain with her best friend had
been great, but as Libby Hamilton drove the last couple
of miles to Swallowbrook village, nestling in a lakeland
valley below the rugged beauty of the fells, she was
happy to be back where she belonged.

A month ago, on what was not as frequent an occasion as she would like it to be, she had met up with
Melissa Lombard for lunch in Manchester, and on seeing how pale and tired Libby looked, the only person
she'd ever told what a mistake her tragically brief marriage had been had said, 'I'm going to our villa in Spain
for a couple of weeks. That husband of mine can't go
with me. There is a big audit due at the office and he's
in charge. So why don't you join me, Libby? It would
be lovely if you could.'

She'd hesitated and Melissa had said coax-
ingly, 'Surely they can manage without you at the
Swallowbrook practice for once, and if they can't, they
can get a temp. I'm no doctor but I think I can safely
prescribe two weeks of lazing in the sun to bring some
colour back to your cheeks.'

'It would be a change, I suppose,' Libby had agreed

wistfully. 'I haven't had any time off since Ian had the dreadful accident. It's as if I haven't been able to stop and think since the funeral. I guess I've been using work as an excuse these past few months.'

Melissa had nodded gravely and gone on to say sympathetically, 'So what better reason for joining me could there be than having spent months of hard graft without a break?'

Libby had smiled at her across the table and told her friend, 'You have just talked me into two weeks in Spain, Mel, but not a moment longer. Our senior partner, John Gallagher, retires at the end of the month and I've taken over as senior partner. He has virtually given up already, but I know if I ask him he'll take up the reins again for two more weeks while I have a break.'

Driving back now, alongside the fells beneath a harvest moon, she was feeling much more like her old self after a healthy dose of sun, sea and a complete rest. Yet as was always the case on the rare occasions she was absent from the practice, coming back to Swallowbrook and her cottage across the way from the surgery was heart-warming, and today was no exception.

The practice building had once been her childhood home. In those days it had been a farmhouse, but in her late teens it had been put up for sale due to her father's neglect of it after her mother had died, and it was now the village medical centre in the middle of the lakeside beauty spot.

When the lease had run out on the old practice premises and somewhere else had needed to be found, the spacious farm building had been an ideal choice. The outside of it was mostly unchanged, but the inside had been modernised and now provided health care for the hardy folk of Swallowbrook and the surrounding areas.

When the transfer had been made six years ago John Gallagher had been senior partner, with his son Nathan, also a doctor, working alongside him, and two years later Libby, who had gone straight into general practice after receiving her doctor's degree, had joined them as the third and youngest member of the trio.

But it had turned out that one of them had itchy feet, and where she had been content to stay in the place she loved best, Nathan Gallagher had other ideas in mind. He was three years older than her and she'd worshipped the dark-haired, dark-eyed, dynamic doctor since her early teens, but in those days she'd been just a kid with a brace on her teeth as far as he was concerned.

Though she'd never admit it to him, one of the reasons she'd joined the practice had been so that she could be near him, and another had been because the building had once been her home, and to be as close to it as she could she'd bought an empty farm cottage across the way.

When she'd joined the practice Nathan had seen that the girl who had always been hovering while they had been growing up had become a slender blonde with eyes like brown velvet and the warmest smile he'd ever seen. They'd shared a brief flirtation but he was aware that Libby had long since had a crush on him and didn't want to lead her on.

And besides he'd had his hands full with a fiancée who had been pushing hard for a gold band to go beside the solitaire diamond on her finger and he had begun to feel that the engagement had been a mistake because he hadn't been as keen on the idea as she had been.

When he'd informed Libby that he was leaving the practice to go and work abroad she'd been devastated. 'The engagement is off,' he'd told her, and it would have been news she had been happy to hear if it hadn't been followed by, 'So I'm free to work in Africa, which is something I've always wanted to do. I've agreed to take up a position in a hospital in a small town out there where doctors are needed urgently.'

'How long will you be gone?' she'd asked with the colour draining from her face.

'As long as it takes, I suppose, but my contract is for three years.'

He'd noted the effect that the news of his departure had had on her. 'Why don't you come along?' he'd suggested casually. 'There's always room for one more doctor out there.'

'No, thanks,' she'd replied hastily before she did some crazy thing like letting her longing to be wherever he was take over, and had gone on to say, 'It wouldn't be fair to your father, two of us gone from the practice at the same time, and *my* father is still around, don't forget, forever sick and remorseful at having to sell the farm. Also it has always been *my* dream to practise medicine in the place that was once my home. I feel I owe it to our community.'

She was almost home. As Libby took the next bend in the road it was there, Swallowbrook, beautiful in the moonlight, a familiar cluster of houses built out of lake-land stone, and outside The Mallard, the local pub, there was the usual gathering of fell walkers and locals seated on wooden benches, drinking the local brew.

Down a side turning not far away was Swallowbrook Medical Practice and across the way from it Lavender Cottage, where recently she'd spent far too many lonely nights at the end of long busy days.

The cottage was semi-detached. The property next to it had been on the market for quite some time and as she turned onto her drive she was surprised to see a van belonging to one of the big furniture stores in the nearby town pulling away from in front of it.

Her eyes widened. It was almost ten o'clock, deliveries weren't usually made so late in the evening. It seemed from the number of lights blazing out into the night from the cottage next door that she was to be blessed, or otherwise, with new neighbours.

But she had other things to think about besides that, such as the longing to be back in her own bed after a quick cup of tea. The flight home hadn't taken long, but the airport procedures at the UK end had been slow and then there had been a thirty-miles-plus drive home after she'd collected her car from where it had been stored while she had been away, so now she was ready to flake out.

She hoped that the people who had moved into next door would be sociable and easy to get on with. Yet wasn't she the last person who should be concerned about socialising? She could barely remember what it was like to enjoy herself in the company of others.

After losing Ian in a fatal riding accident, a luke-warm marriage had come to an end, and since then the practice had been the only thing in her life that she could rely on for comfort and stability. As long as the new neighbours didn't intrude into that she supposed she would cope.

The surgery had been in darkness when she looked across, which was hardly surprising in the late evening, and as it was Friday would be closed all over the week-end. But as the head of the practice she would need to be there bright and early on Monday morning. Maybe during the weekend she would get the chance to meet the newcomers, but the main thing on her mind at the moment was sleep.

After the cup of tea that she'd been longing for on the last part of the journey home Libby climbed the stairs to her bedroom beneath the eaves and in moments was under the covers and ready to drift into oblivion when someone down below rang the doorbell.

She groaned softly but didn't move. When it rang a second time she slipped a robe over her nightdress and went quickly downstairs. Before opening the door she peered into the porch and with the moon's light filter-ing in saw the broad-shouldered outline of a man and beside him was a small child dressed in pyjamas.

It all looked innocent enough, she decided. The two of them must be part of the family who'd moved in next door, and without any further delay she unlocked the door.

'Hello, Libby,' Nathan Gallagher said easily, as if it had only been yesterday that she'd last seen him. 'We saw your car pull up a while ago and had no intention of disturbing you, but Toby needs his bedtime drink of milk, won't settle without it, and it's the one thing I've overlooked in the provisions I bought in the store this afternoon. I noticed you had a couple of pints that someone had delivered and wonder if you could spare one?'

She could feel her legs caving in at the shock of seeing him there.

'Come in,' she croaked, opening the door wide, and as they stepped inside she added, 'I'll get you one from the fridge.' With her glance on the tousle-haired small boy at his side she paused in the doorway of the kitchen. 'So it's you and your family who have moved into next door? You found yourself a wife while in Africa? It seems strange that your father never mentioned a thing!'

'Not exactly,' he said with a wry smile, and she wondered what that meant. Maybe the child's mother was a partner rather than a wife and she'd been rather quick to be asking those kinds of questions in any case.

Obviously Nathan hadn't come for a cosy chat about what he'd been doing during the last few years. Taking a pint of milk out of the fridge, she handed it to him and came up with a question of a more basic kind.

'Are your beds made up? Tell your little boy's mother I can lend you some bedding if you haven't had time to get them sorted.'

'Thanks, but everything is fine,' was the reply. 'We've been here since early this morning. As soon as Toby has had his milk he will be settling down for sleep in a small single bed next to mine. It's been a long day so I don't think either of us will need much rocking.'

'How long have you been back in the UK?' she asked as he was about to depart with the little boy clutching his hand tightly.

'A month. We've been in London until now on business, but I was anxious to get away from the crowds. I want Toby to grow up in Swallowbrook like we did, and the vacant cottage next door to yours seemed to be the perfect answer.'

Answer to what? she wondered. Whatever it was it wouldn't be anything to do with her. He'd asked her to go out to Africa with him all that time ago because they were short of doctors, not because he'd wanted her near, and at the time she'd come up with a few reasons for refusing.

It was like a knife in her heart seeing him with his small son. It meant that he'd found someone that he *did* want, while she'd been letting common sense fly out of the window by agreeing to marry Ian, whose interests had revolved around his horses and pleasure, and seen her career as a hindrance to his lifestyle, instead of giving it meaning.

With no wish to remind herself of how all that had ended she switched her thoughts to the mother of the child and wondered where she was. She probably had other things to do, having just moved into next door, and curious though she might be, there was no way she was going to ask Nathan why the sleeping arrangements he'd described didn't sound as if Toby's mother was included in them.

When Libby went back upstairs to bed the feeling of tiredness had been replaced by bleak amazement as she recalled those incredible moments with Nathan and the silent child. Wide-eyed and disbelieving, her gaze was fixed on the dividing wall between the two properties.

He would be sleeping at the other side of it, she thought. Just a short time ago she'd seen him in the flesh, heard him speak, watched him smile a strange smile when she'd asked him if he had married while out in Africa.

He'd said, 'Not exactly,' and she cringed at her unseemly haste in asking the question only seconds after he'd appeared at her door. It would have been the last thing she would have come up with if he hadn't had the boy with him.

Had his father known for the last month that he was back in England and not told her? If that *was* the case, it would have been on Nathan's instructions. John would never do anything like that to her.

Tomorrow she would have to prepare herself for meeting the little boy's mother with pleasantness and a warm welcome to Swallowbrook, while hoping that she would be able to hide her true feelings, and with those kinds of thoughts to cope with she got up and put the kettle on for a second time.

Behind the dividing wall Nathan was not asleep but Toby was, curled up and content after having drunk some of the milk that Libby had provided. As the man looked down at the child the stresses and strains, the sorrow and confusion of past months seemed less dreadful because he was back home in Swallowbrook once more.

The last time he'd seen Libby Hamilton had also been from the shelter of a porch, but not the one next door. It had been in the shadowed stone porch of the village church after he'd flung himself out of the taxi that had brought him from the airport, hoping that he might get the chance to speak to her before she became the wife of Ian Jefferson.

He'd needed to know if it was because of his leaving that she was marrying the pleasure-loving owner of the local stables…on the rebound. Or if the feelings that she'd said she had for himself had been just a passing attraction that she'd soon moved on from and there was no longer any need for him to carry the burden of guilt that his leaving her had created.

A delayed flight had denied him the chance to clear the air between them and he'd arrived at the church just as the vicar had pronounced them man and wife. As he'd watched Libby smile up at her new husband he'd turned and departed as quickly as he'd come, deciding in that moment he had his answer. Her feelings for him *had* been a passing fancy and a prize fool he would have appeared if anyone had seen him hovering in the church porch for a glimpse of her.

When he'd reached the lych gate in the churchyard a bus had pulled up beside him on the pavement and he'd boarded it, uncaring where it was bound in his haste to get away before he was seen.

As he'd waited for a flight to take him back to where he'd come from he'd thought sombrely that his

arrogance all that time ago when in her despair at the
thought of him going away Libby had confessed her
love for him and been told he wasn't interested, had
only been exceeded by him expecting her to want to
talk to him of all people on her wedding day.

She had turned up at the airport on the morning he
had left for Africa and been the only one there. He'd
said his farewells to his father the night before and told
everyone else he didn't want any send-offs, so it had
been a surprise, and he'd had to admit a pleasant one,
to see her there.

They had been due to call his flight any time and during those last few moments in the UK Libby had begged
him not to go. 'I love you, Nathan,' she'd pleaded. 'I always have. Until I awoke this morning I had accepted
that you were going out of my life. Then suddenly I
knew I had to see you just one more time.

'I know the importance of the work you are going to
do in Africa, but there would still be time for that when
we'd had *our* time, some life together in happiness and
contentment and maybe brought up a family.'

She had chosen the most inopportune moment to
make her plea, with only minutes to spare before he
boarded the plane, *and* with the memory tugging at him
of a failed engagement not so long ago that had done
neither he nor his fiancée any credit.

There had been tears in her eyes but instead of making him want to comfort her he'd reacted in the opposite way and been brusque and offhand as he'd told her,
'How can you face me with something like this at such
a time, Libby? I'm due to leave in a matter of minutes.

Just forget me. Don't wait around. Relationships aren't on my agenda at present.'

Then, ashamed of his churlishness, he'd bent to give her a peck on the cheek. Instead their lips had met and within seconds it had all changed.

He'd been kissing her as if he'd just walked into light out of darkness and it would have gone on for ever if a voice hadn't been announcing that his flight was ready for boarding.

As common sense had returned he'd said it again. 'Don't wait around for me, Libby.' And almost before he'd finished speaking she'd been rushing towards the exit as if she couldn't get away from him fast enough.

Aware that his behaviour had left a lot to be desired, and cursing himself for trampling on what was left of her schoolgirl crush, he'd vowed that he would phone her when he arrived at his destination and apologise for his flippancy, but in the chaos he'd found when he'd got there his private life had become non-existent, until he'd received his father's phone call some months later to say Libby was getting married on the coming Saturday.

Then it had all come flooding back—her tears, the loveliness of her, and his own arrogance in brushing to one side her feelings for him by telling her not to wait for him, indicating in the most presumptuous way that *he* wasn't interested in *her*.

But, of course, by then it had been too late. How could he ever forget how happy she had looked when the vicar had made his pronouncement to say Libby and Ian were man and wife? And he'd thought how wrong he'd been in considering that she might be marrying Jefferson on the rebound.

Now, as he looked down at Toby, young and defenceless beneath the covers, he knew that there would be barriers to break down in coming months and bridges to build, not just in one part of his life but in the whole structure of it, because his contract in Africa was up. He was home for good, and coming back to Swallowbrook was his first step towards normality.

He'd done nothing when he'd heard that Jefferson had died. To have appeared on the scene then might have seemed like he'd been waiting in the wings and it would not have been the case. But now he'd had no choice but to come back to England because his best friend and his wife had been amongst tourists drowned on a sinking ferry somewhere abroad. The tragedy had changed his life and that of the sleeping child for ever.

As she sat hunched over the teapot Libby was thinking what a mess her life had turned into in the three years since she'd last laid eyes on Nathan. Anxious to prove to the world, but most importantly to herself, that her feelings for him were dead and buried she'd turned to Ian Jefferson, someone who had already asked her to marry him twice and been politely refused.

And so six months later, with Nathan's never-to-be-forgotten comments at the airport still painfully remembered, she'd agreed to marry Ian at his third time of asking.

They'd been reasonably happy at first, living in Lavender Cottage, across from the surgery, but as the months had gone by she had discovered that Ian had merely wanted a wife, any wife, to give him standing in the village, and the blonde doctor from the practice had been his first choice.

Marriage hadn't made him any less keen on spending endless hours on the golf course, sailing on the lake by Swallowbrook and, while his staff looked after the stables, riding around the countryside on various of his horses, which had left him with little time to comprehend the burden of care that Libby carried with her position at the practice, a position that left her with little time or energy to share in his constant round of pleasure.

It had been one night whilst out riding that he had been thrown from a frisky mare and suffered serious injuries that had proved fatal, leaving her to face another gap in her life that was sad and traumatic, but not as heartbreaking as being separated from Nathan.

When she'd drunk the teapot dry Libby went to bed for the second time and after tossing and turning for most of the night drifted into sleep as dawn was breaking over the fells. She was brought into wakefulness a short time later by voices down below at the bottom of the drive and when she went to the window the dairy farmer who delivered her milk was chatting to Nathan, who, judging from the amount of milk he was buying off him, was making sure that he and Toby would not have to go begging for his bedtime drink again.

Not wanting to be seen watching him, she went slowly back to bed, grateful that it was Saturday with no need to get up if she didn't want to, and as a pale sun filtered into her bedroom she began to go over the astonishing events of the previous night.

Nathan is back in Swallowbrook, a voice in her mind was saying, *but not because of you. He has a family. He has made his choice and it has to be better than the one you made.*

She surfaced at lunchtime in a calmer state of mind and, dressed in slacks and a smart sweater, went to the village for food and various other things she needed from the shops after being away.

There had been no sign of anyone from next door when she'd set off, but Nathan's car had still been in front of the cottage, so either they were inside out of sight or had ventured out for the boy to see where they had come to live, and the man to reacquaint himself with the place where he had been brought up amongst people who had been his patients and friends.

To make her way home she had to pass the park next to the school that strangely for a Saturday was empty, except for Nathan and the boy, who was moving from one amusement to another in the children's play area.

Don't stop, she told herself. *Nathan has had all morning to see you again if he wanted to, so don't give him the satisfaction of thinking you've followed him here.*

The two of them looked lonely and lost in the deserted park. He was pushing Toby on one of the swings, but on seeing her passing lifted him off. Now they were coming towards her and she was getting a better look at the prodigal doctor than in her mesmerised state the night before.

His time in Africa had taken its toll of him, she ob-

served as he drew nearer. He was leaner, giving off less
of the dynamism that had so attracted her to him over
the years, but his hair was the same, the dark thatch of
it curling above his ears, and his eyes were still the un-
readable dark hazel that they'd always been where she
was concerned.

'I can't believe you were going to go past without
speaking,' he said as they drew level.

'Why?' she asked steadily. 'What is there to say?'

'On my part that I was sorry to hear of Jefferson's
fatal accident, and for another—'

He was interrupted by the child at his side tugging
at his hand and saying, 'Can I go on the slide, Uncle
Nathan?'

'Yes, go along,' he replied. 'I'll be with you in a
moment.' As Libby observed him in a daze of non-
comprehension he explained, 'I'm in the process of
adopting Toby. Both his parents are dead. They were
lost when a ferry sank while they were touring Europe.
Thankfully he was saved. His father was my best friend
and I am the boy's godfather.

'I went out to bring him home when it happened and
applied to adopt him as there were no other relatives
to lay claim to him. The paperwork is going through at
the moment and soon he will be legally mine.'

'How do you cope?' she asked as the heartache of
thinking that Nathan had a family of his own began to
recede.

'It was difficult in the beginning because although
Toby knew me well enough, naturally it was his mummy

and daddy he wanted. He is adjusting slowly to the situation, yet is loath to ever let me out of his sight.'

Poor little one, she thought, poor godfather...*poor me. How am I going to cope having Nathan living next door to me with the memory of what he said that day at the airport still crystal clear? He has never been back to Swallowbrook since and now, as if he hadn't hurt me enough then, he has chosen to live in the cottage next to mine.*

He was observing her questioningly in the silence that her thoughts had created, and keen to escape the scrutiny of his stare she asked, 'How old is Toby?'

'He's just five, and the ferry catastrophe occurred three months ago. You might have read about it in the press or seen an account of it on television.'

That was unlikely, she thought wryly. In the mornings it was a quick breakfast, then across the way to the practice, and in the evenings the day's events had to be assimilated and paperwork brought up to date.

'What will you do now that you're here?' she asked, trying to sound normal. 'Enrol Toby at the village school?'

'I've already done so and am not sure how he is going to react to yet another change in his life. I have to tread softly with his young mind. He soon gets upset, which is to be expected, of course.'

She felt tears prick. It was all so sad that Nathan had been forced to take on such a responsibility *and* felt he had to return to Swallowbrook for the child's sake if nothing else.

As they went to wait for Toby at the bottom of a

small slide the man by her side was smiling, which was strange, as given what he had just told her he hadn't got a lot to smile about.

CHAPTER TWO

IT WAS a lot to take in. Only yesterday she had been flying home from two refreshing weeks in Spain with Melissa. Today she was in the park with Nathan and a child that he was adopting, and though she felt great sympathy for their loss she couldn't help but feel relieved that Nathan hadn't found himself a ready-made wife and family during his time in Africa.

If she had known he was coming back to Swallowbrook in the near future she would have had time to prepare herself for meeting up again with the man who had made it so painfully clear on parting that he didn't return her feelings. But instead it was as if she'd been thrown in at the deep end.

She was bending to pick up the bag with her food shopping inside when he forestalled her by saying easily, 'I'll take that,' and to Toby, who was coming down the slide for the umpteenth time, 'Time to go, Tobias.'

When the little one had joined them they walked back to their respective properties in silence. As they were about to separate Libby asked, 'Have you been to see your father?'

He nodded. 'Yes, we went to see him yesterday in a gap between deliveries of furniture and other household goods, and before you came back from wherever you'd been.'

'I'd been to Spain for a fortnight with a friend for a much-needed break,' she said coolly, 'and hope to be on top form at the practice on Monday.'

'Ah, yes,' he said vaguely, as if he had only a faint recollection of the place. 'Dad told me he plans to hand the practice over to you.'

'Yes. I'm delighted to have his trust. I think I love that place almost as much as he does. I couldn't bear to see it close down with his retirement and said as much to him.'

'So you'll be a doctor short now that Dad's gone,' he commented as she fumbled around in her handbag for the door keys.

'Yes. John and I have seen one or two hopefuls, but he was strangely reluctant to make a decision and now I see why. He's been waiting for you to come home.'

He nodded. 'Possibly, but Dad has only just found out about Toby and now realises that it wouldn't work. I need to be there to see him into school in the morning and to be waiting when he comes out in the afternoon.'

'Part time?'

'Yes, unless I was to employ a nanny, but he has had enough changes to put up with already without my putting him in the charge of a stranger.'

She had the keys in her hand now, but before putting them in the lock had one thing to say that hopefully would end this strange moment.

'Your father might want you back in the practice, Nathan, but I'm not sure that I do. I have my life planned and it doesn't include working with *you*. At the moment the doctors in the practice are myself and Hugo Lawrence, who came to us from general practice in Bournemouth to be where he could give support to his sister and her children. She was widowed some time ago and isn't coping very well.

'There are three nurses, three part-time receptionists and Gordon Jessup is still practice manager from when you were there before, and with a district nurse and a midwife attached to the surgery we have an excellent team with just one more doctor needed to make it complete. I'm not enjoying the interview process much—it's not really my area of expertise. Also it's proving difficult to fill the vacancy. We face stiff competition from urban practices, lots of younger doctors seem put off by the remoteness of the community, but we don't want anyone too near retirement either. The patients and the practice need stability. I've already heard a few rumblings from those concerned about your father's departure.'

'But you don't want me?'

'No, not particularly, but as the senior partner I suppose I should forget personal feelings and consider the best interests of the patients. They would most likely be thrilled to see the Gallagher name remain above the threshold. And I suppose you working part time might work very well for us—it wasn't something I'd considered before.' In a voice that sounded as if she was reciting her own epitaph she went on, 'So, yes, if that is what you want, come and join us.'

'Thanks a bunch,' he said with a quizzical smile, knowing she felt he deserved her lack of enthusiasm. Though would Libby still feel the same if she knew about his last-minute attempt to speak to her before her wedding? But no way was he going to use that to turn her round to his way of thinking.

Apart from the practice, which she would serve well as head, there must be little for her to rejoice about in any other sphere of her life now that Jefferson was gone.

He hadn't been expecting a fanfare of trumpets on his return to Swallowbrook, or Libby throwing herself into his arms, but he had been hoping she might have forgiven him for what he'd said in those moments of parting long ago.

It had been partly for Toby's sake that he'd come back to Swallowbrook, but always there had been the hope that one day he and Libby might meet again and a chance to make up for the past would present itself.

'Do you want to come to the practice on Monday morning to discuss your hours? I could make sure I'm free at ten o'clock,' she was suggesting.

'Yes, please.'

He'd said it meekly but the glint in the dark eyes looking into hers said differently.

He hasn't changed, she thought. Nathan Gallagher is still a law unto himself. She put her key in the lock and told him, 'So ten o'clock on Monday it is.'

Bending, she planted a swift kiss on Toby's smooth

cheek and said in gentle contrast to the businesslike
tone she'd used to Nathan, 'We have a lovely school
here, Toby, I'm sure you'll like it.'

He was a wiry child with a mop of fair curls, and
so far hadn't said a word to her, but that was about to
change.

'Are you my uncle's friend?' he asked.

Aware of Nathan's gaze on her, she said carefully,
'No, I am just someone he used to work with.'

Having satisfied himself on that, Toby had another
question that was more personal.

'Have *you* got any children?'

'No, I'm afraid not.'

'Why?'

'Because I have never found anyone nice enough to
be their daddy,' she told him.

'So why—?' The small questioner hadn't finished,
but didn't get the chance to continue the interrogation
as Nathan was taking his hand and preparing to depart.

'Say goodbye to Dr Hamilton,' he said, and with
half a smile for her, 'Until Monday, then, at ten o'clock,
Libby.'

She nodded, and with sanctuary beckoning opened
the door and went inside.

It seemed as if Sunday was going to be a non-event day
and Libby was thankful for it. While she was having
breakfast she saw Nathan and Toby go down the drive
and get into the car with fishing rods and surmised they
were going to spend some time with his father at the
pine lodge he'd recently moved into.

When they'd gone she did what she'd been doing ever since their discussion about Nathan coming back into the practice, which was wishing she hadn't been so overbearing in her manner.

She'd made it clear without actually putting it into words that she hadn't forgotten that day at the airport, and wasn't going to fall into the same trap ever again where he was concerned. Yet if that *was* the case, why had she been so happy to discover that he wasn't married with a family?

What he was doing for Toby was so special it brought tears to her eyes every time she thought about it. Through no fault of his own Nathan had taken on the role of single father with the burden of care that went with it, and all *she* had done so far was cut him down to size about working in the practice, which was where he belonged now that the African contract was finished.

He'd said he was sorry to hear about what had happened to Ian and she'd thought that he didn't know that disillusion had followed swiftly after a marriage that had been a mistake from the start. Remembering Toby's curiosity of the day before, the answer she'd come up with for not having children had been true. She wouldn't have wanted a child from a union as empty as hers and Ian's had been.

With the afternoon and evening looming ahead, she decided to resort to one of her favourite pastimes, a sail on one of the steamers that ploughed through the waters of the lake countless times each day, and on disembarking at the other end would have her evening meal at her favourite restaurant beside the moorings.

The boat was full and she stood holding onto the rail, taking in the splendour of the new hospital on the lake-side as they sailed past and gazing enviously at houses built from the pale grey stone of the area with their own private landing stages and fishing rights.

She could see farms in the distance, surrounded by green meadows where livestock grazed, and high up above, towering on the skyline, as familiar as her own face, were the fells, the rugged guardians of the lakes.

Had Nathan the same love of this lakeland valley as she had? she wondered. Had he ever longed to be back in the place where his roots were during those hot days in Africa? If he had it would be at least one thing they had in common, she thought wryly, and wondered how many fish he and Toby had caught in the river beside John's pine lodge.

The answers to the questions in her mind were nearer than she thought as his voice came from behind and as she turned swiftly he said, 'I used to dream I was doing the round trip on one of these boats when I was far away. Sometimes it was the only thing that kept me sane.'

Before he could elaborate further Toby was tugging at her sleeve and announcing excitedly, 'We've caught some fish, Dr Hamilton.'

'Really!' she exclaimed, suitably impressed. 'How many?'

'Two. A salmon and a pike,' he announced.

'But we had to throw the pike back into the water because it is a special fish,' Nathan explained.

'And so where is the salmon now?'

'Dad is cooking it for us for when we get back,' Nathan informed her, 'but first I wanted Toby to sail on the steamer.' In a low voice he added, 'I'm sorry if you feel that I'm everywhere you turn, Libby. I had no idea you were on board. Would you like to come back and join us? There will be plenty of fish to spare.'

Temptation was staring her in the face, but she was not going to succumb. It was going to be a strictly working relationship that she had in mind for them and nothing else, so she said politely, 'Thanks for the invitation, but I have a regular table booked at my favourite restaurant and wouldn't want to let them down.'

He was getting the message, Nathan thought. Not exactly the cold shoulder, but the 'I have not forgotten' treatment, and he wished, as he had done many times before, that he had got in touch with Libby the moment he'd arrived in Africa and at the very least apologised to the beautiful girl whose heart he had broken.

But the timing had been wrong all along the line, beginning with him discovering at the airport that he wasn't as indifferent to Libby Hamilton as he'd thought he was, followed by the knowledge that his flight was due to be called any moment, and overriding everything else, at the forefront of his mind, had been his commitment to the hospital in Africa.

The outcome of it had been that he'd been dumb-struck by the suddenness of it all, and had sent her away, then months later there had been his dash across half the world to speak to Libby before she became Jefferson's wife but he'd missed his chance by seconds and returned to Africa with his questions unanswered.

But now *he* was home, back in Swallowbrook once more, and s*he* was minus a husband, though undoubtedly still reeling from grief, and he was still no nearer to knowing how deep her feelings had been that day at the airport. It could have been a carry-over from her schoolgirl crush. In fact, it must have been a short-lived infatuation judging from the speed with which she'd married Ian Jefferson, and there had certainly been no chemistry between them since he'd turned up out of the blue with Toby. Plenty of being put in his place but no rousing of the senses for either of them as far as he could tell.

'Fine,' he said easily in answer to her refusal.

She'd looked so solitary standing by the rail, watching the steamer cutting its way through the water on its journey across the lake, that he hadn't been able to resist inviting her to join them at his father's place but again the barriers had been up.

When they arrived at the moorings at the far side Nathan and Toby stayed on the steamer in readiness for sailing back and Libby, after a brief goodbye, went to dine at the restaurant that she'd used as an excuse to refuse his invitation.

The fact that she'd already been on her way there didn't make her excuse to Nathan any less untruthful. Although she dined there frequently she didn't have a table booked on a regular basis, and for once she didn't enjoy the food that was put in front of her.

She caught the last steamer back before the light went and then made her way to Swallowbrook in a sombre mood with the thought of starting work as senior partner with Nathan as her newest employee the following morning.

A knock on the door of her consulting room at precisely ten o'clock announced Nathan's arrival and Libby pushed back her chair and went to let him in.

He was alone and the first thing she said was, 'Where's Toby?'

'He's playing with the children's toys in the waiting room. One of the receptionists is keeping an eye on him,' was the reply.

Seating himself across from her, he asked, 'Did you enjoy your meal?'

'No, not really,' she admitted.

'Why was that?'

'I don't know. Maybe it was because I like freshly caught salmon.'

'But not the guy who reeled it in?'

'I have no feelings either way about *him*,' she said and followed it with, 'I do have patients waiting, Nathan, so shall we proceed? What hours would you be available to join us here?'

'Half past nine to three-thirty when the primary children finish,' he said promptly. 'We've been to see the headmaster before coming here and it's sorted for Toby to start tomorrow. Today I'm going to take him into town for his uniform and a satchell.

'If it's all right with you, I feel that Wednesday would

be a good day for me to settle back into the practice. It will leave me with tomorrow free in case Toby is reluctant to go when the moment arrives. He's had so many changes in his life over recent months I wouldn't be surprised.'

'Wednesday will be fine,' she assured him, and had to admire the way he had his priorities sorted. Getting back to the reason for his presence on the premises, she informed him, 'Your father's consulting room at the opposite end of the corridor is vacant, and as all the staff are new since you were last with us, apart from Gordon, the practice manager, I'll introduce you to them while you are here if you like.'

'Yes, sure,' he said easily. 'It would seem that the only things familiar to me are going to be the layout of the place...and you, Libby.'

In your dreams, she thought. She would accept him as a neighbour because she had no choice, and as a colleague because she knew his worth as a doctor, but that was the limit of it. Familiar she was not going to be.

Nathan didn't stay long after the introductions had been made. He separated Toby from the assortment of toys provided to keep small patients happy and took him for his school uniform of dark green and gold, leaving Libby to ponder on how much, or how little, she was going to enjoy working with him again.

She saw the two of them go past the surgery window the following morning and a lump came up in her throat to see the small boy resplendent in a green and gold blazer and matching T-shirt and shorts with Nathan holding his hand and looking down at him protectively.

She'd once dreamed of a similar scenario for the two of them, loving each other, loving the children they created, but that was all it had been, a dream. In utter foolishness she'd turned to someone else and that had been a *nightmare*, so where did she go from here? she wondered.

Yet she knew the answer to the question almost before she'd asked it of herself. She and Nathan were going nowhere. That way she would steer clear of any more heartbreak connected with the men in her life. She'd shown herself to be a poor judge when it came to that.

She'd thought sometimes during the long years he'd been gone, Why shouldn't he have said what he did? At least he hadn't strung her along into thinking he was interested in her when he wasn't, which was what Ian had done, pursued the attractive young doctor at the practice when she was at her most vulnerable to satisfy his ego.

But there was work to do, patients to see, and she needed normality to keep her mind free from the events of a very strange weekend.

As she rose from her desk, intending to make a quick coffee before the next patient appeared, Nathan was passing again, homeward bound this time. When she waved he smiled, gave the thumbs-up sign and went on his way, leaving her with the feeling of unreality that had been there ever since she'd opened her door to him on Friday night.

* * *

Henrietta Weekes was a regular visitor at the practice with most of her problems associated with a failing heart due to having had scarlet fever when she was a child. A smart, intelligent woman, she usually coped with them calmly with little fuss, but today she was in distress and needing to see a doctor.

After checking her heart, Libby exclaimed, 'How on earth have you managed to get here in this state, Henrietta?'

'My son has brought me,' she gasped.

'I'm glad to hear you haven't walked,' she told her soberly. 'Your heart is completely out of control and is affecting your lungs. I'm sending you to the coronary unit at the new hospital straight away by ambulance. You will be attended to more quickly that way than if your son was to take you. I'll get one of the nurses to help you back into the waiting room to join him while I send out an emergency call. You're an amazing woman, Henrietta, I'm not giving up on you. Once they get you into Coronary Care, you'll be in safe hands.'

'If I live that long,' she said with a grimace of a smile, and Libby thought it was typical of the woman that she was facing up to what might happen with the same sort of stoicism that was always there in every crisis that brought her to the surgery for help. Her family, who were devoted to her, must live on a knife edge where their mother's health was concerned.

As the day progressed like any other busy Monday at the practice there was no time to wonder how Nathan was occupying himself until Toby came out of school, or let her thoughts wander to how a small orphaned boy might be coping on his first day. Maybe she would find out tonight when her day at the practice was over and she was back at the cottage.

She was about to make a snack meal for herself that evening when there was a knock on the door, and when she opened it Toby was smiling up at her and announcing, 'Uncle Nathan says would you like to come and eat with us?'

Clever uncle, she thought. *He knows I won't refuse if he sends Toby with the invitation, but didn't he get the message when we were on the steamer and I came up with an excuse for not accepting the invitation to join them at his father's place?*

He was gazing up at her innocently, waiting for an answer, so she said, 'Yes, that would be lovely, Toby. When shall I come?'

Taking her hand in his, he tugged her towards him and said, 'Now, Dr Hamilton.' And having just been given her full title once again, she thought that if she and Toby were going to be seeing much of each other he must be allowed to call her something simpler than that.

'We're having fish fingers and ice cream, Toby's choice,' Nathan told her when she appeared hesitantly in the kitchen doorway, 'to celebrate his first day at school,' adding in a low voice that was for her ears only, 'which he has enjoyed, thank goodness.'

'I can imagine how relieved you are about that,' she replied with her glance on the boy who had gone into the garden and was kicking a ball around while he waited to be fed.

He nodded sombrely but didn't reply. Instead he asked, 'How do you like my efforts to make it seem like a home to him?'

She looked around her. 'Impressive. Just the right blend of luxury and cosiness.'

'That is what I wanted to achieve. There wasn't much of that about where I was based in Africa, and since I've become involved in adopting Toby we've been living in a rented apartment in London while I've been sorting out his parents' affairs for him.

'Now that we've crossed the hurdle of his first day at school and are settling into this place I'm hoping that we can put down some roots and become part of the community, the same as I was before.'

'You can't be a much bigger part of the community than serving them as a GP,' she pointed out, 'or have you changed your mind about tomorrow?'

'No, of course not. *I'm* looking forward to it even if *you* aren't.'

He watched the colour rise in her cheeks and thought that where she'd been beautiful before, now she was divine. Still, she'd made it quite clear that their relationship was to be purely professional and he supposed he deserved no more after the way they had parted.

But only he knew the truth of the affair that had ended in him going to work abroad. He still shuddered at the thought of it, and the fact that Libby had been dragged into its aftermath that day at the airport would always be on his conscience.

His broken engagement to Felice Stopford all that time ago had made him wary of romantic love. It was an emotion he'd felt he hadn't fully understood, and it had come through in the way he'd been so dismissive when Libby had told him how much she cared for him.

To Felice 'love' had meant money and position, expensive gifts, wining and dining, holidays abroad in plush hotels, and he had begun to realise that she was not for him about the same time that Libby had joined the practice.

He'd met his fiancée at a charity luncheon where he had been asked to speak about health care in the area and she'd stood out amongst the soberly dressed audience like a beacon on a hilltop. Dark-haired, voluptuous and quite charming, she'd made a beeline for him when it had finished and introduced herself as an American fundraiser representing similar organisations back in the States.

Her invitation to lunch had been the beginning of a romance that had started on a high and finished on the lowest of lows because he'd gradually discovered that her values were not the same as his. He'd found her to be greedy and shallow as he'd got to know her better and been uneasy about her eagerness for them to marry.

When he'd called the engagement off she'd gone storming back to the States and shortly afterwards he'd discovered through a colleague of hers that she'd had a doting elderly husband back there that she'd been eager to unload to make way for someone like himself.

That item of news had sickened him, made him feel tarnished, and pointed him in the direction of working overseas, which was something he'd been considering before he'd got to know Felice and been sidetracked. It was into that state of affairs that Libby had opened her heart to him. Felice had made him suspicious of love and ultimately it was Libby who'd suffered. The least he could do for her now was to abide by her terms and respect her wishes where their relationship was concerned.

By the time they'd finished eating Toby's eyelids were drooping and Nathan said, 'It's been a long day for him, Libby. If you'll excuse us, I'll get him tucked up for the night. There are magazines or the TV if you want to wait until I come down.' And picking the sleepy child up in his arms, he carried him upstairs.

When they'd gone she went into the kitchen. He'd mentioned magazines and television but there was the tidying up after the meal that would be waiting for him when he came back downstairs. If there was one thing she could do for him it was that, then she would go as quickly as she had come while her resolve to be distant with him was still there.

The kitchen was immaculate and she was seated at the table, scribbling a note to say thanks for the meal, when he came down. As she swung round to face him he was observing her with raised brows.

'I was about to go and was leaving you a note,' she explained.

'Making your getaway while I wasn't around?' he questioned dryly.

'Yes, something like that,' she told him with cool defiance.

He sighed. 'Go ahead, then, Libby, don't let me stop you. I can see it's going to be a bundle of laughs at the surgery tomorrow.'

'Not necessarily,' she told him levelly, 'as long as we both behave like adults.'

His jaw was set tightly. 'Why don't you come right out with it and tell me that I'm not forgiven for what I said at the airport that day?' *And have regretted ever since.*

This was laying it on the line with a vengeance, she thought, but was in no mood to bring her innermost feelings out into the open. She'd had a disastrous marriage since then and was older and wiser in many ways.

'What you said long ago is in the past. I never give it a thought. We've both moved on after all,' she said flatly. With a sudden weakening of her resolve, she added, 'So why don't we just get on with living next door to each other, working side by side at the practice, and leave it at that?'

The line of his jaw was still tight, the glint still in his eyes, but his voice was easy enough as he said, 'Fine by me. I'll see you tomorrow, Libby.' As she got to her feet he said, 'Thanks for tidying the kitchen. I'll do the same for you one day if I'm ever invited across your threshold.'

Having no intention of taking him up on that comment, she gave a half-smile and, reaching out for the door handle, said, 'I hope that Toby is as happy at school tomorrow as he's been today.' She stepped out into the gathering dark. 'Goodnight, Nathan.'

'Goodnight to you too,' he said as he stood in the open doorway and watched her walk quickly down his drive and up her own.

When he heard her door click to behind her he went back inside and wondered if him joining the practice would cause less tension or more between the two of them.

CHAPTER THREE

Libby tried not to keep looking at her watch the next morning as she waited for Nathan to arrive to start his first shift. In spite of her personal feelings she knew he would be as good as his word. The same as his devotion to Toby would not falter. With Nathan's loving support he seemed to be settling well into his new life. Sadly the one thing he would need the most at his tender age was a loving mother and what his adopted father intended doing about that she didn't know.

But aware that the man in question still possessed the attractions that had drawn *her* to him, she imagined that there would soon be members of her sex queuing to play the mother role.

Not that she was going to throw herself into the running, of course. She'd tried to make it clear once more last night that there could be nothing more between them, but he was the one who had raked up the past and caused her to put on an act regarding something she would never forget, and no way did she want it to happen again.

She was going to be pleasant but aloof from now on—no more harking back to times past, if only because of the humiliation that came with the memory of them. Life had treated her badly so far with two unpleasant experiences that most women would never have to face in a lifetime, and since Ian's death she was resolved never to let herself be hurt again in that way.

Besides, now wasn't the time to be thinking about Nathan—she had patients to see, starting with octogenarian Donald Johnson and when he appeared she asked, 'What can I do for you today, Mr Johnson? Are you here about the tests I sent you for?'

'Aye, I am,' was the reply.

'Yes, I thought so,' she said, and told him, 'I received a letter from the hospital this morning regarding the tests on your kidneys that I requested and was going to phone you. It would seem that one of them isn't functioning and the other, although performing quite well, is not at full strength.'

'I see. So one of my kidneys has had it and the other is limping along,' he commented grumpily.

She smiled across at him. 'It isn't such a gloomy outlook as it seems. Our kidneys do gradually deteriorate as we get older, but lots of people survive with only one. We hear of those who have given a healthy kidney to someone else to avoid renal failure and still live a good life with just the one, and although in your case the one that is still working is past its best, I feel sure that it will continue to do its job.

'The hospital say that they will want to see you every three months, which means they are going to keep a close watch on them, so for the present I would put your worries to one side.'

'I wouldn't have had any worries if you hadn't sent me for those tests,' he protested.

'It's standard procedure for a GP to arrange for those sorts of procedures for the elderly,' she explained. 'It won't have made your kidneys any worse, and now you will have regular checks, which can't be bad, surely?'

'Aye, I suppose you're right,' he agreed reluctantly, getting to his feet. 'I'm going fishing at John Gallagher's place this afternoon, that'll cheer me up a bit, and John let slip that Nathan is back in the village and he has a young'un to care for too. Is he going to be doctoring in this place again?'

'Yes, he starts later on this morning, once he's dropped his son off at school.'

'That *is* good news!' he exclaimed. 'It will be like old times.'

Not exactly, she thought as he went to make way for the next patient on her list.

'It was a stroke of genius, bringing Nathan Gallagher back into the practice,' Hugo Lawrence said when he appeared in the doorway of her consulting room in the middle of the morning. 'Being out of touch with the NHS for so long doesn't seem to have affected his performance. He's on top of the job from the word go by the looks of it.'

She smiled at his enthusiasm, but couldn't help pointing out that it had been more a case of Nathan taking it for granted he would be slotting back into the practice. There had been no inspired thinking on her part with regard to his arrival at dead on half past nine in a smart suit, shirt and tie and oozing cool competence.

The fact that underneath it he was wary of making the wrong move where she was concerned would have amazed her if she had been aware of it. As it was, his presence was a cause for pain and pleasure in equal parts and she would be relieved when the first day of his return to the practice was over.

When she'd asked about Toby starting his second day at school he had said there'd been just a moment's reluctance to go into lines in the schoolyard, as was the custom before the children went to their classes. But he'd seemed happy enough as he was trooping in with the rest of them.

She'd sensed anxiety in him at that moment, although seconds later he'd been seeing his first patient as if he'd never been away from the place and she'd told herself to stop involving herself in his affairs or she would be asking for more heartache than she had already.

'Do you want to do the home visits to reacquaint yourself with the area?' she enquired when the three doctors stopped for their lunch break. 'Or would you rather give it a few days to settle in before you do that?'

He hesitated. 'Maybe tomorrow, if you don't mind. I would rather be around if the school should need to get in touch after the little episode this morning. I know it sounds as if I'm fussing, but...'

Caring wasn't fussing, she wanted to tell him as a lump came up in her throat, but hadn't she just been telling herself to stay aloof from his affairs? So instead she replied coolly, 'Yes, of course. I'll do them, and leave Hugo and yourself to see the rest of the patients on the list here at the surgery.'

As she drove towards the first of the house calls Libby had to pass the school and on seeing that the children were all out in the yard, on impulse she stopped the car and went to see if Toby was anywhere to be seen so that she could report back to Nathan.

Sure enough, she saw his fair curly mop bobbing up and down as he chased around with another child of similar age, showing no signs of reluctance to be there.

He'd seen her standing outside the railings and came running across breathless.

'Are you all right, Toby?' she asked gently.

'Yes, Dr Hamilton,' he gasped. 'I'm having lots of fun.' And off he went to find the other boy that he'd been playing with.

When she got back in the car she dialled the surgery and asked to speak to Nathan. When he came on the line she told him, 'Don't worry about Toby any more. The children were all in the playground when I was going past the school so I stopped the car and went across to see if I could see him. He was fine, running around with another small boy, and came across when he saw me. When I asked if he was all right he said he was having lots of fun.'

There was silence for a moment, then with his voice deepening he said, 'Thanks for that, Libby. It was kind of you to take the trouble.'

'It was no trouble,' she said lightly as if the pair of them weren't in her every waking thought. 'I'll see you later.' And rang off.

* * *

The Pellows were a dysfunctional family who seemed to go from one crisis to another.

Angelina, the mother, was an artist who, when the creative mood was on her, would disappear into her studio for days on end. No shopping would be done or tidying up of the shambolic old house down a lane at the far end of the village where she and her family lived.

Her husband Malik was employed by the forestry commission and during her absences had to do the best he could in looking after their two children and things in general. He didn't complain much because Angelina almost always sold what she'd painted, but there was relief all round when she surfaced again.

The young ones always seemed robust and healthy enough, but not today, it would seem, with regard to one of them. Malik had phoned to ask for a visit to six-year-old Ophelia, who had recently been diagnosed with measles and now had a high temperature, was very dizzy, and was complaining that her ears hurt.

When Libby arrived at the house she found that another of Angelina's disappearances was in progress and Malik was busy making a lunch of sorts for him and the child, who was lying on a sofa in the sitting room.

When she examined her ears with an otoscope it was evident that the eardrums were swollen and when she asked the little girl where they hurt she pointed weepily to the area where her cheekbone met the inner ear.

'I suspect that Ophelia has got viral labyrinthitis,' Libby told her father. 'It's an infection of the middle ear that affects balance and makes the ears quite painful. It sometimes occurs when measles is present and can take some time to clear. There are two kinds of the illness, viral and bacterial. Viral is the less serious of the two but not to be ignored by any means.

'Your daughter needs to rest, and I'm going to prescribe a low-dosage antihistamine course of treatment because of her age, and an equally mild children's pain-relief tablet.

'I see that the measles rash has disappeared so that problem is obviously lessening. It's unfortunate that in its wake has come labyrinthitis. Ring the surgery if any further problems appear, Malik, and I'll come straight away.'

She looked around her at the cluttered sitting room. 'Do I take it that Angelina isn't available?'

'Yes, you do,' he said morosely. 'She's having one of her artistic sabbaticals that can go on for days or even weeks.'

A vision of his wife as she'd last seen her came to mind, dressed in a golden kaftan with beads and bangles everywhere, and Libby hid a smile.

Angelina had looked more like a fortune teller than an artist.

The rest of the house calls were soon dealt with and as she drove back to the practice Libby stopped for a few moments beside the lake that was only a short distance from the surgery, a stretch of water that was so beautiful it always took her breath away. The white sails of yachts were outlined vividly against its calm waters, and a house built from the pale grey stone of the area was clearly visible on a tree-covered island in the centre of it.

Above the lake the fells towered in rugged magnificence, but all those who lived in the area knew that they could be dangerous too, that they sometimes asked a grim price from those who loved to climb them. The mountain rescue services were kept busy all the year round on behalf of those caught in bad weather up on the tops, or with others who lacked the experience to stay safe while climbing them.

Nathan had been involved in mountain rescue when he'd lived in Swallowbrook before. An experienced climber, he'd often been called out when the need had arisen, but she couldn't see that happening now, not with Toby to care for. It was often a risky undertaking bringing to safety those who had succumbed to the dangers of the fells, and poor Toby had already been orphaned once.

As she pointed the car homewards it was a strange feeling to know that when she arrived back at the surgery he would be there, closeted in the consulting room that had been his father's, and along with Hugo further along the corridor would be dealing with the afternoon surgery until, in a matter of minutes, it would be time for him to pick Toby up from school.

As she was about to take his place he said, 'It is so good to be back here at the practice, Libby. You have no idea how much I missed it while I was away.' She stared at him disbelievingly. 'What? Do you think I don't mean it?'

'I'm not sure,' she replied. 'Once you'd gone to Africa you never came back to visit, did you, and you were eager enough to be gone in the first place?'

It was a moment to tell her that he had come back all right, but no one had known about it, and the memory of seeing her as a bride smiling up at Jefferson surfaced from the dark corners of his mind once again. The frustration and dismay of that catastrophic dash halfway across the world to hear from her own lips that Libby had put behind her the hurt he'd caused her was something he wasn't likely to forget.

So it was just the practice that he'd missed, she thought bleakly, not any of those he'd left behind—certainly not her.

But she hadn't waited, had she? She'd done a stupid thing during the long empty weeks after his departure. Let the feeling of rejection that he'd been responsible for cause her to make a wrong decision that had been second only in foolishness to letting herself fall in love with him. They had been two great errors of judgement and she wasn't going to let there be a third.

During that first day of his return they had spoken mainly about practice matters, but Libby had been so aware of him she'd felt relieved when he'd finished for the day and gone to pick Toby up from school.

When she arrived home at a much later hour she was hoping to be able to go in, shut her door and relax with no further sightings of him. It had seemed that her wish might be granted until a ring on the bell when Swallowbrook was bathed in autumn gloaming had her tensing.

It reminded her of the night of his arrival as she went

slowly to the door, and sure enough it was her new neighbour standing in the shadowed porch.

'I know you must have seen enough of me for one day,' he said apologetically, 'but on the point of going to sleep Toby has just told me that it's the harvest festival at the school tomorrow morning and he's expected to take something, and I haven't got anything that would be suitable.'

'Yes,' she said steadily. 'It is the usual procedure for the school children at harvest-time. They bring fruit, vegetables, flowers, and the person who has been chosen to receive their gifts presents them with a harvest loaf, fashioned in the shape of a sheaf of corn. There is a short service afterwards and then they go to their classrooms.'

'I see,' he said slowly. 'I do wish he'd told me sooner.'

'Not to worry,' she told him with the feeling that the fates were not playing fair. They were determined that she wasn't going to avoid Nathan's presence in her life again. 'I have a tree in my back garden that's loaded with apples, and next to it a plum tree burdened likewise.

'If you'd like to come back when I've had my meal and bring a ladder, we should be able to solve your problem.' *But it won't go any way to solving mine,* she thought glumly.

He was smiling. 'Thanks for the suggestion. So far I'm making the grade with Toby, but it wouldn't have gone down too well if he'd been the only kid without something for the harvest, and with regard to your evening meal have you started preparing it?'

She shook her head. 'Not so far. I'm going to have a shower first to wash away the germs of the day from the practice, but I know what I'm having and it won't take long to prepare.'

'And what is that?'

'An omelette, some crusty bread and a glass of wine.'

'I'm quite good with omelettes and I've got the wine, so if you'll bring the bread I'll have a meal ready for us both by the time you come out of the shower. It's the least I can do if you're going to get me off the hook with the harvest. How long before you'll be ready?'

'Er, twenty minutes,' she replied weakly, with the feeling that she was being manipulated and ought to refuse the gesture.

He was turning on his heel. 'All right, Libby. I'll see you then.' And off he went, back to where Toby was sleeping, totally innocent of being the cause of any embarrassment to him.

Libby didn't linger under the shower. In the stipulated time she needed to dry her hair and brush it into some semblance of order, apply some make-up, and find something in her wardrobe that would put the finishing touches to her appearance.

She chose an attractive summer dress of soft blue cotton that clung to her slender curves in all the right places, but as she was on the point of zipping it up the voice of reason was asking, Are you insane? Dressing up for the man who gave you the brush-off all that time ago and is showing no signs of having changed his mind? You need old jeans and a cotton top for climbing ladders and getting the message over that the days of you wanting him are long gone.

So old jeans it was and an average T-shirt to go with them and off she went, carrying the bread that she'd bought at the bakery in her lunch hour.

The table was set and he was on the point of taking the first omelette out of the pan, so she quickly buttered the bread and at his request poured the wine, and all the time she was wishing that she'd kept to her first intention and dressed up for the impromptu meal that they were about to share, especially as Nathan was attired in the smart casual clothes that she'd seen him in once before and been much impressed.

If she had expected awkward silences as the meal progressed she was mistaken. As if he was geared up for no embarrassment, his conversation was all about the practice, Swallowbrook and the coming harvest, and when he asked who was going to be there to receive the children's gifts she said, 'It's me, I'm afraid. The headmaster decided that as so many of the children and their parents already know me from the surgery it would be nice if I could spare the time.

'I would have refused if it had been later in the day, but it will only be for the first half-hour or so in the morning and Hugo is going to hold the fort until I show up. Also you're due at the surgery at half past nine if I'm delayed for any reason.'

'Yes, of course,' he said evenly, aware that she was still putting up a cold front as far as he was concerned.

When they'd finished eating and tidied the kitchen Nathan said, 'While I'm getting the ladder out, would

you mind popping upstairs to check on Toby? He sometimes wakens up crying for his mother.'

'And what do you do when that happens?' she asked
anxiously.

'Hold him close until the moment has passed and
he has gone back to sleep. Understandably there were
a lot of those kind of moments when he first came to
me, but they are gradually reducing and since coming
to Swallowbrook there hasn't been one.'

'Have you any regrets about taking on such a big responsibility?' she asked gently, because when it came to
what he'd done for Toby she could find no fault in him
and had to fight the desire to help him in every way she
could.

But Nathan wasn't asking for her help. She would
die of mortification if she offered it and he turned her
down in the same way as when she'd offered him her
heart.

'No, none,' he said in answer to her question. 'If
ever I have any children of my own, he will be as one
of them to me. Nothing will change my love for him,
and he's brought purpose into my life.'

He was capable of great love, she thought bleakly.
One day some fortunate woman would come along and
she would be truly blessed if he should give his heart
to her.

'Shall we start picking the fruit?' she asked, bringing
back to mind her suggestion for solving his predicament
regarding the harvest. 'I have a safety light at the back
of the cottage, which will help us to see in the dark.'

He nodded. 'I'll go up the ladder and throw the fruit

down to you. Do you want me to take it all off for you, or just enough for Toby to take to the school?'

'All of it, I think, if you don't mind,' she told him. 'I have a large basket that will hold the apples and a big earthenware dish for the plums.'

They were making good progress with the fruit-picking. She was actually enjoying it, Libby was thinking, in spite of the awkwardness she felt in his company, but there was about to be an interruption.

His phone was ringing next door and, jumping off the ladder, he said, 'I need to get that fast before it disturbs Toby.' He ran towards his place. 'I won't be long, Libby.'

When he'd gone she stood around for a few moments and then decided that she may as well go up the ladder and carry on where he'd left off. Engrossed in what she was doing, she didn't see him come back into the shadowed garden until he called up to her. Taken by surprise, she turned swiftly and the ladder, propped against the tree trunk, moved with her, tilting backwards and throwing her off.

In those few seconds she was expecting to land on a flagged patio beneath the trees, but she was reckoning without his quick thinking. Instead of hitting the ground, she found herself safe in his arms with her fast-beating heart close against his chest.

'Wow,' he said softly as he looked down at her. 'Why didn't you wait until I came back?' Their glances met. 'But that's not how you do things, is it?'

She was too shocked for the meaning behind his

words to register. Instead she was thinking that he had only ever touched her twice in all the years she'd known him and both times it had been out of necessity rather than desire.

The first time had been at the airport when an intended peck on the cheek in the form of an apology for his harshness had somehow become a moment of passion, and tonight it had been when he'd saved her from what could have been a nasty fall, and now with her still held close in his arms he was carrying her inside and placing her on the sofa in her sitting room.

'Are you all right after that scare?' he asked, looking down at her anxiously.

'Yes, I'm fine. Just a bit shaken, that's all,' she assured him, which was true, but it was more due to where she'd found herself when she'd been saved from harm, rather than being thrown off the ladder.

He was frowning. 'I'm going to have to go, Libby. I've left Toby alone for long enough, but I do need to know that you're all right. He sleeps in my room at present, so I do have a spare room and a camp bed. Do you want to come and spend the night with us so that my mind will be at rest about you?

'I'll move Toby and I into the spare and you can have my room. I might have caught you, but the suddenness of it could have jarred every bone in your body and it doesn't always take effect immediately.'

She could feel her colour rising. A night under the same roof as him would have been very appealing at one time but not now, because if she ever came as close to him again as she'd been when he'd caught her she wouldn't be able to guarantee keeping to her vows of staying clear of him, and that was already beginning to look like a no-no, as try as she would to avoid him he was invading her evenings as well as her days.

'Thanks for the offer, but I really will be fine,' she told him, 'and do, please, go back to Toby. I can't bear the thought of him wakening and you not being there.'

He nodded. 'OK. I'll go, but ring me if you have any problems in the night and we'll both come over.'

'Don't forget to take Toby some of the fruit for the harvest,' she reminded him with a change of subject, pointing to a small wicker basket on the coffee table beside her. 'If you put it in that, it shouldn't be too heavy for him to carry.'

He did as she'd suggested without speaking and when it was done wished her goodnight and departed.

When he'd gone she sat gazing out into the dark night with her mind in a whirl. So he thought she didn't need him, which was not surprising as she was giving him no reason to think otherwise. She was putting on a good show of indifference, false as it was, because after being in his arms and held so close to him she was realising that it was no use pretending any more. She needed him like she needed to breathe, but Nathan was never going to know that.

He'd humiliated her once, a second time was not to be endured, and as her neck started to ache from the jarring of the fall and a headache was coming on she went upstairs to bed and wished she'd accepted his offer if only to be around when Toby awoke the next morning.

Back at the cottage next door Nathan was also facing up to what he saw as home truths. One of them being that Libby still hadn't forgiven him for past hurts, and another was that she was only tolerating his presence because of Toby who she was so sorry for, and saw himself merely as part of the package.

But he could wait for that forgiveness. Make it up to her somehow. Ever since that day in the church porch he'd been cultivating patience, along with the strength of will that had helped him to give her breathing space after Jefferson had died.

He would have stayed away if it hadn't been for the needs of one small boy. Still, one day he might find the right moment to tell Libby how sorry he was for the way he'd treated her at the airport that day, but with her on the defensive all the time it might be some time in coming.

CHAPTER FOUR

THE next morning Nathan kept a lookout for Libby going across to open the surgery at eight o'clock in preparation for the eight-thirty start, as was her routine. He'd decided that if she didn't appear he would be round at the cottage next door immediately to check up on her, but not until then because he felt that in his eagerness to have her under his roof the night before he might have overdone it.

He would be concerned for anyone who had escaped what could have been a very serious fall and might be suffering from the after-effects of the incident, but this was Libby, blonde, beautiful and the most caring person he'd ever known. He was really getting to know her at last and liking it more than he could have ever believed he would.

He'd only moved away from the window for a moment to give Toby his cereal and when he turned back she was there, crossing the short distance that separated the two cottages from the practice building, wearing a blue dress that enhanced her golden fairness and clung to her slender curves as if it was moulded on them.

It was very different from the plain suits she wore

during surgery hours, but she was doing the harvest thing this morning and must have decided that the children should see her in something less sombre while she was in their midst.

As far as he could see, she seemed all right after the night before, and if where she'd landed had not been to her liking she had concealed it very well.

Hugo had just arrived and as the two doctors met at the main doors of the surgery and chatted for a moment Nathan thought how relaxed she was with him, smiling at something he'd said and showing no signs of the guarded approach that she reserved for himself.

Presumably the other man had done nothing to upset her, which was more than could be said for his treatment of her. But now he was back where he belonged, amongst the lakes and fells, working in the practice once more, and with those things to provide some small degree of togetherness he was really getting to know Libby Hamilton who for as long as he could remember had always been on the edges of his life and was now filling it with all the things he'd ever wanted in a woman.

Unaware that she was being observed, Libby hesitated for a moment when Hugo had gone into the building and glanced across at his place.

What was she thinking? he wondered.

He was soon to find out. She was retracing her steps back to the cottages and coming up his path. When she knocked on the door he was there in an instant, observing her questioningly.

'I've just been to open up at the surgery,' she explained, 'and thought I'd call back to let you know that I'm fine after our fruit-picking episode. No harm done.'

'That's good,' he said, and had to step to one side before he could say anything else as Toby was behind him, wanting to speak to Dr. Hamilton.

As she smiled at the child she said, 'It is rather a mouthful for Toby to have to say every time he refers to me. Can't he just call me Libby?'

'Yes, if you are happy with that,' he agreed, 'though maybe not this morning in front of the whole school.'

'No, perhaps not, but after that it will be fine,' she told him, and wished they could have a conversation that sounded less stiff and formal.

But at least he was there in the flesh, she could see him, touch him if she so desired, but *desire* was not the name of the game where they were concerned. Just because he'd held her close in his arms the night before, it didn't mean that Nathan had any yearnings in that direction.

'I have to go,' she said with sudden urgency. 'I've arranged to see a patient before I go to the school. Patrice Lewis is Hugo's sister. Do you remember me telling you that he left a position in general practice in one of the southern counties to help her through a difficult time?

'She lost her husband round about the same time that Ian died and has been left with two young girls to bring up. She is very gentle and can't always cope with her grief, so Hugo has come to join her for as long as it takes for her to get back onto an even footing.

'I see her once a month for a chat and a repeat of any medication she may be on, and her appointment,

which she relies on a lot, was made before I was asked
to take part in the harvest celebration at the school. So
once she has been I'll see you both there, won't I?'

As she hurried back to the surgery Libby was wishing she hadn't ended that last sentence with a question.
It had overtones of pleading and that was the last thing
she was ever going to do where he was concerned.

The school hall was full when she arrived, with the primary classes at the front, the junior school behind them,
and any parents who had been free to attend seated at
the back.

Toby was on the front row, clutching his basket of
fruit, and as she took her seat on the platform they exchanged smiles. She'd given up on trying not to care
for him too much. How could she not allow herself to
want to see a small boy happy?

Sitting at the back, Nathan had seen those smiles and
she would have been surprised to know that his thoughts
were running along similar lines. That if Libby could
show Toby the love and tenderness that he was missing from his mother, maybe the sad gap in his young
life might be filled. She was living next door to them
and except for actually residing in the same house, she
couldn't be much closer to the child than that.

He knew that she had none of those kinds of feelings
for *him*. Would take a dim view of the way his thoughts
were racing ahead. But it was early days, and time was
on his side. He and the boy weren't going anywhere and
hopefully neither was she.

* * *

Libby and the headmaster were seated behind a long wooden table covered with a white cloth and as the children were helped up onto the platform one by one she accepted the gifts they had brought with a smile for each one of them.

When the last one had handed over their harvest offering she placed her own contribution, a large crusty loaf baked in the shape of a sheaf of corn, in the middle of them, and then a short service of thanksgiving took place.

She saw Nathan leave the hall just before half past nine and remembered her comment to him that if she wasn't back by then she would expect him to be there assisting Hugo with the first surgery of the day.

What did he think of her behind his politely pleasant manner? she wondered. That she was a dried-up, widowed, boss woman, and an unforgiving one at that? The thought brought tears to her eyes. It wasn't how she wanted him to see her, but it was one way of hiding her feelings.

As he'd walked back to the practice with the vision of her on the platform in the blue dress at the front of his mind, Nathan had been thinking that it was as well that Libby had been wearing her old clothes the night before when he'd caught her in his arms, or he might have forgotten that he was supposed to be keeping to their lukewarm reunion and let his awakening consciousness of her ruin everything.

As the golden days of autumn dwindled, with winter's chill hovering late at night and in the pale dawn, he said one morning, 'Is it all right with you if I call everyone at the practice together to make an announcement before the day gets under way, Libby?'

'Yes, of course,' she replied, with dread making her feel nauseous at the thought of what he might be about to say, such as that he was moving on to somewhere new, for which she could be responsible with her lack of welcome and aloofness.

When Nathan had first come back to Swallowbrook he'd been emphatic that it was there he wanted to be, but when he'd said that he hadn't been expecting to find himself living next door to an ice maiden.

When they were all assembled in the practice manager's office he said, 'Just a quick word. As I came back to Swallowbrook almost at the same time as my father was retiring from the practice, I wasn't able to arrange a suitable farewell for him, so I am going to put that right on Saturday evening by inviting you all to a meal in the banqueting suite of the new hotel by the lakeside.'

As relief washed over her Libby's colour was rising. Before anyone else had the chance to reply she said, 'I would like to make it clear that *we* didn't get the opportunity to do something like that when your father left us because he was adamant that he would want you to be there on the occasion of anything of that nature, so we had to leave it in order to abide by his wishes.

'I for one will be delighted to accept the invitation. John Gallagher was more to me than just a colleague, he was there for me always in the good times and bad.' Her voice broke. *'He cared, and caring is a precious thing.'*

There was silence for a moment then everyone began to talk at once, expressing their pleasure at being asked to such a gathering. For the rest of the day the surprise party was the main topic of conversation when anyone had a free moment.

As Libby had gone back to her consulting room Nathan had been close behind and he'd followed her inside and closed the door.

'There was no criticism intended in what I said, Libby. I know what Dad can be like when he digs his heels in,' he told her. 'You wanting to arrange a farewell must have coincided with me getting in touch with him to say that I was coming back with my soon-to-be-adopted son. I presume he didn't pass that information on because I'd been away so long, he felt that he would believe it when he saw it.'

She was smiling. 'I think what you are arranging is a lovely idea. You are making up for the lack of a proper farewell and that is all that matters, yet what about Toby? It will be late for him to be up.'

He nodded. 'Yes, I know, but there is no one I can leave him with that I would trust, except you.'

'I wouldn't mind if you want me to stay behind with him.'

'Maybe you wouldn't, but I would, and Dad will be most upset if you aren't there. Also Toby and Grandfather Gallagher, as he calls my father, are getting on famously. I shall book a room for the night and when he gets tired tuck him up safely in there and keep checking on him every so often.'

'I could do that for you,' she suggested, 'so that you don't have to leave your guests.'

'So shall I book a room for you as well?'

'Yes, why not?' she agreed. 'It will be nice to have a leisurely breakfast that someone else has prepared overlooking the lake on the Sunday morning.'

'I can agree with that wholeheartedly,' he said, and went to start his day, leaving her to greet her first patient with a lighter heart than she'd had for some time. *Nathan wanted her to be at the party, she thought. She didn't know why exactly. Maybe it was just because of her position in the practice. Whatever it might be, it was like balm to her soul because for the first time since widowhood had fallen on her she would be attending a social event and he would be there.*

Laura Standish and her husband had been wanting to start a family for quite some time but without success due to her irregular menstrual cycle and his low sperm count, but today it was a different story. When she seated herself opposite Libby the reason for her consulting a doctor became clear.

She explained tremulously that she was experiencing all the signs of early pregnancy and was desperate for confirmation from a reliable source.

'I feel nauseous in the mornings,' she said, 'my breasts are tender, and I've missed two periods. I know I'm irregular, Libby, but I've never missed two full months before.'

'Have you done a pregnancy test from the chemist?' she asked.

Laura shook her head. 'No. I preferred to come to you for the good or bad news. We'd got to the point where the gynaecologist you sent us to was suggesting IVF treatment. Then suddenly, almost like a miracle, I feel as if I might be pregnant.'

'Shall we see if you're right?' Libby told her gently, pointing to the couch beside them.

When she'd finished the test and examination that would confirm whether her patient's dearest wish was to be granted she shook her head. 'I'm sorry, Laura,' she told her, 'not this time, I'm afraid. It is more likely to be a hormone imbalance. Maybe you should give IVF some thought the next time you see the gynaecologist.'

'Why is it that it is so easy for some people to have a baby and so difficult for others?' Laura said tearfully. 'Mike will be so disappointed.'

'Nature is a law unto itself and can be very cruel sometimes,' she told her with the memory of a teenage girl that she'd seen the day before who had been desperate to terminate an unwanted pregnancy that had been the result of her one and only venture into unprotected sex.

The first delivery of the flu prevention vaccine had arrived, so it turned out to be an extremely busy day for the practice nurses, with the waiting room full of a mixture of those waiting for the jab and the ones who'd just been given it hanging on for the suggested twenty minutes before leaving the premises in case they suffered any ill effects, and alongside them those who were waiting to consult their doctor about other things.

That being so, it was evening before Libby was able to take her mind back to Nathan's surprise announcement at the start of the day. The party was going to be something to look forward to, a pleasant surprise, and with that thought in mind what was she going to wear?

It would be an occasion for being neither over-dressed or understated, something in the middle maybe. Avoiding the clothes she'd worn during her brief depressing marriage to Ian, she decided that it was going to be a black dress with long sleeves, low neck and calf-length full skirt, with appropriate jewellery.

Next door Nathan's thoughts were also about the party but along different lines. He and Libby would be sleeping beneath the same roof for once, he was thinking, not the golden thatch above them as he would have liked on the night when Libby had fallen off the ladder, but the roof of a smart new hotel by the lake.

On the Saturday night he went on ahead to the party venue with Toby so as to be there beside his father as he greeted his guests, and to make sure that all was in order with the arrangements he'd made with the hotel.

Hugo was the first to arrive with his sister, who he'd brought along for company, a childminder having been engaged to look after her little girls. Then came the surgery nurses Robina, Tracey and Coleen with their partners, followed by the receptionists also suitably escorted, and tagging along behind them was Gordon, a confirmed bachelor.

Next to arrive was Alison, the cleaner, and her husband, who looked after the gardens around the surgery and did general maintenance on the building when necessary. Even the man from the pathology lab who came each day to collect blood samples for testing and anything else that had to go to his department was there. He'd been coming for so many years he was looked on as one of them. The last, but not the least by any means, was Libby, stunning in black, smiling her pleasure to be there and taking in the vision of Nathan and his father resplendent in dinner jackets, evening shirts and bow-ties. Even Toby was wearing a short-sleeved shirt with a little tie held in place by elastic.

As each guest had arrived John had shaken hands with them cordially until Libby had appeared and then it was different.

He held her close for a long moment and then said gruffly, 'I'm missing you, Libby. How's it going with Nathan back in harness?'

The man in question was only inches away, observing her with an ironic gleam in his eyes as if daring her to be truthful and admit that she was putting up with him on sufferance.

He was in for a surprise. 'Everything at the practice is fine,' she told his father. 'The patients are delighted to see Nathan back, and the rest of us really appreciate his contribution to the village's health care.'

'That's good,' the older man said, and with a glance at Toby, who was looking around him with interest, 'You won't have much time for anything else with the job and this young fellow to look after, eh, Nathan?'

'It would depend on what it was and how important,' he said evenly, with his glance still on her, and now there was no irony in it, just a question that she didn't know the answer to.

By the time the last course of the meal was being served Toby was ready for sleep, nodding his curly blond head every few seconds, and as she observed him Libby said to Nathan in a low voice, 'You can't very well leave your guests, Nathan. Shall I take Toby and get him settled for the night, if he'll let me?'

'I don't think he'll object,' he replied. 'He likes you, Libby, and would be round at your place every minute of the day if I let him.'

'So why don't you?'

'I'm not sure. Maybe it's because I know that I'm not welcome and I wouldn't want that sort of feeling to wash off onto him.'

As she bristled with indignation beside him he said, 'We'd better take him up now before he falls off his chair.'

'Yes,' she agreed, 'but don't think that by hustling me off with Toby, what you have just said about not being welcome is going to pass without comment.'

He was on his feet and didn't reply. Lifting Toby up into his arms, he whispered in his ear, 'Libby is going to give you your bedtime cuddles tonight—is that all right?'

'Mmm,' he murmured.

When they reached the top of the hotel's wide staircase and turned into the first corridor he pointed to two rooms overlooking the lake and, giving her the keys, said, 'The nearest one is yours, and the one next to it is a twin-bedded for Toby and I. When you've opened the door I'll lay him on his bed and then go back to the others, if that's all right with you.'

'Yes,' she whispered. 'I won't come down until I'm sure that he's fast asleep.'

The moment Nathan had gone Toby opened his eyes and smiled up at her drowsily. 'We need to take your shirt and tie off and put your pyjamas on before you go to sleep,' she told him gently. 'They are here beside you where Uncle Nathan has left them, so if you'll just sit up for a moment we'll put them on.'

He did as she'd asked and gazing around him said, 'I haven't got my comforter, Libby,' and with his bottom lip trembling went on, 'I always hold it close when I'm in my bed.'

'What is it, Toby?' she asked as tears began to flow.

'It is Mummy's nightdress, Libby,' he sobbed. 'It's soft and cuddly and smells lovely.'

She was looking around her desperately, lifting the lid of a small overnight case only to find it empty, checking that the nightdress wasn't tangled up in the bedclothes, opening drawers, all to no avail.

'I think that it must have been forgotten when your uncle was packing your things,' she said consolingly, 'but do you know what, Toby? I have a nightdress that smells nice. You can cuddle up to that if you like, pretend that it's your comforter just for tonight. What do you say?'

'Where is it?' he wanted to know.

'In my room next door.' Not wanting to leave him even for a second after watching his distress, she said, 'Shall we go and get it?'

He nodded, and swinging his small legs over the side of the bed took her hand in his and side by side they went to find the nightdress that was folded neatly on her pillow.

She gave it to him and holding it close to his cheek he said, 'Mummy won't mind, will she?'

'No, of course not,' she told him reassuringly. 'She will be happy that you are happy. So if that is all right, shall we go and tuck you up in bed?'

The room that Nathan had booked for her had a double bed in it and as Toby observed it he said, 'Can I sleep in your bed, Libby?'

The thought of having him safe and close beside her was tempting, and what the outcome would be if she left him asleep in the next room and when she'd gone to join the others he awoke in the distressed state he'd been in earlier didn't bear thinking of, so she said, 'Yes, you can, but first I must write a note for someone who loves you very much to tell him where you are when the party is over.'

'You mean Uncle Nathan, don't you? He is going to be my new daddy, did you know that?'

'Yes, he told me how excited he is to be your new dad,' she told him.

Picking up a pen off a nearby writing desk, she wrote on headed notepaper...

Nathan.
Toby is sleeping with me after a major upset that has now been sorted. It's why I didn't come back

*to join the party. I know you will want to see for
yourself that he is all right, so will leave my door
unlocked until you've been and checked on him.*
   Libby.

When she'd placed it on Toby's empty pillow in
the next room she took him to her bed and held him
close until he was asleep, then, bereft of her nightwear,
slipped off the dress and lay beside him in the black
lacy slip that she'd worn beneath it.

Down below Nathan was watching the staircase as
coffee was being served to his guests, expecting Libby
to appear any moment, but she didn't materialise and
knowing how tired Toby had been he was wondering
why.

He was tempted to go and check on them but didn't
want to be seen as fussing, either by her or by the surgery staff who were in no hurry to go. But at last they
had all said their farewells and he'd seen his father
safely into a taxi, so was free to go to the suites above
to see where Libby had got to.

The first thing that registered was that there was no
Toby in the bed that he had laid him on. The second
was the note on the pillow. As he read it his expression tightened. For God's sake! What kind of upset was
Libby referring to? Then he was out in the corridor and
pushing back the door that she'd left unlocked.

When he looked inside his face softened. His adopted
son was asleep in the crook of the arm of the woman he
could once have had if he hadn't been too blind to see
what had been under his nose.

As he looked down at the smooth skin of her shoulders inside the flimsy slip and the rise and fall of her breasts as she slept beside the precious child who had been catapulted into his life, it was his turn to fight back the tears for the waste of the years and the mistakes that both of them had made.

He hadn't a clue what could have upset Toby to such an extent until he looked at what he was holding in his arms and as he observed it he gave a hollow groan. He'd forgotten to pack Toby's comforter. How could he have done such a thing? Thank God, Libby had come up with a solution.

His exclamation of dismay must have disturbed her. She had opened her eyes and was looking up at him.

'Everything is all right,' she whispered, and easing her arm from beneath the sleeping child she slid her legs over the side of the bed and stood before him.

'I can't believe that I forgot his comforter, of all things,' he said wretchedly, 'and lumbered you with the aftermath of my carelessness.'

'Stop berating yourself,' she told him. 'You are marvellous to do what you do for Toby. He has told me that you are going to be his new daddy and seems fine with the idea. Forgetting to bring his mummy's nightdress isn't going to change that.'

He was not to be consoled. 'You must wish me a thousand miles away, Libby,' he said bleakly. 'I went out of your life a long time ago and have had the nerve to come bursting back into your planned existence as if by divine right.'

She took a step forward and touched his face with

gentle hands and suddenly nothing else mattered except themselves, not Toby sleeping contentedly beside them, the party that she'd seen little of or the practice that was their daytime rendezvous. There was peace between them for a few brief moments with no recriminations or hurts to spoil it, no bitterness or past mistakes hovering over them. It was a moment of supreme need with desire ruling their emotions.

For the third time in Libby's life Nathan was touching her and there was nothing casual about it this time. His mouth on hers was demanding, urgent, and she was responding with every fibre of her being.

He took her hand and drew her towards the door of a small sitting room at the end of the bedroom and once inside turned the catch to prevent Toby walking in on them. Then he was slipping the black slip off her shoulders and kissing the cleft between her breasts.

As their passion increased Nathan lowered her onto a sofa and as she gazed up at him in the moment before the climax of their desire Libby came to her senses.

She'd already made one big mistake where Nathan was concerned, she thought. This could be another. This wild abandonment of common sense could lead to more heartbreak if she let it continue.

He felt her change of mood as painfully as if it was a knife thrust and as she got slowly to her feet he placed the keys of the suite next door in her hand and said sombrely, 'You can't let go of the past, can you, Libby?

'If you don't mind swapping I'll take over here and we'll see you at breakfast. Do you need to take anything with you?'

'Just the things I brought with me for an overnight stay,' she said weakly, and flinging her belongings into her travel bag she wrapped herself in the robe that she'd brought with her and went.

So much for that, he thought grimly when she'd gone. He'd lost the control that he'd been cultivating ever since coming back to Swallowbrook and all because Libby had stroked his face. Yet it hadn't been just that, had it?

His emotions had already run amok when he'd discovered he'd left Toby's comforter behind and Libby had been left to handle the distress that the oversight had caused his little one, and when instead of blame she'd shown him only tenderness the barriers between them had come down.

He'd given in to passion she'd aroused in him and blown it, had been able to tell that the change in her response to his love-making had been because she'd suddenly remembered how he had once let her see that he wasn't interested in any feelings she might have for him, and had told her cruelly to go and forget him.

It had seemed as if she'd taken him at his word when she'd married Jefferson, and he'd stayed away even after he'd died and Libby was free of him, because of what he'd said that day. Was the awful mistake he'd made always going to be there to haunt him?

As Toby stirred in his sleep and held Libby's night-dress more closely to him, Nathan eased himself carefully onto the bed beside him in the place where she had lain and wondered what tomorrow would bring in a relationship that seemed to be going nowhere.

He'd come back to Swallowbrook with no intentions

towards Libby other than telling her, if she would give him the chance, how much he regretted the way he'd behaved that day at the airport when her timing had been so unfortunate.

CHAPTER FIVE

WHEN Libby went down to breakfast the following morning, pale and drawn after a sleepless night, Nathan and Toby were already seated at a table by a window overlooking the lake on the point of finishing theirs.

When Toby called across to her she had no choice but to go to where Nathan was observing her unsmilingly from the opposite side of the table.

She didn't want to sit with them, the happenings of the night before were too recent, too raw, but she could tell that Toby was expecting her to and there was no way she wanted to upset him. So she asked Nathan, 'Is it all right if I join you?'

'Yes, of course,' he said evenly, and she thought that the core of their relationship, *if it could be described as that*, was as past its promise as the fallen leaves of bronze and gold lying beneath the trees that surrounded the lake.

The mellow autumn of Nathan's return to Swallowbrook was past, winter would soon be upon them and where she'd always looked forward to crisp mornings and snow on the fells, this time it was going to be an ordeal to be got through.

A waitress was at her elbow, asking if she was ready to order, and bringing herself back from the gloom of her thoughts Libby consulted the menu.

When she had gone Nathan asked, as if nothing between them had changed, 'Are you staying here for the rest of the day or checking out, like Toby and I?'

'I intend leaving immediately after breakfast,' she told him. 'There are things I have to do when I get back—household chores, paperwork from the surgery to look through, and other matters to attend to.' She made an attempt at a smile. 'I take it that everyone enjoyed the party?'

'Yes, it appeared so, *except for the two of us.* Maybe you will let me make it up to you at some time in the future? I owe you that.'

'You don't owe me anything,' she said in a low voice that was not for Toby's ears. 'I suggest we forget last night.'

'Just like that?' he said evenly. 'It would seem that you have a very low pain threshold.'

'All hurts lessen in time,' she replied, and as the waitress returned with the food that she'd ordered the stressful conversation dwindled into silence.

Nathan got to his feet and said, 'Come along, Toby, say goodbye to Libby.' He looked at her. 'We'll return your emergency "comforter" when it has been washed and ironed. Thanks again for the loan of it.'

She put down her knife and fork and observing him gravely commented, 'I was only too happy to be of use *with regard to that,*' and to Toby who was looking around him, unaware of the undercurrents between them, she said, 'I'll see you soon, Toby. Do I get a kiss?'

'Mmm,' he said, and pursing his lips placed them against her cheek.

As the two of them went out into the car park Nathan thought wryly that it was nice to know that one of them was in favour.

If ever the day dawned when Libby was ready to wipe the slate clean he would feel that at last the wheel had turned its full circle for them. At the present time it was just something that only happened in his dreams.

When she went to Reception to settle her account for the suite that she had occupied briefly she was told that it had been paid by Dr Nathan Gallagher.

He was heaping coals of fire on her head, she thought miserably, with the memory of his cool comment that he would return her nightdress when it had been washed, and now she was discovering that Nathan had paid for the luxurious accommodation that she'd had little time to take note of the night before.

The receptionist had noticed that she'd been taken aback, and volunteered the information that the account had been settled the week previously when Dr Gallagher had paid in full for everything that the hotel had arranged to provide, and as she went out to have a last stroll beside the lake she thought wretchedly that she'd been wrong about the 'coals of fire' and should be ashamed. He had treated her as he would any friend or acquaintance. The fact that the night before had escalated into something totally mind-blowing had been down to her as much as him.

As she walked beside the still waters the house on the island that could only be reached by boat came into view. She'd heard recently that it had become a tourist attraction and was available to rent for those who craved solitude in one of the most beautiful settings for miles around.

The next time she had the chance to take a break from the practice she would stay there if it was available, she decided. Where no one or nothing could take away the confidence in herself that had disappeared completely the night before when Nathan had begun to make love to her and the longing that she'd thought was under control had become a bright flame of desire.

During the week after the party Libby and Nathan spoke only briefly about surgery matters and in the evenings stayed well apart, until the night when Toby turned up on her doorstep with the nightdress neatly wrapped and with a note attached to say, 'Thanks again for the loan, Libby. I'm sending it with Toby as I have a strong feeling that my presence would not be welcome. Sorry I can't make myself scarce during surgery hours, Nathan.'

When she'd read it she looked across, knowing that he would be somewhere near, that he would not let Toby out into the wintry dusk even for a second without being nearby. Sure enough, he was standing in the doorway of the cottage next door where he could see him.

'Can I come in, Libby?' the young messenger asked once he'd delivered the package.

'Yes, if it is all right with your uncle,' she said immediately, and called across to ask if he could stay and play for a while.

Nathan nodded. 'Yes, for half an hour and then it will be his bedtime.'

Exactly thirty minutes later she took him back and when he opened the door to them Toby said, 'We've had lots of fun playing hide and seek.'

'Really,' was Nathan's only comment as his young charge skipped past him. Giving in to the urge to get him talking on a more friendly level, she asked, 'What have you got planned for Toby at Christmas?'

'Nothing at the moment,' was the answer. 'Why, have you got any ideas?'

'Er, no, but I could give it some thought. It will be his first Christmas in Swallowbrook and yours after a long gap, so it should be something special.'

'Not necessarily for me,' he said dryly, 'but for Toby, yes, absolutely. We'll probably go to stay with Dad for the two days. What are you planning to do?'

She knew he didn't care a jot about what she would be doing, that he was merely asking out of politeness. Any frail rapport they'd had was gone, blown away as if the cold winds from the fells were already in their winter mode.

'I haven't made any plans as yet,' she told him, 'though I will be somewhere around. This place is too lovely to be away from at Christmastime, or have you forgotten?'

'I forget nothing,' he said levelly. 'Neither the good or the bad,' and she wondered what that was supposed to mean. Maybe it was a hint that the conversation had gone on long enough with her standing on the doorstep like someone trying to sell him something, unwelcome and unwanted.

'I've got things to do so will say goodnight,' she said abruptly, and he didn't protest.

The October half-term at the village school was approaching and Libby was curious to know what arrangements Nathan was going to make regarding it.

Hugo was going to be away that week. He was taking his sister and her children away for a short break, so Nathan wouldn't be asking for time off as the two of them would be needed at the surgery.

She wasn't expecting him to discuss his plans with her as they only ever spoke about surgery matters, apart from the one occasion when she had asked him what he was planning for Christmas and received an evasive answer.

So she was surprised when one morning as they waited for the surgery to start he said, 'I can't make up my mind about the half-term break. Whether I should enrol Toby for the play group they have at the school during holidays for children with working parents, or take Dad up on his offer to have him while I'm here. What would you do if you were me, Libby?'

'I'm not sure,' she told him, concealing her surprise at being asked. 'I imagine that your father would love to have him, but he *was* looking forward to a complete rest after all the years as senior partner here. On the other hand, he might be finding that he has more time on his hands than he wants now, and from Toby's point of view there is the attraction of the river and the fishing.

'But the play group is well organised and well attended and Toby would be with some of his school friends. Why don't you ask him which he would like the best?'

'I know what he'll say to that,' he replied whimsically. 'It will be Grandfather Gallagher and the river. Maybe it won't be too taxing for Dad if you can manage on your own for the first hour in the morning and the last couple of hours at night. Can you, Libby?'

'Yes,' she told him steadily. 'I'll fit in with whatever is best for Toby. Just let me know when you've decided. I'm having a week off myself early next month but Hugo will be back by then and half-term will be over.'

'Are you going away? Or staying local?' he questioned.

'Local, but not too local,' she told him, 'just far enough away to have some time to myself.'

'And you are not going to tell me where?'

'No,' she said equably, and went to start her day at the Swallowbrook practice with a vision of a house on an island that she had arranged to rent for the week.

The morning was progressing like most other mornings at that time of year, a few coughs and sniffles, mixed with patients who were there because they had more serious anxieties to consult their doctors about, and once again there was the gathering of the willing and the unwilling who had come to have their flu jabs.

One of the patients was a young pregnant woman whose baby was almost due. She'd come to the surgery because of severe indigestion and when her name was called she got slowly to her feet.

Libby was standing in the doorway of her consulting room, waiting to usher her inside, when suddenly she let out a scream of pain and clutched herself around the waist.

'I think it's the baby,' she gasped. 'I thought the pains I've been having every so often were indigestion as I'm not due until next week, but this is different.'

'A week too soon is nothing when it is a first baby,' Libby told her, and taking her by the arm drew her quickly inside.

Nathan was saying goodbye to one of his patients at the other end of the corridor that separated their consulting rooms and took in the situation immediately. As she was helping the distressed woman on to the bed nearby he appeared and stood by as she checked to see if it *was* the baby on its way.

'I can see the head already,' she said quickly. 'See for yourself, Nathan.'

He didn't need to be asked twice and when he'd done so asked with low-voiced urgency, 'Have you ever done a delivery before?'

She shook her head. 'I know the procedure but have never had to put it into practice.'

'I have,' he said reassuringly. 'I've done dozens of them where I've been for the last three years. In those kind of places one has to be jack of all trades.' He turned to the anxious woman on the bed. 'It's going to be all right. What is your name?'

'Jodie,' she informed him between cries of pain.

'So try to keep as calm as you can, Jodie,' he said soothingly. 'There isn't going to be time to get you to hospital before the birth, but I'm used to delivering babies, so not to worry.'

'I need to push!' she cried.

'Yes, I know you do,' he told her, 'but if you can wait for just a few seconds until I tell you to, everything is going to be fine. In just a few moments you'll be holding your baby, so can you do that for me?'

'I'll try,' she gasped, and with Libby beside him holding a clean towel that she'd taken from a cupboard by the bed he said, 'Now you can push.'

With a huge heave she did so and seconds later a perfectly formed baby girl was wrapped in the towel and placed into her arms. As the tiny one expanded her lungs with a lusty cry a cheer broke the silence that had settled on the waiting room and the two doctors exchanged smiles.

In the euphoria of the birth Libby was forgetting everything except how the two of them, Nathan and herself, had shared such a special moment. Turning to him, she held him close for a few seconds before he dealt with the removal of the placenta.

'I can see that we are going to have to do this more often if this is what I get,' he said softly as she let her arms fall away. 'If this is how it feels to see someone else's child come into the world, can you imagine what it must be like with one of your own?'

'No, I'm afraid I can't,' she told him flatly as he brought her back down to earth. 'I stopped wishing for the moon a long time ago.'

'Point taken,' he replied in a similar tone, and turned back to the ecstatic new mother.

'Could someone phone my husband to tell him that he has a daughter?' Jodie asked in awed wonder. 'He's the trauma technician based at the fire station in the town centre.'

The ambulance that had been sent for had arrived and Libby said, 'Yes, of course, and we'll tell him that the two of you are on your way to the maternity unit at the hospital.'

'Have you chosen a name for the baby?' she asked as mother and child were being transferred to the ambulance a few minutes later.

'Yes,' was the reply. 'When we knew that the baby would be born in October, we chose Octavia for a girl and Octavius for a boy.'

'Very impressive,' Nathan commented briefly when Libby told him the baby's name. He had already gone back to his patients, and she hurried back to hers who had waited with much good humour for the morning surgery to return to normal.

After the moment of euphoria when she'd hugged him to her Libby's upbeat feeling about them continued to dwindle as the day progressed because she kept remembering what he'd said about having children of one's own.

At one time she'd dreamt of having a boy like him, dark-haired, dark-eyed, incredibly handsome, and a girl with blonde hair and the kind of ready smile that she used to have, which now appeared as infrequently as the sun in winter.

But long ago he'd dashed those hopes as casually as if discussing the weather, and Ian's lax approach to marriage had stopped any yearnings in that direction, so if the day ever dawned when she held a child of her own in her arms, it would be the age of miracles.

The arrangements for Toby at half-term turned out as Nathan had expected. John and the river had the vote, with his young visitor even sleeping at the lodge in a small bedroom that the older man had fitted out for him.

It meant that Nathan was able to put in a full day at the practice while the two doctors were holding the fort during Hugo's absence. It also gave him some free time for himself, which he hadn't had much of since taking Toby into his life.

As they left the surgery one evening to go to their respective cottages he said to Libby, 'I don't feel like cooking, so am going to get changed and dine at the hotel where we had Dad's farewell. Do you feel like joining me?'

She hesitated. The thought of a delightful meal in equally delightful surroundings was tempting, but keeping up a front of casual detachment in the place where they had been so drawn to each other wasn't. Yet even as the thought was going through her mind she found herself saying, 'Yes, why not? I don't feel like cooking either. I feel tired and drab, so like you I will go and change into something less formal.'

'The blue dress maybe,' he suggested casually. 'It looked good on you that day at the school harvest.'

'Yes. I suppose it would be suitable,' she told him, concealing her surprise at discovering that he'd remembered what she was wearing on that occasion. But this was Nathan who not so long ago had been quick to point out that there was nothing wrong with *his* memory, as if hers might be at fault!

'How long before you want to go?' she asked, getting back to basics.

'Half an hour?'

'Yes, I'm starving, and, Nathan, I want it to be my shout. I remember finding that my account had been paid when I went to settle it the last time I was there.'

'So? You were my guest.'

She was frowning. 'Even so...'

He sighed. 'Do you recall me saying that I would like to make it up to you for taking up your evening with Toby's problems? So please don't argue, Libby.'

'All right,' she agreed at last. Maybe what had happened between them had been an aberration. A moment of madness that had come out of the blue. Tonight it would be just a matter of two busy doctors unwinding over a pleasant meal. There could be no harm in that.

They were separating at the bottom of their respective drives and as she went upstairs to shower and change, out of the wardrobe came the blue dress.

When she went out to join him wearing it he nodded his approval and for the first time in ages she felt beautiful.

The evening progressed just how she wanted it to

be, friendly and tranquil, with no disturbing vibes to make her feel threatened or on edge as she listened to Nathan describing the traumas and the good times of his time in Africa.

'Was it so demanding that you never had the chance to come back home for a break?' she asked at one point.

There was a pause in what had been a relaxed conversation as his mind went back once again to those soul-destroying moments when he'd stood in the church porch and had to accept that he'd had a wasted journey. He'd been an arrogant fool not to act sooner, to assume that despite their parting words Libby would have continued to have romantic feelings for him and would have waited till he'd come to his senses where she was concerned.

But, no, instead he'd acted on impulse and selfish desire. But he'd got his just deserts. He'd arrived too late to stop the wedding, and as he'd watched her smile up at her new husband had thought that there had been no point in his coming as Libby seemed happy enough with Jefferson.

If he was to tell her that he *had* been home during that time, just the once, what good would it do? She'd loved him once, but not any more, and tonight they were at peace with each other as friends, so why spoil it?

'Yes,' he replied, avoiding her glance. 'The pressures were always too great to be able to take time off.'

As they were about to leave the hotel and he was helping her into the warm jacket that she'd brought with her he asked, 'Do you want to take a stroll by the lake?'

'Yes, if you like,' she told him, with the memory of

that other time when she'd done the same thing alone and in daylight on the morning after the party.

It was then that she'd been attracted to Greystone House, the property on the island, where she was going to stay in a couple of weeks' time.

Tonight it was floodlit with lanterns and so was the lake, like diamonds sparkling on water. When Nathan took her hand in his she didn't draw it out of his clasp, but kept it there, warm and safe, in case she should trip in the semi-darkness.

'What is that place?' he asked, glancing across the water to where the house stood solid and unreachable. 'I remember it from way back but don't ever recall what it was used for.'

'I don't know about then,' she told him, 'but now it is a very popular holiday let, though I'm not sure what degree of the services it has, such as lighting, heating and water, but for anyone wanting peace and solitude it's the perfect place. It's owned by a local businessman who lets it out when his family aren't using it.'

If she told him that she was going to stay there herself in the near future he would think she was crazy no doubt. But it would give her the opportunity to be alone with her thoughts, with the reassurance of knowing that she was just a boat ride away from the things she held dearest.

Every moment spent with Nathan in tranquillity was a joy, but there was always the reminder of things past to spoil it. It was why on the night of his father's party, when she'd been ready to give herself to him completely, she'd backed away. There had been no real closeness between them since then until tonight, just as long as they could keep gentling along like this.

Walking alongside her, still holding her hand, Nathan was thinking the same kind of thoughts. He'd been too pushy that other time and spoilt it, but not tonight. They were in a different mode, though still overwhelmingly aware of each other.

'Is Toby enjoying his stay by the river?' she asked as they went back to where the car was parked on the hotel forecourt.

He was smiling. 'Yes. I don't know which of the two of them is enjoying it the most. Having him around has given Dad something to keep him on his toes, but I have to make sure he isn't doing too much, though Toby isn't a demanding child like some are, and Dad says that he brightens up his life.'

'Becoming his guardian has caused you to have to make many adjustments in yours, hasn't it?' she commented.

'Yes, I have to admit that is so. Before he came to me I was used to doing what suited *me* first and foremost, and now my requirements must always come second. Toby seems happy enough with me, but he needs a mother figure too, which I suppose means that I should find myself a wife.'

He was sounding her out, putting out a feeler to see if she would respond, and she did, but not how he wanted her to.

'I'm sure there will be plenty of applicants for the position once you let that be known,' she replied coolly. 'You have the looks, a beautiful cottage, the job...' *And a heart of stone to be discussing something like this with me of all people.*

She was averting her gaze from his, didn't see him flinch, and when he opened the car door for her, she slid into the passenger seat and stared into the distance.

They were back in the centre of Swallowbrook in minutes and instead of inviting him in for coffee, as she had been intending to, Libby thanked him for the meal, bade him a brief goodnight and was gone, closing her front door behind her decisively.

Yet there was nothing decisive about the way she began to climb the stairs with dragging feet and a heavy heart.

Why couldn't she accept once and for all that Nathan only wanted her as colleague, neighbour and someone to play hide and seek with Toby? she thought bleakly.

Throwing off her clothes, she got into bed and wished that it was tomorrow that she was going to the house on the island.

She slept at last, only to dream that Nathan was down below, ringing her doorbell, and when she let him in he said, 'I love you, Libby, can't live without you.' But as she moved towards him, smiling with arms outstretched, she awoke to find that the doorbell *was* ringing and when she went downstairs he *was* there, but he wasn't saying the words of her dream. 'Dad has just phoned to say that Toby is sick,' he said without preamble. 'I'm going there now and thought I'd better warn you that I might be missing from the surgery in the morning.'

'What does he say is wrong with him?' she asked as the doctor in her rose to the surface.

'Temperature, headache, rash—it all sounds worryingly familiar.'

'Meningitis?'

He nodded.

'Give me a couple of minutes to fling on some clothes. I'm coming with you,' she told him.

'Are you sure?'

She was already halfway up the stairs and called down to him, 'Of course I'm sure. Have you got your bag?' He nodded bleakly. 'So go and start the car.'

'When did Toby start to be ill?' she asked as they drove towards the river and his father's lodge.

'Just a short while ago, Dad said. Awoke fretful, poorly, covered in a damned rash and is vomiting. If anything else bad happens to him, I shudder to think how I'll cope,' he said, with his voice thickening, and she thought that love could make strong men weak.

'Nothing *is* going to happen to Toby,' she told him steadily as the complex of retirement homes came into view. 'The two of us, you and I, are not going to let it. We are being given a taste of what it's like for the families of our sick patients. It's the other side of the coin, a lesson to be well learned.'

Toby was how John had described him, but Nathan's father had met them at the door with the news that the rash had come out fully and wasn't the same kind as the symptoms of meningitis. 'My feeling is he's picked up a bug or some sort of virus,' he said as they examined him.

Nathan muttered, 'Thank God it isn't the other thing. This we should be able to cope with, but the problem is I don't know anything about Toby's health before I took him into my care, what or if he had any health problems before I became responsible for him. In normal circumstances parents have firsthand knowledge about anything regarding their child's health.

'I feel pretty sure that his condition this morning is allergy related but am loath to start prescribing anything until someone else has seen him beside ourselves. What do *you* think, Libby?' he asked.

'It could be something he is allergic to,' she agreed, 'but from what to make him so poorly?'

'That's just it, we don't know, do we? It could be from anything—food, toiletries, plants, something airborne.' To Toby, with incredible gentleness, he said, 'Aren't you the lucky one, with three doctors to look after you?'

As she took his hot little hand in hers to feel his pulse he said drowsily, 'When can we play hide and seek again, Libby?'

'Soon,' she soothed, and when she turned round Nathan had been replaced by his father, who said, 'We're not sure what the rash is, are we, Libby? I'm wondering if his condition is due to something that Toby has eaten, and agree with Nathan that we shouldn't prescribe until we are sure what is wrong, which is going to mean taking him to A and E immediately. Do you want to go with them and I'll take the morning surgery for you?'

Daylight was already filtering through the curtains

and she asked, 'Where is Nathan, and what time is it, John?'

'He's on the phone to the hospital, and it is almost a quarter to eight o'clock.'

'I'd like to go with them, but am not sure if Nathan would rather you were there,' she told him.

'Maybe, but Toby is asking for *you* and that's all that matters.'

'Yes, you're right, of course it is,' she said steadily, and wished that John had felt confident enough to re-assure her with regard to Nathan's desire for her company.

She sat in the back seat of the car next to Toby as Nathan drove them to the hospital. Apart from a brief word of thanks from him for accompanying them, and her telling him that thanks were not necessary in such a situation, they hadn't spoken since they'd left his father's place, but she could feel the depth of his anxiety like a tangible thing.

Taking over the care and wellbeing of a child in Toby's circumstances must be nerve-racking enough without this kind of thing thrown in for good measure, she thought. But apart from that moment of weakness when they'd been hastening to his father's place after he had received the phone call, Nathan was in control again.

Yet she did wish that he didn't feel he had to thank her for being there for the two of them. She'd witnessed his distress when she'd opened the door to him in the early dawn, and seen how much he loved the boy when they'd arrived to find him so poorly. *That* was enough to make her want to be with them every second of the trauma that they were caught up in.

CHAPTER SIX

SHE'D never loved them both so much as at that moment, Libby thought as Nathan drove them to the hospital through the morning rush-hour traffic, the child because he was ill, and the man because he was being cast in the role of the frantic parent.

Holding Toby's hand tightly, she ached to do the same for Nathan, but felt that the memory of what he'd said when leaving her after they'd spent the previous evening together didn't give her the right to do anything other than give him the kind of support that anyone would do in such a situation, which wasn't quite what she had in mind.

Tense behind the wheel, Nathan was aware of how much he needed her, how much she brought stability into his disrupted life, but it wasn't just that, he was in love with Libby. The man who had decided that love was not to be trusted had found that with her it wasn't like that. Life could be so good for them if she would only forgive him.

Since he'd returned to Swallowbrook and got to know her better he'd discovered that it was a passionate, caring woman that he'd once sent away. All his doubts were disappearing as he was getting to know Libby for the person she really was and he wanted her in his life for evermore.

Whether she would believe *that* was doubtful after the way he'd talked about finding himself a wife the night before as if *she* didn't come into it.

When the nightmare they were in the middle of with Toby had been hopefully resolved he would take her somewhere special and propose to her amongst candlelight and flowers. Maybe then she would accept that he was totally sincere in what he had to say.

The months had gone by. Working from dawn to dusk out there, he'd done nothing about the moment of raw awareness that she had awakened in him, until his father had casually mentioned Libby's approaching marriage to Jefferson.

It had jolted him into the realisation that he couldn't let it happen without seeing her first, that he had to go back to see for himself if the love she'd had for him was still there. *And much good it had done him,* he thought grimly, with the memory of those desolate moments in the church porch surfacing once more.

He was watching her in the car's rear-view mirror, noting how gentle and reassuring she was with Toby, and as the turning for the hospital loomed up ahead the tight band of anxiety across his chest increased its stranglehold.

When they arrived at Accident and Emergency he carried a drowsy Toby inside, with Libby close by his side. Two of the staff had been alerted by his phone call and were waiting for them, and once they'd been shown into a cubicle a doctor appeared.

'I don't recognise your youngster's symptoms immediately,' he told them when he'd examined Toby, 'and I take it that neither of you are sure or you wouldn't be here. If I had to make a guess I would say that whatever is wrong with him is allergy related, but we don't rely on guesses so we're going to admit him for a couple of days while we do some tests.'

Turning to Libby, he said, 'We have met before, haven't we, Dr Hamilton, at some meeting or other? And this is your family, I take it?'

'I'm afraid not,' she told him with an anxious look at Toby, who was clinging to Nathan and looking really poorly. 'This young patient is Dr Gallagher's ward. We are both employed at the Swallowbrook Medical Practice and live next door to each other.'

'Ah, I see,' he said, and turned his attention to what Nathan was saying.

'One of the reasons we're here is because I'm in the process of adopting Toby,' he explained, 'and have not yet received his medical records from the practice where he and his parents were registered before they were involved in a tragic accident. So I felt that the hospital needed to see him before we began to treat him.'

'Has he eaten anything that could have caused this? Or been near any plant life that could have a sting in its tail?' the other man asked.

'Not that we know of. He spent yesterday with my father and he doesn't let Toby out of his sight.'

'Hmm. So what do the two of you think it might be?' he asked as they bent over the small figure on the bed.

'I thought of urticaria,' Libby told him. 'When he is at his grandfather's place Toby sometimes plays in a field nearby and if nettles are present he could have been stung by them.'

'Yes, but there would have been tears if that was the case and Dad would have picked up on that,' Nathan said sombrely. 'If we are looking at plant life I think that it might be something he has eaten.'

Looking down at Toby, he asked, 'Did you play in the field yesterday?' And got a drowsy nod for an answer.

'And did you eat anything that you found there?'

'Only the grapes,' was the weak reply.

'What kind of grapes were they, Toby?'

'Black and shiny.'

His next question cut into the tension in the room like a knife. 'How many...er, grapes did you eat?'

'Two. I spat the others out because I didn't like them.'

'That's all right, then,' Libby told him gently, and as the three doctors observed each other there was the same thought in their minds. Toby's symptoms could be those of the poisonous plant belladonna, or deadly nightshade, as it was sometimes called due to the serious effects it could have if the berries were eaten.

As Libby stroked his hot little brow gently the doctor took Nathan to one side. 'It does sound as if your young one has been in contact with the so unsuitably named belladonna, or something similar. The vomiting will have brought some of it up, but I'm afraid that we will have to resort to water lavage if blood tests show the belladonna poison is present. Stomach washing out is an unpleasant prospect for anyone, especially a child, but that is what needs to be done immediately if our premonitions are correct.'

The answer they were dreading was there with the test results and the doctor in A and E said, 'Fortunately Toby doesn't seem to have eaten many of the berries, which is a godsend, but the situation is still critical. Hopefully once his stomach has been washed clear of the poison it will prevent any further complications, but it must be done now.'

Nathan nodded bleakly. 'I'm in favour of anything that will save Toby's life so, yes, let's proceed as quickly as possible. Time has been wasted because neither Dr Hamilton or myself had any idea that Toby might have been near belladonna and been tempted by what he thought were black grapes.'

The doctor was already arranging for a theatre to be made available with staff there ready to assist by the time Toby was brought down, and as he was being transferred there, with Libby still holding his hand, Nathan said with his face a grey mask of horror, 'I'm going to insist that I'm there while they do what they have to do. I've done plenty of theatre work while I was abroad, it won't be anything new. But you should get back to the practice, you're needed there more than here. I'll see you when this is over, Libby, and thanks for coming.'

'Will you please stop thanking me? I don't want your thanks,' she told him, stiffening at the abruptness of his dismissal. 'What I *do want* is to know that Toby will soon be well again and that the pain and the nightmare that is there for the parents of any sick child will soon be over for you, and now I'll do what you suggest and go back to my patients, which will leave your father free to come here.'

As Toby's bottom lip began to tremble she said gently, 'I won't be long. I have to go and see to my other sick people now, but I'll bring you something nice when I come back.'

'What will it be, Libby?' he asked with a momentary brightening of his small pale face.

'It will be a surprise,' she told him, and turning to Nathan as the feeling of being no longer needed persisted, 'I would appreciate a phone call when you have a moment to spare.'

'That goes without saying,' he said evenly, and as she went out into the corridor with a heavy heart she didn't hear him groan at the way he'd told her to go as if she'd served her purpose. It *had* been the right thing to do. It was Libby's responsibility as senior partner to be back at the practice, but it had been the wrong way to do it. What was the matter with him? He'd been floundering about like a quivering jelly ever since they'd found Toby in this state, while she'd been like a rock to hold onto, and now he'd sent her away.

They'd arrived at the theatre on the lower ground floor and after that everything else was forgotten as the great machine that was the NHS took over.

The moment Libby arrived back at the practice she was greeted by John, with an extra furrow of worry to add to those that age had carved across his brow.

'So what's the news, Libby? What did they say at the hospital?' he asked.

'It seems as if it might be belladonna poisoning,' she told him. 'When Nathan asked Toby if he'd eaten anything while he was playing in the field, or anywhere else for that matter, he said, yes, he'd eaten some shiny black "grapes", which we think came from a belladonna plant as it describes its berries exactly and his symptoms fit in with what we know of the poisonous effects of it.

'Fortunately he didn't eat many of the berries, just one or two, but he's finding it rather difficult to swallow and is drowsy. Then there's the fact that he has sickness and diarrhoea and his temperature is up, so the doctor in A and E is going to have to wash his stomach out to get rid of any poisonous substance. Nathan is insisting on being there while it is being done so Toby will have him close all the time, thank goodness.'

John was observing her, dumbstruck. 'I was with Toby all the time he was in the field. The only time he was out of my sight was when he was playing at hiding in the bushes and I had to find him, so it would have to be then that he found the berries. I feel dreadful that it should have happened while he was in my care, or that it should have happened at all.'

'You must *not* feel like that,' she told him firmly. 'These things can happen without any blame attached to anyone. How were you to know there was deadly nightshade nearby and that he would mistake the berries for grapes? It is typical of a child to eat what they shouldn't.'

About to set off for the hospital he paused and asked, 'Nathan—how is he coping? These are times when a child needs a mother. I have the feeling that somewhere in the past he took the wrong turning with regard to that. I don't suppose he's ever said anything to you to that effect, has he?'

As if, she thought grimly, and told him, 'No, John, he's never said anything like that to me.'

'I thought not,' he said with a sigh, and drove off to see his adoptive grandson.

There were still a few stragglers in the surgery waiting room and when Libby called the first of them in she was confronted by middle-aged Thomas Miller, leaning heavily on a stick.

He owned the outdoor equipment store in the centre of the village, patronised by many of the walkers and climbers who were attracted to the lakes and fells.

Once a keen climber himself, he was no longer able to enjoy their delights due to a serious leg fracture that he'd sustained while up on the tops. He had been missing for days until the mountain rescue team had found him at the bottom of a gully.

The delay in getting him to hospital for the surgery needed on the injured leg had left him only partly mobile on it, so now he was doing the next best thing to climbing the fells by providing those who still could with everything *they* might need to keep them safe, dry, and fed.

He was a likeable man with a wife and two teenage

sons who had no yearnings to become involved in the sport that had once been their father's favourite pastime.

As well as the store Thomas was chairman of the community centre in the village and almost always had something interesting to pass on when he saw her about what was being planned by his committee.

Before she had time to ask what had brought him to the surgery he was asking for information, rather than giving it, in the form of wanting to know, 'What's wrong with the laddie that Nathan's bringing up, Libby? I've just seen John setting off for the hospital looking very downcast, said he hadn't time to chat as the young'un was very poorly.'

'Yes, he is,' she agreed. 'We had to take him there this morning as we weren't sure what was wrong with Toby. Nathan is there with him now and I've just got back. When something like this happens and the adoptive parent knows nothing about the child's previous medical history it's very worrying.

'Maybe you'd like to pass the word around for the benefit of other children and their parents that it seems as if he has been poisoned by eating the berries of the belladonna plant and at the moment the situation is serious.

'And now what about you, Thomas? What brings you here on this chilly winter morning?'

'I've got a swollen foot on my good leg and thought I'd better come and see you.'

When she'd examined his foot Libby said, 'It looks like an infection of some sort. Have you had a sore or a cut on it recently?'

'I bought some new shoes a few weeks back and they rubbed the skin off one of my toes. It healed up all right, but still felt tender and then the swelling appeared.'

'Hmm, the infection could have originated from that and lain dormant for a while,' she told him as she felt the swollen fleshy part of the top of his foot. 'I'm going to give you a course of amoxicillin. Are you all right with that? You're not allergic to it?'

'No,' he said easily. 'I've had it before without any side effects.' He got up to go. 'Do tell Nathan that I hope the boy will soon be better. We're having a big barbeque on bonfire night on the usual field behind the park and the young'un won't want to miss that.'

'Hopefully we'll all be there,' she told him, with the dread of what Toby had told them heavy on her, and wished that Nathan would phone, but as it was barely an hour since she'd left him maybe she was expecting too much.

She'd been anticipating having to dash around in the lunch hour to find something to take back with her for Toby, but the nurses had forestalled her and one of them turned up at that moment with sweets and toys that they'd collected amongst the staff.

'Is it right that Toby might have been eating the berries of the deadly nightshade?' she asked. 'I heard you telling Dr John something like that and it sounded really awful.'

'Yes,' she told her. 'He only ate a couple, but it is very worrying just the same as the berries can kill.'

At that moment Nathan came through on her desk

phone and the practice nurse departed. 'How's Toby?' she asked urgently.

'Sleeping more naturally,' he replied. 'His tummy should now be washed clear of the poison, and if what they've done at the hospital is sufficient to make him better, we might see some improvement soon. It makes me shudder to think what he would have been like if he'd eaten more than just two of the ghastly things.

'How are things at your end?' he wanted to know. 'Had Dad finished morning surgery when you got back?'

'Yes, more or less. He is on his way to the hospital now. John was devastated when I told him what Toby had been up to and is most upset that it had happened while he was in his care. He said it could only have occurred while they were playing hide and seek in the bushes on the edge of the field. So do please have a kind word for him, Nathan.'

There was silence at the other end of the phone for a moment and then he said dryly, 'Why, what do you think I'm going to do? Blame him for being kind enough to look after Toby during the half-term break?

'I can tell that you're not very pleased with me, Libby, and I apologise for being a tactless fool when I told you to go back to the surgery, but there are others who need you besides Toby. We can't expect to monopolise you all the time. So am I forgiven? I never get it right with you, do I?'

'There is nothing to forgive, just as there is nothing to thank me for,' she told him with a lift to her voice. 'I'll see you this evening as soon as I've finished here.'

When she'd replaced the receiver another patient was waiting to be seen and after that there were twice as many home visits to do because she was the only doctor available. But that was what it was all about and Nathan had been right as usual in insisting that she make the surgery her priority in spite of her longing to be with the two of them.

When she arrived at the hospital in the evening he was sitting beside the bed, watching over Toby, who was sleeping once more with his small chest rising and falling steadily, unlike the distressed breathing of earlier in the day.

But he was still very pale and poorly-looking and as she came to stand beside them Nathan looked up and said with a wry smile, 'He has asked a couple of times when you were coming with the "goodies" so it would seem that Toby's thought processes have not been affected.'

She was bending over the child in the bed, observing him with a glance that was a mix of the keen eye of the medic and the tender concern of someone who cared a lot for the small motherless child and the man watching over him.

It had been a long and tiring day, but it was as nothing compared to what Nathan had been going through, she thought. Yet when she turned to face him the smile was still there, somewhat frayed at the edges but a smile nevertheless. She wasn't to know that just the sight of her after one of the worst days of his life was comforting beyond belief.

However, Libby's thoughts were centred on the urgencies of the moment and she asked, 'So what is the verdict on the gastric lavage and Toby's condition in general?'

'Improving,' he replied soberly. 'The lavage should have washed the poison out of his system and we have to hope that he will gradually recover. Dad has been and gone in an awful state. He's going to investigate all the plant life where Toby was hiding and see it off when he finds the belladonna so that no other child will be tempted to eat what they think are juicy black grapes.

'And what sort of day have you had?' he asked. 'Or shouldn't I ask?'

Nightmarish would be a truthful answer to that question, she thought, with the two of them constantly in her thoughts and a huge workload to cope with.

Instead she told him, 'I've had better, but Hugo will be back tomorrow and then the pressures from the surgery will slacken off, and as for now would you like me to sit with Toby while you have a break?'

'No, Libby. I'll be fine,' he said, not wanting to miss a moment of being with her now that she was there.

He was doing it again, she thought, pushing her away, keeping her on the edge of the trauma he was going through. Was he afraid that she would see their togetherness at this awful time as a bond that might tie him to her?

She wanted to run away and hide, but not before Toby saw that she had kept her promise. Producing the bag of toys and goodies, she said levelly, 'The surgery staff have sent these, everyone is most concerned for Toby and yourself.' And still persisting, she asked, 'Have you had anything to eat since we came here this morning?'

'No. Food would choke me. I've had a few cups of coffee, which are all I've needed so far.'

She nodded and, pulling another chair up at the opposite side of the bed, sat facing him in silence for what seemed like an eternity until Toby opened his eyes and on seeing her asked, 'Have you brought them, Libby?'

'Yes, my darling,' she told him. 'I've brought lots of things for you to eat and play with as soon as you're feeling better. They're in this big bag.' She held it up where he could see it and he nodded then closed his eyes and dozed off again.

Nathan had been silent during their short conversation. As he'd watched the two of them together all his vows to wait until the right moment to open his heart to her had disappeared.

As she was placing the bag in the locker at the side of Toby's bed he rose to his feet and, fixing her with his dark hazel gaze, said in a low voice that she alone could hear, 'Libby, will you marry me? It would be so much the right thing to do.'

'Nathan, how can you ask me that now? Of course I can't,' she breathed, taking a step back on legs that had turned to jelly. 'I'm not in the market for another marriage of convenience, this time yours!' She moved even further away from him. 'I will be here to see Toby this time tomorrow, or before if he needs me, and it would help if you aren't around.'

'You still haven't forgiven me for rejecting you all that time ago, have you?' he said flatly.

'This is not about forgiveness,' she told him in an anguished whisper. 'It's about a word that seems to be missing from your vocabulary where I'm concerned, so subject closed!' And once again she set off down the hospital corridor with pain in her heart.

But this time it was for the *two of them*. It was crystal clear that Nathan's lukewarm proposal had been because he *was* considering her as a mother figure to help him bring Toby up, and this crisis had settled any doubts he might have had. If that was the limit of his affection for her, the miseries of the past would seem as nothing compared to those of the future.

As he'd watched her go he had wanted to chase after her and tell her that his love for her was a clear and constant thing, that since he had got to know her better she was never out of his thoughts. But it was clear from Libby's reaction to his ill-timed proposal that *her* thoughts were not running along the same channels as *his*.

And so what had he done? Let his heart take over his mind and asked her to marry him in the worst possible setting. At a time when she was bound to feel that he wanted her in his life to help with Toby, who was lying beside them recovering from an illness that could easily have killed him, and when all around them was the smell of antiseptic when it should have been lilies or roses.

The only good thing to come out of his crazy impulse was to know that she was still on Toby's case, loving and gentle towards him, *caring for him like a mother*. So if he, Nathan, had put himself beyond the pale in

Libby's estimation, at least her feelings towards Toby weren't going to change.

He loved everything about her, he thought achingly, the golden fairness of her, the soft brown velvet of eyes that were only ever watchful and wary where he was concerned. He admired the way she ran the practice and treated the staff, and sometimes wondered how that father of hers could bear to be so far away from his only child. Yet fool that he was, hadn't *he* stayed away from her for three long years and now was desperate to make up for it?

As Libby drove back to Swallowbrook at the end of one of the most stressful days she'd had in a long time, her spirits were at a low ebb. It had started badly and got steadily worse, the final straw being Nathan's impromptu and emotionless proposal.

Her refusal had been prompt and painful, and she'd had control of the situation until now, but on the last mile of her journey home she was weeping at the futility of her feelings for a man who understood her so little.

Roll on her short vacation in the house on the island in the middle of the lake, she was thinking as she put the car away for the night. Just a couple of weeks and she would be away from everything that hurt.

Hopefully by then Toby would be better, because if he wasn't she wouldn't want to be away from him no matter how desperate she was for some time on her own, and if Nathan was back at the practice along with Hugo she would be able to go away with an easy mind. But for the present the sting of being proposed to because of her usefulness rather than her appeal was not easy to cope with.

Normality was coming back into his life in everything except his relationship with Libby, Nathan reflected on the morning that Toby was discharged from hospital. That had died a death on the day that he'd asked her to marry him and been well and truly put in his place.

It had been crazy to throw away the closeness that had been developing between them in a moment of intense longing, and now there was not a lot left between them, he decided as he drove home with an excited Toby beside him.

She had been diligent in her visits to the boy, and he'd done as she'd asked and kept out of the way in the early evening of each day, which was when she came, using the break from his bedside to go home and have a shower and a change of clothes.

By the time he'd got back she had been and gone. Sometimes they'd passed each other on the way and he'd thought grimly that it wasn't a crime he'd committed. He could think of one or two local, unattached women who would jump at the chance of marrying him, but he didn't want them. He wanted Libby beside him in the dark hours of the night and across from him at the breakfast table. What it was going to be like when he returned to the practice he shuddered to think.

It had been a Friday when he'd brought Toby home from the hospital and he would be going back to school on the Monday. Nathan had seen little of Libby over the weekend, but Toby had spent some time with her as it seemed that she'd promised him on the night before his discharge that he could go across to her place to play whenever he wanted if it was all right with his uncle.

Nathan hadn't had any quarrel with that, just a wish that he might have been included in the invitation, and now it was Monday morning and after seeing Toby safely into school Nathan presented himself at the practice once more with the determination inside him that as far as he was concerned he was there to work, ready to slot himself back into the busy medical centre where at least he would be able to see Libby, even if *she* didn't want to see *him*.

He was in for a surprise. Along with the rest of the staff she greeted him cordially enough, as if nothing between them had changed, and he observed her thoughtfully when she wasn't looking in his direction. He was getting the message. It was going to be business as usual at the surgery and the cold zone at any other time.

It was the first time she had seen him properly in days she was thinking as the morning got under way and noticed that although Nathan was dealing with his patients with his usual brisk efficiency he looked tired and gaunt, like someone carrying a heavy burden, and she felt that her love would be a poor thing if she didn't do something about it, because love him she did, she always had, and no matter what he did or said, nothing was ever going to change that.

CHAPTER SEVEN

AT the end of the morning surgery she said to him, 'Would the two of you like to come for a meal tonight? It would save you cooking as long as you don't mind eating somewhat later than you usually do.'

He was observing her with raised brows but his reply when it came was easy enough. 'That would be very nice, except for the fact that Dad is picking Toby up from school and taking him back to his place for his evening meal to celebrate him being well again. Thanks for the thought, though.'

As she'd listened to what he had to say she knew that the obvious thing to do was to say that the invitation was still open if he wanted to come alone, but she'd been relying on Toby as the bond between them to keep the atmosphere less taut than it had been since Nathan had asked her to marry him as those hurtful moments haunted her constantly.

He was tuned into her thoughts on *this* occasion and said, 'I'm sure you would prefer it if he was with us, so perhaps another time would be better, and by the way, as I don't have to pick Toby up from school, I'm available until we close here if you want an early finish for a change. I can imagine what the workload has been like while Hugo and I have both been absent.'

It was *her* turn to refuse *his* offer. 'I asked you to come for a meal as you look as if you haven't been eating much over recent days, and as this evening will be your first free time since Toby was ill I wouldn't want you to be putting in extra time at the practice on my behalf. So do we understand each other? The offer still stands if you would like to come on your own tonight.'

She wasn't going to tell him that she was achingly aware of the strain he'd been under, and that she could not stop herself from caring about him just as long as he understood that was where it ended. He'd spoiled the rest of it by making her feel that he wanted her as a mother figure for Toby and was seemingly prepared to go along with the *wife* part of it for the child's sake.

He couldn't refuse again, Nathan was thinking. The thought of having Libby to himself for a couple of hours until his father brought Toby home at his bedtime was not to be refused twice, so he said, 'Yes, all right, I'd like that, but before I set off on my house calls I'd like to make it clear that I *will* be working the extra hours this afternoon in spite of what you say.

'I know that you would rather see less of me than more, which makes your invitation to dine with you tonight somewhat of a surprise, but with regard to this place I'm part of a team and am already conscious that my contribution is a lot less than yours, so today I am on full steam.' While she digested that he went out to his car and within seconds drove off to visit the sick in the cottages and in the bigger houses on the leafy lanes that surrounded the village.

Hugo followed him shortly afterwards to do his share of the house calls and while they were gone Libby went across to Lavender Cottage and prepared a casserole, which she put in the oven on a low setting.

Once that was done she laid the table with the cutlery and crockery that had been her mother's pride and joy. Then it was back to the practice where the waiting room was filling up again for the second surgery of the day.

As she crossed the space that separated the cottage from the practice building the lake was glinting in the distance beneath a pale winter sun and the house on the island was caught in its rays as a reminder that soon she would be there, away from the practice for a little while and from the man who was never out of her thoughts.

Maybe when she wasn't seeing Nathan all the time at the surgery and in his comings and goings to the cottage next to hers she might find some peace of mind, if only briefly, she thought, but loving him had become a way of life, a reason for living, even though she was miserable most of the time because of that same love.

At the end of the day they left the building that had once been her home together and separated outside the cottages while Nathan went to change and Libby hurried inside to check that the casserole hadn't dried up.

It hadn't, so she dashed up the stairs, flung off her

working clothes, and after a quick shower put on pale grey slacks and a black silk top and was coming down the stairs when he rang the bell.

Her eyes widened when she saw the bouquet of all the flowers she liked best that he was holding, and as she stepped back to let him in, with her composure slipping into confusion, he handed them to her and said whimsically, 'I'm not going to use the "thanks" word, but I don't know how I would have got through the last couple of weeks without you, Libby. You were my rock to hold onto in the midst of the horror of Toby's illness.'

He was explaining the other side of that ghastly proposal, she thought with tears pricking, and unable to stop herself she reached forward and kissed his cheek.

As he turned his head, surprised by the gesture, their lips met and the moment became a torrent of longing as his arms tightened around her and she gave herself up to kisses that were a much better thing than her lips against his cheek.

The ringing of the doorbell broke into the moment and Nathan groaned as they drew apart. 'Are you expecting someone?' he asked.

She shook her head. 'No, but I'd better see who it is.' Moving towards the door reluctantly, she pulled back the catch to reveal John in the porch, holding a heavy-eyed Toby by the hand.

'Sorry to arrive so soon,' he said apologetically. 'When Nathan rang to say that he would be eating here tonight I told him that I would bring Toby back at half past seven as he'd already been asleep for a couple of hours after school, but his first day back has taken it out of him and he needs to be tucked up in his bed.'

Nathan had appeared behind her. 'It's all right, Dad,' he said, and with a smile for Libby, 'Would you consider bringing the food over to my place while I get Toby settled for the night? It would solve the problem.'

'Yes, of course,' she agreed weakly, still under the spell of his kisses and the joy of being in his arms. There had been none of the awful feeling of being used, just the supreme delight of a moment that had come out of nowhere and might have progressed into something special maybe.

Yet, she thought as John said a brief goodbye and Nathan picked Toby up into his arms ready to take him to where he belonged, some things that happened came in the form of a lesson from life and were meant to cause those involved to stop and think before committing themselves.

As the door closed behind them she took the casserole out of the oven and placed it on a tray, then followed them across, and while Nathan was putting Toby to bed set the table in his dining room instead of hers.

'The sleepy one is asking for a kiss, Libby,' he called down some minutes later. 'Can you come up?' When she appeared in the doorway of the smaller of the cottage's two bedrooms Toby was smiling at her from the pillows and clutching his comforter, which had been with him all the time he'd been in hospital.

As tears pricked she thought how wonderful it would be if she was there every night at his bedtime because Nathan loved her for herself and not her usefulness.

Nathan was watching her expressions change and knew that what his father's ring on the doorbell had interrupted was not going to happen again when Toby was asleep. It had been a moment of bliss that had ended as quickly as it had begun. Once again the timing had been wrong.

His surmise was correct. As they ate the meal that Libby had prepared the conversation was about everything except those kisses, such as their day at the practice and village affairs, including the barbeque and bonfire that was to take place on the coming Friday night.

'There has been that kind of thing on Bonfire Night ever since we were young, hasn't there?' he commented, remembering how she had always been somewhere near on the night. 'That is what is so enchanting about this kind of community. I would imagine that everyone rallied around like they do when you lost Jefferson.'

'Yes, they did,' she said quietly, wishing he hadn't brought up the awful mistake she'd made out of loneliness and rejection while they were in the middle of chatting about general things, and that wasn't the end of it.

'You never talk about your marriage, Libby. Did you love him?' he asked gravely, and more importantly, 'Did he love you?'

He was remembering them again, those ghastly moments in the church porch, and suddenly he had to know if he'd made the second-biggest mistake of his life in thinking that Libby had been totally happy on her wedding day.

'I think I was more in love with love than I was with Ian,' she said, as if the words were being dragged out of her. 'I was in my late twenties with no family around me. I'd lost my mother, and my dad had moved away because he couldn't stand the thought of how he'd had to sell the farm due to his own carelessness.'

There was a pause and he felt himself tense as she continued, 'And you'd made it clear that you had no feelings for me. You never came back. Not even for a visit.

'Ian had already proposed to me twice and I'd turned him down, but the third time…well, you know the rest. With regard to if *he* loved *me*, not in the true sense, I felt. He wanted a wife. I was sitting there on the shelf. In truth it wasn't the marriage I wanted it to be, but the way it ended was a tragedy and not something I'd wish on anyone. It's not something that I like to talk about, Nathan, so can we please change the subject?'

'Yes,' he said with the gravity still upon him, 'but just one thing before we do.'

'And what is that?' she asked tonelessly.

'How in a thousand years could you have ever thought you were on the shelf? Not every guy in Swallowbrook was as blind as I was at that time.'

She shrugged slender shoulders inside the black silk top. 'Maybe they just didn't appeal to me. Ian was different, he didn't ask a lot of me because he was so absorbed in his own lifestyle. I asked him once why he'd married me and he said he'd felt he was at the stage in his life where he should have a wife, and I obviously fitted the bill for him. So you see, neither of our hearts was ever in it. If Ian hadn't died we would have been divorced by now, I'm sure of it.'

They were closer than they'd ever been in these few moments, he was thinking, but Libby wanted to talk about something less revealing and he had promised her that he would, so returning to the subject of Friday night he asked, 'What about the bonfire and barbeque? Have you got something planned, or should the two of us take Toby? Today has exhausted him, it was plain to see, but by Friday he should be more his usual self and if he's not we won't take him. Agreed?'

'Yes,' she told him. 'I haven't made any plans regarding it. I don't have much time, *or inclination*, for socialising these days.'

'So can't we do something about that? When things are really back to normal with Toby, and Dad will have him for the night, why don't we live it up somewhere in the town, or hereabouts if you know of somewhere special?' As she observed him doubtfully he said dryly, 'With no strings attached.'

'Yes, maybe we could do that some time,' she agreed, and thought it wasn't *strings* she was concerned about, it was *bonds*, the bonds of the love that bound her to him, while for all she knew Nathan might be wanting to use her for some light relief in the restricted life that was now his.

She didn't stay long after that. His questions had opened old wounds, brought back the uncertainties of the past that were always there somewhere in the background, and just because the moment they touched they became two different people she wasn't going to turn back into the romantic innocent that had been given her marching orders that day at the airport.

Her timing had been so horribly wrong. There had been weeks before he'd gone when she could have told him how much she loved him, and when he'd casually suggested that she go with him she'd begun to hope.

But in love with him though she was, her loyalties to the practice, his father, her father and to the place she loved most on earth had made her refuse. Hoping all the time that he would change his mind about working abroad if only for a little while, and begin to see her as something other than just a face at the practice.

When she opened the door to leave there was a chill wind blowing and Nathan took a jacket of his off a hook in the hall and wrapped it around her protectively. When she looked up at him from the circle of his arms it was there again, the awareness that was so strong between them. Turning it into trivia before it took hold of them again, she said, 'My door is only yards away. I'm not going to catch cold.'

'Nevertheless,' he said, releasing her from his hold, 'you wouldn't be out in it even for such a short distance if it wasn't for my affairs, and there's no rush to return the jacket. I have others.'

He gave her a gentle push. 'Away with you, and thanks for the food. It would seem that the next time we dine together will be at Friday night's bonfire, subject to Toby not being too tired. Every time I think about what he has recovered from I feel weak with thankfulness.'

'Yes, you must be,' she said gently. 'I was only on the outside of things and I was transfixed with horror, so what it must have been like for you I shudder to think.'

'You helped us to get through it, Toby and I. Without you I would have been in despair. I am so sorry I presumed on your good nature by asking you to marry me, Libby. Obviously we aren't on the same wavelength about that sort of thing and it won't happen again.'

'I would prefer not to talk about that if you don't mind,' she said with sudden coolness, stepping out into the darkness. 'Goodnight.'

He nodded, he'd got the message. After watching her safely cross the distance between their two cottages and close the door behind her, he went in and did the same.

As the week progressed Toby was getting stronger with every day and the three of them going to the bonfire on the Friday evening was becoming a certainty that Libby was looking forward to in one way, but not in another.

She hadn't forgotten the conversation she'd had with Nathan on the Monday night. How he'd wanted to know how much Ian had meant to her. If she'd known that within seconds of her becoming Ian's wife Nathan had rushed through the churchyard and onto a passing bus to get away from the scene he'd just witnessed, she might have understood his questioning better, but as it was she'd found it unnerving.

The morning after the bonfire she was going to the island for the long-awaited break that she'd arranged, and on the Thursday night was intending going into the

town to do a big shop as there was no way she wanted
to be going backwards and forwards between Greystone
House and the village or the privacy she was looking
forward to would be gone.

She'd arranged to be taken there and brought back the
following Saturday by one of her patients who owned a
boatyard on the lakeside and also offered transport on
the water to anyone requiring it.

'I'd be obliged if you could take me to the island early
Saturday morning before anyone is about,' she'd asked
him. Easygoing Peter Nolan, who saw her from time
to time for diabetes checks, had said, 'Sure, Libby, I'll
take you in the middle of the night if you want, and you
can park your car at the yard if you like, so it won't be
on view. But are you sure you'll be all right out there
on your own?'

'Yes, I'll be fine,' she told him. 'I just want a rest and
some privacy.'

'All right,' had been the reply. 'I'll be waiting for
you at crack of dawn on Saturday, and by the way the
other day I went for my yearly retinol check that the
NHS insist we diabetics have.'

'And?' she asked with a smile for the burly boatman.

'The optician said everything was OK behind my
eyes and she'll be writing to you with the results.'

'Good. Keep on watching your weight still, won't
you, Peter?' she reminded him gently.

Whenever anyone at the surgery asked Libby where
she was going for the winter break that she was planning she was evasive and Nathan decided that it was

because of him. What did she think he was going to do? he thought sombrely. Ask if he could go with her, like some hungry dog begging for a bone?

After her chilly farewell the other night he felt that their relationship was back at square one again and no way was *he* going to ask what her plans were. Sufficient that they were going to spend Friday evening together with Toby, who was counting the hours.

But a week without her was going to be a long one, though he supposed he shouldn't complain as originally her winter break had been going to be two weeks instead of one.

He didn't know that quixotically she was desperate to be away from him to sort out her thoughts about the two of them. Ever since the night he'd rung her doorbell to ask if she had any milk to spare for Toby's drink Nathan had never been far away.

Yet she also felt that a week would be long enough without seeing him, so she'd reduced her winter break to one week instead of two and saved the other one for Christmas.

He'd seen her arrive home with a big shop from one of the supermarkets on the Thursday evening and decided that wherever she was going it would seem that it was self-catering. When he'd told Toby on the Friday that Libby was going on holiday the following week he'd asked with the uncomplicated mind of a child why they weren't going with her, as to him her presence was now an accepted part of his life.

Toby knew that she loved him just as much as he,

Nathan, did, so he would be unhappy too while she was away. He told him gently that it needed two doctors to look after the people of Swallowbrook, especially in winter time, which meant that he was needed at the surgery while she was away and that was why they weren't going with her.

He wasn't going to explain to Toby that his father was always available in a staffing shortage, and that it was because Libby wanted some time away from himself that she was taking a break. So to take his young mind off her comings and goings he'd drawn his attention to the bonfire, which was no longer in the future. It was glowing and crackling not far away on the field behind the park.

Practically everyone from the village was there in party mood, but not in party clothes. Strong shoes, warm jackets and woolly hats were setting the dress code for the evening.

The members of the event's committee were in charge of the fireworks and Toby's eyes were wide as they exploded in brilliant-coloured cascades in the night sky. Above his head Libby and Nathan exchanged smiles at the extent of his wonderment, and Hugo, who was standing nearby with his sister, said that it was only last year that her two girls had been in a similar state of wonder, but tonight they had promoted themselves to helping with the sale of treacle toffee from a nearby stall.

Their mother was chatting to a neighbour who had appeared beside her and Libby said in a low voice, 'Are things any easier with Patrice? Is she any nearer to accepting Warren's death?'

He sighed. 'Sometimes I think she is and then it all goes haywire again, which makes me wonder if she ever will. She hasn't got your ability to face up to what life hands out to us, Libby.'

She almost laughed. Hugo hadn't been in Swallowbrook long enough to be aware of how she'd married in haste and repented at leisure, and before that had been in love with the man beside her who had come back into her empty, organised life and turned it upside down.

She didn't feel as if she was facing up to anything at the moment and when she turned and met Nathan's dark, inscrutable gaze she wondered what *his* opinion of her was.

Did he think she was a tease who blew hot and cold with him? Or a frigid widow who wasn't going to thaw out just because there were brief moments of sexual chemistry between them?

He wasn't thinking anything of the sort. His thoughts were travelling along different tracks. One of them was the fast line to envy because Libby and Hugo made such an attractive couple, and with the memory surfacing of his inopportune marriage proposal, *also the other guy didn't have a ready-made family, like himself.*

Another track of thought, which was much more basic, was that the smell of the food on the barbeque was making him feel hungry, and when Toby voiced *his* thoughts by asking, 'When are we going to have something to eat, Uncle Nathan?' Libby took the hint and they left Hugo and his sister to carry on doing their own thing.

Unlike previous Bonfire Nights when often rain had sheeted down, the weather was perfect for this one. A winter moon high in the sky was shining down on the scene below, and although the night was chilly, it was warm around the fire and beside the barbeque, and the community spirit that was an essential part of Swallowbrook was giving off a warmth of its own.

As the two doctors and Toby stood amongst the crowd waiting to be served with sausages and beef burgers, followed by parkin and hot drinks, Nathan said, 'It's so good to be back. The work in Africa was hard yet very fulfilling and before Toby came into my life I'd thought I might extend my contract, but everything has changed and it is here that I want to be.'

He was giving her a lead, she thought, an opening to say how she felt about that. If it was what *she* would want him to do, yet he shouldn't need to ask. Did Nathan think she kissed every man who might put his arms around her the way she'd kissed him?

'Growing up in Swallowbrook would certainly be the best thing for Toby,' she told him, keeping it impersonal. 'It was a heavenly place to me when I was young and still is for that matter.'

'I can remember you when you were small,' he said, aware that he'd been sidetracked. 'A chubby little blonde kid with your hair in bunches who always seemed to be tagging along with me and my friends.'

He'd described her exactly, she admitted to herself, and thought how well *she* remembered *him*, dark-eyed, dark-haired, agile leader of the young ones of that time. He used to call her 'pudding' and groan when she appeared.

Years later, when she had joined the practice as a slender, dedicated young doctor with the same golden fairness, her attractions had registered with him, but familiarity had made her seem less appealing than she was because to him she'd still been the kid who'd followed him around like a lap dog all that time ago.

It wasn't until she'd surprised him by turning up at the airport that it had hit him like a sledgehammer with only seconds to spare that he didn't know the woman that she had become as well as he thought he did, and ever since he'd wanted to put that right.

Reminiscing was the last thing Libby had in mind on this cheerful, noisy night beside the bonfire, so she changed the subject and brought the moment back into the present by asking, 'So how do you think Toby is doing now that he's on the mend?'

'He's doing well considering what happened, but it will be a long time before I stop having nightmares about it, and will never cease to be thankful that he ate so few of the berries.'

He would have liked to tell her on a lighter note that he'd kept a promise he'd made to Toby when he'd been in hospital and had bought a boat for the three of them, so that they could sail the lake whenever they chose, but felt that when she heard about it Libby might see it as presuming too much, so bringing his attention back to the bonfire, the fireworks and the food he gave himself up to the pleasure of being there with them both.

The fire had burnt itself out, and all that remained were a few glowing embers.

All the food had been cooked and eaten, and as the three of them walked slowly back to the cottages Nathan said, 'I hope you enjoy your break from the practice, Libby, and also hope that you have given someone details of where you will be staying just in case of any emergencies.'

She shook her head. 'There is no necessity. I won't be far away and will be able to get back quickly if the need arises.'

When they were about to separate she bent and hugged Toby with a feeling that she was making a big thing about a few days on her own. There was nothing to say that she wouldn't be bored out of her mind alone out there on the island, but she needed the respite.

When Nathan had returned to Swallowbrook she had been in a state of joyful amazement. But over recent years she had grown to be wary of life's twists and turns. If there was one thing she didn't want any more, it was heartache.

As he watched her holding Toby close, the feeling that she was eager to get away from him was strong, or else why would she not tell him where she would be for the next seven days?

As she straightened up their eyes met and he said coolly, 'You never used to be so secretive. Is history repeating itself and this time *you* are telling *me* not to wait around?'

It was the first time he'd referred to that since coming back into her life and she replied steadily, 'Not at all. I wouldn't presume to think that I am of such importance.'

On that they separated, with Toby waving sleepily as Nathan unlocked the door and ushered him inside, leaving Libby to step into the quiet of Lavender Cottage with the feeling that their relationship had just taken another backward step.

CHAPTER EIGHT

ALL was still around the lake as Libby drove to the boatyard the next day in the dark of an early autumn morning. She'd loaded her car the night before with all her requirements for the week ahead while Nathan had been occupied in tucking Toby up for the night, and after a quick breakfast had been ready to leave before there had been any signs of life next door.

Now she was wondering if shutting herself away from Nathan for a week was going to make the confusion of her feelings for him any easier to cope with, but the decision was made. When she arrived Peter Nolan was waiting with the motor of his boat spluttering in the quiet morning and once they were off she didn't look back.

When she stepped onto the landing stage at the island and felt the peace of the place wrap around her the doubts disappeared. The boatyard owner observed her dubiously and said, 'Are you sure about this, Libby? It's a bit remote to be out here on your own.'

'Yes, I'll be fine,' she told him confidently, and on that reassurance he began to unload her belongings off the boat and carry them inside while she explored the house.

It was warm and cosy. The fires might be wood-burning stoves not yet lit, but there was also heating and lighting from the house's own generator, which was a pleasant surprise.

She was going to love it here, she thought as she went to watch Peter prepare to set off back across the lake, but still uneasy he said, 'So have I got it right that if folks are curious about where you are, I haven't got to say?'

'Yes,' she assured him, 'you have got it exactly right.'

'So you don't want me to pop across now and then for a cup of tea?' he said jokingly.

'Don't you dare,' she threatened mildly, 'I might be tempted to prescribe castor oil the next time you come to see me if you do.'

When he'd gone she unpacked and then cooked herself a hot breakfast on the top of a magnificent stove to make up for the hasty tea and toast she'd had a couple of hours ago, and her first day at Greystone House began to get under way.

It was daylight now and as she explored the house thoroughly she thought how lovely it was in a cool, uncluttered sort of way. All the inside walls were painted white, with curtains and carpets dark gold to match modern furniture of relaxing designs.

Around the house was the lake on all sides and though the island was not large it had lots of trees and bushes with walks amongst them. *This is paradise,* she thought, or would be if she knew what lay ahead in her life. She wondered if the property ever came up for sale.

The village school was visible in the distance with the playground empty because it was Saturday. How were Nathan and Toby going to spend their weekend? she thought, and had to remind herself that she had come to the island to have some time away from them, not to be pining, otherwise the whole purpose of her being there would be wasted.

Her relationship with Nathan had moved along then taken a step back a few times since his return and amongst all the other uncertain thoughts that filled her mind was the memory of how he'd commented that if ever he had any children of his own, Toby would be loved just as much as they were. He'd said it with just a hint of regret, as if a family of his own wasn't a certainty for a man who already had a child to bring up.

As darkness fell in the late afternoon and the lanterns came on around the lake, she put down the book she'd been reading and thought she was just as uncertain as he was with regard to whether she would ever have children and experience the joys of motherhood.

For her to do so he, Nathan, would have to be their father and the way they were blowing hot and cold with each other was not going to bring that about, yet she couldn't stop herself from thinking about him no matter how hard she tried not to.

She would have been amazed if she *had* known how he was going to spend his weekend. That after a quiet day for Toby on the Saturday at the end of his first week back at school after the deadly nightshade scare, he had arranged to take him to his father's on the Sunday morning for the rest of the weekend and pick him up from there for school on Monday.

Once he had dropped him off at the lodge by the river he was going to Peter Nolan's place to take possession of the boat, so that when Toby came out of school on Monday afternoon the big surprise would be waiting for him at the moorings at the far end of the lake where privately owned boats were kept.

When he'd purchased the boat and been asked what name he would like painted on it, in a crazily insane moment of euphoria he'd said '*Pudding*' and wondered what Libby would think of *that*. Would she understand that it had been chosen in tender humour, or see it as another reminder of how lukewarm had been his interest in her, not just when she'd been small but right up to him going to work abroad?

If she did think that she would be wrong, but she was hardly going to believe that in a matter of seconds at the time of his departure for Africa, he had realised how much she was a part of his life.

On Sunday morning when he went to complete the sale and take the boat out on to the lake, the first thing he saw in the yard was Libby's car parked in front of the office. He observed it in amazement, thinking that his eyes were deceiving him, but the details on the number plate were correct and when he went into the office and asked what Dr. Hamilton's car was doing there, Peter Nolan replied evasively that she'd needed somewhere to leave it while she was away and he'd offered to let her use an empty space on the forecourt.

'But why would she bring it here in the first place?' he persisted as the other man cast a quick glance in the direction of the island.

'Ah,' he breathed as light was beginning to dawn. 'She wanted you to take her somewhere by boat, didn't she, but where?' He looked out onto the lake through the office window. 'Not the island surely!'

The other man nodded reluctantly and said, 'I wasn't happy about leaving Dr. Hamilton there but she insisted she would be fine and it wasn't for me to argue.'

'No, of course not,' he agreed, 'but what is that place like? Is it fit to live in?'

'Absolutely,' was the assurance he was given. 'It is an elegant, away-from-it-all retreat.'

'Hmm,' he murmured doubtfully, and thought he would be getting a close look at it as he sailed the boat past on his way to where he would be keeping it when not in use. Would he be able to resist the temptation to call on the hidden lady of the lake? He doubted it.

Libby and Toby were the two most precious things in his life, the boy because he, Nathan, was the pivot on which his young life revolved, and the woman because of her strength and integrity and the desire she aroused in him. During the last few years he'd come across women who would have been there in an instant if he'd beckoned. But the one that he had on his mind was for most of the time out of reach because of their quixotic past.

As he set sail the sky was dark above and a strong

wind stung his cheeks as the boat ploughed through grey water. The weather was in keeping with the gloom that had settled on him when he'd discovered that it was to the island that Libby had gone in her desire to have some time away from him.

The pleasure of acquiring the boat had been swallowed up by discovering that, but the thought of Toby's delight when he saw it was still there and he was smiling as *Pudding* cut through the water with a comforting chug.

He was nearing the island and straining to see if there was any sign of her. Smoke was rising from the side of the house and as he drew nearer she was there, stoking a bonfire of loose branches and leaves that had been lying around, and he thought grimly that Libby must be desperate for something to do if she was having to do that to pass the time.

The landing stage for the island was close. Risking a rebuff, he began to pull in beside it and was now near enough for her to hear the noise of the motor above the wind.

She turned sharply and as she did so the long skirt she was wearing wafted onto the fire and a tongue of flame curled upwards from the hem.

'You're on fire!' he shouted, and had never moved so quickly in his life. Leaving the motor running, he jumped over the side of the boat onto the stone landing stage and flung himself at her, beating out the flames with his bare hands.

When he was satisfied they were out he looked down

at her sagging in his arms and saw horror and amazement in the eyes looking up into his.

'Where did you come from?' she croaked. 'How did you know I was here?'

'Shall we save that for another time?' he said tersely. 'Right now we need to go inside and treat any burns we might have.' His voice got even tighter. 'What on earth were you doing, having a fire in a gale-force wind?'

She turned her head away and asked in a low voice, 'Where did you get the boat from?'

'It's mine. I've bought it. I picked it up from the boat-yard an hour ago.'

'So that's how you knew I was here. Peter told you.'

'Not exactly. I saw your car parked there and wormed it out of him. When Toby ate the poisonous berries and was so ill I promised him I'd buy a boat and tomorrow when I pick him up after school he will see that I've kept my word. He's staying at Dad's place tonight, so I've got some time to myself today.' He looked down at his hands. 'They're beginning to blister where I beat out the flames. What about you, Libby?'

She looked down at the charred fabric of the skirt and said, 'I think you appearing so quickly saved me from anything like that. I'll go upstairs and strip off shortly but first, Nathan, let me look at your hands.' As he spread them out in front of him she saw that he wasn't wrong. The skin was bright red and blisters were appearing.

When she cried out in dismay he said dryly, 'Don't fuss, Libby. Do you have your medical bag with you?'

'Yes,' she replied as the wind howled around them.

'I brought it in case of emergencies, but was not expecting anything of this kind. I'll go and get it.'

He nodded. 'While you're doing that I'll see to things out here before I come inside, such as putting the fire out. I've got a bucket on board and with the lake on your doorstep there's no shortage of water, and then I'll see to the boat, which is reasonably secure as I flung the loop end of the rope over the mooring post as I jumped onto the landing stage. But the motor needs switching off and the rope tightening until I'm ready to leave. It looks as if it's going to be a rough night out there.'

When she came back downstairs carrying the bag he was coming in from outside and looking around him with interest. Pointing to a nearby kitchen chair for him to be seated, she thought that his hands must be really painful, but he sat patiently without a murmur while she put dressings on them that were specially for burns and then brought him a glass of water and painkillers.

'I'm sorry to inflict myself on you like this,' he said when he'd taken the tablets. 'I knew you were here, but wasn't intending calling until I saw you out there stoking the fire. When I saw your skirt was alight I had to do something even though you'd been so secretive about where you were going to spend your break and were so adamant that you wanted to be left alone.

'I was originally on my way to anchoring the boat at the moorings where I'm going to keep it when not in use. It's there that Toby will see it for the first time tomorrow after school, so I will be off shortly and once it is secured will take a taxi back to the cottage.'

'I don't think so,' she said gently. 'Do you honestly

expect that I would let you leave here with dressings on your hands and in pain because of me? You must stay the night and if your hands are no better in the morning I'll fill in for you at the surgery so that Hugo isn't the only doctor there.'

Dark brows were rising as they were apt to do when he had other ideas to what were being suggested. 'I'll accept the offer of a bed for the night,' he said levelly, 'but I've already butted into your holiday once and if you think I'm going to do it again by letting you stand in for me tomorrow at the practice, you're wrong, Libby.

'I'll have an early breakfast, after which I'll moor the boat as I intended doing this afternoon, and then go back to Swallowbrook by taxi. Are we agreed on that?'

'Yes, if you say so,' she said meekly.

He laughed. 'No need to sound so placatory. I'm the one who should be using that sort of tone, having broken into your Greystones idyll. I have to admire your taste, this is a beautiful house.'

'Yes, it is,' she agreed, looking around her. 'It would be fantastic as a weekend home for someone.' *Like us, for instance, if only you would say the 'love' word and convince me that I won't ever have my heart broken again.*

With those words left unspoken she asked, 'How long is it since you've eaten?'

'I had breakfast at seven o'clock.'

'So how about an early lunch?' she suggested, aware that although the quiet she'd been enjoying had been broken into she didn't mind in the least. Nathan was there and she was rejoicing inwardly, not just because he'd saved her from being set on fire but because they would have these precious few hours together that might never happen again.

Looking down at the tattered remnants of her skirt, she said, 'I'll go up and get changed and then we'll have some lunch if that is all right with you.'

'That would be great.'

While they were eating she asked with her glance on the dressings on his hands, 'Do you think we should have gone to the burns unit at the hospital to have your hands treated?'

'Not in this weather,' he said as the wind howled outside. 'I'll see how they are when I get back to the practice in the morning. For the moment the pain is under control. I'll take some more painkillers later before I go to bed,' and with a question in the eyes looking into hers, 'Where will I be sleeping?'

'There are three bedrooms. I've got the big one on the front. There is a ground-floor room just across the hall and a smaller bedroom opposite mine. The one on this level is very attractive. I think you would be most comfortable there.'

I would be 'most' comfortable in yours with you, he wanted to tell her, but didn't know how much of Libby's warmth towards him sprang from gratitude rather than affection because he'd stopped her from getting burnt and been scorched himself in the process.

She may not realise that he wasn't bothered about that as long as *she* was unharmed, but was not going to tell her as the last thing he wanted was to worm himself into her affections by playing the hero. But at least he would have her to himself for a while. *He was inside the fortress.*

After dinner in the early evening they spent the next couple of hours watching a drama on TV and chatting about life in general. Libby brought up the subject of Christmas again and was surprised to find that after her previous mention of it Nathan was well ahead of his shopping for the event, which was more than she was, and rather knocked on the head any ideas she might have had about them doing their Christmas shopping together.

'Would you like to have a look at your room?' she asked when they'd exhausted every topic of conversation they could think of that wasn't about them.

'Yes, sure,' he said easily, and when she'd shown him around he nodded without a great deal of enthusiasm and said with a change of subject, 'I need to check that the boat is safe for the night before I turn in. I won't be a moment, Libby.'

She held out a restraining hand and told him firmly, 'No, I'll see to it. You don't know the layout of the landing stage in the dark like I do.' And before he could protest she'd gone.

The thought of any more harm coming to him was just too much to bear, she thought as she made her way towards where the boat lay still safely tethered. As it rocked to and fro on the surface of the lake a shaft of moonlight brought the name that he had given it into focus and her face stretched.

Painted in black on its dazzling white timbers was the word 'Pudding'.

He had followed her out of the house and as he came up behind her saw that her shoulders were shaking and knew why. *You idiot!* he told himself. *You've upset her. Libby doesn't see it as a joke. Or maybe she does and finds it in bad taste. You aren't going to woo her with that sort of humour.*

She was turning to face him and it was his turn to be taken aback.

It was laughter that her shoulders were shaking with. 'Are you sure you want to call it that?' she gurgled in the dark November night. 'You could run a competition to guess what it means.'

'So you're not mad at me, then?'

Her eyes were wide and luminous in the lights of the landing stage and she said softly, 'Just as long as you don't think I'm a pudding now, how could I be angry with you when you've been hurt because of my carelessness?' Laughter still bubbled. 'I don't think you'll find another boat with a name like that.'

When he took a step towards her she didn't side step or back away. She just stood there and waited for him to take hold of her and when he did it was as if they were on another planet where only they existed as he kissed her until she was limp with longing.

'How am I going to make love to you with hands covered in these things?' he murmured as with arms still entwined they stopped every few moments to kiss on their way back to the house.

'I'm sure you'll find a way,' she breathed with all her

doubts and uncertainties disappearing as the wonder of the night closed in on them.

When they were inside he pointed to the downstairs bedroom and said, 'Do I *have* to sleep in there, Libby?'

'Not unless you have powers that I am not aware of and are going to make love to me by remote control,' she said softly, and taking his hand led him towards the stairs.

It was how she'd always known it would be if they ever got that far, she thought as they made love. The wasted years were forgotten, the future was beckoning, and when at last she slept in his arms it was with the knowledge of just how much Nathan loved her.

Until she awoke the next morning to find him gone, and a note on the pillow beside her that turned a grey November day into a black hole. It said,

Libby,
Am ashamed that that I took advantage of your gratitude with regard to the incident with the fire, and those brief but memorable moments when you saw your childhood name on the boat.

I had invaded the privacy that you were so desperate for and then proceeded to use it to my advantage. At the time that I was doing so it seemed the right thing to do, but when I awoke in the dawn and found you curled up beside me I wasn't so sure. None of what happened was how I'd planned it was going to be since I came back

*to Swallowbrook. I do hope you will understand
that and we can still be friends.*

*Be careful on your own out here and don't light
any more fires,*

Nathan.

When she'd read the note Libby sank back against
the pillows, too stunned for tears. Surely Nathan wasn't
saying that the night before had been just a one-off that
he'd engineered because he'd known she was vulnerable and willing due to what had happened previously,
and now he'd gone, leaving a note instead of telling her
to her face that he was still not willing to commit himself?

Fair enough, he wanted them still to be friends, did
he, so friends they would be when Toby was around and
at the practice, but for the rest of the time he would not
exist as far as she was concerned. He'd made her feel
cheap and cheap she was not!

Nathan had left the island at six o'clock with the motor
of the boat not at full throttle so as not to awaken her,
but once he was clear of the place he sailed at full
speed and once the boat had been moored did as he'd
said he would do, took a taxi back to his cottage in
Swallowbrook where he showered and changed before
picking Toby up for school and then on to the practice.

Everything was going to plan at this end, he thought
as he ate a hasty breakfast, but what about Libby on the
island? She would have read his note by now and he
prayed that she understood what he'd meant by it.

He'd wanted her so much and when she'd responded to him the night before like she had he'd taken the moment, made love to her and it had been fantastic. But afterwards he'd wished that he hadn't got carried away and had waited as he'd planned to do until he knew that she was sure of him, trusted him not to break her heart again, and now he was thinking that by leaving her the note he might have done that all over again.

Toby was full of what he and Grandfather Gallagher had been doing by the riverside when he called at his father's place to take him to school and John, who knew about the surprise he was planning for him, said when he wasn't within hearing distance, 'You look a bit down. Did you get the boat?'

'Yes,' he replied, forcing a smile. 'I'm taking him to see it this afternoon after school. Do you want to come?'

'No,' was the reply. 'Let it be just the two of you there when he sees it for the first time. I'm going to put my feet up for the rest of the day. Your boy takes a bit of keeping up with, but I wouldn't want to miss having him here for the world. He's given me a new reason for living, and for Toby you're giving him everything you can to make him happy except maybe a woman in his life, a mother figure.'

'Yes, well, they don't sell them down at the supermarket, you know.'

'Which is perhaps all to the good,' his father commented dryly. 'He talks about Libby a lot. Is there anything that he and I can look forward to in that direction?'

'There might have been once,' he said flatly, 'but I made a mess of things and she is wary of me now, so don't raise your hopes only to have them dashed. Maybe Santa might have a mummy for Toby when he comes.'

'Now you're being flip about something very important,' he was told, and Nathan thought that his approach to Libby was anything but flip. If it was he would already be making capital out of the happenings of the night before instead of taking a step back to give her time to take a long look at what had happened in the house on the island.

As if to give emphasis to the conversation he'd just had with his father, Toby asked on the way to school, 'Will Libby be there when I get home this afternoon?'

'I don't think so,' he said gently, 'but I've got something to show you that I think you will like.'

'What is it?' he wanted to know.

'It's a surprise.' And as the school gates were looming up ahead Toby had to be satisfied with that.

When Nathan arrived at the practice Hugo asked in surprise, 'What's wrong with your hands?'

'I had an argument with a bonfire,' he said with a dismissive shrug of the shoulders, and then had another question to answer when the other man said, 'I don't suppose you've heard from Libby at all, have you?'

He sighed. For some reason she was the main topic of conversation this morning when all he wanted was to be left alone to gather his thoughts, which had been almost impossible since he'd left the island at half past six to anchor the boat, then gone home to change, and finally had driven to the lodge by the river to pick Toby up.

But Hugo was asking out of genuine concern and, knowing that Libby would not want her whereabouts to be public knowledge after the way he'd gatecrashed her quiet time and turned it into a night that she would either want to remember always or be in a hurry to forget, he said, 'No, nothing as yet, Hugo, but she has only been gone a couple of days.' And then steered the conversation towards practice matters.

The two of them had decided that today Hugo would do the house calls, while Nathan took Libby's place, with one of the nurses to assist, at the Monday morning antenatal clinic. When she had dealt with blood-pressure checks and sent off any urine or blood samples that were required he would see each one in turn to make sure that the pregnancy was progressing satisfactorily and he found that even there Libby's name was cropping up.

'Where is Dr. Hamilton today?' one of them asked. 'It's unusual for her not to be here.'

'She's taking a short break,' he said levelly, 'and will be with you as usual next week.'

Most of them were in good health and giving no cause for alarm, but when the nurse informed him of the results of the blood-pressure reading for one of them, he told an apprehensive forty-year-old who was expecting her first child, 'I'm afraid we're going to have to give you some bed rest as your blood pressure is very high. I'm going to send for an ambulance to take you straight to hospital because you need to be under their immediate supervision.' As the colour drained from her face he told her reassuringly, 'It can happen to any pregnant woman that their blood pressure gets out of hand. Once you are resting it should level out and it will be monitored constantly all the time you're there.'

'It's our first baby,' she told him, dabbing at her eyes. 'We've waited so long for me to become pregnant, we couldn't bear to lose it.'

'Of course not,' he sympathised. 'That's why I've sent for an ambulance. While you are waiting, have a word with the receptionist if you want your husband to be contacted, or anyone else that needs to know what is happening.'

When the ambulance had been and gone and the clinic was over it was back to seeing his own patients and the first ones to present themselves were a young mother with a little girl of a similar age to Toby.

'So what is the problem?' he asked with a smile for the child when they'd seated themselves opposite. He'd seen her following Toby around in the school playground like a small golden-haired shadow and had thought it was like history repeating itself.

'Cordelia has got a sore eye,' her mother said. 'She was poked in it by one of the boys in her class yesterday. I bathed it when we got home but it doesn't seem to have had much effect. When she woke up this morning it was all red and sticky around the bottom lid.'

'Can I have a look at your eye, Cordelia?' he asked gently, and she nodded solemnly. It was as her mother had said, quite inflamed, and when he'd finished checking that the eyeball wasn't damaged and that the soreness was reserved for the membranes of the socket he told her mother, 'I'll give you some drops that should clear it up in a day or two, and if you still aren't happy when you've used them all, come back to see me again.'

As they were about to go he said to the child, 'It wasn't Toby who poked your eye, was it, Cordelia?'

She shook her head emphatically and her blonde ponytail swung from side to side with the movement as she told him still in solemn mood, 'No. Toby is my friend.'

Her mother butted in at that moment to say, 'Everyone thinks you're doing a wonderful job with the boy, Dr Gallagher. It can't have been easy.'

He didn't reply, just nodded, and as they departed he considered that compared to sorting out his love life, caring for Toby *was* easy.

CHAPTER NINE

WHEN they arrived at the moorings in the late afternoon it was a much better day than the one before. The wind had dropped and a pale sun was shining down onto the assortment of craft there. When Nathan pointed out the boat that was theirs, Toby's delight and excitement was a pleasure to behold and would only have been made more gratifying had Libby been there to share it with him.

Before he took Toby on board he fastened him into the life jacket that he'd bought from the Outdoor Pursuits store. Nathan knew he could swim, his parents had seen to that, but he was taking no chances as they pulled out onto the lake.

This time he didn't go anywhere near the island. It would soon be dark and he didn't want Toby to have any diversions on his first sail on *Pudding*. That was what he was telling himself anyway and it was true in part. The last thing he wanted was for the child to be involved in the complexities of his relationship with Libby while on his maiden voyage, but it was an effort not to keep casting his eyes across to where the island stood remote and still on the autumn afternoon.

* * *

If Nathan's day had been full, Libby's had been an aching, empty void. She'd thought the night before that it was all coming right between them at last until he had done what he always did, pushed her away again with just a few words on a scrap of paper. Thank goodness she was here on the island away from everyone, she thought as she gazed out onto the lake's now calm waters. She needed this time alone more than ever.

It was her third day at Greystone House, and she had the rest of the week to concentrate on putting up her defences once more. She'd done it before often enough and would do it again when next the two of them met, she decided determinedly, so why was she weeping all the time and in the late afternoon straining for a sight of Nathan as he took Toby out in the boat for the first time?

She knew what his plans for the day were, and it went without saying that he would be taking the excited five-year-old for a sail about that time, but there was no sighting of them and she went back into the house knowing he wasn't going to be coming calling again unless she asked him to—*and she was not going to do that!*

It was Saturday morning and she was packed and ready to depart, leaving the house as she'd found it, a place to dream in, but not, it seemed, for her.

Peter was due any moment to take her back to Swallowbrook, back to the bosom of a busy practice, back to a relationship that was more of an endurance test than anything else since Nathan had come back into her life. She couldn't believe that he'd thought she'd let him make love to her out of gratitude, or because of their brief rapport when she'd laughed at the name he'd chosen for the boat.

Yet she had to admire him for one thing. Most men would accept what had happened between them without giving a second thought to the whys and wherefores of it, but not so Nathan Gallagher. What he'd said in the note he'd left had hinted that the night they'd spent together had been a mistake and it had besmirched the memory of it, made it seem cheap and fortuitous. She could not forgive him for *that*.

When Peter arrived his first words were in the form of an apology for letting Dr Gallagher find out where she was. 'He guessed when he saw your car parked at my place,' he told her awkwardly, 'and I couldn't deny it. I hope it didn't cause any problems, Libby.'

'No, not at all,' she assured him. There was no way she was going to let Peter be dragged into their affairs, neither was she going to tell him what it was all about. The folks in Swallowbrook had already watched her make one mistake by marrying Ian and, as they always were for their own, had been there for her every step of the way.

It would grieve them beyond telling if they had to watch her make another mistake. It did at least seem as if Nathan's hasty departure from the island and 'the note' had saved her from doing that.

The cottage when she got back was how she'd left it, attractively furnished, tidy and soulless. There were no signs of life next door but as it was Saturday morning she wasn't surprised. Nathan would either have gone into the town to shop or taken Toby to the park, she decided, and if that was so she would have a few more hours' grace before their next meeting.

She was wrong on both suppositions. When she went to the local store to shop for fresh food to replenish her stock after being away, Libby could hear music, and when she turned the corner to where the village hall stood back beside the shops, the fact that Christmas was only a few weeks away was brought to her notice with a jolt.

Morris dancers, dressed in bright colours with bells jangling in the crisp morning, were performing on the forecourt of the hall, and behind them was the Christmas market that the shops and stall-holders held at this time of year.

When she stopped to watch them she saw Nathan and Toby in the crowd on the opposite side of the road and was about to turn away when it seemed that she'd been seen. She heard Toby shout, 'There's Libby!' When she looked up the two of them were coming towards her, with Toby beaming his delight and Nathan observing her gravely.

The urge to depart with all speed was strong, but Toby was not to blame for her fixation for his guardian. He was straining to get to her through the crowd and when they stood in front of her she swept him into her arms and hugged him.

'So how is my beautiful boy?' she asked laughingly, as if she hadn't a care in the world. 'What have you been up to while I've been away?'

'That's what I want to tell you,' he said excitedly. 'We've got a boat, Libby!'

'Wow! When did this happen?' she asked, looking suitably surprised.

'Monday after school,' Nathan said as if she didn't know.

'And guess what it's called?' Toby cried.

'I'm sure I have no idea. What *is* it called?' she asked, as if it wasn't imprinted on her mind for ever. She'd laughed when she'd first seen it, but now she felt it was another reminder of how Nathan still saw her as someone on the edge of his life, rather than at the forefront of it.

'It's called *Pudding*,' he said, unaware of its origin, and turned to Nathan. 'Can Libby come with us the next time we go sailing?'

'Yes, of course,' was the reply, 'if she wants to, that is. How about tomorrow morning?' he suggested promptly, not wanting her to go and knowing that Toby would give him no peace until she'd sailed on it with them.

'I could never say no to Toby,' she told him. 'I've got a life jacket somewhere.'

Libby would be so good to be around him while Toby was growing up, Nathan thought. She was just what the child needed to fill the empty place in his young life. He knew how much she loved him, but would she want himself as part of the package? That was the question. From the frost in her voice when she wasn't speaking to Toby it was almost certain that the answer to *that* would be no.

She'd made it quite clear that night at the hospital when he'd asked her to marry him that she was not in the market for a marriage of convenience and what he was thinking now was that kind of thing.

She would always love the child devotedly, but not the man. Unless he could convince her that the caution he displayed in his approach to her was because of the past flippancy he'd shown for her love for him and the careless words that he'd dismissed it with.

Added to that was always the thought that she would never have married Jefferson if he, Nathan, had not been so blinkered. But maybe he'd been playing it *too* cool, that he'd been patient long enough and was hurting her once again in the process.

He was by nature a man of action, not a ditherer, and as he brought his thoughts back to where Libby and Toby were chattering away, happy to be together again, he felt that his cautious approach had gone on long enough.

On observing that he was back from wherever his mind had been during the last few moments, she said, 'I'm afraid that I have to go. I'm here to do some food shopping as my larder is bare. I'll see you both in the morning, but before I go, Nathan, what about your hand, how is it now? Did the dressing prevent the blistering and take the soreness away? I've been wondering all week if you had to go to A and E.'

'My hand is fine.' He was holding it out in front of him for her to inspect and commented dryly, 'You could have phoned.'

'So could you,' she parried. 'Yet maybe it was as

well that neither of us did. We might have said things that we regretted afterwards.'

'Such as?'

Toby was engrossed in what was going on around him at that moment and she said in a low voice, 'Such as how could you liken the first time we'd ever made love to a vote of thanks on my part and an opportunity not to be missed on yours?'

He was not to be ruffled, was actually smiling, and she thought despondently that he didn't care. Nathan didn't care what he did to hurt her, and with a brief word of farewell and a kiss for an innocent Toby she left them and went to shop.

She drove into the town to do some Christmas shopping in the afternoon after watching the morris dancers and buying food from the stalls of the Christmas market in the morning, and after a quick lunch in a bistro went to choose gifts for Toby, John, her father far away in Somerset and the practice staff, and then there was Nathan. It would be the first time she had bought him anything on her own and it wouldn't be easy.

When he'd been part of the practice before she'd contributed as a junior doctor to the gifts that the staff bought for the partners, which had been an impersonal sort of arrangement, but now there was nothing impersonal in their dealings with each other, far from it, but neither was it a situation for bestowing on him the kind of gifts she'd always wanted to buy, so how was she going to get around that? Certainly not a voucher from one of the big stores, their relationship wasn't so cut down to size as that.

For Toby, whatever she chose she would have to consult Nathan, first, to make sure that he hadn't got the toy already and, second, to check that Nathan hadn't bought it for him as part of the delights of Christmas morning.

It had been a phone call she'd been reluctant to make, but it would be easier than speaking face to face, she'd decided, and when his voice had come over the line it was almost as if the rift in their relationship hadn't happened. When they'd discussed what Toby would like at length he'd said casually, 'And what would you like for Christmas, Libby?'

That had brought the conversation back down to basics and her reply had even more as she'd told him, 'Just peace of mind would be fine.' And before he'd been able to pursue that line of reasoning, she'd rung off.

He hoped to present her with more than that, he thought in the silence that followed, and was already taking steps in that direction. Asking her out to dinner was going to be the first. He'd once suggested that they go out somewhere if his father would have Toby for the night, so the idea wasn't going to come as a complete surprise when he came up with it, but whether Libby was still in the same frame of mind as she'd been then remained to be seen.

When he saw her return in the late afternoon he went out to ask her, and as she faced him with the car behind her full of packages he said, 'Do you remember we once discussed going out on the town if Dad would have Toby for the night?'

'Yes,' was the reply. As if she could ever forget anything he'd said, though it might be better if she could.

'So what do you think? Would you like me to take you for a meal to somewhere of your choice? I've already squared it with Dad that he'll have Toby.'

'Yes, I suppose so,' she told him, hating herself for being so easily swayed. 'If that's all you're suggesting, I suppose we could. As we said at the time, neither of us has much opportunity for socialising so it would be a change, but as far as I'm concerned that is all it will be, a nice meal in pleasant surroundings.'

'Sure,' he agreed, 'but it would be a treat if you wore the blue dress.'

'Why, what for?'

'Because it suits you maybe.'

'I'll think about it, but don't be surprised if I don't.'

There was still frost about, he thought, and as if unaware of it asked, 'So where do you want to go and when?'

'My favourite place is on a wide ledge high up on one of the fells. It's called the Plateau Hotel,' she replied, 'and if we're going there I think it should be soon as it gets booked up very quickly at this time of year.'

'So what about tomorrow night, sailing on the lake in *Pudding* in the morning and dining at the Plateau in the evening?'

'Er, yes, I suppose so,' she said, taken aback at the speed with which he was ready to act on her suggestion.

'So that's sorted, then,' he replied, and again she despised herself for being so amenable after recent events having been so hurtful.

He was eyeing the car and asked, 'Can I give you a hand with your shopping?'

She shook her head. 'No, I can manage, thanks just the same.'

He didn't persist. 'All right, I'll go and see what Toby is up to, then.' And off he went to get in touch with the restaurant.

A phone call while she was sorting out her purchases of the afternoon was to say that he'd made the reservation for eight o'clock the following evening, which would give them time to drop Toby off at his father's place and drive up to the high plateau from which the hotel had got its name.

Back in her own bed that night Libby was finding sleep hard to come by. She'd agreed to go sailing on the lake with Nathan and Toby the next morning and how awkward was that going to be? she kept thinking. The three of them in close proximity with Toby happy and excited because she was there, and Nathan playing it cool as he always did, *except for that night on the island.*

And now to add to her sleeplessness even more, she'd agreed to dine with him in the evening and could see that being another nerve-stretching occasion.

Sailing the lake the next morning in the smart new boat was Toby's special time, she thought, and put her anxieties to one side as the two of them smiled at his excitement.

Living near the lake, they'd both been brought up amongst sailing craft and it was like history repeating itself from the days when they'd been young and *their* parents had smiled at *their* excitement on the occasions when they'd been on the water in *their* boats.

They stopped for lunch at one of the restaurants beside the water and as Libby looked at his young face glowing from the nip of the wind she hoped that if Toby's parents, taken from him so tragically, were anywhere nearby in the ether, they would be content to know that he was being loved and cherished by the two of them.

If her relationship with Nathan could be as strong and sure as the one they both had with Toby, life would be so wonderful, she thought wistfully, and hoped that she wasn't inviting more uncertainties on herself by accepting his invitation to dine with him that evening. *And it wasn't going to be in the blue dress.* It belonged to a better understanding between them than the present one.

Dressed in warm trousers and sweaters, and with wind cheaters beneath their life jackets, the three of them spent another hour on the lake when they'd had lunch and at one point the house on the island came into view.

Libby was conscious of Nathan's glance on her as the memory of what had happened between them there on a magical night came back, and she turned away. As always at the end of that mind picture was the moment when the putdown had occurred the following morning.

She was tempted to tell him that the dining-out arrangement was off. If his sombre expression was anything to go by, he was reading her mind and didn't need telling, but she told herself there was no cause to make a big drama out of going for a meal with him—that was all that it would be, for heaven's sake. She intended to make sure of *that*.

When they'd left the boat behind and driven back to the cottages Nathan said levelly, 'So are we still on for tonight?'

She was bending to give Toby a hug and looked up at him with an expression that was giving nothing away. 'Yes, I thought we had agreed...hadn't we?'

He was smiling. 'Just checking, that's all.'

As the afternoon wore on she was restless and on edge. Why had she agreed to this evening's arrangement? she kept asking herself. It was bound to be an ordeal, making polite conversation with Nathan when the only words she wanted to hear from his mouth were 'I love you'. If it wasn't for Toby she would steer clear of him altogether, and doing that would not be easy.

Working at the surgery with him, living next door to him, what chance would there be of that? There *was* a solution, of course—leave Swallowbrook, go elsewhere to practise medicine and start a new life. But to do that she would have nothing left of the things dearest to her and that would be worse than what was happening now.

On impulse she put on the warm jacket and the hat she'd worn for the sail on the lake and went out into the village to try to banish the blues.

There was hammering coming from the square in the

centre where the war memorial was situated, and next to it council workmen were erecting the big Christmas spruce that they brought every year to be a focal point in the village.

In the fading light she saw that fairy lights were already beginning to appear in cottage windows and on trees in the gardens. Inside the grey stone properties were her patients and her friends, and next door to her was a man who held her heart in his careless hands, always had, always would.

If it wasn't for it being Toby's first Christmas in Swallowbrook and the first one since he'd been orphaned, she would go away for the two days that were all they allowed themselves at the practice, and that would be a first, absent from the village at Christmas. But if she was filling one of the gaps in Toby's life to some small degree, she had to be there for *him*.

The vicar and his family were arriving home from a drive out in the already frost-covered countryside and as she was passing the vicarage they invited her in for a hot toddy.

As they chatted, the man who loved Swallowbrook almost as much as she did was reminded that so far there were no Christmas weddings arranged to take place in the village this year, which was unusual, and with his glance on Libby hoped that one day, whatever the season, he might have the pleasure of officiating for the caring young doctor who had her own special niche in the life of the place.

Surrounded by the warmth of the vicarage family's welcome and the hot drink they'd provided, Libby's spirits were lifting and as dusk became the darkness of night she made her way home with a lighter step than when she'd set out.

Yet it didn't stop her from remembering how what she'd thought had been the beginning of bliss had turned out to be a raw and aching memory of a non-event that Nathan had felt warranted an apology, and now she was committed to an evening of polite conversation and strained smiles.

Before she went up to change she wrapped the Christmas gifts she had bought for Nathan and Toby, a cashmere sweater for the man and for the boy a battery-operated replica of the boat called *Pudding* that he would be able to sail in the bath. There hadn't been any need to consult Nathan again as to what she should get him. Once she'd seen it in one of the toy shops her mind had been made up.

As she'd been about to wrap the sweater she'd held it close for a moment and wished that Nathan was inside it, that she could hold him close and tell him how much she loved him, but the road of rebuff was a painful one to travel, and she'd been down it too many times.

For her father she'd bought a smart towelling robe and as she wrapped it wished she saw more of him, but he seemed contented enough where he was, so there was no point in fretting.

A camera was her gift for John, who had a special place in her heart, and now all that she still had to shop for were gifts for the practice staff.

Christmas was only a month away and what it would bring with it she didn't know, but had a dismal feeling that Santa wouldn't have any nice surprises for *her* in his sack.

Yet she wasn't quite right about that. The thought had no sooner entered her head than the phone rang, and as if by wrapping his gift she had conjured him up, her father's voice came over the line and it was more buoyant than it had been for a long time.

As he explained the reason for his call his upbeat tone was easily understood. It seemed that he was coming to Swallowbrook for Christmas and bringing someone with him, the new woman in his life. They would be staying with John at his invitation and he hoped she would be happy for him when she met Janice. 'It doesn't mean that I've forgotten your mother, you know,' he said awkwardly. 'I've been like a lost soul since she went.'

'Yes, I know you have,' she told him reassuringly, 'and, Dad, of course I'm happy for you.'

When they'd finished the call she put the phone down slowly. She'd meant what she'd said to him, but couldn't help feeling that she really was going to be the odd one out during the festivities.

But there was no time to mope. The clock said that it was time to start preparing for the evening ahead and the final result was far from what she would have chosen if she'd been looking forward to it.

She'd decided to wear a starkly simple black dress that fitted her mood, relieved only by a gold necklace and matching earrings, and on observing herself in the mirror thought that it went well with the pale face looking back at her and the lacklustre expression.

One thing was clear, she decided, after tonight

Nathan wouldn't be falling over himself to wine and dine her again after her performance of death's head at the feast.

They had taken Toby to the lodge by the river, complete with 'comforter' and his favourite teddy bear, and now Nathan was pointing the car in the direction of the hotel on the plateau beneath the tops of the fells.

He had made no comment about the absence of the blue dress, had just observed her thoughtfully when he'd answered her knock on the door of his cottage and suggested that she get in the car as he and Toby were ready so they might as well get mobile.

Of the two of them he was the most distinguished-looking in a smart grey suit with matching shirt and tie. Where Libby had felt she was underdressed for the occasion she thought that his clothes were a bit over the top for a casual night out, but could not deny that his appearance was heart-stopping, with regard to *her* heart anyway.

Since they'd kissed Toby goodnight and taken the road out of the village there had been no conversation between them and now Nathan's only comment was, 'There is snow on the tops and the forecast isn't good. Gale-force winds and sleeting rain are moving in and if it turns to snow at this level it will be tricky.'

'So do you want to turn back?' she asked quickly.

'No. I'm used to this road,' he said levelly. 'I won't let you come to any harm.'

She almost groaned out loud. Some night out this was going to be, with ghastly weather blowing in and

Nathan as chatty as one of the large stones that in a by-gone age had been strewn along the side of the road by the elements. She wasn't to know that his insides were clenching at the thought of what he would do if tonight, which he'd had such hopes for, turned out to be a fiasco in the storm-lashed hotel that Libby had chosen. Not so long ago he'd decided that he was being too wary of the past in his dealings with her and a more forthright attitude was called for, so he'd suggested that he take her out to dine with a view to clearing the air between them once and for all, and the earth would have to open up and swallow the Plateau Hotel before he would be willing to turn back.

Their table was ready and as they looked around them it was clear that the weather had made others think twice about dining there on such a night, and they had either cancelled or not been willing to make the effort without a booking in such weather.

Nathan's smile was wry. He'd wanted to have her to himself this evening and he'd got it, but it wasn't exactly as he'd hoped it would be as they ate in silence in the empty restaurant, and when they were seated in the hotel lounge with coffee and petit fours amongst a scattering of people who had just stopped by for a drink to take away the chill of the winter night, there was still no rapport between them.

This was catastrophic, Libby was thinking. She should have followed her instincts and refused the invitation to dine with Nathan, yet it would soon be over, it would have to be. Neither of them would want to be stranded up here with nothing to say to each other in this ghastly weather. As soon as they'd finished their coffee they needed to be off.

A gust of cold air in the reception area close by and the loud voices of new arrivals broke into her thought processes and almost simultaneously two men dressed in mountain rescue gear appeared in the doorway of the lounge.

'I know these guys,' Nathan said. 'I used to be part of their team before I went to work abroad. What are they here for, I wonder?' Rising from his seat, he went across to speak to them.

'We're looking for a volunteer to go up to the tops with us as we're short on members tonight,' one of them told him. 'Two teenagers are missing from a group who are staying at the youth hostel on the bottom road. Should have been back hours ago. Their friends reckon they aren't experienced or well equipped, so fast action is needed. How are you fixed for joining us, Nathan? We might need a doctor if we find them.'

'Yes, all right,' he agreed soberly. 'But as you can see I'm with Libby Hamilton from the surgery in Swallowbrook, I need to explain what is happening… And what about equipment? I can't go dressed like this.'

'The hotel has a stock of clothes for this kind of situation. We'll sort that out while you make your apologies to Dr Hamilton.'

'What's wrong, Nathan?' she asked anxiously when he came back to her side.

'Two youngsters lost on the tops,' he said grimly. 'They want me to go with them, Libby. I hope you'll forgive me for leaving you like this but, whatever you do, don't set off homeward bound, will you? I'll come straight back for you once we've found the teens.'

She was observing him aghast. 'I'd rather be up there with you,' she protested.

'No way. I want you here out of the cold, waiting for me, when I return.'

'You're risking your life up there. Suppose you don't come back?'

'I *will* come back,' he said steadily, 'because I have so many things to say to you that I've left unsaid, and then there's Toby, who needs us both so much. I know the fells as well as anyone and I'm trained for this sort of emergency. There's no way I can leave two kids stranded any more than you could. I have to do this, Libby.'

The manager of the hotel was approaching with the necessary equipment that he would need and minutes later he was gone in the company of the two mountain rescue team members with a long backward look in her direction.

CHAPTER TEN

WHEN the three of them had opened the door to go out into the night the wind had been howling even more and, crouched by the fire in the lounge, Libby prayed that it would stop.

Over the years high gusts had been known to blow the unsuspecting off ledges to almost certain death in rock-strewn gullies below, and she thought there would be parents somewhere, frantic to think that their young ones had been caught out by the weather and their own inexperience.

Or it might be that the folks in question didn't yet know that there was a problem and had that frightening moment yet to come.

A hush had fallen over the room with their departure and as she stared blindly into space all she could think of was how the evening that had been so empty and unsatisfying had become a time of praying for the safe return of the victims and their rescuers.

Supposing Nathan didn't come back, she kept thinking, and she'd never told him how much she really did love him? The future would be a black hole if she never saw him again.

The hotel staff were keeping her supplied with hot drinks and as the hours crept by, as if in answer to her prayers, the wind was lessening and the snow that had threatened earlier hadn't yet fallen, but it didn't give any indication to those waiting below what it might be like higher up.

They had no way of knowing what was happening until the door burst open and the two mountain rescue men appeared, carrying a lightweight stretcher with a teenage girl on it wrapped in blankets.

They were followed by a youth of a similar age who was also draped in a blanket, and Nathan was bringing up the rear.

When she saw him Libby's heart leapt with thankfulness. He held out his arms. She ran into the safe circle of them like a homing bird and as he looked down at her their love for each other was there, strong and sure.

'Are you all right?' he asked in a low voice.

'I am now,' she told him joyfully as her life righted itself, 'but I wasn't before. I kept thinking what it would be like if we never saw each other again after wasting so much time.'

'Me too,' he said sombrely. 'As I took one long look at you before I walked out of the door with those two guys, I was thinking that it might be my last, that I might never see you again. We have so much catching up to do, my darling.'

'And all the time in the world to do it,' she said softly,

then back in doctor mode asked, 'What about the poor girl, Nathan? Is she injured or too cold to walk?'

'She'd fallen up there, hurt her leg badly, almost certainly has a fracture, so couldn't walk back down the fell side. She's also suffering from hypothermia due to not being able to move around in the cold, and needs her body heat brought back up in front of the fire, but not too near as it has to be a gradual thing to prevent shock.'

'And the young guy, what about him? He looks dreadful.'

'Yes, I know. He is totally traumatised by what has happened, thought they were going to die as their mobiles couldn't get a signal up there—it's totally impossible to do so. I'm going to give him something to calm him down. My bag is on the back seat of the car and I've got a relaxant in it that should do the trick. The guys from Mountain Rescue have phoned for an ambulance and as the weather has improved it should soon be here.'

She had been examining the girl's leg with gentle fingers and when he said, 'So was I right?'

She nodded. 'Yes, I would say a fracture of the tibia.'

He'd given the other teenager the relaxant and the youth was in a less traumatised state by the time the ambulance came. As it was about to set off with the two of them on board the boy's father phoned, having only just heard about the day's happenings, and promised that both he and his mother would be waiting for them in A and E when they got there, which helped to complete the calming-down process.

By the time that Nathan had changed back into his

suit and the three men and Libby had eaten the cooked breakfast that the hotel had provided, the night was almost gone. Soon it would be time to return to their homes, back to reality, work, school, and who knew what lay ahead of them now?

When they arrived back at her cottage he said jubilantly, 'Alone at last! I have things to say to you, Libby, that should have been said long ago. Come and sit beside me while I tell you all that is in my heart.

'I asked you to marry me once for the wrong reasons, didn't I?' he said soberly when she'd done as he asked. 'I was totally distraught knowing that Toby had been poisoned by the belladonna plant, and also because you were there like a rock to hold onto.

'I'm going to ask you again to be my wife, but there are things you need to know before I do that. When you told me that you loved me that day at the airport I realised that for the first time I was seeing you how you really were, beautiful, desirable and uncomplicated, but the timing was all wrong.

'When I kissed you goodbye after having told you in supreme arrogance that I wasn't interested in you, and that you should forget me, I knew that I wanted to stay and carry on from there with you. That I'd been blinkered, hadn't seen what was in front of me, since the kid who was forever at my heels when I was young had grown into the woman standing before me in tears.

'But I was so taken aback by the sudden revelation that I let you walk away and went to catch my flight, which was already being called, intending to get in touch the moment I arrived at my destination.

'When I got there I arrived to such a state of chaos at the hospital where I was going to work that I found that private lives were non-existent out there. We were on the job sometimes for twenty-four hours non-stop and even though I hadn't forgotten you I let the weeks and months go by. Dad used to phone me from time to time while I was out there and on one occasion he mentioned that you were marrying Jefferson on the coming Saturday. I knew then that I had to get to you before you married him and there was very little time to do so.

'I needed to ask you if you'd stopped loving me after the airport episode and had decided that he was the man you wanted. If you'd been able to tell me that he was, I would have left you in peace and lived with my own stupidity for the rest of my life.

'But my flight was delayed. I arrived at the church while the wedding ceremony was taking place. As I entered the porch the vicar had just pronounced you man and wife and you were smiling up at Jefferson like any happy bride would, so I had my answer, or thought I had.

'I couldn't get out of the church quickly enough and jumped onto a passing bus to get as far away as possible, then caught the next flight back to where I'd come from. So you see, Libby, I did come back for you, but not soon enough, and I've lived with the misery of knowing that ever since.'

She was listening to him aghast, with tears streaming down her face, unable to believe what he was saying, yet she knew Nathan wouldn't lie, he had no reason to. And he hadn't finished.

'I don't know if you will understand what I'm saying now,' he went on, 'but it was because of that and the hurt I did you that day when you came to see me off at the airport that I stayed away for so long.

'When I came back to Swallowbrook with Toby you had become just someone from my past, and since I've really got to know you I've found myself holding back all the time in case I hurt you again. Even after that fantastic night on the island I couldn't let *my* feelings, *my* needs ruin your life again.

'When you described what your life with Jefferson had been like I could have wept. But it was the smile you had for him that day in the church that threw me, which made me think you had married him for love.

'So now that you know how much I love and adore you, Libby, can we wipe the slate clean and start afresh with a wedding of our own, a life of our own, with Toby and our own children when they come along?'

'I married Ian on the rebound,' she said in a low voice, 'because you had made me feel so unloved, and the smile you saw was to convince those who I knew *did* care about me, such as both our fathers and other friends of long standing, that I wasn't making a big mistake, which of course I was.

'Yes, I will marry you, my dear love. To belong to you for always is all I've ever wanted. It will be all my dreams coming true, and with regard to giving Toby brothers and sisters I haven't checked it out properly yet, but mother nature is telling me that we might have taken care of that already on that wonderful night at Greystone House.'

'You mean that you might be pregnant? Oh, Libby, that would be fantastic!'

'It only occurred to me as I was getting ready this evening that I'd skipped a period for the first time ever, and I consoled myself with the thought that if you never did want me, at least I might be going to have some part of you in a child that we'd conceived.'

'Want you! I've never wanted anything more than you in my arms, in my bed, in my life for ever, so how about a Christmas wedding? But before that I have something to put on your finger.'

He produced a small velvet box from the inside pocket of his jacket and when he lifted the lid a beautiful emerald ring was revealed. As she gasped with delight he said, 'I chose it because the emerald is glowing and beautiful like the woman I love, but we can change it to a diamond if you wish.'

'How can you think that I would want to change something that you have chosen especially for me?' she asked breathlessly, and he took her hand in his and slipped it onto her finger.

As she looked down at it she said, 'I would love a Christmas wedding in Swallowbrook, Nathan, to be married in the village church with the bells ringing out across the snow that hopefully will have fallen to complete the day.'

He took her in his arms again and it felt like coming home after a long journey. Tears glistened on her lashes as the wonder of the moment took hold of her, and this time they were tears of happiness.

'You said that you also had something else to tell

me,' she reminded him in the last few moments before they had to separate while Nathan went to collect Toby from his father's house.

'It's just an idea that has been in my mind ever since I saw the house on the island, and I've followed it up by asking if it is available to rent for the Christmas period, and it is. So how would you like us to have our wedding reception there? Many of our guests will have their own boats and we could hire something bigger to transport those who haven't across the lake?'

'That would be magical,' she cried. 'Shall I ask the vicar if he can call round this evening to talk about the arrangements? He was saying only yesterday that he was disappointed that no one was planning a Christmas wedding, so he will be pleased to hear our news.'

The ring on her finger did not escape the notice of the surgery staff when she got into work later that morning and congratulations came from all sides. Nathan had told his father their good news when he'd gone to pick Toby up, and John called at the surgery during the morning to express his delight to his prospective daughter-in-law.

'You'd better tell your father to bring his best suit with him if he's going to be giving his daughter away,' he said laughingly, and remembering her father's pleasure when she'd rung him earlier with her news she thought that for once he was happy. Happier than he'd ever been since they'd lost her mother.

* * *

The vicar came round that evening as requested, and was, of course, delighted to hear that he was going to have a Christmas wedding in his church after all, and by the time he was ready to go the foundations of a wedding ceremony to take place on the morning of Christmas Eve had been laid.

'The main formality is that the banns, which are in the form of giving notice to anyone and everyone that a wedding has been arranged, must be read three times on three separate Sundays in a church before it can take place,' he told them. 'The rest of the procedure you will already know, I'm sure.

'December the twenty-fourth will be a special day for the folks of Swallowbrook this year,' he said as he was leaving. 'Two of its own marrying on that day, and both of them doctors from the health centre that is one of the main focal points of the village.'

Toby was fast asleep upstairs and when the vicar had gone they went up and stood by his bed. As they looked down at him Libby said, 'I wasn't wrong about us being in the baby business, Nathan. I've done a test and I'm pregnant.'

'Life is getting more wonderful by the minute,' he said chokingly. 'It wasn't so long ago that I wasn't sure if I would ever have children of my own because they would have had to have you as their mother and at the time the chances of that weren't looking good.'

'I was having the very same thoughts,' she told him, 'that if ever I had any children they would have to be yours.'

They sat talking long into the night, making plans,

dreaming dreams, and amongst them was the idea of making the two cottages into one.

The invitations had been sent, the details of the music they wanted given to the vicar, and the banns were being read. Libby's father would give her away. Hugo was to be Nathan's best man and Toby a pageboy.

Libby's best friend Melissa was cast in the role of matron of honour, and Keeley, a friend she'd always kept in touch with since they'd been at medical school, was to be a bridesmaid.

The ceremony would take place late morning and when it was over Libby and Nathan would sail cross the lake in *Pudding* to the house on the island where the reception was to take place in the afternoon. Outside caterers had been hired to prepare a buffet that would go on until everyone who wanted to come had been.

When they had all gone Toby would be tucked up in bed early to be ready for what Santa had brought while he'd been asleep. The problem of how he would get his sledge across the water had been on his mind at first, but they'd told him that he would bring it down from the sky on to the island and it would give the reindeer a chance to have a nibble at any grass that was lying around.

The day had dawned and though the sky was heavy and grey there was no snow, but Libby told herself it was expecting too much that the weather would adjust itself to her special requirements. She already had blessings by the score.

She was marrying the only man she'd ever loved in the church, in the village, where she'd lived all her life. She was carrying his child and was going to fill the gap, God willing, in the life of the small boy who was so dear to her heart.

That morning Nathan had told her that he was the interested party who had been quick to agree to a price when Greystone House had come onto the market, and that soon it would be theirs for holidays and weekends, and as she'd held him close she'd thought, what more could she want?

The church was full, the organist was playing the wedding march, and the bells were pealing out high above as Libby stood holding her father's arm on the same spot in the porch where Nathan had seen his hopes scattered all that time ago.

Today none of what had gone before mattered, they were together at last, and with a smile over her shoulder for her small pageboy and the two friends who had both travelled quite some distance to be with her on her special day, she lifted the hem of a wedding gown of heavy white brocade and, holding a bouquet of red Christmas roses, met her father's enquiring gaze and whispered, 'I'm ready, let's go.'

With every step she took towards Nathan, standing straight and still before the altar with Hugo by his side, the rightness of the moment increased. As he placed the gold band of matrimony on her finger next to the glowing emerald, the future was stretching before them as a wonderful dream that had become reality.

* * *

She was back in the church porch, holding onto the arm of her new husband this time, and as they stepped out into the open to be photographed they began to fall, soft and white, whirling and twirling—snowflakes from the sky above.

They were coming across the water, boats of all shapes and sizes, amongst them a big launch with lots of seating, and as Libby and Nathan waited to greet their guests on the landing stage of the island, with Toby holding both their hands, the lanterns around the lake came on early as a token of congratulation to the newlyweds.

'That will be one of my patients who works for the lake authorities making a gesture,' she said. 'People are so kind. If any of their craft go past we must signal for them to stop and invite them in for a bite, don't you think?'

'I *think* that you are wonderful,' he said laughingly. 'The whole world can stop by as far as I'm concerned as long as you are here with me to greet them.'

It was over. Their guests had gone back across the water with the moon to light their way home as well as the coloured lanterns.

Toby was asleep, having supervised leaving out wine and a mince pie for Santa Claus. Libby and Nathan had the night to themselves and as he removed the soft white cashmere stole from her shoulders, which she'd worn to keep out the cold, and unzipped her out of the long white dress, he held out his arms and after that it was

just the two of them, loving and giving each other all
the joys they had longed for and had sometimes thought
would never be theirs.

* * * * *

ONCE UPON
A GROOM

KAREN ROSE SMITH

With fond remembrance of Joan.

Prologue

July

As Zack Decker approached Jenny Farber in the cafeteria, decorated with blue and yellow streamers, memories washed over him. He struggled to maintain the cool facade that had enabled him to direct the most temperamental actresses…that had allowed him to hide the turmoil that had churned inside him since he'd left Miners Bluff fifteen years ago.

In a strapless yellow dress that accentuated her slim but curvy figure, Jenny was dancing with a classmate. The way she was smiling up at the man lit the wrong fuse on Zack's usually controlled temper.

He clasped Brody Hazlett's shoulder, dredged up a smile he didn't feel and ignored the hushed surprise of other classmates he hadn't seen in years. "Can I cut in?"

Brody let go of Jenny's hand and faced Zack, his expression friendly. "Hi, Zack. It's good to see you. The reunion must have meant a lot to you."

"The reunion, and a few other things," Zack said off-handedly, his gaze on Jenny as the silver disco ball spun, casting flickering lights across her heart-shaped face. She'd left a message on his cell phone last week. He remembered her words. *Zack, please come home for the reunion. I need to talk to you about Silas's health.*

And here he was.

Taking Jenny's hand in his, he circled her with his arm and steeled himself. As his hand brushed over the bare skin of her back, golden sparks lit her expressive brown eyes, bringing back too many buried memories.

"How long can you stay?" Jenny always went straight for the bottom line.

"Until tomorrow afternoon. I have to be on location in England on Monday."

"That's all the time you can spare?" Her voice was less accusatory than wistful...or regretful.

"I hadn't intended to come to the reunion, but with your call, I revamped my schedule."

The rhythm of the music overtook them for a few moments. It was a nineties ballad he recalled too well. The melody had wafted from the radio in the hayloft as the two of them...

He shut down the movie in his mind, leaned away from her slender body that had caused an instantaneous and powerful reaction in his. "Do you want to go somewhere quieter to talk?"

Quickly glancing around, she motioned toward the shadowy corridor lined with lockers where they had once exchanged heartfelt secrets...and kisses.

He led the way as he always had, trying to forget that fifteen years ago, she hadn't followed.

Jenny attempted to calm her racing pulse and swallowed hard. Being in Zack's arms again upturned her world until she became almost dizzy! He *couldn't* still do that to her. She wouldn't let him.

She watched him stride toward the corridor leading to the stairwell where he stopped and waited for her. He obviously wasn't used to waiting for anyone. He'd left her behind once before. She imagined he wouldn't hesitate to do it again.

Remember, he asked you to go with him.

Yes, he had. But she'd been eighteen and had finally found roots with Zack's parents. As for Zack, he'd wanted to escape both his roots and his mom and dad. All he'd focused on were his dreams and a film school scholarship in L.A. She hadn't been able to pin their future on something so intangible. Her own father's dreams had disappointed her too many times to count. Her job as a groom at the Rocky D, Olivia Decker's faith in her and Silas Decker's promise to give her more responsibility in the future had been grounding forces much more powerful than her fear of what lay ahead with Zack.

But she *had* loved him in the ferocious way only an eighteen-year-old could love.

As she walked beside Zack, her high heels clicking on the waxed tile, her arm brushed his. The shiver that rippled through her almost loosened the mass of blond curls she'd pinned on top of her head. How could the brush of her skin against his suit jacket cause such a reaction?

He stopped halfway down the corridor, obviously hoping for privacy.

She gazed up at Zack, reminded again of how tall six-foot-two could be, how broad his shoulders had become, how slim his hips still were. He'd always oozed a James Dean kind of sensuality and that hadn't changed. With a small cleft at the center of his jaw, his tousled, almost raven-black hair just barely tamed by an obviously expensive cut, his stormy-blue eyes, she realized the tabloids always got it right—he *was* a heart-breaker.

But then, she knew that from personal experience.

She felt tongue-tied with him, and he seemed to be at a similar loss for words until he said, "I spoke with Dad when I arrived. Sorry I missed you, but I was delayed."

Had father and son finally had a heart-to-heart and found common ground? "And?" she prompted, instead of saying what she was thinking.

"And," he drawled, "I don't understand why you needed me to come. He's as contentious as ever. He wanted to know if I flew all this way for a few dances for old times' sake."

"What did you tell him?"

"The truth—that you thought something was wrong with him."

"Oh, Zack, you didn't! I wanted you to observe him when he wasn't aware of it. If he knows you're watching, he'll act all macho."

"Jenny, I don't have time to follow him around and act as if I'm not. Like he wouldn't catch on to *that* in about ten minutes."

Men! She was ready to throttle the two of them.

Zack hadn't been home for eight years—not since his mother's funeral.

"Something is wrong with him," she insisted with so much vehemence, loose tendrils of hair fluttered along her cheeks. "He can't walk from the house through the barn without getting winded. He hasn't taken Hercules riding in weeks. He doesn't even watch me train anymore. I spent every day in that house with him for the past sixteen years and I know when he's off his game. He's off, Zack, and I think there's a physical reason."

"Then make him a doctor's appointment."

"I did, several times. He won't go. A few days before, he always cancels it."

Zack blew out a long breath and looked as if he were drawing on a short store of patience. "What do you want from me, Jenny?"

The first answer that came to mind was—*Not a blasted thing.* Then she remembered the manners Olivia had taught her...the wisdom that she'd get what she wanted more easily with a light touch than with a heavy one.

"Silas is getting older. What I think he needs most from you is your forgiveness."

They both went silent, then the surprise on Zack's face quickly faded. "What do you want me to forgive him for?" he asked, in a low but angry voice. "For the gambling and drinking? For the affairs that hurt my mom? For his lack of faith in my abilities and my career path? Or for the big one—for being responsible for my mother's death?"

Jenny barely opened her mouth to protest before Zack moved closer. "Don't give me a sympathetic, 'Oh, Zack, that's not true.' Her plane went down because of a storm, but she was on it because my father had driven her away."

Jenny had been in the barn that day when Olivia had confronted Silas, holding the credit card statement showing the hotel bill, and the flower order she'd never received. Half the ranch hands had overheard their argument.

All Jenny could say was, "He's a different man now."

"Different? He's the same man he's always been. So what if he doesn't gamble anymore?"

This might be her only chance to make Zack understand. "When he lost Olivia, he didn't just lose his wife, he lost *you*. All of that changed him."

Zack shook his head. "You're as naive as you've ever been."

The arrogance in Zack's voice nettled her. "No, I'm not naive, but I've watched him and worked beside him every day for all these years. He's changed. He not only doesn't gamble, but he doesn't drink, either."

Instead of responding, Zack peered down the hall to the reunion going strong in the cafeteria. Then very quietly, firmly, he insisted, "I don't belong here, Jenny. You fit in better than I ever did. My father didn't want a son who escaped his parents' fights by videotaping the scenery on Moonshadow Mountain, by recreating an old Western with some of his friends in Horsethief Canyon."

Tears burned her eyes because he was right. Zack and Silas had never understood each other very well. Still, she answered his vehemence with softness. "Silas wanted a son to take over the Rocky D. That's all he ever expected of you."

"You know I loved training the horses, almost as

much as you did. But I never wanted this to be the extent of my world. I had bigger dreams than that."

"And you've made them come true."

After a lengthy pause, he responded, "Yes, I have."

She heard the pride in his voice and knew his success was as important to him as the Rocky D was to Silas. "Then be a little generous," she pleaded. "Be kind, and forgive what neither of you can change. Find out what it is to be father and son as grown-ups."

"You're still an optimist who won't step outside of her little world."

"Don't talk down to me," she returned hotly. "I found the life I want in Miners Bluff. If you want to travel the world, be my guest. But I'm perfectly happy right here on the Rocky D."

"You're like him," Zack maintained. "You both have tunnel vision. The two of you believe the Rocky D is the only world that matters, but you're wrong. You're also wrong about Dad needing my forgiveness. Granted, I haven't been in much contact with him since Mom died—I phone now and then because he *is* my father— but he's *never* reached out to me."

If her plea was for herself, she'd let Zack walk away. But it was for Silas. "Please, Zack. Can't you at least stay for a few days? Or at least come back after the shoot."

"The shoot will take three months."

The walls in Zack's eyes were as solid as the armor he wore on his heart. "So why did you bother to come home?"

"Because you asked, and so I could get a quick peek for myself. I think you're overreacting. Dad might simply be growing older and you don't want to recognize that."

"You're wrong."

"Time will tell. Make him another doctor's appointment. That's all you can do."

"He might listen to you."

"To a son he's never listened to before? I doubt that."

"You're as stubborn and blind as he is!" Her voice had risen and she hoped it hadn't carried down the hall.

"I'm not going to argue with you, Jenny. I have a plane to catch tomorrow afternoon."

She was outraged that he cared so little about Silas and the Rocky D that he wouldn't stay long enough to see the full picture.

"This project is important to me," he went on. "It has to get off to a good start."

"And you don't care what ends *here?*"

"Everything here ended for me a long time ago." With those words, and a last long look, Zack walked away.

Jenny stared at his back, remembering the first time he'd left her. Six weeks later, she'd discovered she was pregnant. Six weeks after that, she'd miscarried.

Zack Decker might think he knew everything, but he still didn't know *that.*

Chapter One

Late October

Finally back in L.A., Zack studied the stack of script revisions on his desk, the mound of messages not important enough to return while he'd been on location. He started with the most recent, saw Dawson Barrett's name and smiled. He and Dawson had kept in touch over the years, and they'd reconnected briefly at the reunion a few months ago.

He'd call Dawson when he returned to his penthouse later that night. From the amount of reading on his desk, he would be staying in the city this weekend.

He swore. He'd been looking forward to a couple of days at his house in Malibu. That was the one place he could relax. Usually he derived satisfaction and a sense of accomplishment after a movie was in the can. But this time, his mind had kept drifting. The adrenaline rush had been missing and he didn't know why.

His cell phone vibrated against his hip. He considered ignoring it, then pulled it from his belt and studied the caller ID on the screen, surprised to see it was Jenny. A sense of foreboding zipped from his head to his loafers.

"Jenny?"

Words came tumbling from her. "I was afraid you'd still be out of the country."

"I just got back yesterday. What's wrong?"

He heard her take a steadying breath and he braced himself for what was coming.

"Silas collapsed. I rode with him in the ambulance to Flagstaff—" Her voice caught.

Zack went numb, absolutely numb. Images of his dad riding Hercules, giving the hands orders, smoking a Cuban cigar, flew through his mind. The idea of Silas being loaded into an ambulance... How could Jenny have been so right when he'd seen no evidence of a problem? *Was* he blind where his father was concerned?

He pushed out the words lodged in his throat. "I'll catch the first flight out."

"Zack..."

To his surprise, he still felt connected to Jenny and could read her thoughts. "I know you're scared. Try to take a deep breath and hope for the best. Call me with updates. If I'm on the plane, I'll get your message when I land."

"What if you can't get a seat?"

"Then I'll charter a plane. You don't have to go through this alone."

"Thank you."

Her voice wobbled in a way that was so unlike Jenny that Zack's throat tightened. "No thanks necessary. I should have listened to you."

She said nothing.

"I'll be there as soon as I can. Hold tight."

She murmured her thanks again and ended the call.

Conflicting emotions battered Zack as he turned to his computer to make a reservation. What would he find when he got to Flagstaff? *Hope for the best,* he'd told Jenny.

Just what *was* the best?

Late that night, Zack rushed into the emergency room entrance of the stucco and brick hospital in Flagstaff, his pulse racing. He'd thought he'd distanced himself from his father. He'd thought he simply didn't care anymore. Maybe that's why he hadn't seen the symptoms Jenny had noticed when he'd been home for the reunion. Or maybe his father pretended as much as he himself did.

It was possible his father had put up a front for Zack's benefit, but Zack's coolness and reserve toward Silas wasn't a pretense. They'd had many arguments before Zack had left for film school. Growing up, he'd often seen his dad inebriated after a high-stakes poker game. He'd heard his parents' arguments and known his dad was always at the root of them. When Zack had learned what had happened the day his mother died, why she'd taken off in that airplane to visit her sister in Montana, he'd disowned his father just as his father had practically disowned him when he left the ranch to pursue a film career.

After inquiring at the desk and showing ID, he headed for the cardiac intensive care unit and found Jenny in one of the waiting rooms. Even looking distraught and pale, she was a beautiful woman. At thirty-three, maturity had touched her in attractive ways. Her glossy blond, shoulder-length hair framed a heart-shaped face that had taken on a more haunting beauty. Her deep brown eyes, always wide with emotions, were stunning as she looked up at him.

"I'm so glad you're here. They've stabilized him but—" The quick shutdown of her thoughts told Zack just how upset she was.

Shrugging out of his leather jacket, he laid it over the back of the sofa.

"Did you even have time to pack?" she asked.

"No. I keep a duffle in my office with a change of clothes and workout gear. I just grabbed that."

"Are you going to try to see him now?"

"Yes, for a few minutes. Thanks for giving me his doctor's number. I called him after I landed. He said he'd noted on the chart that I could see him when I arrived."

"Zack, you *can't* upset him." She looked as if that was hard for her to say, but yet she knew she had to say it.

Her regret didn't help the sting, though, and he replied, almost angrily, "Do you think I would? My God, Jenny, I don't wish him harm."

"How would I know what you wish him, Zack?"

She was right. How would she know? They hadn't really talked except about the most mundane practical things when he called his father now and then. He'd felt it was his duty to keep in touch even though he hadn't wanted to. Sometimes Jenny would answer. Sometimes they'd exchange pleasantries. Others she'd just tell Silas he was on the line.

We live in different worlds, he reminded himself, not for the first time. Yet standing here, facing her again, years dropped away and lingering nudges of what they'd once shared startled him. Memories ran through his head of the two of them sitting on the corral fence talking...of gentling a foal together...of graduating... of making love in the hayloft. No—not making love. Having sex. If it had been love, Jenny would have gone with him to L.A. when he'd asked her.

"How long are you going to stay?" she asked, and he could see she was already preparing herself for the fact he might be here merely twenty-four hours again.

"I don't know. Let's just see what happens after to-morrow. I'll conference with the doctor and then de-cide."

She appeared to want to say something, maybe ask him if he could stay longer than a day, but she didn't. Instead she murmured, "I'll get a blanket and pillows while you're gone. I'm bunking here tonight."

Zack knew his father had become a dad to Jenny, the way her own had never been. It was ironic that Silas couldn't be a real father to Zack when Zack was growing up, but with Jenny—Silas Decker had never been anything but supportive, positive and encouraging with her even before his wife had died. Maybe that's because Jenny hadn't been a disappointment to him. Or because she had stepped into the role that Zack had been groomed for but had refused.

"I'm going to see him now." Zack steeled himself

for the visit, knowing he did have to distance himself from this experience and whatever happened next.

Surprising him, Jenny crossed to him and touched his forearm. It was just a whisper of a touch, no pressure at all. Yet Zack felt the fire of it. He felt his body respond to it, and he pulled away before she could guess what was happening. But not before he saw the disappointment on her face that they couldn't have a heart-to-heart about this.

There would be no heart-to-hearts, not tonight, not in the days to come. He didn't do that because letting himself be vulnerable would only invite pain. He'd seen it with his parents. He'd felt it with Jenny, and he'd certainly experienced it in L.A.

He headed for his father's cubicle, not knowing what to expect.

Zack walked into the glass enclosure and stopped short. Silas's eyes were closed and his complexion was ashen, almost as gray as the hair fringing his head. His mustache was still black but streaked with gray, too. His father was a strapping man—six foot tall and husky. He'd gained weight over the past ten years. Seeing him like this, lying in a bed in a hospital gown, hooked up to IVs and God knew what else, Zack had to absorb the fact his father was aging.

What had Zack thought? That the years would keep passing and his father would remain the same?

His dad's eyes fluttered open, and he stared at Zack for a few seconds without speaking. Finally he said hoarsely, "You came."

Still struck by his father's appearance, Zack didn't respond.

"You didn't want to come, did you?" Silas asked, sounding more like his old self. "This is a duty call."

Was that true? Not entirely, but he didn't admit it. "You had a heart attack," he said without answering the question.

Silas gave a slight shrug. "That's what Jenny tells me. The doc uses words that don't make any sense, and tomorrow, well, I don't know what's going to happen. There's always a chance—"

Zack stepped closer to the bed. "No, there isn't. You're going to have what's called a cardiac catheterization. It's going to show what's wrong and your doctor is going to fix it."

"Sometimes you can find out what's wrong and *not* be able to fix it."

"You can't think that way going into it."

"And here I thought you'd like it if I just faded away and you didn't have to deal with me anymore."

"Don't be ridiculous." Zack said the words, but he *did* feel guilty. Hadn't he often wondered what life would be like without his father's carping?

"Don't lie to me. The truth is the truth is the truth."

No matter what had happened before, Zack said with certainty, "I want you to be well. I want you to be healthy again. Jenny is worried sick about you and she needs you."

His father swallowed, looked away for a moment, then back at him. "She's the daughter I never had. Her own father's a fool for not realizing what a gem he has in her."

Silent, Zack considered Jenny's background and the year he'd been closer to her than he'd ever been to anyone.

Silas asked, "What are you thinking about?"

After a few moments' reluctance, he answered, "How much Jenny meant to Mom and you." And how she'd refused to go with him to L.A. That thought still had the power to bring back bitterness and regret.

"I need you to promise me something," his father entreated in a low, serious voice.

"What?" Zack asked warily.

"With me out of commission, Jenny can't handle the burden of the Rocky D on her own. She's taken over even more responsibility the past couple of months with management of the ranch as well as training the horses, but it's all too big for any one person. So no matter what happens tomorrow, will you stay a month, six weeks, and help her get a handle on whatever has to be done?"

"Dad—"

"I know it's a lot to ask. I know this isn't your life. You have big fish to fry. Well, the Rocky D has big fish, too. I know you think I have no right to ask anything of you. That might be true. But Jenny's going to need some help, and you're the only one I trust to give her that help."

If his father had asked for his own benefit, Zack might have been able to turn him down. But the way he'd put it, how could Zack refuse? Still, he had commitments of his own.

Silas continued, "You could set up shop at the Rocky D for a while. There's plenty of room. You could have your own office in the east wing." He hesitated. "I have a home theater there now, too."

The sliding glass doors of Silas's cubicle opened and a nurse bustled in. "Time's about up," she said gently but firmly. "Your father needs his rest."

Zack knew that was true. He also knew state of mind could make a big difference if his father was to recover. No, he didn't want to stay. No, he didn't want to get roped back into a life he'd left behind. No, he didn't want to be around Jenny and feel that old tug of desire they'd shared.

"Think about it," his father said.

Zack knew he wouldn't be able to do much else.

The following morning, Jenny paced the waiting room while Zack worked on his laptop. She didn't know how he could concentrate with his dad undergoing the heart catheterization. Even during the night as she'd tried to doze on the sofa, she'd caught glimpses of images flickering on the laptop screen where Zack studied them and tapped the computer keys. He hadn't slept at all.

When he'd returned from seeing his dad last night, he'd been remote and silent. This morning, after visiting Silas again, he'd been the same. Just what was going through his head? Once, so many years ago, she would have known. For the past fifteen years, she hadn't had a clue. For the gazillionth time, she thought about what might have been if she hadn't lost their baby. Quickly she shut down those thoughts.

With a long, blown-out breath, Zack closed the lid of the machine, pushed it deeper onto the side table, stood and rolled his shoulders. His muscles rippled under his black T-shirt. Above the waistband of his khakis, she could glimpse just how flat his stomach still was.

"Do you do that often?" she asked, feeling wrinkled and rumpled and not as put together as he had always looked no matter what he wore. The lines around Zack's

eyes were deeper now, but other than that he looked…
as charismatic and sexy as ever.

"Work through the night? Oh, yeah. Especially when
we're on deadline."

"For a movie?"

"For a movie, for an edit, for a casting." He shrugged.
"It's the nature of the business."

"Here I thought you lounged in a chaise at the beach
most of the time," she joked.

He gave her a long considering look. His blue eyes
were so direct with an intense focus that hadn't changed.
"My life isn't what it seems from the outside."

"The outside?" She was genuinely curious.

"What you see and hear. The premieres, the public-
ity for the movies. It looks as if it isn't staged, but all
of it is."

"Even those photos of you on the beach?" She
wouldn't mention the drop-dead gorgeous models and
actresses he was always photographed with.

"Exactly."

Pausing only a second, she prodded, "Does Silas
know about your real life, or do you only tell him about
the outside?"

"Dad hears what he wants to hear."

"But do you talk about your actual work with him?"

"You probably know how much we talk. It's mostly
about the weather, his horse buyers, if I'll be nominated
for another Oscar."

"If you made a point of telling him…"

Zack scowled and even that expression was sexy
as the corners of his mouth turned down. "You're not
going to be on my back about talking to Dad the whole

time I'm here, are you? Because if you are, I'm going to spend most of my time working."

If he'd intended to frame that bomb of information into his response, she didn't know. But she surely realized the implication. "The time you're here? How long will that be?"

"We'll figure it out after he's back up here giving orders again."

"We're talking about more than a few days?"

"It depends on his condition. I'll let you know after I speak with his doctor."

For just a moment, Jenny felt her heart fall. She really didn't have a right to be here, or to any information. No matter she spent every day with Silas, saw his symptoms develop, and cared deeply that they had. She wasn't a relative. Zack was his son. She was not Silas's daughter.

That thought brought to mind the inevitable one of wondering where her own father was right now. Maybe she cared so much about Silas because her own dad didn't seem to want her to care about *him*. And she shouldn't, because he always left...he never stayed. But she did care.

"What are you thinking?" Zack asked, as he crossed to the sofa where she sat. He moved the magazine she had tried to concentrate on, lowered himself beside her, yet not too close.

Did he feel any remnant of the attraction that had rippled between them as teenagers? The attraction she felt now? "I'm not thinking. I'm just worried."

"Bull. Something was ticking through that pretty head of yours besides worry."

His attitude both shook and angered her. "You don't

know me anymore, so don't try to read me like a mentalist at a carnival."

"So you think I don't know you?" His voice was lower as he said, "When you're thinking, little frown lines appear right here."

He touched the space between her brows and her heart rapped against her ribs.

"But when you're worrying—" he slid his finger across the side of her mouth "—this dimple disappears and sometimes your lower lip quivers."

She was mesmerized by the pad of his finger on her skin...trembling from skimming her gaze over the breadth of his shoulders, his beard stubble, the past memories in his eyes.

Grabbing her composure for all she was worth, she straightened her shoulders and leaned back. "You're making that up."

"Nope. You haven't changed all that much. You grew up fast and were always direct, curious and sassy. Give me one way you're different now than when you came to live at the Rocky D when you were seventeen."

Instead of an off-the-cuff flip reply, she considered his request. "Now I think before I speak. I hope I've learned to have as much patience with people as I've always had with horses."

He smiled and she wished he hadn't. Zack smiling was almost impossible to resist.

"You think before you speak and have patience with everyone but *me*."

She was about to protest, to tell him he was all wrong, but she considered what he'd said. "I guess with you, my good intentions get short-circuited."

His smile faded. "So tell me what you were thinking."

Zack had always been determined. Maybe this time she shouldn't fight his desire to know. "I was thinking I have no official right to be here...to know Silas's condition. But I'd like to be included."

The cold detachment she'd sensed in Zack when he'd arrived, dissipated altogether. "Of course you'll be included. Has anyone told you differently?"

"Oh, no. The staff and doctors have been understanding."

Zack was studying her as if he knew old insecurities still haunted her. She couldn't let him see that sometimes they did. Most of all, she couldn't let him see that she was still attracted to him.

Rising to her feet, she said, "I'm going to get coffee. I'll bring you a cup."

"Black," he told her as he rose, too, and returned to the laptop.

He'd always taken his coffee black, but she wouldn't let him see she remembered that...along with everything else.

Chapter Two

When Jenny returned to the waiting room with two cups of coffee, Zack wasn't there. She didn't know what to think. Had there been news about Silas? She set down the coffee, noticed Zack's laptop wasn't on the table and was about to ask for information at the nurses' desk when he strode into the waiting room, cell phone in his hand.

"Is Silas finished?" she asked.

"Not that I know of. I locked my laptop in the car and went to make a call." When she glanced at his cell phone, he clipped it onto his belt.

"Business?" she asked, not sure why she was asking. Maybe she just wanted to probe a little.

"Actually, no, it wasn't."

"Someone who wondered where you disappeared to?" She knew she shouldn't be inquiring about this.

His life was none of her business, not anymore. Still, she was curious.

Amused, he asked, "You want details?"

"Only if you want to get them off your chest."

He cast her a wry smile. "No, I don't think I do."

She felt the disappointment like a weight. She should have known better. For all she knew, he was dating three different women at once. That was certainly what the tabloids led everyone to believe. One of the most eligible bachelors in L.A. didn't need to be married or even in a relationship because he was having too much fun. Though from what he'd said last night—

He approached her until he stood close enough to touch. "I left L.A. in a rush. I have lots of loose ends that aren't tied up."

Including a relationship with a woman? she wanted to ask, yet didn't. The one thing she'd learned long ago was never to make the same mistake twice. That was how she'd learned to accept disappointment where her dad was concerned. That was how she'd learned to move on, always looking for a new way to solve a problem, a new way to handle a loss. She'd lost Zack once. She wouldn't make the mistake of feeling too much for him again. It really was as simple as that. Practice had taught her well. Now she had to just keep her wits about her and pretend that being this near to him didn't send a tingle of awareness through her body.

Since she couldn't—wouldn't—ask anything personal, she forced a smile and inquired, "Do you really have a house in Malibu, a penthouse in L.A. and a condo in Vail?"

"Now where did *that* come from?" His forehead furrowed but there was a sparkle of curiosity in his eyes.

"I'm just wondering how much of the tabloid stories about you I can believe."

"Well, at least the real estate I have is one thing they got right. Yes, to all of the above."

"And you've been to every continent?" she pushed.

"I have, for either work or pleasure."

"You actually vacationed in Antarctica?"

At that, he let out a chuckle. "Yes, I did. Why are you so amazed?"

"Because I can't imagine why anyone would want to vacation there."

His blue gaze became more probing. "Jenny, don't you want to see the world?"

"Why would I? I'm happy here."

He shook his head as if he couldn't understand that philosophy at all. "Don't you want to know how other people live? What work means to them…what gives their lives meaning?"

"Does your curiosity get satisfied in your travels?"

He considered that. "I don't know. But I always find answers to some unanswered questions I didn't even know were lurking in my mind. That probably doesn't make any sense to you."

She could see he wasn't talking down to her, but really trying to clarify his point of view. "When *I* want an answer, I just work at finding it right here. But then I guess that's why I gentle horses and you make movies."

"The movie-making might change now."

"How? Why?"

Suddenly, Zack's focus shifted from her to the doorway. When she peered around him, she saw Dr. Murphy,

Silas's cardiologist. He looked serious and she couldn't tell from his expression exactly what had happened.

The cardiac surgeon said, "Zack has signed appropriate forms and instructed me you're to be kept up-to-date on everything that concerns his father's condition."

She murmured to Zack, "Thank you."

His gaze briefly met hers and she gained a momentary glimpse of the young man she'd once loved. The next moment his attention focused on the cardiologist as he asked, "Good news or bad?"

Although Zack might be a visionary behind the camera, Jenny realized he was a pragmatist, too.

"A little of both. There has been heart muscle damage, which we suspected from the myocardial infarction. But we inserted two stents and with a change in lifestyle, I think he'll regain his energy and maybe some of the verve he's lost in the past few months. He's a lucky man…lucky this happened when someone was with him and fortunate an ambulance got him here as soon as it did. No one is ever happy about life changes they need to make to continue good health, but your father seems like a practical man. I'm hoping with the two of you to help convince him, he'll see this as a positive life change, not as something he has to dread. I'll have a nutritionist talk to him before he leaves."

"Can I sit in?" Jenny asked. "He has a housekeeper and I'd like to relay any information to her. Maybe we can devise meals that he doesn't think are too boring."

The doctor smiled. "Diet and exercise will be the two main components of his life changes and…" He motioned to Zack. "Zack told me you'd be a big help with that."

"What about a cardiac rehab program?" Zack asked.

"I'll be speaking with your father about that, too. There are a couple of different ways we can handle it. He'll have to choose what's right for him."

"He'll probably want a private nurse and a home gym," Zack muttered.

The doctor didn't look fazed. He just said, "Whatever it takes."

Jenny knew he was right. She would do whatever it took to keep Silas on the road to good health. Seeing how quickly Zack had responded to her call, she was hopeful he would, too, even if it was only so he could get back to his own life.

"How long do you think it will be until he's able to do the things he wants to do again?" she asked.

"We're going to have to see how his recuperation comes along. But if you're asking in general terms, I'd say four to six weeks at least. Maybe longer until the changes he makes take effect."

Jenny saw Zack frown and didn't know what that meant. Would he consider staying in Miners Bluff that long? If so, why? Did he feel she couldn't handle Silas on her own? Or was he simply worried about his father and didn't want to admit it?

"I'm going to keep him in CICU for today. Tomorrow, if all goes well, I'll transition him to an intermediary room. I want to keep an eye on his blood oxygen level. Then we'll decide what happens next."

Zack extended his hand to shake the cardiologist's. "Thank you."

Jenny did the same, saying, "I wish we weren't so far from the hospital."

"Miners Bluff has a superior urgent care center. Don't hesitate to go there or call me if there are any problems." The doctor moved toward the door. There he stopped. To Zack he said, "Your dad is a tough customer. It might take both of you to convince him to do what he needs to do." Then he exited the room, leaving Zack and Jenny alone—each wondering what came next.

Four days later, Jenny stepped through the mahogany French doors to Silas's parlor, surprised to see Zack cleaning out the cupboard behind the wet bar. "What are you doing?"

Zack didn't know if this was going to be a fight or not, but he wouldn't back down from it. He stacked bottles of liquor into a carton. "I'm clearing away temptation. Dad's resting, I hope?"

They'd driven into Flagstaff together to pick him up when he was discharged. Both wanted to hear what the instructions were for after-care. He was supposed to take it easy for the next week. Zack wasn't sure that meant the same thing to his father that it meant to him.

He continued to remove bottles from the cabinet and shove them in the box. "I know he doesn't like staying in one of the guest bedrooms down here, but it's for his own good. I'll stay down here, too, then I can keep an eye on him."

"He can use the intercom system if he needs you."

Zack stared down into the box so long, Jenny finally asked, "Zack?"

"Sorry. I was remembering… This isn't the first time I've done something like this."

She looked puzzled. "What do you mean?"

Did he want to get into this with her? Why not? The past didn't matter anymore. If she didn't know the gritty details, maybe it was time. "Dad drank and gambled for as far back as I can remember, then he'd come home and fight with Mom. When I was around ten, I got this mistaken impression that if I went through the house and got rid of some of the liquor, that might make a difference. So I'd take out a bottle here, a bottle there and I'd dump them behind the barn. I couldn't wipe out the whole cupboard, there would've been hell to pay. But at least I felt I was doing *something*."

He saw the softening in Jenny's brown eyes and he knew what that meant. It was pity. He certainly didn't want her pity, not for the boy he'd been, and certainly not for the man he was now. "That taught me one very important lesson," he added, suddenly realizing exactly why he was telling her this story. "You can't make a difference in someone's life unless they want you to."

She crossed the hunter green and burgundy Persian rug, rounding a suede and leather sofa. "That's not true, Zack. Don't tell me you believe that."

When she stopped in front of the bar, he focused his gaze on her. "Do you think you've made a difference in his life?" He knew Jenny had poured everything she was and everything she could have been into Silas and the Rocky D.

"I *have* made a difference. Because I've become a substitute for you."

This time there was no pity in her eyes but there was something else he couldn't decipher. That bothered him. He used to understand Jenny so well...why she yearned for bonds she could depend on.

Jenny's father had done his duty by her when he'd had to. His love had always been the rodeo. Early on,

Jenny had had her mom, but had only seen her dad when he came in from the circuit. After that…

Jenny's mom had suddenly died of a brain aneurysm when Jenny was eight and her father had been devastated. Jenny had known, even though he wasn't at home that much, that he and her mom had really loved each other. After a year of Jenny taking care of Charlie, rather than Charlie taking care of *her,* he'd left her with a neighbor more and more, always chasing a rodeo purse and a dream. That's the way it had been until Jenny had done an internship on the Rocky D the summer before her senior year in high school. She'd loved horses, handled them expertly and calmed them, showing up his father's best grooms. His mother had started giving her other responsibilities and had let her handle some of the bookwork. When his mom learned her history, she'd asked Jenny if she wanted to live with them her senior year of high school. Charlie had easily agreed, handing off some of the responsibility for his almost-grown child. Jenny became like a daughter to the Deckers.

Zack's attraction to Jenny and hers to him had revved up the moment she'd set foot on the Rocky D. Zack had known it wouldn't be fair to start something with her, when he intended to leave Miners Bluff as soon as he could. Jenny, on the other hand, wore her heart on her sleeve, which had made it easy for him to confide in her, go on long walks and rides, become close to her in a way he'd never been close to a girl before. The night of their high school graduation, they'd gone to the all-night party, come home around 3:00 a.m. and climbed up to the hayloft, which had become their private place. They'd been so excited. He'd won the National Young

Filmmakers Scholarship and his dad had hired her to be one of his horse trainers and handlers. In that excitement, their threshold of restraint had fallen low. They'd made love in that hayloft. He'd asked her to go with him to L.A. She'd refused. That had been the end of them.

"You didn't have to be a substitute for anyone," Zack protested, feeling as if she were blaming him for something about her life, too.

"I didn't say I didn't want to be here, because I *did*. But I also realized that after your mother died, Silas gave up on the idea that you'd ever come back."

Staying in this house again, recollections from that difficult time in Zack's life pummeled him. As he'd tried to do since he'd returned, he shoved them away. "Even if Mom hadn't died, I doubt if I would have come back. When she visited me in L.A., she made sure to tell me she was proud—of me, of my work… But have you forgotten that when I left for film school, my father cut me off? He didn't want to know how the classes were, or what kind of projects I was doing. He didn't want to know if I was successful. He just didn't care. He'd planned for me to take his place someday. He blamed her for my absence because she gave me my first video camera."

Jenny leaned closer, the bar still a barrier between them. "You're both carrying too many shadows from the past. It's time to let go of all of it."

Just a whiff of Jenny's perfume unsettled Zack and lit fires he'd rather douse. "What about *your* dad, Jenny? Have *you* let go of all of it?" He saw immediately that he'd struck home and he shouldn't have. He shook his head. "I had no right to ask that."

With a sigh, she leaned away. "Maybe you did. After all, I'm giving *you* advice."

With a shrug, he admitted, "I have no advice, not about fathers and their kids." Closing the top of the carton, he taped it then started filling another.

Finally she said, "I've learned something over the years, Zack. I do have to accept reality. Wishing my dad would change only brought me heartache, so I accept him for who he is and don't expect anything. That way I don't get hurt."

Her acceptance of her own father's shortcomings made him feel like a jerk. He shouldn't have complained about the childhood he'd had when Jenny's had been so much worse. Losing her mom as a kid couldn't have been easy. Staying with a neighbor who really wasn't interested in babysitting while her father was gone had to have made Jenny feel unwanted.

She proved that as she told him, "After Mom died and I had to stay with Mildred when Dad left for the circuit, I disappeared into the library downtown and learned everything I could about horses…to fill up my life and I guess my heart, too. I didn't have the guts to come to a place like the Rocky D to learn what I needed to know to become a horse trainer, but I went to smaller ranches, asked if I could help with chores and got paid enough to buy clothes for school. I didn't care about the money as much as I just wanted to be around the animals, to know more about them. Some of those horses were my best friends until I went to high school and really got to know Mikala and Celeste. Up until then I shied away from the other girls because I felt they made fun of me…and looked down on me. Celeste and I had a lot in common because we were both girls from the wrong side of the tracks. I'm not sure how Mikala hooked up with us, maybe because her mother wasn't around much when she was growing up. But they became my safety net—they were always there for me. How did you and Dawson and Clay become friends?"

"The reverse of you and Celeste and Mikala, I guess. Our families went back to the founding fathers of Miners Bluff. In one way or another, we were all rebelling against authority, against our fathers, our families. Don't get me wrong, we didn't talk about it. Guys didn't do that." He shot her a wry grin. "But we knew we all wanted to be independent and forge our own course, no matter what anybody else thought."

"Rebels *with* a cause?" she joked.

"Minus the motorcycles. Clay and I used horses. Dawson had a Mustang."

She laughed at the pun.

Whenever he and Jenny found a nonvolatile subject, he enjoyed the ease of talking to her, just as he had when he was a teenager.

In high school, they'd all hung out at Mikala's aunt's bed and breakfast where her refrigerator and pantry was overstocked with everyone's favorite drinks and snacks. As he and Jenny started spending more time alone after she moved in at the Rocky D, long talks about anything and everything had taken place in the barn and hayloft. Long talks…and plenty of kisses.…

But they weren't kids anymore and the shadow of him leaving and her refusal to go with him sidled in and out between them now, along with the electricity that never seemed to cease buzzing.

"Is there anywhere else you think I should look for a stash like this?" He waved at the remaining bottles.

"You could ask me," Silas said from the doorway. Both Zack and Jenny jumped, startled by his appearance.

"All right," Zack agreed quickly, deciding to face his father head-on in everything now. "Is there anyplace else you'd like me to clean out?" He tried to ignore the fact that his father was leaning on a cane and looking pale. His physician had warned them not to expect too much too soon, but it was hard seeing his father like this.

Silas entered the room and straightened up to his full six-foot height. "You don't have to clean anything out. I haven't had a drop of liquor for a year. I keep that assortment for my friends, or for cocktail parties, like the one I had to introduce Clay Sullivan to some possible clients. It was the same night we all watched your new movie."

That derailed Zack's thoughts. "You got a pirated copy?"

"I did. I didn't want to wait for the premiere."

Sometimes Zack forgot how well his father was connected. "You never told me you watched it."

"Does it matter?"

Good question—and he really wasn't sure of the answer. Did he want to know what his father thought about it? Chances were good Silas would have something critical to say. Not that Zack couldn't take criticism. He'd had to take plenty of it to get where he was now. But coming from his father, it would be nice to hear something positive, some sort of encouragement or pat on the back he'd never gotten as a kid.

Silas stroked his mustache. "If you're looking for cigars in addition to the liquor, you'll find a box in my bottom desk drawer in my office. They're underneath the Bible. I haven't had a smoke in the past six months."

As Zack looked into his father's eyes, he wished he could believe him. But after years of hearing his dad lie to his mother so many times, he knew trust hadn't even been a word in his father's vocabulary.

Deciding to leave this discussion for the present, Zack asked his dad, "Is there anything I can bring you from upstairs to make you more comfortable down here?"

"I'll only be comfortable when I'm in my own room again," Silas grumbled.

Jenny, who'd been absorbing the conversation, stepped in. "It's only for a few days, Silas. Besides, you'll have a great view of the back pasture from the guest room. You can watch the yearlings when we let them out on the nice days."

"Nice days?" Silas barked. "You won't be seeing many more of them. I heard we're in for snow next week."

"So you can watch them frolic in the snow when I exercise them," she responded, unfazed.

"While I eat sawdust and vegetables."

"Do you think I'd let Martha serve you sawdust and vegetables? I'm smarter than that. We're going to make such tasty recipes you won't be able to resist."

Finally, Silas broke into a slow smile. "If anybody can do it, you can." He sighed and ran a hand through his halo of gray hair. "Already I'm more tired than if I'd ridden out to Feather Peak. Jeez, how long is this going to last?"

"You know what the doctor said. It could be a while—a month, two, maybe even three. But with a new diet and some exercise when you're ready, you'll be feeling better soon, Silas. I promise you."

He looked at her the way a doting father looks at a loving daughter. "Your promises I believe."

With a last glance at Zack, he said, "I'll make that list."

After Silas had gone, his cane tapping on the hardwood floor down the hall, Zack turned to Jenny, feeling somewhat unnerved by witnessing the bond that had developed between her and his dad. Was he envious of it? Yet how could he be when it had been *his* choice to put his dad in the recesses of his life for so many years?

"What if he doesn't feel better in three months?" he challenged her. "What if the way he's feeling now is as good as it gets? That happens, you know."

"Maybe so. But I can't think that way and Silas doesn't need *you* thinking that way. We have to encourage him, day by day." She studied Zack for so long it made him uncomfortable.

"What?"

"I don't think you're used to encouraging *anyone,* are you?"

"That's not true. I deal with temperamental actors all the time."

"That isn't the same thing at all. I'm talking about common kindness, compassion and an optimistic attitude to make someone *want* to get better, want to do their best in life, not in a make-believe world."

"Do you think I deal with make-believe? Have you even *watched* any of my movies?"

That made Jenny's cheeks flush. "Of course I have. I'm sorry. That didn't come out right. I know you don't just produce and direct entertainment. There's always more than that to it, a bigger cause, an issue under the surface."

So she'd realized that about him, had she? He didn't know whether he'd expected her to be perceptive about his motives or not. "That's one reason why I'm moving into documentaries. I don't want to hide the cause anymore. I want to go after it. I have the clout and the money to do that now. I can film the stories I want to film."

"Did you ever think about what you'd be doing if you hadn't won that award in high school? Where you'd be now?"

He couldn't tell if she was really asking about *them* or his life in general. Anytime they got near the personal, the vibrations between them picked up, the attraction he still felt for her ignited. "I still would have found a way to get to L.A. with or without my dad's approval, with or without his money. You know that. It was that important for me to get away from here and find a life of my own."

"And what if your career hadn't worked out so well? What if success hadn't come easy?"

"Easy? Is that really what you think?"

Moving around the bar, she helped him pull bottles from the cupboard. "It seemed like it. You went to film school, then you were directing your first movie which was a hit. Then you directed another and then another."

When Zack reached into the cupboard, his shoulder grazed hers and a jolt of awareness hit him in the gut. He leaned away before she could see how that minor contact rocked him.

Clearing his throat, he said, "It did seem like that from the outside, didn't it? That first film was a technical success, but not an industry success. For a year I worked in the stables outside of Anaheim to make money to keep a one-room apartment. I was still sending out résumés, reading scripts, thinking about what to do to make a career work. I directed a rock video that caught notice and put me in touch with the right people. One of them hired me as an assistant director. After that, I worked day and night, took any project I thought would get some notice until finally, I got my chance. A director backed out and I was in. *That* movie was an industry success. That movie won me my first Oscar."

"I never knew you had to work so hard. Did Silas know?"

"Are you kidding? When I left, he told me he knew I'd come running back with my tail between my legs. There was no way in hell I wasn't going to make my life out there work."

And he'd been willing to make the two of them work, too. If only Jenny had come with him. If only she had tried, maybe then he wouldn't still feel resentment and bitterness along with an attraction that wouldn't fade. The sooner he was back in L.A. again, the better. But he'd made his father a promise, to stay here long enough so Jenny wouldn't have the burden of running the Rocky D all on her own. He regretted that promise now. Looking into Jenny's soft brown eyes, feeling his body respond to her, he knew his stay was going to be nothing but torture—on many fronts.

"What's wrong?" she asked softly. "You look... angry."

"You don't want to know."

"I wouldn't have asked if I didn't want to know."

He was quiet for a moment. "Did you ever imagine what your life might have been like if you had come with me?"

She looked surprised, as if she'd never expected that question to pop up. "I...I never wanted that kind of life."

"How did you know when you hadn't tried it?" Then he lifted his hand in a dismissive gesture. "Never mind. I shouldn't have asked. During those couple of tough years, you wouldn't have stuck by me. I know what you went through with your dad. You would have thought it was just more of the same."

She looked as if he'd slapped her. There was real hurt in her eyes. He'd never meant to cause that. Or had he? Did he want her to feel the same pain he'd felt when she said she couldn't go with him? This was so ridiculous, revisiting history that couldn't be rewritten.

He shook his head. "I shouldn't have brought it up. We made the decisions we did."

In a quiet voice, she asked, "Where has your heart gone, Zack? You talk as if you have nothing but your work. Is that the way it is?"

"Work is everything, isn't it, Jenny? Isn't that why you stay here? What else do *you* have?"

She was quick to answer. "I have Silas. I also have friends and a sense of belonging in Miners Bluff. I have a life here, Zack. All of that is more important to me than just work."

Zack's cell phone buzzed and he was actually relieved for the interruption. Taking it from his belt, he checked the caller ID. "Speaking of friends, it's Dawson. He's returning my call. I'd better take this."

Jenny studied him as if she hadn't expected him to stay in touch with old friends.

He explained quickly, "Dawson, Clay and I kept in touch over the years. Dawson flies out for Lakers games now and then. Clay sends me photos and video clips of Abby. I can't believe she's growing as fast as she is."

He opened his cell and would have passed Jenny without a glance, but she caught his arm, saying, "You stay. I'll go." The impression of her fingers burned through his sweater. The room felt hot and he knew it was definitely time to put distance between the two of them.

She hesitated as if she wanted to say so much more, but clearly thought better of it as she released his arm. "I'll see how Silas is making out with that list."

Zack wished she would take his memories and regrets with her.

"Hey, Dawson," Zack said, watching Jenny leave the room. The scent of jasmine that always seemed to surround her still lingered in the air.

"Sorry for the phone tag," Dawson apologized. "Construction's picking up again and we're swamped."

"How's Luke?"

There was a long hesitation on Dawson's part, as if he didn't talk about his son easily these days. It had been over a year and a half since Dawson's wife died and Zack knew the boy was having problems getting over his mom's death. Dawson had talked to him about it when Luke's school grades had tanked, when he'd started getting in trouble, when Dawson was at his wit's end because counselors hadn't seemed able to help.

"That's why I'm calling, Zack. Come January and the start of a new school term, I'm going to move us back to Miners Bluff."

"You're kidding."

"No, I'm not. I've been considering it ever since I spoke to Mikala Conti at the reunion. You know she's a music therapist."

"I knew she was a counselor. I just didn't realize what her specialty was."

"Luke is into music. He spends more time with the piano and his iPod than with schoolwork or with me. When I mentioned that to Mikala, she said it could be a starting point. I'm willing to give anything a shot. Nothing here is helping."

Zack knew Dawson's life in Phoenix was high stress, long hours, with lots of monetary rewards. He had a huge house in Fountain Hills and more money than he'd ever need. But money wasn't doing his son any good.

"Luke needs a supportive community around him," Dawson continued. "And Mikala has a high success rate, according to the psychologist who has been treating Luke here. If Mikala could just get him started turning around so that he and I could at least communicate, that would mean everything."

"What about the business?"

"I can handle it lots of ways. Dad's a great manager when it comes to my crews. I can run everything long distance, at least temporarily. I have to try this, Zack, because I don't know what else to do. It's the first time in my life I've felt powerless. I hate it."

Dawson was the CEO of his own construction company. He handled workers, payrolls, new design projects, architects. Zack had an idea of his frustration now.

"I'm back in Miners Bluff for the moment," he revealed to his friend.

"You're kidding! You've been away for years, now suddenly two visits in a few months? What happened?"

"Dad had a heart attack."

"Zack, I'm sorry. How is he?"

"He just came home today. I'm going to be here for the next few weeks, so if there's anything you need to know before you make the move, just give me a call."

"Do you have work to keep you busy while you're there?"

"Some. There's a new project I'm thinking about doing. I can do a lot of the research from here."

"Give your dad my regards."

"I'll do that. And you call me if you need anything."

"I will. I'll be driving up there some time after the first of the year to look at the school. If you're still there—"

"No way will I still be here."

Dawson chuckled. "Try not to go stir crazy. I'll give you a call in a couple of weeks to see how your dad is."

"Thanks, Dawson. I'll talk to you soon."

Zack closed his phone and clipped it onto his belt, wishing he could do something concrete to help his friend. He couldn't imagine having a child and watching him suffer.

He hadn't thought much about being a father...until now. He didn't date women who had motherhood on their minds. Maybe he should think about dating a different type of woman. A woman like...

Jenny?

No, he told himself. They were over.

Chapter Three

Golden sunrise drifted over the pastures of the Rocky D, defying the colder weather that had moved in since the beginning of November. Jenny loved early mornings this time of year, when one season teetered on the brink of another. This early, Silas's three permanent hands, Hank, Tate and Ben, were already at work. The horses weren't yet restless to be let out, to be let free. She could forget about what problems the day might bring with Zack and Silas under the same roof and have some time for herself.

She led Songbird from her stall, rubbed her nose and asked conversationally, "Ready for a rough and tumble ride?"

"And just what *is* a rough and tumble ride?" a deep male voice asked from behind.

Jenny turned and saw Zack coming down the walkway. "You're up early," she said lightly, ignoring her racing heart.

"I usually am. I thought I'd go for a ride instead of doing an early-morning workout. Mind if I join you?"

Had anyone told Zack she rode every morning? Had he come out here purposely to talk to her about something? He seemed to be waiting for an answer so she responded, "I don't mind. Which horse would you like?"

"Tattoo."

He'd already picked one out? "How do you know you're compatible?"

He laughed. "Only *you* would ask something like that. I was down here last night. Tattoo and I struck up a conversation and we're well along to becoming friends. So...any problem with me taking him out?"

"No." She hesitated, then asked, "Why did you come down here last night?" When he gave her a studying look, she said, "Sorry, none of my business, I guess."

"It was after dinner. You were discussing new recipes with Martha. Dad was on the phone with Clay's father. I thought I'd take a look around. Everything's been kept up well. I noticed the mares' barn had a new roof."

"Last year."

"Are you still attracting clients from across the country who want cutting horses for competitions?"

"Yes."

"And the boarders' barn is full."

"Always."

Zack had to pass her to reach Tattoo's stall. He was dressed in jeans, boots and a sheepskin jacket this morning.

"You couldn't have brought that along," she said gesturing to his coat.

"Nope. It was hanging in the closet in my old room. I'd forgotten about it. It was huge when Mom bought it for me. Now it fits."

Jenny could almost see the memories in Zack's eyes, some bittersweet, some warm and some painful. She wasn't sure what to say.

"We can talk about her, Jen. All my memories of her have been limited to the photographs I took along and the videos I made. I have never had anyone to talk to about her. Do you know what I mean?"

"I do. I mean I talk to Dad about Mom when he's around, which isn't often, but I don't really have anything of hers except the funny hat she used to wear to church. I took it from the bag Dad was giving to Goodwill after she died. I know things are just things, but they seem to mean a lot after someone's gone. The pearl earrings your mom gave me for high school graduation are one of my prized possessions."

"You wore them the night of the reunion."

"You noticed?"

The quiet of the stables seemed to breed intimacy, and this morning was no different. This was the everyday barn, where favorite horses were lodged, where personal tack was kept, where the hayloft up above whispered about the kisses shared there when she and Zack were teenagers. And not only kisses. On that graduation night—

"I noticed," he responded, and she didn't know now if they were talking about earrings or so much more. This was dangerous territory for both of them. Especially for her. Since his return, her secret seemed to be on the tip of her tongue, ready to spill out. But there was no reason to tell him about her pregnancy and miscarriage... no reason to hurt him with something they couldn't change. With him standing there, looking down at her, all brawny and handsome in the sheepskin jacket and jeans, she knew she needed some cool air to capture her equilibrium once again.

"Let's saddle up," she suggested a bit shakily.

Zack just gave her an imperceptible nod and moved away.

Ten minutes later they were on the trail. This time of year, the most impressive aspect of the landscape was the mountains in the distance—Moonshadow Mountain and beyond it, Feather Peak.

"Have you ridden to Horsethief Canyon lately?" Zack asked.

Horsethief Canyon led up to Feather Peak. She and Zack had spent time there as teenagers, exploring, hiking, making out.

"No, not lately. Celeste and Clay have. They spent a honeymoon weekend there."

"You were at their wedding?"

"*In* their wedding. It was beautiful. They exchanged vows in Clay's backyard even though his parents probably would have preferred something more elaborate."

"Clay was always good at standing up to his dad."

"I think he and Mr. Sullivan have come to a new understanding since he and Celeste married."

They rode along the fence line until it gave way to rockier terrain. Both horses snorted as if begging to be let loose. Jenny felt the same way. Riding side by side with Zack, she felt edgy, awkward, unlike herself.

"So how about that rough and tumble ride?" he asked with a grin that could always make her breath hitch.

She tossed him a smile over her shoulder and then took off.

She heard Tattoo's hooves behind her steadily, easily keeping up, not trying to overtake her. She thought this might become a race, but Zack wasn't racing. When she cast a glance back at him, he looked intense as he usually did, but also as if he was having a good time.

The morning cold reddened her cheeks, numbed her nose, cooled her breath, but she loved every exhilarating moment of it. Zack galloped past her at one point and she strove to overtake him again, but she couldn't. He didn't just keep riding ahead, however. At a grove of pines he reined in his horse and waited for her. She knew this stand of trees quite well. She and Zack had sought their shade and cool comfort that final spring, when everything just seemed to be beginning. His face was ruddy, too, now from the cold, his hair windblown, his sheepskin collar turned up against the breeze.

"This is magnificent country," he said, almost to himself.

"I can't imagine anywhere as beautiful as this." The sky was already topaz-blue, devoid of clouds, hovering protectively over the landscape.

"Do you want to dismount for a few minutes? The trees will provide a buffer against the wind."

Something about being on the ground within the barrier of trees where they'd once spent time seemed dangerous to Jenny. Yet she wasn't going to be a coward about this. She'd just be very careful.

Zack tethered his horse to a low-slung branch and waited as she did the same. Then in the golden morning light, he found the old path covered with pine needles and dried leaves from the aspen in the not-too-far distance. There was a hushed quality within the grove that Jenny had always liked, that gave her a sense of peace.

Zack followed the path until they were deep inside the grove where sunlight and shadows dappled the ground.

"Soon this could be covered in snow," she reminded him. "If we've had a snowfall, sometimes after the kids finish their lessons, we come out here and play. They bring their saucers and tubes, and it's great fun."

"What kids?" he asked with a curious look.

"I give riding lessons. I do it on a sliding scale and take a few pro-bono students who can't afford to pay. They learn how to ride and groom, and just forget anything that's troubling them."

"Like you did."

"Horses have many lessons to teach, but I give these children goals and they have a sense of accomplishment when they learn how to master riding. I'm hoping those skills will stay with them well into the future."

Zack was standing beside a tall fir. She went still when she recognized it.

"What is it?" Zack asked, following her gaze. Then he saw the bark of the tree. Their names were carved there, deeply enough to have lasted all these years.

"I can't believe the weather hasn't worn them away."

"Or a lightning strike," Zack said nonchalantly. But she knew he was remembering the day he carved them there. They'd had exams at school that week and had come riding out here one day to let off steam, to forget about studying, to be together. She'd been so innocent. He'd been so noble. They'd kissed and made out, and she'd known he wanted her. Yet more than once, he'd insisted it wouldn't be fair if they became really intimate because he'd be leaving.

"You carved our names there, so there would be something lasting of our friendship." They would have had so much more that was lasting if she hadn't had the miscarriage. Yet what would they have done? Even if she had told Zack, would she have joined him in California and regretted it?

"Not much is lasting, is it?" he asked rhetorically.

"Friendships last. We both have proof of that."

"Maybe our high school friendships are the ones that matter most. I don't have friends in L.A. like Clay and Dawson. Even though we don't see each other often, we can pick up wherever we left off."

"Are you *sure* you don't miss Miners Bluff?"

He didn't answer right away, just studied their names, the tall firs, the land that he'd roamed when he was younger. "You can miss something but not need it or count on it or want it in your life anymore."

She wondered if he was feeding himself a line, or if he really believed that. "I think you don't want to admit you miss it. I think you don't want to admit you miss your father."

"Miss the arguments and his disagreeable view of my life?"

"He's proud of you."

"Maybe you've heard that, but I haven't. When I scored the most points in a basketball game, he was proud of me. When I gentled a horse he couldn't get near, he was proud of me. But when I picked up a camera, when I attempted to give him a look at the visions

I wanted to create, he turned the other way. A kid can only take so much of that."

"But you're not a kid anymore."

Zack's gaze became set and somber. "No, I know what I want. I detached from Dad and what he thinks of me." As if he'd grown tired of being on the defensive, he motioned to the land beyond the tree growth. "And what about you, Jenny? Just why did you stay? Out of loyalty, or out of a chance that all this could be yours someday?"

There was something in his voice that disconcerted her. Suspicion? "What do you mean?"

He only hesitated a moment before he said, "I left. I wasn't coming back. The longer you stayed, the more entrenched you became. You loved my mother and she loved you. But after she died, then why did you stay?"

"Because Silas needed me. Because by then the Rocky D was part of *me,* too."

He studied her as if he was looking at a scene he didn't quite know how to edit. "Tell me something, Jenny. Are you included in Dad's will?"

She was absolutely shocked by the direction of his thoughts. Did he believe that she'd hung on to a job here because it would pay off someday? That with him gone, she'd seen an opportunity and she'd taken it? That after his mother died, she could somehow convince his father *she* was the heir?

Insulted beyond measure, she couldn't even speak. Had her refusal to go with him caused this cynicism? Had his sense of betrayal grown into something insidious that made him think of her as an opportunist?

Without a word, she spun around and headed for her

horse. She'd already untethered him when she heard Zack call, "Jenny."

Ignoring the sound of her name on his lips, ignoring the voice that could always affect her so deeply, she mounted Songbird, clicked her tongue and took off for the Rocky D. The boy Zack had once been had been taken over by a man she absolutely didn't know.

The crunch of tires on gravel from cars and trucks pulling into the space between the everyday barn and the mares' barn on Saturday morning pulled Zack from his office where he sat listening by the intercom in case his father needed him. As if that would happen. Silas wasn't asking for a thing from him, not even a glass of water. He was relying on Jenny and Martha.

The door to his father's room was slightly open. Zack peered in and found Silas working on a crossword puzzle. "Dad, I'm going out to the barn." Zack lifted his cell phone. "You have my number on speed dial, right?"

"Filling out a crossword puzzle isn't too strenuous for me," his father muttered, waving him away. "I'll be fine."

Leaving his work behind, Zack headed for the kitchen door. Martha was already sautéing something for lunch.

"Smells good," he said with a smile for her.

"Jenny and I concocted this recipe. We'll see if your dad's ready to become part vegetarian." Martha had brown hair with blond highlights and was in her late forties. She'd been the Rocky D's chief cook and housekeeper since Zack's teenage years. Her quarters were behind the kitchen and like everyone else on the Rocky D, she was more like family than an employee.

"If you can win him over to vegetables, you deserve a raise."

She gave him a quick grin as she shuffled the vegetables in the pan.

As if his sixth sense about Jenny was still functioning, Zack spotted her outside the barn talking to a group of kids. She'd just pointed them toward the arena when she stepped aside to have a conversation with a woman who looked to be about her own age.

He knew he should apologize to Jenny, but whenever he thought about it, he realized that wouldn't be quite honest. He'd voiced some of the thoughts that had niggled at him for all these years. Why had she stayed? Because his mother had become the role model she'd missed? Because Silas was a substitute father? Or because she'd seen the opportunity to become part of a family that in the end could benefit her in so many ways?

When Jenny had refused to go with him, he'd thought about all of this. The longer he'd been in L.A., he'd thought about it even more. From his own experience, he'd learned women often wanted to latch on to him because of what he had to offer, not because of who he was. In fact, he'd broken off a relationship before the reunion. He'd learned a woman he'd been dating for a couple of months had used his name as a reference when she'd gone to a bank to apply for a small business loan. Rachel Crandall had never mentioned a loan to him, never asked him if it would be okay to use his name. Afterward, when he'd told her he was going out of the country soon and didn't feel their relationship was going to work, she'd arrived at his penthouse, all perfumed and tempting, her dress so tight he didn't know how she'd gotten into it. She'd pouted, she'd pleaded and finally she'd come right out and asked him for money. He'd known then their matchup had been all about money for her, or at least what she could get.

He'd again nixed the idea of any investment in her on his part and she'd left in a huff. As soon as the door had closed, he'd known he wasn't going to miss her.

On the other hand, while he'd been in England, he hadn't been able to stop thinking about how beautiful Jenny had looked at the reunion in her yellow dress, or how she'd looked in jeans with a bandanna around her neck and a straw hat on her head fifteen years before.

Approaching the women at the barn, he froze when he heard the brunette say, "Stan doesn't want me to bring the kids for lessons. He insists he won't take handouts. I just don't understand the man anymore. We're behind on our utilities and the rent. I can see Michael and Tanya are worrying about us. They hear us arguing about money, talking about where we might go if we have to leave the house, and I just want to give them some happiness. They love your lessons. I want to be on the same page as my husband, but with this, I can't be. We're not going to have money for Christmas gifts this year and this is the least I can do for them, thanks to you."

Jenny reassured her. "Helen, if your husband calls me, I'll do my best to convince him to let Michael and Tanya keep coming."

Helen gave Jenny a wan smile. "Thank you."

"Is there anything else I can do for you?" Jenny asked her. "You know the community will be delivering food baskets for the holidays. I can put your name on the list."

"Stan would never accept a food basket. He went into

Flagstaff today to apply for a job at an electrical company. Say a few prayers for us that it comes through."

"I will," Jenny said, and Zack knew that she meant it. He waited until Helen went to the car and said over her shoulder, "I'll be back at noon."

Jenny spotted him then. Their gazes met briefly but she turned away, heading toward the arena.

He caught up to her easily. "Tough conversation," he said.

She glanced over at him, but she kept silent.

"You've given me the cold shoulder for forty-eight hours. Is this the way it's going to be?"

This time she stopped, hands on her hips. "I don't know. You tell me. Why would you want to talk to someone with ulterior motives like mine?"

She was angry, but he could tell from the expression in her dark brown eyes, she was hurt, too.

"Damn it. Do something for me," he suggested. "Try to imagine yourself in my shoes. I thought we had something to build on and you refused to take a chance with me. All these years you've stayed here when you're young, beautiful and talented. You could go anywhere and do anything you wanted. So from my perspective, what would *you* think?"

"So you didn't accuse me of being an opportunist because I was backing you into a corner? You really *meant* it? You really *don't* trust me?" She seemed horrified at the thought.

Before he considered how to word his answer, she asked, "Do you trust *anyone?*"

"I trust Clay and Dawson."

"You don't trust your accountant, your lawyer, people

who work for you?" She shook her head. "What kind
of life do you have out there?"

He wasn't sure what he heard in her voice, but he
didn't like it. "I have a life I like—the life I've always
wanted."

She searched his face. Her gaze dropped to his lips.
Then she turned away from him so he couldn't see her
thoughts in her expression and headed for the arena
again. "I've got to get to those kids. Hank can get them
started, but they're a lot to handle."

"How many in the class?"

"It varies."

"Ages?"

"Eight to eleven."

"Mind if I watch?"

"I don't mind as long as you don't get in the way."

He grinned at her. "You won't even know I'm there."

Twenty minutes later Zack's words echoed in Jenny's
head. Oh, she knew he was here all right. In his black
crew neck sweater, jeans and boots he was an imposing presence whether she wanted to admit it or not. At
first, he'd stood at the arena's entrance watching her
and Hank help the children mount, making sure their
helmets were secure. But then he'd come closer, studying what they were doing. Jenny was on her horse leading the class in a circle while Hank was on the ground
watching for any problems. One of the boys' boots kept
slipping out of his stirrups and Hank had gone to help
him adjust them.

However, the next time she looked behind her shoulder, Zack had Helen's son, eleven-year-old Michael, to
one side and was talking to him in a low voice, show-

ing him something with his hands. She didn't want to break the circle and distract the other kids, so she kept giving directions, leading them in a figure eight. Soon, however, Michael joined them and he seemed to have better control of his horse. He was all smiles and she couldn't help but wonder what had taken place between him and Zack.

She'd never seen Zack with kids. What kind of father would he be? What kind of father would he have been? One thing was certain—she was never going to tell him about the miscarriage. She just wasn't. Only Silas and Olivia had known. She hadn't even told Mikala and Celeste. Her pregnancy had been such a scary secret that she'd only confided in Zack's mother. Then when the miscarriage happened, Silas had to know, but that was as far as it had gone. Except, of course, for the doctor Olivia had rushed her to.

Now, crazily, the wave of loss came rushing back. Years had passed. She had to admit when she babysat Clay and Celeste's little girl, Abby, longings tugged at her heart. "What ifs" rushed into her head. She'd had lots of practice with staying in the moment. The problem was, Zack's return had mixed the past with the present.

True to his word, Zack didn't interfere with the class. He just sat on one of the bales of hay, his long legs stretched out in front of him, ankles crossed, as if he didn't have a care in the world. But Jenny sensed more was going on under the surface than he'd ever admit. Returning to the Rocky D had obviously stirred up old feelings and resentment, old bitterness, maybe even a feeling of home he hadn't experienced for a while.

At the end of class, Hank and Jenny helped the kids

with their mounts and their tack, then Zack did, too. When he saw the children were going to groom their horses, he passed out the brushes.

A moment later, he stopped to talk to Michael. Zack said something and Michael laughed and she wondered how the two of them had formed a bond so quickly. Sometimes Michael and his sister had worry written all over them. She was glad to see Zack could help Michael forget some of what was going on at home.

She said easily, "I see the two of you have met."

"Yeah," Michael answered. "Zack taught me how to hold the reins so Firecracker listened. I was having an awful time turning him."

After a glance at Zack, Jenny asked, "What did he tell you?"

"He didn't tell me. He *showed* me. I was confusing Firecracker. Zack said my hands had to be gentle and easy, yet clear. If I wanted him to go right, all I had to do was tug the reins that way and give him a little nudge with my left foot, and it worked. I kept up and didn't get out of line once."

"Well, I'm glad to see you're pleased, but you don't always have to stay in line. And if you need help, all you have to do is ask me."

"I know." His voice lowered. "I don't want to seem stupid to the other kids."

"I don't think any of them would think that, Michael. You catch on quickly. I'm glad you learned gentleness with Firecracker works best."

"Did you know Zack makes movies?" Michael asked her, wide-eyed and in awe.

"Apparently, his dad told him someone famous was staying at the Rocky D right now," Zack interjected. "I guess the whole town knows about Silas's heart attack and why I came home."

"My dad said it was on the news channel," Michael offered helpfully.

Zack grimaced.

"His picture was on there and everything," Michael added. "That's how I knew he was the one my dad was talking about."

"I have a job like most people. Mine just happens to involve shooting film," Zack explained.

Michael looked down at his shoeboots. "I wish my dad had a job, then maybe he wouldn't be so grumpy."

Zack exchanged a look with Jenny. "It's hard for a man not to have the work he likes to do. Work not only pays the bills, but it makes a man or a woman feel like he or she is accomplishing something. What do you want to be when you grow up?"

"I don't know, but I sure do like riding and taking care of horses."

Zack stood again. "I always liked that, too."

"But that's not what your work is," Michael pointed out.

"No, it isn't. I miss being around horses."

"If you're famous and rich, then you could have some," the eleven-year-old said as if life was as easy as that.

Zack laughed. "I suppose I could, but I'm not in one place very long. If I had horses, I'd like to be there to take care of them myself, not let someone else do it."

"My mom says Tanya and I can learn responsibility coming to this class."

"You already are," Jenny insisted. "You're grooming your horse yourself and you take care of your own tack."

"Maybe I could ride my bike out here and help you with chores and I could earn money for Christmas."

Jenny didn't know what to say to that. Finally, she responded, "Instead of earning money to buy things, maybe you could give your mom and dad something they'd enjoy that wouldn't cost anything."

Michael thought about that. "You mean like taking out the garbage without being told?"

"Sure, something like that."

He didn't seem impressed by the idea.

Zack said, "If you think about it, I'm sure you can be creative." Zack held out his hand to Michael and said, "It was good to meet you."

Michael shook his hand, too. "I'll have to tell my dad you're just a regular guy."

Zack smiled. "I'll make the rounds and see if anyone else needs help."

Jenny watched him walk away with a lump in her throat. She told herself again Zack couldn't mean anything to her now. But watching him interact with Michael had made her wonder once more what might have happened if her pregnancy had gone to term. It made her wonder again exactly what kind of father Zack would be.

Chapter Four

On Monday evening, Jenny and Zack drove down Copper Mine Boulevard to the town square. She couldn't help noticing he was moodier than usual, and she was pretty sure of the reason for his demeanor. "You didn't want to sub for your dad at this meeting, did you?"

Straightening in his seat now, his head practically hit the ceiling of the pickup. "Another committee meeting to decide something about Miners Bluff? I *hate* this kind of thing. Besides that, it's not even about something important. This committee is going to decide on the decorations for the gazebo, square and outlying streets. Dad always offered money to back whatever decorations they wanted. He still will, even if he isn't there. So I don't understand why they need my opinion."

Her silence in the cab of the truck seemed to bother him. "Say it."

"Say what?" she innocently asked.

"What's on your mind."

"You should look beneath the surface."

"Of stringing lights on the gazebo?"

"No, of what the season means to your dad…how the part he plays in Miners Bluff contributes to his worth, and I don't mean monetarily. He's tired. He doesn't feel as if he can do anything he used to do—not with any verve—so he's frustrated. If he can't do it, then he wants someone to do it for him."

"Do what?"

"Be there. Have a say. Maybe even give a few ideas that will pretty up the town for Christmas."

Zack rested his hand on his thigh, one very muscular thigh. Jenny remembered the feel of his legs against hers while they'd briefly danced at the reunion. That memory brought back another picture she put away to think about later.

"My dad has always been manipulative. He sees this meeting as a way to get me involved in Miners Bluff."

"Would that be so bad?" Jenny asked.

"It's not bad. It's not good. It's just *not* going to happen. I don't even know if I'll be here 'til Christmas, so why care about the lights and decorations?"

Jenny pulled into a parking slot she found in front of a lawyer's office. Light snow had begun to fall and she knew that wasn't going to help Zack's mood any. He was used to California sun. Yet he didn't complain as they stepped out of the truck.

He checked his watch. "We're early. Let's take a walk in the park before we get cooped up in one of those meeting rooms in the town hall."

"Sure. We can walk to the gazebo."

They ambled across the street to the park that sat at the center of town. Signs detailing the history of Miners Bluff were posted at two of the entrances, and at this hour, walkways through the park were lit by tall, old-fashioned streetlamps that cast a soft glow through bare maple, oak and sycamore branches. The snow floating into the lighted path was absolutely beautiful as it sugared everything it touched.

He suddenly stopped and she could see he was focusing on the here and now and where they were, rather than on where he wanted to be. She had to wonder exactly where that was. His gaze targeted the gazebo that they were heading toward, the benches on the pathways, the white picket fence surrounding the outskirts of the park.

"It hasn't changed," he noted.

"Not much. The gazebo gets a fresh coat of paint every other year. The lamplights have new energy-saving bulbs. But other than that, it's the park of your youth."

"I didn't come into town much as a kid. Everything we needed at the Rocky D was brought to us."

"You never came here to ride those big swings over there? Or climb on the jungle gym?"

"I was always too busy with the horses, or exploring areas of the ranch where Dad particularly didn't want me to go. This park was just a place we came to for special events, holiday celebrations, summer festivals. But it wasn't really part of my life. How about you?"

Jenny was slow to answer because she had to think about what she wanted to say. She could just gloss over the truth, but, after all, this was Zack. "I met my first horse here when I was about five," she said with a smile.

"It was a Shetland pony and it was love at first sight. I remember my mom smoothing her hand over my hair and saying one of these days when Dad won a great big purse, he'd buy me a horse. Someday we'd move out of the trailer and live in a real home."

Jenny shrugged as if it was all really in the past. "But someday never came. I sneaked into the rodeos as often as I could in summers, talked to the owners, got their permission to handle their horses. But from fall to spring when I needed someplace to go, I came here. I know we're talking about hanging Christmas decorations and that doesn't seem important to you. But when I was a kid, I loved to look at the flowers planted around the trees, the ivy growing up and along the fence. It all just seemed special. And at Christmas, the decorations that sparkled made me believe that someday I could give my life sparkle, too." She shrugged. "Maybe lighting up the park for Christmas will give a child a fantasy of what he can be or do in the future."

They had reached the gazebo now. No one else was in sight.

"You really didn't have a home."

She'd never talked to Zack much about her childhood—she'd just given him bits and pieces. The one thing she'd never wanted was for Zack to feel sorry for her. "Our trailer was a home when Dad was there. It was a home while Mom was alive. It was still a home even when only *I* was by myself...until I got lonely. That's when I'd go looking for a horse to talk to."

Zack stopped, eyed the park again, then responded, "I know what you mean. I did the same thing. After all, I had a lot of horses to choose from, and every one of them had their own personality. I learned that about animals before I learned it about people."

"I won't ask which are easier," she said with a laugh.

"Right. We both know the answer to that one. But once I got my first video camera, I could see more about the horses I videotaped and more about people. I could study them from behind that lens more easily. I became part of the scenery and they forgot I was there. I'd be shooting from across the pasture and Duke's ear would flicker because he knew I was around. Yet he still let me examine the way he related to the other horses, the way he ran, the way he just enjoyed a sunny day."

"I remember Duke. You took him on our rides up to Moonshadow Mountain and Feather Peak."

Zack had been attached to Duke. Was he attached to anyone or anything now?

"Do you have anyone special in your life?" Yes, she wanted to know for her own benefit, but she was concerned about him, too.

He put one gloved hand on the gazebo above her head then stared down at her as if he wanted to decipher where her question came from. Finally, as if he'd come to a decision, he answered her. "No, no one special. I broke it off with a woman I'd been seeing before I came back here for the reunion."

"How long had you been dating?" Her voice held just a slight amount of interest as if his reply didn't matter.

"A couple of months. I think I sensed from the beginning we weren't right together."

She could imagine the dilemma he might face. "How do you know if someone's interested in just you or in what you have? Can you trust your instincts?"

"My gut instinct usually pays off. Sometimes,

though, I ignore it, just to have a little...fun. But there are consequences to every action *and* complications."

She knew all about consequences and complications, possibly even more than Zack did.

He nodded to the folder in Jenny's hand. "So tell me about your ideas for Christmas."

If she could get him interested, would he stay? Hardly. But maybe she *could* get him involved.

Opening the folder, she turned toward one of the lights atop the gazebo. He moved closer to her until he was looking over her shoulder at the folder in her hands. Zack wore a more expensive aftershave than he had when he was a teenager, but she still responded to its woodsy scent. She still got goosebumps when his breath fanned her ear.

She swallowed hard and pointed to her sketch. "We have a couple of women's groups who have volunteered to make evergreen wreaths with candy-cane-striped ribbons. They'd be pretty around the outside of the gazebo. Then I thought we could invest in some of those outdoor flameless candles that have timers. They'd go on every evening at dark and stay lit until midnight. We could actually attach a few of them to the ledge around the gazebo."

"So the gazebo would be like a shelter from the storm."

"Exactly. In the trees around the gazebo, I'd like to arrange those nets of twinkle lights. They'll have their energy sources from the lamp posts."

"Any color at all?"

"I'd like to hang some of those solar balls from the trees. They come in all colors."

"What about vandalism and the chance they'll be stolen?"

She rolled her eyes. "This is Miners Bluff, Zack. Low crime. Noah will put the word out in schools that anyone caught vandalizing will have stiff community service. He's the chief of police now. Did you see him at the reunion?"

"Not much more than a nod and a wave. Maybe I'll have the opportunity to talk to him in the next few weeks."

Noah Stone, one of their classmates, was of Hopi descent. He brought unique sensibilities to his role as chief of police, and the people in town appreciated them.

"You can connect with him tomorrow if you'd like. I got a call from him before we left. He rescued a horse and asked if I'd like to gentle him."

"Do you do that often?"

"Whenever we hear of one in need. Silas let me redo one of the old barns and corrals for that purpose."

Silence met her answer. Finally, he tapped a sketch in her folder. "What's this?"

Putting aside the subject of rescuing horses for the time being, she explained, "I know the private businesses will decorate for Christmas, and have their own lights and garlands. But I'd like to put a star on the courthouse's bell tower. Don't you think that would be a striking touch?"

"The bell still tolls at noon on Saturday?"

"And at midnight on holidays. I thought that star would be a nice reminder of what we're celebrating. Kids need to know Christmas is about more than Santa Claus and presents."

When she closed the folder and turned to face him again, he said, "Kids seem to mean a lot to you."

Her heart hammered. This was a subject she really didn't particularly want to talk about with him. She could give something away too easily. "Kids and Christmas just go together."

"It's more than that. I saw you with them during your riding class. Are you worried your biological clock is ticking?" he asked, half-joking.

"Sure, that's it," she said with a shaky laugh.

He cocked his head as if he knew she wasn't telling him the whole story.

They were the only two people in the park, and the velvet sky and the falling snow created an intimate atmosphere. She gazed up at Zack, seeing the boy he'd been and the man he was now. In spite of her best intentions to keep her distance, both tugged at her heart, created warm tingles on her skin, almost urged her to resurrect the past.

Silver light flickered in his blue eyes and she recognized desire when she saw it. She felt an answering heat in her own body and leaned in a little closer. He braced his hand on the gazebo and leaned into her, too.

The sound of a car horn startled them both.

Quickly, Zack straightened. "We should get over to the town hall." He checked his watch. "Everyone else is probably there by now."

Maybe they were, but she didn't care. She was too busy asking herself what had almost happened. Was Zack about to kiss her? Would she have kissed him back? Her mouth went dry at the thought.

Thank goodness some driver had probably wanted a parking space.

Because one of Zack's kisses could change *everything.*

The following afternoon, Jenny heard the horse trailer roll in and was excited at the prospect of gentling a rescued horse. At least doing this would keep her mind off Zack.

She still wasn't sure whether he would have kissed her at the gazebo. What would have happened if he had? How would she have responded? She hadn't been able to focus at the decorations meeting, and she hadn't slept very much, either. Just having Zack in the house made her edgy.

So this morning she'd done something she might come to regret. She'd asked Brody Hazlett to the dance at the firehouse's social hall on Friday night. Needing more distance between her and Zack, she thought this date might do it. After all, Brody had asked her out before, though she'd always come up with a reason to decline his invitation. Although he was an attractive, down-to-earth guy who loved animals as much as she did—he was a veterinarian—her heart didn't race at the sight of him like it had—and still did—with Zack.

Leaving the tack room in the barn, she went outside and let the November breeze brush her face. She headed for the smaller barn that she'd refurbished to house horses who had been mistreated. There were only four stalls. The doors to those stalls could be opened to a corral that gave plenty of room to horses who wanted to be free. When they felt safer, they could enter the stall.

Today, Noah Stone was bringing her a gelding named Dusty. She didn't know what to expect. She never did. This was one of those situations that had to be taken moment by moment.

To her surprise, as she walked to the corral gate, Zack was standing by the driver side of the truck talking to Noah. They'd been classmates once, but Zack and Noah hadn't run in the same crowd. But time and age were great equalizers and the two men seemed friendly now.

As she approached them, Noah sent her a smile. Zack's expression was neutral.

Noah said, "I was telling Zack I'm often the one who gets called when someone around here sees a horse being mistreated."

"You said Dusty was malnourished?" Zack asked.

"That and other things. I had a time of it getting him into the trailer. I had to use blinders. I don't think he's the type of horse who's going to want to be in a confined space."

"Any history?" Zack inquired, obviously interested.

"Just what I told you. The rancher bought him at an auction, fell on hard times and couldn't feed him. He tried to ride him, but Dusty wasn't cooperative."

"I don't think I want to know any more," Jenny said. "I don't think I *need* to know any more."

Zack had been taking in their conversation. "Getting him out shouldn't be a problem. But leading him where you want him to go might be something else."

"I'll open the gate and you can back the trailer in," Jenny informed Noah.

Zack's gaze met Jenny's, and she felt a shiver run down her spine that wasn't from the cold.

After another look that made Jenny remember the closeness of their bodies last night all over again, Zack motioned Noah through the gate opening into the corral.

As Noah backed up the truck and trailer, Zack asked her, "Does Noah's father still have horses?"

"A few. But he's had some health problems and Noah has been helping him with the chores on their ranch."

Once Noah stopped and climbed out of the truck, Zack suggested, "Why don't I go inside and back him out."

For a moment, Jenny felt indignant. "I'm fully capable of doing this, Zack."

"I have no doubt you are. I just thought you might want to take the blinders off."

He *was* right about that.

"All right. Thanks," she murmured, knowing she couldn't be so touchy around Zack. That would tip him off that her feelings were more personal than she wanted to admit.

After Noah opened the back of the horse trailer, he lowered the ramp. "Okay, Zack," he called.

Inside the trailer, Zack called back, "Give me a few minutes, okay?"

"If he thinks he's going to sweet-talk him," Noah said with a shake of his head, "he's sadly mistaken."

"I don't think it's sweet talk. Maybe Zack just wants to get him used to a kind voice."

As she and Noah waited, she wondered if Zack still had "the touch." He'd been so good at handling horses as a kid. But mishandled horses were another matter. It could take many months to calm Dusty down, many months to establish trust. Even the training she did with cutting horses was all about forming a relationship. She'd learned *that* from Noah Stone's father and grandfather. She'd worked there one summer when she was fifteen and learned lessons she'd keep for a lifetime. Not lessons about not owning a horse, but becoming friends with a horse, about not expecting a horse to listen like a human, but about creating communication bonds both she and the animal would understand.

Horses had herd instincts. She had to become leader of their herd of two—a kind leader but a confident, firm leader. She'd had to *learn* her skills, but Zack seemed to have been born with them.

Zack called, "I'm going to back him out."

As soon as the horse's back legs were off the ramp, he was kicking out, pulling at the lead, defying everyone around him. Zack held on and wouldn't let him rear up.

"Blinders off," he called to Noah and Jenny. "They're driving him crazy."

Before Noah could move, Jenny had slipped up beside Zack, unfastened the blinders and let them drop into her hands. All the while, Zack kept a firm hand on the lead and spoke in gentle tones.

Jenny could have cried. Dusty, a buff-colored gelding with a black mane and tail, was trembling. She felt so sorry for him. Yet she knew she couldn't get too close too fast. She knew she had to bide her time. The horse's gaze couldn't seem to settle anywhere.

Zack suggested, "You and Noah drop back. Let me lead him in."

The horse had stopped kicking, though he was dancing around, moving fretfully. Jenny knew better than to try and touch him yet. She had to let him come to her.

"All right," she said. "Noah, do you think you can ease out of the gate? Once I close it, Zack, you can take off the lead and let him run free."

Jenny held her breath as Noah eased the truck out of the corral. Dusty tried to rear up but Zack held the lead and his strength was obvious.

As quietly as possible, as slowly as possible, she shut the gate.

Zack asked, "Are you going into the barn?"

She knew he wanted her to, but that wasn't going to happen. "No, I'll just climb to the other side of the fence. Are you sure *you* want to do this? As soon as you let go, he might become even wilder."

"It's okay, Dusty. No one's going to hurt you." Zack's voice was almost hypnotic. In the same tone he assured her, "I'll be fine. I'll see what he does when I unhook the lead."

Scaling the fence to the outside of the corral, Jenny watched as Zack continued to talk to Dusty in the same low tones, as he tried to keep the horse's attention focused on him, as he tried to start building trust.

He reached toward the fastener slowly, unhooked it and stood perfectly still. For a second or two, Dusty didn't seem to know what to do. But then he snorted, pawed and kicked up his back legs again.

Jenny was afraid he might simply gallop into Zack. But Zack just stood there, speaking softly, not moving a muscle, until finally Dusty wheeled in the other direction and ran like the devil was chasing him to the other end of the corral. Zack took that opportunity to cross quickly to the fence, climb up and settle on the top rung.

Dusty ran across the corral, aimed straight for him, then at the last moment veered away, running again.

Looking up at Zack, she murmured, "You took a chance."

"Better me than you," he muttered.

"Don't turn protective on me, Zack. You've no right."

He climbed down off the fence to stand before her and look her straight in the eye. "Yes, I do. My father depends on you. I'll do what I have to do to keep you safe."

Maybe he'd keep her physically safe, but he couldn't keep her heart safe.

"Come on," he said. "Let's watch him from the barn. You don't even have your jacket on."

She was about to protest she was wearing an insulated vest, but knew that would do no good. She *was* cold, now that the adrenaline had stopped rushing.

They hurried to the side door and Zack let her precede him into the barn. Her arm brushed against his sheepskin jacket, but she didn't look up at him. She didn't want to remember that moment last night when they'd stood so near, their breathing synchronized—

Taking her phone from her pocket, she speed-dialed Noah. "Thanks. Do you want to come up to the house for lunch? Martha probably has it ready."

"No, thanks, Jenny. I have to get back to my office to handle paperwork."

"You spend your life there."

He laughed. "It's my job. I don't tell you that you spend too many hours working, do I?"

"That's because you know it wouldn't do any good."

"Right."

"I'll accept your refusal this time," she conceded.

"But let's just say I owe you lunch. Thanks again." After Noah said goodbye, she closed her phone and stuck it back in her pocket.

Zack said, "You and Noah are friends," as if he were confirming something in his mind.

"Yes, we are."

"He's very different now than he was in high school," Zack decided. "He's confident, not rebellious and defiant."

"I never would have thought he would have gone into law enforcement, but he had his reasons," Jenny responded. "Training and working in the Phoenix police department changed his outlook on a lot of things."

"I can imagine," Zack said, as if he could.

She didn't know why she'd thought Zack had no empathy left anymore. Maybe because he'd put up a barrier between himself and his dad that was so high neither of them could breach it. Yet, she was seeing now that barrier didn't necessarily define Zack's character any more than it defined Silas's.

Crossing to the feed bins, Zack picked up two wreaths of golden bells that were lying there. "I haven't seen these for years."

"You remember them?"

"How can I not? My mother loved bells, especially at Christmas—sleigh bells, garlands with bells, wreaths with bells."

There was such fondness and affection in Zack's voice, Jenny was drawn toward him. "And red velvet ribbon," she added. "She tied big red bows on anything to do with Christmas."

"What are you going to do with these?" he asked, a bit roughly.

"I hang them on the barn doors, just like she did. Then we hear the jingle of bells up at the house. It's a nice sound when the wind is howling or when the snow is falling."

"I didn't know you'd kept up some of her traditions."

"If you would have come home—"

The look he gave her made her cut off her words. "I loved your mom, Zack, and I want to keep remembering her. We put up a Christmas tree and I use the ornaments she collected over the years. She had favorite recipes for the holidays and I made sure Martha makes those. Your father wants to remember, too."

An almost angry look shone in Zack's eyes. "Don't tell me he loved her. He couldn't have loved her and treated her the way he did."

Instead of heading into the eye of *that* storm, Jenny asked, "Do you know how your parents met?"

He thought about it. "Her father was buying her a cutting horse as a birthday present."

"Your grandfather had recently died and your dad was trying to keep the Rocky D afloat," she said, filling him in.

"I remember Mom talking about those years," Zack responded, a far-away look in his eyes.

"From what I understand, your grandfather had let it go south," Jenny explained. "Your dad took over, had a couple of bad years but managed to turn it around by expanding the breeding facilities and the training opportunities. That's when everything took off for him. But at the beginning…"

"At the beginning, what?" Zack seemed genuinely curious.

"Picture this, Zack. This beautiful, raven-haired

woman with more poise than any model comes to the Rocky D with her very rich father. Your mom had received her college education back East and was going to teach at Northern Arizona University. Your father, to his way of thinking, had gotten through high school the best way he could, with no real love for books. He was scrimping to pay the bills. Yet the two of them, as different as they were, were drawn to each other."

"What are you trying to tell me, Jenny? That my father felt inferior to my mother?"

"I think he did…in a lot of ways."

"That doesn't excuse the gambling and the affairs. Was he trying to prove he could become richer easily? Was he trying to prove he was deserving of her somehow, because other women wanted him, too? That doesn't make any sense."

"It might not make sense to *us*. But to a man in his position back then, maybe it did. It's not an excuse. But it might be a reason. When a man doesn't feel worthy, his world is pretty lopsided."

"What was my mother supposed to do? Disown her family? Pretend she wasn't educated?"

"I'm not saying there was a solution, Zack. But maybe if they'd understood each other better, talked more, realized each other's fears, your dad wouldn't have been so obsessed with becoming a giant in the community any way he could."

"My mother should have left him. She wouldn't be dead if she'd walked away."

"And what would she have done about *you?*" Jenny protested. "Would she have taken you with her? Would she have left you with your father? If she took you, would she be denying you your birthright? Denying you the Rocky D and everything it represented? There's no easy decision for a mother in that position."

He was looking at her as if he was trying to figure her out. "You sound like you know."

She shook her head but couldn't take her gaze from his.

He was leaning toward her slightly, one hand over the back of the stall, the other free to do whatever it wanted. She suddenly wanted his arms around her. She suddenly wanted a lot more than that.

As if he was reading the message in her eyes, he did put his arm around her—and he bent his head to hers.

The first touch of Zack's lips wasn't anything like Jenny expected. She'd expected hard, possessive and arrogant. His lips were firm as if he knew what he wanted. But they were coaxing, too…encouraging her to respond. If she had thought further than that, she might have saved them both a lot of trouble. But she didn't, because all of her concentration was on the feel of his mouth, the touch of his tongue against hers, the strength of his arms as he pulled her closer, enveloping her fully in his embrace.

She couldn't fall in love with Zack again. She couldn't let her future be affected like that again. She *wouldn't*.

Wrenching away, she looked up at him and shook her head. "No. You're not going to make me want you and then turn around and leave again. It won't happen, Zack. I won't let it. I deserve more than that."

Without waiting for a response from him, she returned outside to watch Dusty. If Zack built any sense of trust with this horse, it would be broken when he left.

Neither of them needed Zack Decker, and she'd better not forget that.

Chapter Five

At midnight, Zack stood on the back veranda of the east wing overlooking the rose garden. A frosting of snow coated the bare branches of the bushes that slept during the winter. This had been his mother's favorite spot. Her rosebushes had been her pride and joy. He wondered if Jenny collected blooms, in colors from yellow and coral to light pink and magenta, for each of the downstairs rooms as his mother had.

No matter how much he wanted to forget it, he could taste Jenny's kiss on his lips. He'd been reckless and impulsive in the barn, two qualities that hadn't been part of his life as an adult. But Jenny had always turned him inside out. Most of all, she made him *feel*. As a kid, he'd turned off his feelings as his parents fought. He'd turned off his feelings when Jenny had decided not to go with him to L.A. He'd turned off his feelings in anything that approached business. In all these years, he'd only let them free when he was behind the lens.

When he heard the French doors open and close, he almost exhaled a frustrated breath. He knew the sound of that heavy tread. "You shouldn't be out here, Dad. It's too cold. You don't want to overtax—"

"Stow it," his father mumbled. "I needed some fresh air."

"At midnight?"

His father came to stand beside him, looking out at the garden. "I'm feeling claustrophobic. A man's not made to be cooped up in the house."

"It's not for long. As soon as you're feeling stronger you can walk wherever you want. Just don't push it."

Instead of reacting to Zack's words, Silas gestured to the fountain in the middle of the rose garden. "Jenny put in one of those solar fountains. She prunes the rose-bushes herself. She won't let anyone else near them."

"I don't see how she has time for that with every-thing else she takes care of."

"That girl has energy. Always has."

"She's not a girl anymore."

After a few moments of quiet, Silas asked, "Do you ever regret what you left behind?"

Zack wasn't sure how to answer that one. Certainly his father didn't want to get into an argument about any-thing that had happened. He kept his answer simple.

"I don't have regrets about leaving. I had to find out who I was without the Decker name and wealth. You never understood that."

"Maybe I understood more than you thought. Maybe I hated that camera of yours because I knew it would take you away from here."

Which, of course, it had.

"And what about Jenny?" his father asked gruffly. "Do you wish you had taken her along?"

Zack felt more than saw his father turn toward him and study him in the shadows. He wasn't about to start confiding in a man who might use those confidences against him.

At Zack's silence, Silas grunted. "She hasn't told you everything yet, has she?"

Nothing else could have gotten his attention as that did. "What are you talking about?"

"You need to ask Jenny that yourself. Did she happen to mention she's going with Brody Hazlett to the dance at the fire hall Friday night?"

Zack didn't want to admit he knew nothing about the dance or about Jenny and Brody Hazlett. Except that they'd been dancing together at the reunion when he'd cut in. "No."

"Apparently, a lot of your old classmates will be there. Jenny's friends for sure. You can buy a ticket at the door…if you're interested."

Was he interested? If not in the dance, in finding out if anything was going on between Jenny and Brody?

Zack let his pride slip a little and asked, "Has she been dating him?"

"Nope. He's asked but she always says no. I don't know what happened to change her mind." Silas coughed, then coughed again. "I guess I've had enough of this air. I'll see you in the morning."

Zack almost caught his dad's arm…almost asked, *What hasn't Jenny told me?*…almost felt something more than the bitterness and resentment toward his father that he'd nurtured all these years.

But he didn't ask. He just said, "Good night, Dad."

He heard the French doors close behind his father. Zack was an outsider here and he'd never felt more like one than he did tonight.

A harvest theme prevailed in the fire hall Friday evening. Stacked bales of hay were supposed to give the room a barnlike ambience. A section of rustic fencing had even been set up along one side of what was supposed to be the dance floor. A fiddle was playing now, a man on a mike called out square dancing moves. Zack hadn't been square dancing since high school, and he doubted that he even remembered how.

So what the hell was he doing here?

That was a no-brainer. He spotted Jenny easily in a red checked blouse and denim skirt, do-si-do-ing with Brody. He'd thought about his father's words all last night and all today. *She hasn't told you everything yet, has she?* What exactly did Jenny have to tell him? Or was his father just causing trouble?

Zack had spent a good part of the day with Dusty, just talking to him, letting the horse get used to the sound of his voice. When Jenny had come around at lunchtime to tell him she'd take over, he'd let her, without any conversation. He wasn't sure what he wanted to say to her, and she was just as awkward with him. Awkward or not, he wanted to kiss her again. But she wasn't coming too close and he knew that was for the best. Had she come to the dance tonight to put another wall between them? Or was she really interested in Brody?

What did he care when he wouldn't be staying?

He knew already he couldn't spend the evening

watching her. Clay and Celeste, who were seated at one of the long, red cloth-covered tables, waved and motioned to him. Zack smiled as he studied the couple. They were newlyweds and anyone could tell. Seated close together, shoulders touching, their hands entwined on the table.

A few of the townsfolk recognized him, smiled and nodded as he crossed to his classmates. One called out, "I hope your dad's back on his feet soon," and another said, "Good to see you're back." There were no gawkers here as he might have encountered in L.A. if anyone had recognized him. That was one benefit to being in Miners Bluff. He felt ordinary again. To his surprise, he actually enjoyed that feeling.

The fiddling was loud and Zack knew conversation would be tough. He went to the Sullivans' side of the table and stood between them. "You two look happy."

"Life is good," Clay said with a satisfied smile. "How's your dad?"

"As ornery as ever. Liam O'Rourke came over to visit with him tonight. Martha was still there, too, so I know he's being watched over." He tapped his phone in the pocket of his shirt. "He has my number on speed dial, but he'd probably call Jenny if there was an emergency."

The three of them glanced over to where she was still dancing with Brody, her blond ponytail swinging with the music, her skirt flaring out around her when she moved.

After Celeste and Clay exchanged a look, Celeste said, "You'll have to stop over when you get a chance. I could make dinner. I'm sure my cooking isn't what you're used to, but we'd love to have you."

"I do a lot of take-out," Zack responded with a wry grin. "I'll give you a call when Dad's feeling better. I'm not going to stay very long tonight."

Mikala Conti suddenly appeared at Zack's side. "It's good to see you here."

"Hi, Mik. How's your aunt?"

"She's good. She'd be here tonight but she has a cold she's trying to beat."

Zack had always liked Mikala. With her wavy black hair and tobacco-brown eyes, she had quiet beauty and listening skills that made her easy to talk to. He wondered if she knew more about Jenny and Brody.

As the fiddling stopped, the announcer let everyone know they were slowing things down with an old Patsy Cline standard. Zack suddenly asked Mikala, "Would you like to dance?"

She was totally surprised for a few seconds, and then smiled. "Sure."

"Talk to you later," he said to Clay and Celeste, as he led Mikala to the dance floor. Mikala waved to Riley O'Rourke and Noah who were standing by the snack table talking to Katie Paladin, another of their classmates.

"Almost like the reunion," Mikala said with a smile, as Zack put his arm around her and took her hand in the standard ballroom position. Mikala *was* a beautiful woman, but Zack didn't feel the attraction he'd felt with Jenny when he held her in his arms. Lust that had started as a teenager shouldn't still be alive fifteen years later! But it was, and he couldn't help glancing toward Jenny again. She and Brody were dancing close, and Zack's gut clenched.

"Earth to Zack," Mikala called softly.

Feeling embarrassment for the first time in a long time, Zack brought his attention back to his dance partner. "Sorry. What did I miss?"

Mikala laughed softly and shook her head. "I asked if you heard from Dawson lately? At the reunion, he told me the two of you kept in touch."

"Actually, I did. Did you know he's thinking of moving back here? In fact, he's pretty sure about it."

"Is he really going to do it?" Mikala's eyes seemed to take on an extra sparkle and Zack wondered about that. He didn't remember Dawson and Mikala being an item in high school. Dawson had hung out with everyone at Mikala's aunt's but also dated the popular girls. Zack didn't think Dawson and Mikala had been more than friends. But what did he know? He'd been too smitten with Jenny.

"If he moves back here, I think you're one of the reasons," Zack admitted to Mikala. "He thinks you might be able to help Luke."

The sparkle left Mikala's eyes and her expression became more polite than friendly. Zack guessed why. "You can't talk about that, can you? Because of patient confidentiality?"

"That's right."

Zack knew he could hold his own on the dance floor. He had to for all the social functions he attended. He took Mikala through a few intricate steps and found her to be an excellent partner. "I should have known you'd be good at dancing. After all, you're all about music."

"Music has been my salvation on many an occasion." She tilted her head and eyed him thoughtfully. "Just as film-making has been yours."

This close friend of Jenny's understood more than he expected. "Was I so transparent as a teenager?"

"No, not to everyone. Maybe I just understood because I used music to escape the same way you used that video camera. Besides, even now I can see the intensity and desire to make the world a better place in your films. Jenny and I have talked about that."

"You have?" He kept his voice neutral, not knowing if he wanted to know what Mikala and Jenny spoke about concerning his films and his life.

When he glanced toward Jenny and Brody again, he saw they were laughing, seemingly having a good time. As he turned away from them and Mikala caught sight of them, she said, "Jenny and Brody are friends."

"The way you and I are friends?"

"Possibly. Brody spends some time at the Rocky D treating the horses."

"It's none of my business," Zack muttered, knowing it wasn't, yet feeling pangs of jealousy anyway. He might as well call a spade a spade.

Mikala's understanding expression told him he wasn't fooling her one bit.

After the ballad ended, Zack escorted Mikala back to where Celeste and Clay were seated. He sat with them for a while, listening to the women describe Celeste and Clay's wedding. He couldn't help being cynical about marriage. Years ago, he'd decided he'd *never* marry. He never wanted to end up the way his mom and dad had, fighting all the time, looking at each other with resentment, playing the social game for others to see. Yet Clay and Celeste certainly seemed happy. The way they spoke about their daughter and their life together gave Zack pause.

After another hour chatting with people, he decided to call it a night. He had to admit, reconnecting with old friends had been enjoyable. Yet his gaze had never been far from Jenny and he was on edge about her relationship with Brody. After he retrieved his jacket and hat from a rack, he exited through a side door. Shoving his hands into his jacket pockets, he took a few deep breaths and gazed up at the night sky. This wasn't a smog-filled California sky. It was a Miners Bluff sky, with too many stars to count.

When he rounded the side of the building to head to the parking lot, he heard voices around the corner—Jenny's and Brody's.

She said, "Thanks for coming with me tonight."

"You surprised me when you called. The last couple of times I asked you out you were busy."

Zack didn't hear Jenny's answer to that. He didn't *want* to hear it. What if she said her feelings toward him had changed and she was interested in dating him for a while, to see how their relationship would progress? After all, isn't that what she should do? Especially if she wanted to have a family.

Zack strode through the parking lot, his thoughts all in a jumble. He shouldn't care. He didn't care. Yet he remembered Mikala's knowing look. He knew denial was a strong defense against unwanted feelings.

His life was in California and Jenny had no desire to leave Miners Bluff. Those were the same facts that had divided them once before.

Back at the ranch a half hour later, Zack checked on his father. Silas was sleeping. In the kitchen, Martha was setting the table for breakfast. Now that Zack was home, she went to her quarters without worrying Silas might need her. Zack thanked her for looking after his father, then made a pot of coffee, expecting to be up for a while. He had work to do and he was always productive at night.

He'd just poured himself a mug of the freshly brewed coffee when Jenny came in the side door from the garage. She looked startled to see him standing there.

"Decaf?" she asked, nodding toward the coffee pot.

"Nope. I found the real thing in the freezer."

She laughed, but it was an uncomfortable laugh. An I-know-there's-something-we-need-to-talk-about laugh. Except she tried to exit the kitchen so quickly, he understood she didn't want to talk. Tough. He did.

"Jenny?" he called before she was through the doorway.

She stopped but she obviously didn't want to. "It's late, Zack. I have an early morning. I need to exercise a few of the horses in the arena before Michael and Tanya come for their lesson."

He took a moment to absorb that. "I was going to work with Dusty, but if you need my help—"

"I don't."

The tension between them pulled taut.

She added, "If he learns to trust you and then you leave, I'm not sure your time with him is going to be beneficial."

"If he learns to trust me and then I leave, he'll have learned at least one human being can be kind to him. I don't see that it will hurt, as long as you work with him, too."

Jenny kept silent, but unbuttoned her turquoise-and-red-patterned wool jacket. He might as well ask her what was on his mind. "So are you and Hazlett going to see each other now?"

Her eyebrows quirked up. "What gave you that idea?"

"You seemed to be having a good time with him."

"Brody and I go back a ways, Zack. We're friends. That's it. I pretty much told him that tonight."

"You did?"

"Yes."

"I accidentally overheard some of your conversation with him before I left the fire hall. Why did you ask him to the dance? Why didn't you just ask me to take you? Aren't *we* friends, Jenny?"

She didn't answer him and that bothered him more than he wanted to admit. So he left his mug on the counter and crossed to her. "Dad and I had a conversation the other night."

He could see she was listening wholeheartedly now, wondering what was coming next. He wondered the same thing. "You know how he likes to make cryptic comments. He said to me, 'She hasn't told you everything yet, has she?' and I asked him what he meant. He wouldn't answer. He said I should ask you."

Jenny suddenly looked panicked, just like Dusty did sometimes when he was cornered…when Zack approached him and he wasn't sure what Zack would do.

Zack reached out and took Jenny by the shoulders, partly to comfort her, partly because he wanted to know the truth. Had she been married and divorced in the fifteen years he'd been away? Did something happen to her while he was gone?

He had no idea what to expect. He certainly didn't expect the tears that came to Jenny's eyes, and her attempt to pull away.

"Jenny, what's going on? What was Dad talking about?"

Her lower lip quivering, but her head held high, she finally answered him. "I found out I was pregnant after you left. Six weeks later, I had a miscarriage."

Although Zack heard the words, it took a few moments for their full impact to hit him. He was stunned by the thought of Jenny being pregnant—and even more stunned that she hadn't told him.

"Tell me what happened." Emotion filled his voice—he couldn't seem to hold in the turmoil Jenny was creating.

Her face went pale as if she hadn't expected him to ask that. Her eyes looked for an escape, but there was none because he wouldn't let her turn away from him. She confessed, "I had a fall."

He guessed right away. "From a horse?"

"Yes."

"My God! Why did my parents let you ride?"

"Only your mom knew. Your dad didn't until the day I fell."

"Why were you riding when you were pregnant?"

"I couldn't quit my job here. I needed the money."

"The money? You lost our baby because of money?"

Her eyes flashed and her whole body tensed. "Don't sound so self-righteous, Zack. You don't have the right. You left."

"Why didn't you tell me?" The question came slowly because he had such a hard time getting it out. He was filled with anger and disappointment and loss.

"I didn't tell you so you could chase your dream. I didn't want to be a burden on you or hold you back. I didn't want you to resent me for trapping you."

The reasons spilled out of her as if she'd been holding them in for fifteen years. He supposed she had. "Did you know before I left?"

"Not until a few weeks after. Your mom saw me throwing up behind the barn one day and she guessed. She tried to convince me to tell you, and I was going to, but then I lost the baby and there just didn't seem to be any point."

Everything she was revealing swirled in his head. Looking at her, at the face that had been in his dreams more times than he could ever count, he saw the honesty he'd always expected from Jenny. Yet she'd kept this secret for *fifteen* years.

"Who else knew?" he asked, feeling betrayed.

"No one else. Only your parents…and a doctor your mom took me to."

No wonder Jenny and his mother had been so close. They'd had this secret between them as well as everything else. If only she'd told him. If only he could have been here for her. He murmured, "I can't believe you never told me."

She must have taken his complete shock at her disclosure as an accusation, because she asked, "How was I supposed to tell you, Zack, when you were miles away in a different life? What happened didn't matter anymore. I was young and stupid and devastated when you left. Along with that, I had to get over losing a baby. It wasn't as if you came home or wrote or phoned. Your parents and I were just part of your old life. We didn't matter anymore."

He wanted to deny that, but he'd embraced his future with all the energy he'd possessed, leaving behind his father's disapproval and Jenny's refusal to go with him. Yet she said she'd been *devastated* by his leaving. It all seemed so incomprehensible now.

"What happened mattered," he protested. "The fact you were carrying my baby *mattered*. The loss of our child *matters*. It's true, I don't know what I would have done. But I wish I'd had the chance to find out."

Now when Jenny tried to pull away, he didn't hold her. He couldn't bear gazing into her brown eyes, filled with the pain of what she'd experienced.

As she left him in the kitchen, her pain gripped him and became his.

Chapter Six

After Zack had spent some time with Dusty, he had gone on a cold morning ride, trying to sort out everything Jenny had told him last night. He'd stayed up most of the night, lost in the past, remembering too much about their senior year in high school, remembering too much about the night he and Jenny had made love in the hayloft. He'd been naive back then, more experienced physically than emotionally. He'd believed that night had meant as much to her as it had meant to him. He had to admit that he'd been bitter and resentful about her refusal to go with him ever since. But now—

Returning to the Rocky D after a fast ride he'd hoped would numb his thoughts, he spotted Jenny entering the arena with Michael and his sister.

As he lead Tattoo into the everyday barn, Hank saw him and waved. "I'll take him for you if you'd like."

"Are you sure?" Zack asked. "I know you have enough to do." Hank was a few years younger than Silas but never seemed to slow down.

"No problem. I see how much time you're spending with Dusty. He won't let me get anywhere near him."

"We'll have to change that. Maybe tomorrow if you have a little time, you could come with me and I'll show you some of the things I've learned about him."

"Like?" Hank asked with an arched brow.

"Like if you sit on the fence long enough, he'll come over to see what you're about."

"*You,* not me."

"We just have to show him there are a lot more nice humans in the world than cruel ones."

Hank laughed and shook his head. "You never *would* believe you had a special gift. But I'll come out with you tomorrow in that dang cold just to prove my point."

Zack shook Hank's hand and agreed, "It's a deal." Then he left Tattoo with a man he'd learned to trust when he was just a boy.

Zack took out his cell phone as he strode to the arena and speed-dialed his father.

Silas picked up on the second ring. "Where are you?" his father asked without any preamble.

"I'm going to the arena to see what Jenny's up to. I just thought I'd check in, to see if you needed anything."

"I need some energy and a good dose of stamina."

"When are you coming down to the barn?" His dad had been walking on the paved paths in back of the house. He also now climbed the stairs to his bedroom each night. That was progress even though his dad didn't seem to see it that way. But he hadn't taken a stroll down to the barns yet and it was time.

The silence was so lengthy, Zack asked, "Dad?"

"Not when there are people around. Jenny's got those kids there and their mom will be coming to pick them up. Ben went to Flagstaff today but Hank and Tate are around somewhere, too."

"What are you afraid will happen?"

"I'm not afraid of anything."

Becoming more comfortable at the Rocky D again, Zack had forgotten he needed to watch his words. "What are you *concerned* might happen?"

"I can't *do* what I used to do. I don't know when I'll be riding again and I don't want anybody asking me about it. Jenny said something about going to lunch with Mikala and Celeste on Monday. Hank will be going into town to place a feed order. The temporary hands won't care what I'm doing. Maybe then I'll take a walk over."

"All right, whenever you want. You know what the doctor said—build up each day."

"Go do what you gotta do," Silas muttered. "I'm fine here for now." Then his father hung up.

Go do what he had to do. Talk to Jenny about what had happened fifteen years ago? Not likely with two kids around. Yet he felt drawn to the arena where he knew she'd be.

Opening the heavy door, he stepped inside. Jenny was riding Goldenrod, one of the horses she'd be putting up for sale in the spring. Michael and Tanya were following her in a circle on two of the mares Jenny trusted with kids. One of them, a chestnut with a white blaze, was her own horse—Songbird.

He heard Michael say, "I wish we could come out here and ride every day."

Zack heard Jenny laugh, a sweet sound he'd always

enjoyed. She responded, "You have to go to school, and I have horses to train."

"It's great you have an arena," he said. "That way if it snows, we can still ride."

"That was the idea when Mr. Decker built it."

After a few moments, Tanya informed her, "Daddy doesn't like when we come here."

"That's just because he can't pay," Michael explained. "I heard him arguing with Mom again about taking handouts. He doesn't want anything for free."

Jenny stopped leading and waited until Michael brought his horse up beside hers. "Your mom will be here shortly. Let's dismount and unsaddle. If we have time, you can help me groom."

Jenny dismounted first and then helped both of the kids. As Zack watched her, he realized she was as gentle as a caring mother. Last night, when she'd told him about the miscarriage, there had been such sadness in her voice. Did she long to have children now? Did she want a family?

As they walked the horses to their stalls along the edge of the arena, Zack joined them, ready to help with their saddles.

"Hi, guys."

"Hi, Mr. Decker," Michael said, as Tanya grinned shyly. "Carson and Danielle couldn't come, so it's just us today! I was hoping I'd see you," Michael went on. "Can I talk to you?"

Jenny gave Zack a look that asked what it was about, but Zack shrugged, having no idea. Their gazes stayed connected longer than necessary, but then she broke eye contact and almost too eagerly helped Tanya. Michael joined Zack by a set of feed bins.

"What's up?" Zack asked.

"You know how to make movies."

Zack suppressed a smile. "Does making movies interest you?"

"Not really. I mean, I don't want to make a movie exactly. I want to make a video of me and Tanya to give to my mom and dad for Christmas. My mom said we're going to have to be inventive this year and think of things to give each other that don't cost money. Well, my dad has a video camera and there's some blank tapes with it he never used. So I thought it would be really cool if you could help me and Tanya make a movie for Mom and Dad. What do you think?"

The last thing Zack was thinking about was the holidays. He was obviously going to be here for Thanksgiving. But Christmas? That was still up for grabs. He thought about what Michael had said, about the family being inventive so they could give each other gifts that didn't cost anything. Wasn't *that* a novel concept? He didn't give many Christmas gifts. For the most part, Christmas was just another day. He remembered again how special the holidays had been to his mother.

He didn't know why he was even considering this boy's request. It wasn't something he'd ever do if he was back in L.A. But the sparkling hope in Michael's eyes, the idea his parents would derive joy from this present that was much needed in their lives encouraged Zack to say, "Let me think about the best way to do it. Can you get the camera here without your parents knowing?"

"Sure. I can put it in my backpack. It's a little heavy, but not that big. It has real small tapes."

Zack understood exactly what kind of camcorder Michael was talking about. "We have some time. Christmas is still weeks away. Bring the camcorder along next Saturday when you come. Maybe Jenny can tell your mom the lesson's going to run longer than usual. That way we'll have a chance after the other kids leave. Okay?"

Michael was beaming. "I can't believe you said yes."

"Why is that?"

"Because my dad said you're really an important person and you're not going to be here long. He said you're just here because your dad's sick, and then you'll fly off and not be seen for another five to ten years."

Zack was used to tabloid news about him, rumors that weren't true, stories that were exaggerated from the telling. He knew there had to be gossip around Miners Bluff about his return. Apparently, this was some of it.

"I won't be here too long," he told Michael. "But I'll be here long enough to help you make a present for your parents. That's a promise."

"Cool!" Michael grinned from ear to ear.

Zack felt good about his decision, better than he'd felt about anything in a while.

As Michael and Tanya groomed their horses, chattering away as they did, Zack approached Jenny. She was running the grooming brush over her horse's back.

"Can you tell Michael's mother that their lesson will run longer next week?"

Jenny didn't look at him as she asked, "Why?"

"Because I'm going to help him with something after the other kids leave."

Now she did turn her gaze up to his. "Zack, they're under my care. You're going to have to tell me what you're planning."

"What do you think I'm going to do, take them on a

trail ride to Feather Peak in the snow?" He didn't know why her lack of trust made him angry, but it did.

She sighed and turned to face him. "Does it have to be a secret?"

"No. Michael wants me to help shoot footage of him and his sister as a present for their parents for Christmas. That's it. Nothing nefarious."

"And you said *yes*?" She seemed really surprised and that did nothing to take the edge off his annoyance with her attitude.

"I said *yes*. What do you think happened to me in L.A., Jenny? Do you think I became a different person than the one you knew?"

She looked over at the kids to make sure they weren't listening. They weren't. They were engrossed in what they were doing and talking with each other. "All I know is that you left and didn't look back."

Stiffening, he kept a lid on his temper, remembering what had happened to her and the pain he'd glimpsed in her eyes. "Last night, fifteen years after the fact, you told me why I should have looked back. I wasn't a mind reader, Jenny. I didn't know what was happening back here. Obviously, you didn't want me to know. I stayed in touch with my mother. I would have stayed in touch with you if you'd given me any indication you wanted that. But you didn't. So tell me who's to blame in all this."

"We can't talk now," she said in a whisper.

"Do you want to make an appointment?"

"Zack—"

The arena door opened and Helen Larson walked in. She called, "Michael, Tanya. I'm here."

Zack realized his moment with Jenny had been lost again.

Jenny said in a low voice, "I'll tell her the lessons will last longer next week. We can talk later."

Jenny said the words, but when Zack studied her face, he saw she didn't want to talk later any more than she did now. Would they accomplish anything at all if they spoke about what had happened? Or would speaking about the past widen the gap between them?

Late that night, Zack finally got a private moment with Jenny.

She'd eluded him all day, but she wasn't going to elude him now. He stood outside her bedroom door and knocked.

"Zack!" She looked startled when she opened her door.

She was already dressed for bed in a flannel nightgown that on anybody else might not look enticing, but on her, the pink background and small flowers, the short ruffle around the neck, the way the flannel lay over her breasts was alluring.

"Can I come in?"

"I'm ready for bed. I have an early day tomorrow."

"We need to talk, Jenny, about a couple of things. I really don't want Dad to overhear us so I thought your room would be best." He was now ensconced in his old room near his dad's master suite.

After a moment's hesitation, Jenny backed up and let him inside. She was the type of woman who toughed things out. She'd make a point, even though she might be uncomfortable doing it. The point tonight was—she could stand in her flannel nightgown in front of him and not look nervous.

The gas fireplace in her room was lit and she settled on the mauve and sage-green, flowered sofa, pulling the pale pink afghan from the back and covering herself with it. The room was a little chilly, but he doubted if Jenny would have used that afghan if she were alone.

Whatever. This wasn't a date. He sat down on the sofa about a foot away from her. Her gaze swept over him. He was wearing a navy flannel shirt, jeans and boots, usual attire for the ranch in the winter. He couldn't tell what she was thinking, but her gaze on him made him feel much too warm.

"Did you know Dad invested in a horse farm in Kentucky?" he asked.

That obviously wasn't a question she'd been expecting. "Yes, I knew. Why?"

Her surprise kept her from being defensive and he was glad of that. "Because it's losing money faster than any of the thoroughbreds they're raising there can run a mile."

She gave a small shrug. "He didn't invest in it just to make money."

Zack narrowed his eyes. "Why did he invest?"

"Because the family owned the ranch for generations. It's been going downhill for the past ten years and they were going to lose it. Silas tried to help keep that from happening."

"I noticed expenses for a trip there a year ago. Has he been there since?"

"No. But the family sends him pictures and they keep him updated."

Zack grunted. "Pictures. You can't get a good perspective from a few pictures."

"They also send videos of two of the most promising two-year-olds."

Zack shook his head. "This is a sinkhole, Jenny."

"It was your father's decision to invest in the ranch. Why are you discussing it with *me?*"

"Because you keep the books. You can see what's happening. The Rocky D is still making a profit, but that profit is down, too."

"We don't just do this for the money," she reminded him softly.

He approached the ranch's finances from another angle. "Dad still has a full staff when a lot of the other ranches have cut back."

"Our horses need the care we give them. I'd cut *my* salary before I let anyone go."

"Do you have say over that or does Dad?"

"We make joint decisions. If you were here, he'd give your opinion weight, too."

"I doubt that. I don't think he's going to give it any weight now. *You're* not giving it any weight."

Her finger came to her lips and she looked as if she were about to weigh her own words. His gaze targeted that finger and her lips. She had such a kissable mouth. With her hair long and loose on her shoulders, he was more tempted by her wholesome beauty than he ever believed he could be.

"If you were going to stay involved in the Rocky D, everything would be different," she returned quietly.

"Stay involved from long distance or close up?" he asked, trying to see into her mind.

But she wasn't even giving him a glimpse. With another little shrug, she responded, "Either."

"You wouldn't want me looking over your shoulder." He was sure about that.

"It wouldn't be like that."

"Wouldn't it?"

The defiant look came into her brown eyes and she turned away and started to rise from the sofa.

He caught her arm. "We're not done."

"You're in my room, Zack, and if I ask you to leave—"

"You know I *would* leave. But I'd also be waiting for you in the morning to finish this."

"Finish what? We don't have anything to finish."

He waited a beat, let her think about the evening before. "Last night you told me the bare essentials. You've told me the minimum. There's obviously more. You couldn't hide the sadness in your eyes. So tell me about the miscarriage."

Slowly sitting on the sofa again, she lowered her gaze to her hands in her lap. "I can't. It still hurts."

"Jenny."

That bit of caring in his voice must have gotten to her because she finally raised her eyes to his. "Fifteen years ago when it happened, I thought it was over. I thought it was done. Your mom and dad both helped me concentrate on other things. They gave me more responsibility around here. Your mom practically let me take over the bookwork. Your dad gave me more horses to train and let me become involved in the PR of selling the ones we bred. Years passed and then your mom died, and all of it came rushing back."

Zack could feel his chest tighten with a years-old ache of his own.

"When you came home for your mom's funeral," she went on, her voice low, "I thought about telling you then. But you were hurting so much, why make you hurt more? Now, most days, I think I've forgotten about the miscarriage. I think I've moved on. But then I see a child with her mom. I spend time with Celeste and Clay and Abby. I teach kids how to ride. All the while I know that I'm getting older, and I wonder if I'll ever have another chance at motherhood. Maybe it will be better now that you know. But I don't think so. Because last night when I told you, I saw a change in *your* eyes, too."

The emotion in her voice drew him closer to her. He couldn't help sliding his arm around her.

She resisted at first, but then she relaxed against him and he held her.

They sat there a long time, watching the flames in the fireplace, feeling but not talking.

The warmth of Jenny's body seeped into Zack, heating up the cold chambers of his heart. The change felt odd and uncomfortable and unnerving. He'd distanced himself from his emotions for so long, it was hard to process what he was feeling. But there was one sensation that was familiar and easier than all the others.

He slid a hand under Jenny's hair and turned her face up to his. He didn't have to say a word because he found a response in her eyes that matched the desire she'd always ignited in him. He bent his head, giving her time to move away, stopping for just a moment to let his breath mingle with hers. When she closed her eyes, he knew she was giving in to an attraction that had started so many years ago.

He began the kiss slowly, with just the coaxing taste of what passion could be. After all, he'd learned finesse since they were teenagers. He'd learned what women liked. But then Jenny gave a soft sigh, opened her mouth and everything he thought he knew vanished. This kiss wasn't about technique or titillation. It was about raw feelings they'd once shared and a hunger that still remained. He knew he shouldn't kiss her. He did know that. But Jenny was old memories, old feelings, feelings he hadn't experienced after he'd left her.

His thoughts shifted into such a high gear they were no more. Kissing Jenny was all that seemed to matter. The desire he felt was so startlingly strong, it drove him where he didn't want to go. They'd had something together. They'd lost something even greater. They'd lost a child. And now for a few moments, he had to try to get something back.

She seemed just as eager to try. Her hands were at the back of his neck…in his hair. She gave a little moan that he remembered all too well. Heat poured from him into her and back again that had nothing to do with that fire in the room. That was a fake fire anyhow. What was happening between them was *real*.

Jenny's body was soft against his. His fingers went to the tiny buttons on her gown as his tongue searched her mouth. He felt like a fumbling idiot when he couldn't open them fast enough. He was experienced at this. He should be doing a quicker job…a better job. Finally, he'd undone a quarter of the buttons and he could slip his hand inside her gown. He felt her start and wondered why. After all, she was thirty-three. She must have had partners, a few at least. It was no secret that men found her beautiful.

Yet she'd been a virgin when they'd had sex the first time…the only time. It shouldn't have happened. He'd intended to leave without going that far.

When his fingertips touched her breast, his hunger for her shook him. She pressed into his hand and rubbed against his palm. He wanted their clothes off. He didn't even care if they made it to the bed. The floor would do. His mouth twisted over hers and angled until his tongue explored deeper. It seemed to matter that he possess her.

Suddenly, everything stopped. Jenny tore away, pulled her nightgown closed and looked at him as if he were a stranger.

"No," she said on a sob. "This can't happen. I won't *let* it happen."

"Jenny." He reached for her trying to draw her to him again.

But she leaned away. "What do you think you're doing, Zack?"

The question swam around his head until he realized he couldn't answer it with any kind of logical response. Finally he admitted, "I'm not sure." His own voice was too husky, too filled with emotions he didn't want to acknowledge.

Where she had looked angry and almost defiant before, now her expression softened.

He reached out and took her hand, just held it in silence for a few moments. "We're still attracted to each other."

"That doesn't matter," she said quickly. "We know there's nowhere to go. Maybe I should have told you about the baby so many years ago. But I didn't want to hurt you then and I didn't mean to hurt you now."

Had he kissed her because he didn't know where to go with the feelings the loss had caused? Because the fact that they'd lost a child hurt too much to express in words? Finding out about the baby had cracked the shell he'd built around his heart. Cracked it, but not broken it. He knew better than to open up his heart again, especially to Jenny. She was so sure there was no world outside of the Rocky D. She was so sure that security was so much more important than dreams. There was no such thing as security and all anyone ever had were dreams.

"I didn't know how to react," he confessed. "I guess we both just got caught up in…the moment." Actually, he was embarrassed he hadn't been the one to stop it. He was dismayed that the same thing could have happened tonight that had happened in the hayloft on their graduation night. No, it wouldn't be the same at all. Now he carried a condom.

"What are you thinking?" she asked quietly.

"Nothing important."

"Your face went all dark. Your eyes changed."

"Don't try to read me like one of your horses."

With a sigh, she buttoned her nightgown. "I didn't want you in my room for a good reason."

"Then you shouldn't have run away from me all afternoon and evening."

She looped her hair over one ear. "You won't be home for that long, Zack. This shouldn't be so hard."

"This isn't hard. The fact that you didn't trust me enough to tell me about the baby before now is hard. The fact that my parents kept it from me is hard. What you've been through had to have been unimaginably hard."

His understanding brought vulnerability back to her face, and he realized now he'd taken advantage of that vulnerability, something he'd never done with a woman before. The women that he dated on the west coast knew the score. He chose women who didn't want entanglements any more than he did.

His personal life was a train rushing nowhere. Had he dated Rachel because he'd been bored? Restless? Searching for something he couldn't find? Had he dated Rachel because she was the extreme opposite of Jenny? Was that a pattern with him?

He swore and rose to his feet. "I should have gone outside and made some headway with Dusty. I didn't mean to...turn my sense of loss back at you."

All buttoned up now, she stood, too. To his surprise, she took a step closer and lightly touched his jaw. "We could have just talked, Zack, about what you felt and about what I felt. You express yourself so well in films, but you have such a tough time in person."

Wasn't that just the crux of it? Jenny had always seen too much. He didn't like the fact that she seemed to see through to his soul now.

He was the one who moved away this time. He crossed to her door, opened it and left her room. When the door shut with a click, he wondered just how soon he could return to California—because his staying here at the Rocky D wasn't good for him or his dad or Jenny.

Chapter Seven

With a sideways glance so his father wouldn't know he was watching him, Zack took a quick assessing look at Silas as they walked down the uneven stony path from the house to the barn. Zack suggested easily, "Maybe you should have brought your cane."

His dad scowled at him. "Don't even suggest it. I'm not an invalid. It's bad enough I have to take all that medication."

They walked in silence until they crossed the road and ambled up the loose gravel to the side door of the barn.

Once inside, Zack asked, "How do you feel?" This was his father's first sojourn to the outbuildings.

"I'm fine."

Zack had known his dad would say that, but he looked a bit winded. "The equipment for the exercise room is being delivered this afternoon. A nurse will be coming tomorrow. My guess is, she'll start you on the treadmill."

"I wonder what people do who can't afford an exercise room and a nurse," his father grumbled.

"You could be going into Flagstaff."

"That's a trek. Maybe I should donate enough money to build a cardiac rehab center at the urgent care place in town."

At first, Zack didn't think his father was serious, but as he studied his face, he saw that he was. "You'd consider that?"

"I'd consider giving a chunk and letting somebody start a fund drive. It's not as if when I die, you're going to need the money."

"No, I won't, but Jenny might. Have you included her in your will?"

"Do you think that's something you deserve to know?"

"I'm just asking. If you don't want to tell me, that's fine."

"Stop being so damn diplomatic," his father ordered with some of his old fire. "You've been treating me like a favorite uncle who's suddenly on his deathbed. I know that's not how you feel. Don't you think honesty between us would go a lot further?"

"And what do you want me to be honest about?" Zack asked, bracing himself for the inevitable.

"For starters, how angry you are you had to come back here in the first place. I know you don't want to be here."

As Zack remained silent, his father weighed his expression.

"You don't, do you?"

"No, I don't," Zack admitted. "But...this time being back here, remembering Mom being here, feels good in some ways."

Silas thought about that. "I think about her over the holidays most of all." Silas stopped at Hercules's stall and rubbed the horse's nose. The gelding snuffled and nuzzled Silas's hand as if he'd missed him.

"You know, Dad, you're going to have to make better investments than that horse farm in Kentucky if you want money to give to charity *or* money to leave to Jenny."

"I didn't buy in to that farm for an investment."

"You expected it to *lose* money?"

"*Expected* isn't the right word. I'm just not surprised. You know, not everything's about winning or making money."

"Since when is that your philosophy?"

His father didn't bristle at the comment. "Maybe the past few years. You should see those thoroughbreds, Zack. Their beauty is a gift to this earth."

His father never used to talk like this. He never thought about charity or doing something for his fellow man. Could Jenny be right? Was his father changing?

"And when do you think you're going to see those thoroughbreds again?"

"When I'm feeling better than I am now."

Zack glanced over the horses in the everyday barn, thought about the other barns, the foals up to the two-year-olds. "You have beautiful horses here, Dad. Why isn't that enough?"

"Why do you keep making movies?"

"You think there's a connection?"

"If you think about it long enough, you'll find the connection. It's about *more* and *what is* and experiencing every little thing while you can. Big things, too. Did you and Jenny have a talk?"

Understanding the leap in his father's thought processes from what was important to precious moments, he said, "We talked. She told me about her miscarriage. You don't have to worry about keeping the secret any longer."

"So you're mad at me for that, *too.*" Silas exhaled with a sigh.

"I don't know. I'm still trying to take it all in. One moment I hear she was pregnant, the next she tells me she lost the baby. Do you think she did it on purpose?" That had been the question rolling around most in Zack's mind.

But at that inquiry, his father turned away from the horses and looked squarely at him. "You *know* Jenny. How could you even think that?"

"She was young and scared and didn't know what to do. That's how I could think it."

His father was already shaking his head. "Jenny has more guts than that. I do think, like most teenagers, she might have believed she was invincible. She thought she could ride and train and everything would be okay. But she had too much on her mind, got distracted, lost control of the horse for just a minute. That's all it took. Afterward, she was so sad I didn't know if she'd come out of it. Your mom stayed with her, talked to her, sat with her, made her eat and finally she started to heal."

Silas capped Zack's shoulder. "If you're half the man

I think you are, you're going to need to grieve, too. It's like it happened when she told you, right?"

Zack knew now that last night with Jenny, the sexual storm that had driven him, had been about grief and reclaiming life. But he hadn't confided in his father in much longer than fifteen years, so it wasn't something he could do easily now.

Stuffing the turmoil he felt about Jenny and the miscarriage, he gave a shrug. "I'll deal with it." In the next breath, he asked, "Are you ready to go back in?"

Silas shook his head and muttered, "You really are your father's son. Whether you like it or not, Zack, you're a lot like me. But you don't have to make the same mistakes I made."

Zack wasn't going to ask his dad to elaborate on the similarities between them. He concentrated on the differences…because that was a lot easier.

Snow had started falling again the night before. After Michael and Tanya's lesson on Saturday, Zack asked Michael what he'd like to shoot. The eleven-year-old announced he'd like to make snow angels with his sister. If Zack would help, they could videotape each other.

Zack checked the settings on the camcorder, remembering his own when he was in high school. He was used to much more sophisticated equipment now but this would get the job done for Michael and Tanya. He didn't know where Jenny had disappeared to but maybe she just didn't want to be out here doing this with him. He really did understand. If they got within a foot of each other, they'd melt the snow all around them.

Michael took hold of the camcorder to tape his sister.

He told her, "Say hi to Mom and Dad and wish them a Merry Christmas."

Tanya obeyed with a happy smile and a wave, then she lay down in the snow to make her angel.

Zack hefted Michael up onto his shoulder.

"Shoot it from up there. You'll get a better angle."

"Looks great!" Michael said as he let the tape run. He started humming "Jingle Bells" as he taped Tanya and that gave Zack an idea. When Tanya's turn came, Zack lifted her up onto his shoulder so she could do the same thing.

Suddenly, Jenny came around the corner from the barn. She stopped short when she saw Zack with Tanya on his shoulder. He could imagine what she was thinking. A child of theirs would be fourteen now, would be learning his talents, or her abilities, would be becoming an independent person, might be rebelling against parental authority.

Zack caught a glimpse of what Jenny was pulling behind her and felt as if someone had kicked him in the gut. It was the oddest sensation. She was pulling the sled he'd used when he was a boy. His father had bought it for him when he was seven and his mother had warned him too many times to count that he should be careful. Of course he hadn't been and she'd had to bandage him up. But he and his dad had taken that sled to the highest hills on the property. His father had approved of Zack's flying over hillocks and around brush, only to trudge up to the top of the hill again and start all over. Where had those memories been hiding all these years?

But Jenny couldn't know about that, could she?

When Tanya finished taping, he swung her down to the ground. She ran over to Michael and tried to hold the camera steady as he wrote "Merry Christmas" in the snow.

Pulling the sled, Jenny stopped beside Zack. "Look what I found."

"Where did you find it?" Zack asked, his voice huskier than he'd like it to be.

"It was in the storage barn behind some old tools. I'd seen it there when I was looking for Silas's toolbox. I thought the kids would like to use it in their video." She studied Zack thoughtfully. "Should I have not brought it out?"

"No, it's fine. In fact, it will be perfect."

Snow had begun falling again. Jenny wore a red knit cap, a crimson scarf around her neck and a yellow down jacket. Snowflakes settled on her bangs and eyelashes and Zack suddenly wished he had a camera in his hand to take a video of *her*.

"Come on," he encouraged her. "Let's get this done before their mom arrives. We wouldn't want to spoil the surprise."

He turned away before she could see too much on his face, too much he was trying to hide yet couldn't.

First Michael pulled Tanya on the sled, singing "Joy to the World" and waving. Then Tanya tried to pull Michael but had a tough time of it even though she was a good sport. Zack knew the recorder was taping their laughter as well as their Christmas carols and the fun they were having. That laughter would be the best present they could give their parents.

Jenny suggested, "Now both of you get in the sled. I'll pull it while Zack shoots."

Zack framed the moving picture, Jenny pulling the

two children in the sled. She would make a terrific mother. He felt the hard hand of fate squeeze his heart.

He called to them, "We'd better call it a wrap, or your mom's going to catch us doing this."

The kids tumbled from the sled and ran over to Zack.

Michael beamed up at him. "Thank you so much for helping us do this."

Zack had reviewed some of the footage on the camera. "You did really well, both of you. Now I have a question for you. If I can find a machine that will transfer your video onto a DVD, are you interested?"

"Really, you can do that?" Michael asked enthusiastically.

"Sure. I can even put a beginning and end on it like a movie. Would you like that?"

Both kids were jumping up and down now. "That would be great," Michael enthused. "We have a DVD player. We'd still have the tape, right?"

"Right. You'd have both. Your parents might like that."

"Thanks so much, Mr. Decker," Michael said, giving him a huge hug. "You're going to make our Christmas super."

Tanya was a little more sedate about her thanks, but she gave him a hug, too. Zack couldn't remember when he'd last been hugged like that by kids. His heart seemed to warm up and grow and forget about everything that wasn't good and innocent and carefree.

"I'll take the sled back to the barn," Jenny said.

"Better stow the camera in your backpack," Zack reminded Michael.

Before he did, Michael removed the tape and handed it to Zack.

They had just reached the arena when Michael and Tanya's mother drove her truck onto the gravel. The two children went to join her. She waved, watched them climb into the truck, then took off.

Zack turned the tape around in his hand. What more could parents want than memories of their children in living color?

Staring down at the tape, Zack didn't hear Jenny when she came up beside him, but he did feel her hand when she placed it on his jacket and squeezed his arm. "What are you thinking?"

"I'm thinking losing a child isn't a pain that goes away easily."

"Oh, Zack." She stepped into his embrace, letting him hold her again because he was the one person who understood better than anyone.

They gave comfort to each other, oblivious to the snow landing on their noses and settling on their cheeks. When Jenny looked up at him, he saw the tears and he knew her telling him had opened the old wound wide. He hugged her again and she snuggled into his shoulder. She fit there so perfectly.

"Kiss me, Jenny."

"Do you think the pain will go away if I do?"

"No. I tried that last night. It didn't work. But when you do kiss me, I forget about everything else for a little while."

"So do I," she admitted, lifting her mouth to his.

He didn't mean to deepen the kiss. He didn't mean to coax every ounce of life out of it. He didn't mean for the world to fall away until only the two of them stood there. But that's what happened.

He broke the kiss, leaning away to look at her. "Attraction's hard to deny."

"But we're both trying to, and we have to. Maybe it will be easier this week with Thanksgiving and all. I want Silas to know he's loved and cared about. So I'm asking Mikala and her aunt Anna to join us. They really have nowhere to go for the holiday, either. We can celebrate together and maybe Silas can see he still has a lot of years to go. That can be meaningful."

"Are you going to have help other than Martha for this dinner party?"

"No. Mikala said she'd help."

"So you want an old-fashioned Thanksgiving?"

"Yes, I do. Don't you?"

"Holidays don't mean much to me anymore, Jenny."

"You don't go anywhere special for Thanksgiving or Christmas?"

"I might not even be home over a holiday. I'd rather be shooting a film somewhere. I don't see holidays the way Mom did, the way you do."

"Holidays should be a time to spend with family and friends, to appreciate the reasons you're together."

He frowned when he realized that's exactly what she truly believed. "I think you've read too many greeting cards."

"It's the way I feel, Zack. It has nothing to do with greeting cards, or what the commercial world is trying to sell me. It's about the feeling I have in here—" she tapped her chest "—when I'm with people I know care about me."

"We have such different views of life," he said.

"They don't have to be so different. Promise me something."

"What?" he asked warily.

"That at the end of Thanksgiving Day, we'll talk about this again."

"You're serious."

"Yes, I am. Is it a promise?"

Looking into Jenny's coffee-brown eyes, reading the pleasure she got from standing out here in the snow with him, talking about things that mattered to her, he said, "I promise."

But as soon as he said it, he wished he hadn't. He didn't make promises anymore. They were too easy to break. But with this one, he had a feeling Jenny wouldn't let him break it.

What kind of holiday would Thanksgiving Day be?

On Thanksgiving Day, Jenny trimmed holly leaves from a branch, washed them and used them as decoration on a large fruit tart. The delicious aroma of roasting turkey filled the kitchen. She hadn't seen Zack all morning. He had a habit of closeting himself in his office when he didn't want to deal with her or his father. Of course, she hadn't searched him out, either. Being with Zack was too exciting, too painful, too regret-filled.

Martha checked the cooking potatoes one last time and said, "I'm going to make sure the dining room is ready," then left Jenny alone in the kitchen.

Not long after, Zack strode in. "Everything smells wonderful," he said. "Dad wants to know if he gets a free pass for today."

"Not exactly a free pass. We won't be using cream in the whipped potatoes. The turkey's good for him and I made apple stuffing instead of the usual sausage. We're good to go." As Zack approached her, the heat level in the kitchen seemed to go up a few degrees.

"And what about the desserts?" he asked with a quirked brow, as if normal conversation was all they needed between them, as if normal conversation could solve everything.

"Martha made a low-fat, low-sugar pumpkin pie, and the fruit tart has a whole wheat crust. He can have a sliver of each."

Beside her now, Zack checked her handiwork. "Did you do this yourself?"

"I did."

Slowly, Zack reached toward her, his thumb brushing her upper lip. "I think somebody was tasting the fruit."

She laughed self-consciously, because his touch made her tremble all over. "You caught me. Strawberries."

The simmering desire in his blue eyes told her he wanted to do more than touch her. He wanted to kiss her again. But he wouldn't, and she wouldn't let him. She had to do everything in her power to stay away from him.

The timer went off on the stove. "That's for the turkey," she said a bit shakily.

"Do you want me to get it out?"

"That would be a help. Martha and I wrestled it into the oven, but we certainly wouldn't want to drop it now."

Zack chuckled as he went to the oven, opened it, then took the oven mitts from the counter. He lifted the pan so easily, Jenny wondered how much he worked out in L.A. He'd always been all muscle, with broad shoulders and a lean torso. The past fifteen years hadn't changed that. It hadn't changed a lot of things. He was wearing a snap-button shirt today and black jeans, just like he used to. His boots were ever-present now.

She'd dressed carefully, telling herself she wanted to be festive for their company. She'd worn the pearl earrings Olivia had given her. In her turquoise sweater and skirt and suede high-heeled boots, she felt festive and put-together. After all, today was Thanksgiving. She'd felt like dressing up.

She'd thought about all the times her father had missed holidays with her. Would he even call today? She couldn't expect him to. And without the expectation, she wouldn't be disappointed.

"Did you get much work done?" she asked Zack as he took the lid off the turkey and took a whiff in appreciation.

"I wasn't working, at least not in the office. I was out there with Dusty. He actually took a piece of apple from my hand."

"Oh, Zack, that's wonderful! Did he run afterward?"

"Of course. He wasn't going to wait around to see if I wanted it back."

She laughed. "You're making such progress with him. I just hope when you leave—"

"He's not as skittish with you anymore, either. Is there anything else you need me to do?" Zack asked, looking around the kitchen, unwilling to address the subject of his leaving.

"Not right now. Everything else is last minute. As soon as I see Mikala's car in the drive—she's bringing veggie casseroles—I'll put the water on for tea." When Zack would have turned to go, she asked him, "If you were in L.A., what *would* you be doing?"

He shrugged. "That's hard to say. I might have been alone, walking the beach, taking advantage of the day off, or I might have spent it working on script notes for my next project. Or I might have gone north for some skiing. Why?"

"I just wondered. Most of the things you mentioned, you would have been doing alone, except for the skiing if you took someone along."

"Did you ever ski?" he asked her.

She shook her head, wondering if he was thinking again how limited her life experiences were.

"You should try it. It's great exercise. But for the most part, it's a solitary sport."

"You wouldn't have taken someone along?"

"Not if I wanted to ski."

Jenny realized exactly what *that* meant. Zack was a focused person. If he went to the mountains to enjoy the outdoors and to ski, that's what he'd do. If on the other hand, he went to the mountains to hook up with someone in a cozy little cabin and have sex, that's what he'd do.

The kiss in her bedroom played in her mind all over again and she felt her face getting hot. "I'd better see to the potatoes," she told him, going to the stove and cutting off their conversation. But Zack couldn't be shut down that easily. He came up behind her and turned her around to face him.

"There's nothing wrong with the way I live my life or the way you live yours. They're just different lifestyles."

Were they so different? He walled people out and kept them at a distance. Because he'd gotten hurt too many times in the past? Because she'd been one of those reasons he'd put up walls? She let people in, but not men, at least not men who wanted a relationship. Because she was afraid they'd let her down…as her father had always done? Because she was afraid they'd leave… as Zack had done?

She said the truth running around in her head. "I think your life is lonely, Zack, and maybe mine is limited."

Just then, the three-tone chime on the front door echoed through the entire house. They'd been too engrossed in each other to hear a car driving up outside. If they became engrossed in each other again, would their walls come tumbling down? Or would they simply be opening themselves to more heartache?

Chapter Eight

Jenny loved holidays, especially when they were like this one, with friends and people she cared about sitting around the dining room table. She'd dreamed of a Thanksgiving like this when she was a child. Now it was a reality.

Yet, sometimes she felt as if she were living someone else's life. This wasn't her house. These weren't her horses. Silas wasn't her father. Really if she got down to it, she was an employee on the ranch, just like Hank and Tate and Ben and the other workers.

Still, when her gaze met Zack's she felt a sense of... belonging. How crazy was that? She didn't belong with Zack. They were way too different...and five hundred miles apart. As she passed the green beans to Mikala, she noticed Mikala watching Silas and Anna. They hadn't stopped talking since Anna arrived and Silas looked more animated than he had since his procedure.

"They're getting along well," Jenny said in a low voice.

"I think they dated once upon a time," Mikala said.

"What happened?"

"Aunt Anna has never told me much. I mean, I always knew she and Silas went to school together. But he worked so hard trying to give the Rocky D a good reputation. He was always on a horse, in the barn, going to sales, traveling to other ranches meeting clients. So I think his ambition got in the way. Then he met Olivia Reynolds. Aunt Anna told me she'd never really had a chance after that."

"Look at them now. Even your aunt seems to be… sparkling."

"Hmm," Mikala said, noncommittally. "Zack doesn't look as if he's happy about it."

As Jenny watched Zack, she had to wonder what he was thinking…what he was feeling. She'd lost her mom, too, and missed her desperately. No one could ever, *ever* take a mom's place. Yet, as she'd grown older and her father had been away more and more, she'd wondered if he'd met the right woman, if they could have formed a family. The thing was, he never had, or at least he'd never brought anyone home.

Zack's experience, on the other hand, had been altogether different. He'd known his mother into adulthood, and the sun had risen and set with her. His father had been the bad guy, the disapproving distant dad who had done his mother wrong. Now she wondered if Zack would resent seeing his father happy, or if he just didn't want to see a woman fill his mother's place.

Mikala engaged Zack in conversation. When Jenny tried to do the same and their gazes met, she couldn't seem to find any words. At one point, when they all seemed to be finished with the main course, Silas focused his attention on Jenny.

"What do you think about having dessert in the living room?"

This was a departure from their usual routine, but Jenny liked the idea. "Sure, we can do that." She wondered if Silas thought his guests would stay longer if they were comfortable.

Silas rose to his feet. "Wonderful! Coffee and dessert in the living room, and maybe Anna and I can share some of the legends circulating around Miners Bluff from when we were kids."

"The Preservation Society is trying to gather them all," Anna explained. "Celeste Sullivan is helping us put them all together in a book."

"Celeste is also working on a book with Clay's mom about the Sullivan family history, isn't she?" Jenny asked.

"She is. And I understand even Harold is contributing his time. Celeste's marriage to Clay has brought that family together. It's wonderful to see."

"I suppose a good marriage can do that," Jenny responded with a quick glance at Zack.

His expression was so blank she knew he was really working at keeping it that way. He'd once told her that after seeing his parents' arguments, he would never marry. Maybe that was the real reason why she hadn't gone with him to L.A. Maybe because she'd wanted to believe in the power of marriage—and wanted to be with a man who believed in it, too.

Over coffee, fruit tart and pumpkin pie, Anna and Silas told some of the legends of Miners Bluff. Zack appeared totally engrossed. He'd obviously never heard them from his father before. They were stories about the miners who worked the first copper mine, tales about the drums some visitors heard when they were exploring Feather Peak. Jenny wondered if Zack was seeing his dad in a new light, but was almost afraid to hope.

After Anna and Mikala left, Silas gave Jenny a hug. "I'm grateful you made this Thanksgiving special." He looked at Zack. "And I'm glad you're here." Then turning away from both of them, he said, "I'm tired. I'm going to my room and fall asleep in front of the TV."

Once Silas had turned away, Zack stared after him.

"He and Anna seemed to get along well." Jenny thought she'd just throw the comment out there and see what was going on in Zack's head.

"What are you suggesting?"

"That hinting to your dad that he might want to go on a date with Anna could be a good idea."

"Jenny..." Zack's tone was filled with warning.

"What? It's not so far-fetched. Dating Anna could give Silas some of his old verve back."

"Verve? Look what he did to my mother!"

"Can't you see the man he is now?"

Zack raked his hand through his hair and she realized it would probably take a lot more than a few weeks for him to see how much Silas had changed.

She knew she should keep her mouth shut, turn away and go to her suite. But she couldn't. "You know, Zack, your dad made bad decisions, but your mother did, too. She stayed with him instead of holding him account- able for his actions. I think she liked her life here, and

she didn't want it to change. She's the one who got into
that small plane, knowing full well the weather could
be bad. You're blaming him for the decision *she* made
that night. Is that fair?"

"I thought you loved my mother," Zack said, accusation written all over his face.

"I did. I do. And I love your dad. That doesn't make
me blind. That just makes it even more important that
I accept who they were and who they are. It takes two
people to fight, two people not to resolve the problems
in their marriage."

The house phone rang breaking the dense silence
between her and Zack. "I'll get it," Jenny said, "in case
Martha already went to her quarters." Checking the
caller ID, she murmured, "It might be my dad."

Her heart lifted at the thought.

"Go ahead and take it. I'm going out to take Dusty
a Thanksgiving treat. Hank, Tate and Ben should be
back, but I'll check the bunkhouse to make sure."

With a nod, he left her in the foyer.

Phone in hand, seeing the caller ID said OUT OF
AREA, she answered, "Hello?"

"Hey, baby. Happy Thanksgiving!"

Hearing her father's voice always created a mixed
rush of feelings. She kept telling herself it didn't matter if he called. She no longer waited for calls or visits.
Yet when she heard his deep baritone, she remembered
the times he'd hoisted her on his shoulders, took her to
the rodeo to watch the horses, looked at her mother as
if she'd been the most important person in his world.
Now she felt…relieved that his latest job of teaching
techniques to rodeo clowns and cowboys hadn't gotten him injured. "Thanks. What are you doing?"

"I'm here at a restaurant with some of my rodeo bud-dies—great turkey and pie—just outside of San Anto-nio. You ought to come down here sometime. You'd like the Riverwalk."

She'd read about the Riverwalk and its shops and boutiques and restaurants. Her dad just didn't under-stand that the traveling bug had never bit her, probably because he'd always been gone so much that he didn't realize she saw traveling as a way to escape responsi-bility. Because of the life her dad had led, she'd always wanted to put down roots, to dig in her heels, to make a life that was sturdy and safe.

"How long are you going to be in San Antonio?" She couldn't stop herself from asking. "Do you think you can get back to Miners Bluff for the holidays? It would be great to spend Christmas together." As always, she issued the invitation without getting her hopes up.

"I don't think so, darlin'. I'm going to be one of the teachers at a training camp between Christmas and New Year's. The money's too good to turn down."

At her silence, he went on, "You'll have a big ole Christmas tree at Silas Decker's place, and probably any present you could ask for. You don't need me mucking around."

Maybe her father had just never understood how much she needed him. "Silas had a heart attack, Dad. He's recovering now, but I'm not exactly sure what we'll be doing for Christmas. Zack came home while he was in the hospital and he's staying a few weeks."

"Zack, huh? How do you feel about that, having him there again?"

Her father had known she'd been smitten with Zack. She hadn't been able to hide it. But he hadn't known about the pregnancy or the miscarriage, or how broken-hearted she'd been when Zack had left. "This is a big place. We run into each other now and then."

He laughed. "Oh, I bet you do. Does he act all high and mighty like he's better than everybody else? That's the way those celebrity types are."

As she thought over exactly how Zack did act, she found herself thinking that it wasn't like a celebrity. "No, he's not like that. He's more introspective, more cynical, more…alone."

"That's hard to believe. Hey, maybe I should ask him to back my idea for starting up a clown camp."

"Oh, Dad, you wouldn't."

"Why not? He could be part investor."

"Everybody wants something from him. I think that's partially why he is the way he is. So don't even think about asking him for money."

There was a very long pause, then her father said, "I understand."

She was glad he understood at least. He'd never really understood her. Ever since her mother died, she'd had no one to depend on. When she tried to depend on her dad, he'd let her down, not once but over and over and over again. Her life just wasn't important enough to him to be part of it. Yet she could never close the door.

"I wish you could come back for Christmas," she said, trying to keep the wistfulness from her voice. "You know if you change your mind, you're welcome."

"You know I wouldn't be comfortable staying there."

"You could always stay in the bunkhouse. I don't think Hank, Tate and Ben would mind."

"We'll see, darlin'."

Jenny swallowed hard, then blurted out, "Why don't

you want to get close to me, Dad? You never have. I always thought something was wrong with me."

"Jenny, no! There's nothing wrong with *you*. You're beautiful and smart. You always have been." He stopped, maybe trying to rearrange his thoughts, and she gave him the time. Finally he admitted, "You look like your momma. Even when you were a little girl, you did. After she died, I couldn't look at you without seeing her. It hurt. If I'd stayed home with you, I would have drunk myself into an early grave."

She didn't know why she'd brought this up. Because Zack's return had stirred the pot?

"What about now?"

After a few beats of silence, her dad sighed. "Aw, Jenny. When you love someone and you lose them, the pain never goes away. It comes back in a wave when you least expect it."

"Can't you just appreciate the ways I'm like Mom, but also know the ways we're different? Can't you separate us? Can't we just be a daughter and a dad getting to know each other?"

"That was a mouthful."

"No, it was a heartful." She waited a beat and added, "Silas is great, and he does act like a father. But he's *not* my father. *You* are."

"Jenny, life is what it is. People are who they are. You're old enough to accept the fact that I'm a wanderer. I don't stay in one place. You do."

After a long pause, he said, "I've got to go."

"All right, Dad. Thanks for the call."

"You take care, you hear?"

Before she could even say "I love you, Dad," he was gone.

* * *

Jenny wasn't sure why she went to the exercise room later that night. Usually when she couldn't sleep, she went to the barn, or at least outside on the balcony that overlooked the rose garden. There she could remember happier times with Olivia. She could remember strolling with Zack in and out of the paths, stealing kisses under the arbor. But tonight, she thought Silas's new elliptical trainer might be what she needed. Maybe she could work off steam, calories and exhaust herself so that when she fell into bed, she'd go to sleep.

Her dad's phone calls always troubled her, and this one was no exception. When she was a kid, she'd watched out the window, waiting for him to come home. She'd waited for phone calls that had never come. She'd longed for daddy-hugs at bedtime when he was gone. As a teenager, she'd gotten used to being disappointed by him. She'd sloughed off his absences and just pretended they didn't matter. But the truth was, when he'd so readily agreed to the Deckers taking her in during her senior year, she'd just felt unwanted.

You're an adult now, she told herself. *Get over it.* Isn't that what she expected Zack to do?

She heard the hum of the treadmill before she reached the exercise room. Silas certainly wouldn't be in here this time of night, not without someone to watch over him. So it must be—

As she stood in the doorway, Zack was unaware of her presence. He was shirtless with a towel slung around his neck. He was jogging on the treadmill and she couldn't help but stare at the straightness of his spine, the smooth motion of his hips, his powerful thighs as he ran the difficult course he'd selected. Zack would never take an easy course. He would challenge himself with the hardest one.

His black hair was mussed as if he'd rubbed the towel over it. He stared ahead at the TV screen on the wall—the sound was turned down low and she didn't know how he could even hear it. But then she supposed he might just be reading the crawl across the bottom of the news channel. She knew she didn't make a sound when she entered. Her athletic shoes were silent on the wood floor. Still, he glanced over his shoulder spotting her. He appeared surprised, slowed his pace to a fast walk, then switched off the machine.

"I didn't mean to interrupt your workout."

He stepped off the treadmill and ran the towel over his face and down his chest. She couldn't look away. He'd had broad shoulders as a teenager, but now they were even broader. His chest was wider, covered with black hair tapering to a spot below his navel. The drawstring of his shorts kept her transfixed.

"I'm finished."

As her gaze traveled back up his torso to his eyes, her breath caught at the sheer virility emanating from him. Being in the same room with him had always affected her. But now, being in the same room with him looking so primal made her pulse quicken and her breath come in short puffs.

"Did you come in to work out?" he asked her, noticing her attire. She'd worn leggings and a tank with her hair in a topknot.

She motioned to the elliptical trainer. "I thought I'd try that out. I'd firm up different muscles than I use when riding."

He gave her a quick once-over. "I think you're firmed up just fine."

She felt the heat of the blush.

He grinned at her. "Aren't you used to compliments?"

"Not that kind," she admitted.

He shook his head. "I think you're running with the wrong crowd of men."

"I don't run with a crowd of men." And the implication was there—*like you do with women.*

His grin faded. "I know you don't. That was a stupid thing to say."

Admitting he'd made a mistake was something she didn't expect from Zack. Flustered, she searched for something substantial to hold on to, something that would distract her from the chemistry between them, the sexual vibrations beating along with her heart as loud as a primitive drum.

"Anna and I were discussing something I thought you might want to help with this year."

"Oh, yeah. What's that?" he asked warily.

"It's not another committee. Actually, we could really use another pair of hands."

She accompanied her words with a glance at his shoulders and arms and now he shifted as if he might be uncomfortable with her appraising him. Wasn't he used to women staring at him?

"I'm almost afraid to ask."

"Next Friday, we're meeting at the social hall at the firehouse to fill holiday baskets for needy families, and then we'll be delivering them. Do you think that's something you could help us with?"

When he was nonresponsive for a few seconds, she assumed he wanted to say no. "That's okay," she said, "I just thought I'd ask." She moved to the elliptical trainer and began to study the settings.

He moved quickly and was there beside her before she could blink. "I didn't say no."

"But you want to."

"You're reading me wrong, Jenny. I'm just wondering how the people in the community will like me pushing in when I'm not an insider anymore."

"Are you kidding me? You could never be an outsider here."

"You mean because of my father's name?"

"No. Because of your reputation. My gosh, Zack, don't you believe the residents here would be honored to work beside you? They might ask for your autograph!"

"Not in Miners Bluff."

"I've seen women go up to Silas in the feed store and ask for an autographed picture of you."

Zack laughed out loud. "And what does he say to that request?"

"He usually tells them you're too busy to take time to sign photographs, that you're working on your next blockbuster. He's proud of you, Zack, and anyone can hear it in his voice. So don't think for a minute that you wouldn't be accepted here. You're Miners Bluff, born and bred, and that's all that matters."

In the silence that followed, his gaze held hers. No words passed between them, but a whole history did. Finally she found her voice again, and said, "It would mean a lot to Silas if you stayed until Christmas." She remembered she'd told him they'd talk about holidays again at the end of the day. "Didn't you enjoy being here today?"

She almost thought he wasn't going to answer. But then he said, "Even if I did, staying wasn't in my plans."

"I know. But can't you think about changing them?"

He reached out and laid his hand alongside her neck, his thumb rubbing her jaw. Although she knew she should move away from his touch, she couldn't.

"Do *you* want me to stay?"

If she said she did, she'd be in trouble. If she said she didn't, she might be in just as much trouble. Either way, her feelings were going to show. Could he see she wanted to be held in his arms? Could he sense the tingling awareness that tempted her to lift her lips to his? She could feel his body heat, was familiar with his scent, knew that he had a birthmark on his right upper thigh, and a scar on his right knee.

If he kissed her now, they'd end up on the floor, tearing each other's clothes off.

The chirp of Zack's cell phone was an unwanted distraction. She realized he'd hooked it to the control panel of the treadmill. He must have been expecting a call.

"Take it," she said breathlessly.

When he leaned in closer, she shook her head. "Take it, Zack."

After hesitating one more moment to decide whether he wanted to acquiesce to her wishes or kiss her anyway, he sighed, swung away from her, and grabbed the phone. He recognized the number on the screen and he put the phone to his ear.

"Hi, Grant. How did it go?"

Jenny unabashedly listened. After all, Zack was right there and he wasn't moving away, so it must not matter if she heard.

"I thought the terms were settled."

He listened for a while. "Damn it, Grant, this isn't a good time."

He listened again. "You're sure we can handle this in one more meeting?" Zack frowned. "Not a conference call or a video conference? All right, let me think about it. I'll get back to you tomorrow morning." He ended the call and laid the phone on the treadmill control panel once more.

"Problems?" she asked, curious.

"Complications." He studied her for a few very long moments.

"What?" she asked, unnerved by his intense concentration on her.

"You want me to stay until Christmas, so I'll make you a deal. If you fly to California with me for a few days, I'll stay until the holiday. What do you say? Will you go to L.A. with me?"

Fly to L.A. with him. He'd asked her to go with him once before and she'd refused. If she refused now—

"You have to go back now? Is it really necessary?" Or did he just want to get away from the Rocky D and Silas? Had he had enough?

"My next project is important to me because it's a departure from what I usually do. If I went for marketable again, funding wouldn't be a problem. But a documentary? I have to get one particular investor to sign on the dotted line. He's hesitant. I have to convince him by giving him my vision in person."

She could see how sincere he was. His work gave purpose to his life. But that still didn't explain the deal he was proposing.

"Why do you want me to go with you?"

He hesitated for a few moments, then admitted, "I want you to get a glimpse of my world."

Of what she'd missed by refusing him so long ago? Silas needed him to stay until Christmas. They seemed to be relating to each other and a few more weeks could strengthen new bonds between them. And, to be honest, she wanted more time with Zack, too. She couldn't refuse him this time.

Inhaling a deep breath, both excited and a little fearful of venturing out of her realm, she agreed. "Okay. I'll go with you to L.A. if you'll stay until the new year."

When he smiled and extended his hand, she let his fingers envelop hers. Then an idea hit her with some force. She'd be staying at Zack's house—alone with him.

This trip to L.A. could be the biggest adventure of her life.

Chapter Nine

The Saturday after Thanksgiving, Jenny studied Zack's house, part of an exclusive community near Malibu. Surrounded by coastal trees and shrubs, it was unique and surprisingly welcoming.

"What do you think?" Zack asked as she stepped into the entrance, wondering exactly why she'd come, why she'd left Silas, why the ground beneath her feet seemed to be shifting.

When she didn't answer right away, he came up beside her and put his hand on her shoulder. "Are you still worried about Dad?"

"No," she answered honestly. "We'll only be gone two nights. Martha said she'll stay within shouting distance and Hank promised to stop in often, too."

Jenny returned to studying the architecture of Zack's house. Its intriguing quality lured her deeper inside.

The stone-accented and wooden-beamed exterior led into a high-vaulted, A-framed ceiling with those same accents inside. It was an open plan and she could see beyond the living room to the sunroom, deck and ocean. Taking a few steps deeper inside, she spotted another set of sliding glass doors off the kitchen with its granite counters and stainless steel appliances, its dining area with a glass table and comfortable-looking blue and green fabric-covered chairs. The colors inside the house reflected the sea, accented by natural materials mirroring hues of the outside landscape. Zack had obviously added his own preferences—dark wood bookshelves with rows and rows of videotapes and DVDs, a group of framed photos depicting various scenes from movie sets, an oil painting of a rocky cliff reflecting shadowed moonlight.

The photos on the mantel were telling. There was one of his mother in the corral of the Rocky D, one of Dawson and Clay and Zack outside a sports arena, probably in L.A. There was also an older one of Zack and Clay and Dawson standing around his first car in the parking lot of Miners Bluff High School. Jenny remembered taking that photo herself with Zack's camera. Yet there were no pictures of Silas or of her.

Zack came up behind her and dropped her overnight case to the sunset-colored scatter rug.

"What do you think?" he asked again gruffly, so close to her, she could feel his body heat.

She wasn't exactly sure what he wanted her thoughts on. When she turned to face him, her heart thumped madly. "Your house is beautiful, Zack. It could be a retreat from the world." She gestured to the view of the ocean. "I can imagine you sitting here, peering out there, seeing scene after scene of a new movie flashing in your mind."

"That's exactly what I do. And the beach, for the most part, is private. My closest neighbors are away for months at a time."

A picture of the two of them on a private beach with no one around suddenly occupied her thoughts. Is that why she'd come? For intimacy with Zack? Or *had* she come to catch a glimpse of his lifestyle and find out whether he was simply the movie director and producer now, or still the boy she'd once known and loved?

She'd worn espadrilles to travel, along with jeans, a T-shirt and a windbreaker. He'd told her nights at the beach could be fifty degrees in late November. She'd been surprised that Zack had worn his boots instead of Italian loafers along with his jeans and a snap-button shirt. Was this the first time he'd brought something from the ranch here with him? Were his bitterness and resentment about the way he'd left the Rocky D fading away?

Standing there, gazing at each other, his blue eyes going darker, her own blood running faster, she might have asked him, but she didn't get the opportunity because his cell phone buzzed.

Grimacing, he took it from the holster on his belt. "I have to get this. It's about my meeting."

"I'll unpack," she said easily. "Just point me to the right room."

"Down the hall, second door on the left. Make yourself at home."

This didn't feel like home at all, because it was so different from what she knew. The ranch was dark paneling and leather, rawhide, suede and corduroy. Its rugs had Native American flair in jewel tones that were deep and dark and beautiful.

However, she *did* like the ocean.

Trailing the travel case behind her, she stopped in the kitchen and gazed out those sliding glass doors. To have the salt air and breeze and the beautiful colors right there was amazing. The sound of it must be, too. She couldn't wait to feel the sand between her toes. Yet, she felt a little strange in this house full of light and cream walls, glass and chrome and appliances that were shiny and new. She didn't know what to think about Zack and his life here, what he did to relax and what he did to connect.

From what she could tell, there was a master suite and two guest bedrooms. When she opened the second door on the left, she found a beautifully decorated room anyone would have felt at home in. There was a coral reef mural on one wall, a rich coral spread on the bed, a pale yellow carpet and distressed pale green furniture. When she opened the closet, she found it empty. Apparently, he didn't even need to store anything in it. It seemed Zack lived luxuriously but sparingly. Of course, he had a penthouse in town and a chalet in Vail. His life seemed unimaginable to her. Yet, when she watched him work with horses on the Rocky D, she knew he'd been denying a part of himself for a long time.

Forgetting about her suitcase, she crossed to the window. When she looked at the property next door— though next door was a relative term—it was a large estate and Jenny doubted whether neighbors borrowed a cup of sugar from each other around here.

She heard Zack coming down the hall, heard him

coming into the room, but she didn't turn around. Her Zack-radar knew when he was about a foot behind her.

"A different view from the one at the Rocky D," she murmured.

"We have roses here, too," he responded, his voice nonchalantly mellow.

Still, she didn't face him. "But you don't have four seasons. Do you see Christmas trees around here? I mean, do people have them in their homes?"

"Some do. You know, Jen, I didn't bring you out here to make comparisons." Something like impatience edged his tone. "I thought you might like to see beyond the boundaries of the Rocky D, beyond the boundaries of Miners Bluff. Open your eyes, Jen. There's a whole world out here."

She motioned to the estate outside, to the room, and the house beyond. "And what's in that world, Zack? I saw a few pictures out on the mantel, but nothing else that was really personal. Do you have many personal things at any one of the places where you live? Do you really *belong* anywhere?"

After a few beats of silence, he asked with a bit of exasperation, "Do you want to fight?"

Maybe she did want to rile him up. Maybe she wanted to make him feel. She took a deep breath and shook her head. "No, I don't want to fight. I just want to know where you really live. Which place do you call home? Which place reflects who you are? Which place makes you feel warm and cuddly and makes you feel as if you don't want to leave?"

His eyebrows arched. "Warm and cuddly? Did you ever know me to want warm and cuddly?"

She thought back to time spent in the barn when they'd cuddled in the straw.

He must have been revisiting the same memory because he muttered, "Scratch that. I'm not like you. I don't carry memories of my childhood with me to take out and look at. I don't hang on to possessions thinking they'll bring me good luck. I don't store things, hoping I'll use them one day."

"And why is that, Zack? Connections and bonds and dreams and memories are *not* bad things. I understand memories can bring pain, but they can bring happiness, too, even if it is a little nostalgic. When did you let go of needing roots? When did you stop having dreams?"

"My dreams are just different from yours. We're not the same. We never were."

"Except for one summer when we thought we belonged to each other," she refuted quietly.

She saw she'd hit home with that one. His eyes darkened and the corners of his lips turned down. She could see he was about to respond, maybe with a bit of temper, when his cell phone buzzed again.

She was sorry it had because she figuratively would have liked to have duked this one out.

He checked the screen, said, "Excuse me," and exited the bedroom.

While she heard the murmur of his voice down the hall, she started to unpack. A few minutes later, he reentered her room. "My driver will be here in about fifteen minutes to take you sightseeing. I have a meeting here this afternoon that will last a while."

"Does that mean I shouldn't come back until your meeting's over?"

His lips thinned. "Of course not. You can see as

much as you want to see, or as little. I thought you might like to go shopping on Rodeo Drive, see the stars' handprints at Grauman's Chinese. But if you prefer something quieter, and you just want to sit out on the deck and watch the ocean, that's fine, too."

She thought about it. "When Mikala came back from a conference out here, she told me about Olvera Street. She said the leather goods there are wonderful. And I'd like to visit the Getty Museum."

"Just tell my driver where you want to go. When the meeting's over, we can go out to a restaurant or have a picnic on the beach."

"I should think about that, too?"

"It's the only major decision you'll have to make while you're here." Now amusement danced in his eyes, but then he sobered. "You asked a question before my telephone interrupted. You wanted to know where I felt really at home. I feel at home on the production set. I feel at home in my editing studio. I can be at home anywhere with my laptop and the right software. Home doesn't have to be a specific place."

She wasn't sure about that. She couldn't imagine home being anywhere but on the Rocky D. "Home to me will always be the Rocky D. That's where I learned to have self-worth. That's where I found out what I was really good at, about what I loved to do. Work for me is part of who I am. The bigger part comes from the people around me, how much I care for them and how much they care for me. My life isn't all about work. It's about loving your dad and caring for him, being with my friends and caring about them and even my own father, too. Your world might be bigger on the outside, but I think my world is bigger on the inside."

Cocking his head, Zack assessed her as if he didn't really know her, and maybe he didn't. Just because they'd once been intimate and in love, didn't mean the bonds had lasted, didn't mean they still acted and reacted like those teenagers, didn't mean anything but sexual chemistry remained.

"You could be right. But while you're here, try to enjoy everything so that you can take it back to the inside with you."

As Zack left the room, she realized he'd missed her point. The inside for her wasn't the Rocky D...it was her heart.

Jenny returned to Zack's house as two sleek, black luxury vehicles exited his driveway. After she gathered her packages, she thanked his driver and went inside.

Zack was picking up empty old-fashioned glasses sitting around his living room. "Timed perfectly," he noted, as he tossed her a smile and went to the kitchen.

"I'm going to take these to my room," she said as she passed him.

But he'd already set the glasses in the sink and he caught her arm. "Did you enjoy yourself?"

She would have enjoyed herself more if he'd been with her. "I did. I found great Christmas presents for Celeste, Mikala, Abby and—" she hesitated "—even my dad."

Zack's fingers became more gentle. "Do you think he'll show?"

"I can hope."

Zack took a few of the bags from her arms. "Here, I'll help you."

When the back of his hand grazed her breast, the

contact was searing. His gaze locked to hers, and she didn't think either of them breathed.

Carefully, he grabbed the bags and strode down the hall. She followed him slowly, still tingling from his inadvertent touch. How would she feel if it was more purposeful? How would she feel if she let herself respond as her body wanted to…as her heart wanted to?

He plopped the bags on the yellow settee. "What do you want to do next?"

"How about a walk on the beach?"

He looked surprised she might want to do that and she added, "I want to get a real feel for the ocean."

He tilted his head in agreement. "A walk on the beach it is. Better grab a jacket. It's getting colder."

"Cold is Miners Bluff in January. I think I can handle this."

Again he studied her with something close to penetrating attention. How she wished she knew what kind of thoughts clicked through his mind. But Zack had become an enigma to her and she only caught glimpses of the boy she'd known once in a great while.

The sun was hanging close to the horizon. Gray and purple stole into the sky as they walked without talking from the deck and down the steps to the beach. She thought she might not be able to keep up with Zack, but he didn't seem to be in a hurry.

"Do you do this often?"

"Whenever I can. I often jog on the beach in the morning when I'm here."

"You know what Michael said was true. As much as you like horses, I'm surprised you don't have a place with a couple of them here. You could ride whenever you wanted."

"I'd probably have to move farther north and have a longer commute."

"Wouldn't it be worth it?"

He stopped in the loose sand and faced her. "What are you trying to do, Jenny? Get me to admit I miss the Rocky D?"

"I'm not trying to do that. I just think, well…if I moved my life from the Rocky D, across the country somewhere, I'd still want to be around horses. Our passions are part of us, and whether you admit it or not, when you're gentling Dusty, your passion still shows."

"Out here I have to worry about paparazzi," he grumbled. "Back at the Rocky D, I have to be concerned about you and my dad watching every move I make."

"It's not like that," she protested.

His brows arched. "Try to fit your pretty feet in my shoes."

"You actually think my feet are pretty?" she teased, turning backward, still trying to talk to him as she walked that way. She didn't want to fight. Teasing was more fun.

"I always thought they were. Take your shoes off and feel the sand. Or are you afraid to because your nails are painted fuchsia or lime, or some fashionable color?"

Actually, they were. They were a sparkly purple this week but she certainly didn't want him to know that.

He saw something in her face, though.

"They *are* painted a wild color and you don't want me to know."

"Now, Zack."

He started running after her and then she did take off, running for all her life.

The loose sand and high tufts of grass made running

difficult and she had to make sure she didn't twist an ankle.

He was used to jogging on the sand, used to catching up to anyone he wanted to catch up to.

"You're pretty good," he said when he caught her and twirled her around. "But I beat you, so I get to see your feet."

"I don't think I remember that being part of the deal!"

"We can wait until we go back to my house and I could explore them there."

Out of frustration and some embarrassment, she sank down onto the sand and pulled off her shoe, then her sock. He witnessed the glory of purple nail polish on a foot that seemed demure in every other way. Back in high school, he'd known she wasn't demure, not by the way she responded to his kisses and touches, not the way she'd responded that night they'd made love. Now he looked at her as if he were considering his next move.

His smile crookedly boyish, he said, "I think we should really explore your wild side."

"I don't like that look in your eye."

"You wanted to experience the ocean, right?"

"Zack…"

He scooped her up off the sand and she felt like a rag doll in his arms. She kept protesting, but he didn't hear. Or if he did hear, he was intent on doing what he wanted to do anyway. That was Zack.

And she loved him. She was in love with him all over again.

That realization hit about the same moment he plunged into the cold waves, drenching them both in surf. She screamed, but she found it wasn't in dismay. She screamed, then laughed, because she was enjoying this wild idea of Zack's as much as he was. Laughing, too, he twirled them around and the surf splashed them all over. Then he was running with her back to the shore, back to the safety of just his arms and the California night. She held on tight as he sprinted back to his house. At the bottom of the steps, he set her down but she didn't let go. Her arms were still around his neck as she stood on tiptoe, reaching up to him.

There were no words for that moment. Yes, they were wet and she was starting to shiver, but she could feel Zack's warmth and wanted more of it.

As soon as his lips came down on hers, she wasn't cold. All she could feel was the heat the two of them generated. All she knew was that she didn't want to be separated from this man.

He broke the kiss only to come back for more, again and again and again.

The breeze blew by them and Zack tightened his arms and separated from her for a moment. "We have to get inside and get these clothes off."

She didn't disagree. She took his hand as they ran up the steps, as they crossed the deck, as he tugged her inside the sunroom, away from the surf and the wind. As he kissed her again, her fingers tunneled under his shirt, seeking the warmth of his chest.

He trailed kisses down her neck, but then asked in a murmur, "Are you sure?"

"Oh, yes," she answered, "I'm sure." She'd been fighting to keep her feet under her for too long. She'd been fighting all the feelings that had never been resolved. She'd been fighting the idea of loving Zack again. In his arms, she couldn't imagine why. Responding to his kiss, she didn't even want to think about it.

As they undressed each other, she could hear the ocean. As she rid Zack of his shirt, the last glimmer of daylight faded away. They were surrounded by windows, views of the sea and the scent of each other, damp from their dip, heated from their desire, magnificently unique to them. Zack's body heat almost singed her as she ran her hands over his muscularly developed shoulders, his arms, his flat stomach. He easily stripped her clothes from her, kissing her everywhere skin was revealed until he was kneeling before her, kissing her where she wanted him to touch her most.

Jenny felt weightless as he brought her to orgasm, then caught her as she sank to the floor with him. The rug was soft and silky against her back. Zack was strong and hard and hungry as he stretched out on top of her. They'd been coming to this for weeks, ever since he'd returned. She'd been pushing it away, pushing *him* away, but now she just wanted to be part of him, just wanted to know that what they had was real.

It felt real.

Zack's beard stubble against her face was erotic. The glimmer in his eyes when he tore away from their kiss expressed the passion he was feeling. His lips teased and titillated her body until sensation was her world. He caressed between her legs, checking to see if she was ready for him. She'd been ready for him for years. Although she didn't want to admit it, her dreams were filled with him, her memories of their time together a golden treasure she cherished. She'd done him wrong by not telling him about the baby. She'd done them both wrong.

Zack rose above her, looked deep into her eyes and then entered her. She rose up to meet him, wanting to give him so much of herself she had nothing left. For a few spectacular moments of giving and receiving and joining, they were one. She clung to Zack as her body tensed and then unwound into bliss. After his shuddering release, there was no time or distance between them and they held on, savoring the beauty of what they'd just given each other.

As they lay there, the ocean sounds seemed to grow louder, the night darker, the temperature cooler. Rationality returned with a vehemence when Zack raised his head. "I can't believe I didn't protect you. I can't believe this happened again."

Of course, she knew what he meant. She was concerned, too. But those weren't the first words she wanted to hear out of his mouth. What about, *I still love you?* But as she saw the worry in his eyes, she realized he felt betrayed by her not going with him, and that betrayal could mean he'd never trust her again. The truth was—*could* she follow him anywhere? Could she ever think about leaving the Rocky D?

"I let it happen," she said on a soft sigh. "Protection wasn't only *your* responsibility. Not before and not now."

He rolled to his side but reached for her and brushed her hair behind her ear. "You'd welcome a child, wouldn't you?"

She had to admit she would. Zack's child would mean everything to her. "I didn't let this happen on purpose, if that's what you're thinking. I mean, I wasn't using you to have a baby."

Her blunt words silenced him for a little while.

"Tell me something," she said quietly. "Have you changed your opinion of marriage?"

"You know how I feel about marriage, how I watched Mom and Dad fight. And I've witnessed more divorces than successful unions."

The reality was—she could never change Zack's mind. But she could tell him how she felt about commitment and vows. "I look at Celeste and Clay and I know marriage is about what two people make it. I want to be a wife and mother, doing work I love to do."

"You need commitment."

"I need *more* than commitment. I need vows and a steadfast love."

"That you never had from your dad."

She bristled a little. "I'm an adult now, Zack. I know what I didn't have as a kid. But I know what I want as a woman."

His gaze was steady and probing. "Are you telling me you don't have affairs?"

"I don't have affairs, not unless you count the one I had with you." She sat up and would have risen, but he caught her arm, looking vexed and unsettled.

"I can't be what you want me to be," he said with certainty. "I've made a life here. I brought you to L.A. so you could see it. One of the actors I know is having a premiere tomorrow night. I want you to go with me."

She had to give his life a chance, didn't she? She at least owed him that. "I'll go with you."

"And to the party afterward?"

"And to the party afterward." She would get a good look at Zack's life, up close and personal. But… "I didn't bring anything dressy."

"We can go shopping in the morning. There are plenty of designer boutiques. I'm sure you can find something."

"You'll go with me?"

"Why not? I owe you another pair of shoes. Yours got lost with the tide."

It wasn't only her shoes that had gotten lost with that tide. Memories and thoughts and her convictions had floated away, too.

Tomorrow, maybe she'd like what she saw of Zack's life. Maybe she *could* think about leaving the Rocky D.

Chapter Ten

Jenny ducked into the sumptuously equipped pink-and-black-marble bathroom, heaving a sigh of relief. The red carpet had been exciting yet intimidating. Dressed in an off-shoulder, black beaded designer gown, she'd had more confidence than she'd expected with camera flashes, reporters, fans and paparazzi creating chaos around them. She'd held on to Zack as if he were her lifeline. *He'd* taken it all in with confidence and nonchalance, introducing her to whoever stopped them, making her comfortable when a conversation swirled around them. It was easy to see he was in demand when he was out and about.

Still…she'd gotten the feeling he kept himself removed from all of it. They'd come to this party at the home of one of his "friends" but she'd gotten the feeling they were more acquaintances than really friends.

Jenny studied her reflection in the mirror and spotted a work of art on the wall behind her. It was probably a very *valuable* work of art.

As she plucked her tube of lipstick from her purse, the door to the bathroom opened.

"Oh, sorry," the tall, attractive brunette said. "I didn't know anyone was in here."

Jenny hadn't locked the door since she was just going to freshen up. "No problem," she said with a smile. "As soon as I fix my makeup, I'm out of here."

"I'm Sheila Jameson. You're Jenny, right?"

"Yes," Jenny answered with some surprise, shaking the woman's hand.

"My husband and Zack are business associates. He was at Zack's house yesterday for a meeting on an upcoming project."

"I see." Jenny wasn't sure what else to say.

"There will definitely be talk about you being Zack's flavor of the month."

"Flavor of the month?"

"In the tabloids. When they find out you stayed overnight at his place…" She let her words trail off and shrugged. "Well, you know how it is."

Tabloids. Lord, was she naive. Was her picture going to be in supermarkets? "I'm just an old friend."

"Your history will be laid out if there's any history to find."

Jenny's shock must have shown.

"You're new to this, aren't you? Zack should have prepared you for the aftershock. The truth is I don't think he takes one look at anything anybody writes about him, but everyone else does."

That sounded like Zack. "Have you and your husband known Zack long?"

"A few years, but I can't say we really know him. He's a hard man to get to know." Sheila stepped up to the huge double vanity beside Jenny. "As an old friend, how long have *you* known Zack?"

Jenny hesitated to answer.

"I'll find out tomorrow in the gossip columns," Sheila said with a sideways glance. "It's amazing what a reporter can discover on the internet with a picture and a name."

Jenny applied lipstick to her upper lip and then her lower lip, feeling as if she'd been swallowed up by an alien world. "I've known Zack since high school."

"Oh, there *is* a story here."

When Jenny was about to protest, Sheila shook her head. "No use denying it." She produced a compact. "There's been a lot of speculation about Zack and the women he dates. Rumor has it, he starts an affair with an end in mind. Maybe you're the reason."

In spite of the ring of truth in Sheila's supposition, Jenny felt the need to defend him. "Maybe Zack's just a private person and the rumors are all wrong."

"Maybe, but there's always a hint of truth there."

Dropping her lipstick into her purse, Jenny snapped it shut. "I'd better get back to the party."

"Back to the party...or back to *Zack?*"

Jenny was silent.

Sheila laughed. "You're learning already. It was nice to meet you, Jenny. It's good to know there might be someone in Zack's life who's a little special to him."

Jenny really didn't know what to say to that. After a murmured, "It was good to meet you, too," she exited

the powder room, wishing she *had* locked the door behind her.

Reaching the enormous living room with its open gas
fireplace and sunken sections, she noticed Zack was in
one of those areas speaking to an actor she recognized
from a sitcom. Should she approach him or leave him
to his conversation? Last night had made everything
awkward between them. Not more intimate, not more
clarifying, certainly not more definitive.

To her relief, she didn't have to decide whether to
approach or not, because Zack saw her, excused himself from his conversation, mounted the two steps and
came toward her.

His easy stride, the way he looked in that tuxedo, the
concerned look in his eyes practically melted her. He'd
wrapped his arms around her heart again. If she tried
to wriggle away, if she tried to cut him out of her life
once more, she really wasn't sure what would happen.

What if she was pregnant with his baby? Oh, she'd
want his child, but a relationship with Zack would become even more complicated than it was. How had she
gotten herself into this mess?

By *loving* him, that's how.

When he reached her, he gently took her arm and
guided her toward a set of French doors leading to a
patio around the pool. Shrugging out of his tuxedo
jacket, he dropped it around her shoulders, then opened
the door. They stepped outside into a backyard that
was as unreal as the rest of the luxurious appearance
of the house. A gigantic triple-tiered fountain bubbled
and gurgled in blue light while the pool itself shim-
mered a blue as perfect as the seas. They walked to the

wrought-iron railing and stared into the grandeur of
marble benches, manicured paths and garden arbors.

"Did you enjoy yourself tonight?" he asked, staring
out over all of it.

"It was exciting, being a part of a premiere."

Now she could feel him studying her. "That's not
what I asked."

When she turned to face him, she knew she couldn't
hide the truth. "It was an experience, Zack, one I'll always remember. I was dazzled. I was busy absorbing
it all, trying to keep myself from gawking at all the ce-
lebrities, at the designer dresses, at the fabulous shoes."
She gave him a smile that was the best she could mus-
ter.

"But you wouldn't want to do this often, and you
could live your life without it."

She stayed silent until finally she asked, "Did *you*
enjoy yourself?"

He didn't answer quickly as she thought he might.
"This kind of thing has become such a part of my life,
I take it for granted, I guess."

"Can I ask you something without you getting defensive?"

"I don't know if that's such a great way to start. It
makes me defensive before you ask. But go ahead."

"How many people do you know here?"

He furrowed his brow. "Oh, Jenny. I work with some,
do business with others, attend cocktail parties and ben-
efits with friends of their friends."

"But how many of them do you know? I mean, *really* know? Do you ever sit down and have a conversation about what you did when you were a kid? Do they
know you like horses? Do you know what really mat-

ters in their lives? Is there anyone here that if you didn't talk to them within the next month, it would matter?"

He went silent and that silence developed into the remote wall that she'd felt since the reunion. "You're becoming defensive, and you're backing away."

"How do you expect me to react to a question like that?" Frustration was evident in his voice.

"I was hoping you could answer it. I was hoping that there was someone here who matters as much as Dawson and Clay, Mikala and Celeste, me and your dad."

"Maybe I've decided that those kinds of ties cost too much."

She gazed into the end-of-November night, not knowing what to say.

Taking hold of her shoulder, he nudged her around to face him again. "Can't you let go of the Rocky D and Miners Bluff for just one night?"

Biting her lower lip, she sifted through her feelings before she confessed, "I let go of it last night, Zack, only to find out I had nothing else to hang on to when I did. I'm ready to go home."

He looked frustrated with her, but the fire was back in his eyes as if he wanted to kiss her. Then, all at once, his face became neutral, his tone even. "I'll find our host and we can say our goodbyes."

She was afraid she was saying more than goodbye to L.A. She was afraid she was starting to say goodbye to Zack all over again.

Instead of bales of hay and the rustic look of a barn, the firehouse's social hall was buzzing on Friday afternoon with volunteers who were filling food baskets and taking deliveries to needy families in the area. Back in Miners Bluff again, Jenny and Zack worked side by side, speaking to the other volunteers but not each other. There was a crackle in the air when their gazes met, current rushing between them if they inadvertently touched. But Jenny was keeping her thoughts and words to herself and so was Zack.

Anna stopped beside Jenny and gave the two of them a wise, knowing look. "Silas says he's doing well with his rehab."

Zack responded, "He says his nurse is a slave driver but he's looking better every day."

"That's wonderful. I hope he can start looking forward again and see what he can accomplish. He thinks his best years are behind him, but that isn't so." She paused, then said, "Mikala tells me you were in California for a few days." She looked at Zack. "I bet you miss it."

"I miss the ocean and the long walks on the beach. But as far as work, I'm amazed at what I can accomplish long distance. With smart phones and video conferencing, work really is portable."

"Mikala does that video conferencing on her computer. I don't understand the first thing about it." Anna tapped her pocket. "But I wouldn't be without my cell phone. It's my connection to Mikala and all my friends. I even text."

Jenny laughed. "Maybe you can teach Silas how to do it. I've tried to, but he just gives me one of those looks and says talking's good enough for him."

"I'll keep that in mind." Anna's eyes twinkled. "I'll be seeing him Sunday. I'm picking him up and we're going to dinner."

At Jenny and Zack's astonished silence, she said, "I see he didn't tell you."

"It's wonderful you're going out!" Jenny said, recovering from her surprise.

Anna blushed a little. "Just to the Feather Peak Diner."

"An outing will be good for Dad. I should have thought of it myself," Zack said, seeming sincere.

"We made plans while you were gone. But I thought he'd tell you."

Jenny suspected why Silas hadn't. Maybe he thought Zack wouldn't approve.

Anna noticed the baskets Zack and Jenny had almost completed filling. "Would you mind delivering some of these? We've so many this year."

Jenny gazed up at Zack and he gave a small shrug and a nod. "Sure, I have the truck," he agreed. "We'll load it up and we'll be on our way."

Fifteen minutes later, they were on the road, Zack expertly driving.

"What do you think of your dad and Anna going out?"

Zack gave an offhanded shrug. "He enjoyed Anna's company on Thanksgiving. Maybe while we were gone he decided he can have a real life again."

"How will you feel if they become serious?" she pressed.

"Dad's never consulted me about his decisions. I don't think he'll start now."

Zack was so good at evading what he felt as well as talking about it. Jenny let the subject alone for now. "I tagged one of the baskets for the Larsons."

Zack gave her a quick sideways look. "From what Michael says, I don't think his dad would appreciate it."

"I don't know if he'll appreciate it or not, but they need it. Maybe they won't be home and we can just leave the basket at the door."

"If Mr. Larson is home, we'll deal with him." Zack's quick look was confident.

"Just because you can convince Dusty to come inside the barn now, doesn't mean you can get Stan Larson to accept a handout without protest."

"There's a secret. Dusty doesn't have to stay inside the barn. That door to the corral is always open. He can come and go as he pleases. You just have to give a person an out so they don't feel trapped."

"And what's the out we're going to give Stan Larson?"

"Let me work on it," Zack said with a wry smile.

Jenny just shook her head.

After a few quiet minutes, Jenny knew she had to fill Zack in on plans she'd made for Sunday. "Clay, Celeste and Abby are coming over Sunday afternoon. Will you be around?"

"*Should* I be around?"

She shifted uncomfortably because she realized he probably knew she had something in mind besides a simple visit. "I told Abby we'd make cookies and I thought maybe you and Clay could set up the tree. Hank and Ben found one that's perfect. It's in the storage shed for now."

Zack's silence was telling. He'd already explained holidays meant little to him. But she was trying to change that and he knew it.

Finally, he answered, "It will be good to spend some time with Clay and Celeste."

She noticed he didn't mention Abby. Because it was too painful to think about the child they'd lost and dwell on what could have been?

Two hours later, they'd delivered all the baskets except for the one Jenny had put together for Michael and Tanya's family. Zack had been on his phone on and off in between deliveries and had even let her drive some of the way. She wasn't sure what the calls were about. She couldn't quite tell from his side of the conversations.

As they approached the address Jenny had secured from her lesson roster, she began to feel a little nervous. What if Michael's dad *was* home?

Once again in the driver's seat, she asked Zack, "Are we making a mistake?"

"This is food we're talking about, Jenny. I suspect this family is making do and not by very much. We can at least try. If the help is rejected, we'll find another way to help."

After they disembarked from the truck, Zack pulled the lone basket from the back. Then he slammed the truck's bed door shut. When they reached the front door, Jenny punched the bell and waited, hoping Helen would answer.

But luck wasn't with her today. Stan Larson opened the door, studied them for a few minutes, then scowled. "Aren't you from the Rocky D?"

"Yes, we are," Jenny answered, her shoulders squared, her gaze meeting the proud man's. "But really, today we're just from Miners Bluff. We're passing out food baskets and we'd like to give you one."

"My family is fine," he said stiffly. "Go give your basket to someone else."

"Maybe we should introduce ourselves," Zack interjected. "This is Jenny Farber and I'm Zack Decker."

"I know who you are. Don't you think I hear from Helen how great Miss Farber is with the kids? Don't you think I know she's giving them lessons for free? And you...I've seen your face on TV and in magazines. I don't want your food. I don't need it."

Zack set the basket down on the porch floor then straightened slowly. "You're a father, Mr. Larson. Isn't it your job to provide the best you can?"

Jenny took hold of Zack's elbow. "Zack."

But Michael and Tanya's dad shook his head. "Let him say his piece, then he can leave with his basket. I'm not a charity case."

"Isn't it true you're out of work?" Zack pressed.

"I am, but I'll have a job soon. I'm waiting to hear from a couple of friends."

"How far are you behind on your rent, your utilities?"

"That's none of your business."

"Maybe not, but I don't think you want to lose everything, including the respect of your family, do you?"

"What would *you* know about it?"

The way he said the word "you," Jenny was sure Michael's dad thought Zack lived in another universe.

"You're right, I don't know how you feel," Zack admitted. "I had plenty lean years when I didn't have work. Thank God, I didn't have a family to take care of then. But you do. So I don't think you can afford to let pride rule your life."

"You think a ham and some canned goods are going to make a difference?"

"It might in the way you spend your holiday, and what you have to be thankful for. But maybe I'm here to offer you more than a food basket."

Jenny dashed a look at Zack in total surprise. What was he talking about?

From Stan Larson's expression, he wondered the same thing.

"Are you willing to change your life?" Zack asked.

"What does that mean?" Stan was definitely wary.

"Are you willing to move to Phoenix?"

Michael's dad took a step back. "I...I don't know. Why?"

"I have a contact in Phoenix who owns a general contracting company. He's managed to ride out the economic downturn when other companies have gone under. He has several crews and he could use a qualified electrician. Are you interested?"

Stan looked speechless, and then he looked mystified. "Why would you do this? You don't know me."

"I know Tanya and I know Michael, and they seem to think you're a good dad who just needs a break. I know they'll miss everyone here if you move, but in the long run, life could be better for them. Right?"

Zack produced a card from his pocket and handed it to the man. "Dawson Barrett is the CEO of the company. His dad, Greg Barrett, is his crew manager and right-hand man. Both of their numbers are on there. Give either one of them a call today and they'll give you the details. They're looking to hire soon, so you have to make up your mind."

Stan studied the card, turning it over in his hand. "I have to talk to Helen."

"Of course you do," Zack acknowledged. "Dawson said you could call their cell numbers."

"Helen took the kids downtown to McDougall's Department Store to see Santa. I told her it wasn't any point. She was setting them up for disappointment."

"Maybe now they won't have to be disappointed," Jenny said softly. "There's a gift certificate to McDougall's in the basket. Please don't look on this as charity. Just try to look at it as the people of Miners Bluff standing together to help each other."

Stan stared down at his sneakers. "I suppose the rich folk of Miners Bluff donated all this."

"No," Jenny told him quickly. "That's not true. Everybody in town gave what they could. Maybe sometime soon, you'll be able to help someone who needs a hand up."

Stan's gaze went to the basket, rose to Zack's and then Jenny's. "I don't know how to thank you."

"Dawson's a high school buddy of mine," Zack told him. "Just do a good job for him."

Stan stooped to pick up the basket and then smiled at them for the first time. "I can't wait 'til Helen gets home."

As they turned away, Jenny tossed over her shoulder, "Tell her I'll see her tomorrow for the kids' lessons." He waved as they climbed into the truck. He was still waving as they drove away.

On the road again, out of the corner of his eye, Zack could see Jenny swing around as far as she could with her seat belt attached. "You didn't tell me you were going to do that," she accused.

"I didn't know if it would come together. Dawson might not have needed anyone. He had to check with his dad and wait to hear back. I didn't want you to be disappointed."

Jenny was quiet as Zack drove back to the Rocky D, and he didn't know what to think. Did she believe he had been too high-handed? Sometimes it was hard to tell with her these days. She was doing a better job of keeping her guard up.

He thought about their walk on the beach and what had happened afterward in Malibu. No guard up then... for either of them. Was that why he backed away from everything she'd tried to tell him? Was that why the idea of commitment urged him to work through the night and most of the day, too? She wanted so much and he felt as if he could give so little.

He kept thinking everything would have been different if she'd gone with him to L.A. when he'd asked her. Yet, would everything *really* have been different? Would she have stayed? Or would she have bailed? Would she have gotten tired of waiting for him to ask her to marry him when that had never been in his plans? Would he have started thinking differently about a life with her? Especially if she was pregnant.

And what if she was pregnant now? That thought practically made him panic and he wasn't the panicking type.

He'd always known his own mind. He'd always had goals and known exactly what they were. Now, his life was fuzzy. He was restless and not much made sense.

He drove under the wooden sign for the Rocky D that marked the front boundary of the property as he had done thousands of times before. At least, since his dad's heart attack, he didn't feel so estranged from his life here as a kid. He definitely didn't feel as estranged from Jenny.

The lane was rutted with tire tracks. He tried his best not to give them a rough ride, but he knew they were in for one anyway. They couldn't put a stop to this attraction any more than they could stop breathing. Staying away from each other, in some ways, just made the chemistry even more obvious.

Chemistry. He'd never felt this kind of chemistry with any woman other than Jenny and that was way too telling on its own.

Zack had no sooner pressed the remote to park the truck in one of the garages, when Jenny unfastened her seat belt. He thought she was in a hurry to jump out and get busy doing whatever else she wanted to do for the day. Jenny was like that. She never sat idle. Yet, instead, she waited for him to switch off the ignition. To his surprise, she leaned over, wrapped her arms around his neck and kissed him full on the lips.

Reacting instinctively, he unhitched his seat belt with one hand and wrapped his other arm around her. Kissing across the console wasn't the most comfortable position in the world, but comfort was the last thing on his mind as fire raced through him, as sensations jammed his brain and all he could think about was leading Jenny to his bed.

She let up first and he told himself this wasn't the place to go crazy, tear her clothes off, or to pretend they were those teenagers again.

When his thoughts got unstuck, he took a deep breath, righted himself in his seat and asked, "What was that for?"

"That was for the wonderful thing you did for Michael and Tanya. Do you know what this means for them and their future?"

He felt heat creeping up his neck at her praise and strived to be offhanded. "I checked around Miners Bluff and even in Flagstaff before I made the call to Dawson. I couldn't find him anything else."

"If they get back on their feet, the economy picks up and they want to move back here in a few years, they can. But they'll build a life wherever they go and that's what's important," she concluded.

"Is that what's important?" he asked and watched to see if Jenny caught the underlying meaning of his message.

Before she could answer him, his cell phone buzzed. Jenny motioned for him to take it and he checked the caller ID.

"It's work," he said, wanting to hear her answer.

But she was already climbing out of the truck. He knew why. She didn't want to answer his question because it came too close to the root of the problems between them.

Ten minutes later, he went into the house, knowing his call would make everything between them more complicated. Jenny was in the kitchen having a glass of orange juice at the counter. She'd taken off her coat. Her Western-motif red and green sweater hugged her slim body at the waistband of her jeans. Her high boots showed off her slim legs. She'd worn her hair in a ponytail today and with the cold air still pinking her cheeks, she looked like the all-American western girl. The kiss was still with him and he was glad his sheepskin jacket fell midthigh. He didn't unsnap it.

She must have been able to tell something from his expression because she asked, "Problem?"

"No. In fact, it was good news about the documentary project I want to do."

"Concerning veterans?"

"Yes, the funding's there, but…I'm going to be traveling for the next few months."

"Traveling?"

"I can put the production company together long distance from here. I know who I want on my team. But this is all about the men's stories so I'm going to have a lot of interviews to do, many of them in D.C., some across the country."

"Do you want to do the interviews yourself?"

"I'm not sure about that yet, but I do know I want to run the project, as well as edit it, not stay in the background. It will air in about a year on a cable network."

The disappointment in Jenny's eyes was obvious and he approached her and stood beside her. "I can't delay the timing of this. It's too important."

"Silas is on the mend," she offered with sudden neutrality that made him want to shake her.

"I was hoping I could convince you to spend some time in California, maybe in the spring," he offered.

"That's when the Rocky D's the busiest."

"The Rocky D is busy all year." He had to let her know she couldn't use that as an excuse.

Her eyes were brimming with the turmoil she was feeling. "And if I spend time with you in California in the spring, what would that mean?" The question came spurting out of her as if it had just been waiting to erupt.

"I don't know, Jen. I don't have the answers."

She backed away from him. "Well, I need some answers, Zack. Soon I'll know if I'm pregnant or not, but that doesn't make our situation any clearer."

"Life isn't about clarity. It's about taking what you have and working with it," he responded gruffly.

"You don't want marriage and a family and traditions to pass down. I do."

But Jenny didn't want to leave the Rocky D. They were back to square one.

Chapter Eleven

Zack wasn't sure when the idea of Christmas approaching had started to mean something to him—when he'd seen his mother's golden bells in the barn, heard them jingling in the wind, or when Jenny had hung a wreath on the front door.

As he held a huge, nine-foot fir steady in the Rocky D's living room on Sunday afternoon and Clay Sullivan tightened the screws holding the trunk in place, he smelled the aroma of cinnamon and cookies baking emanating from the kitchen.

Christmas. What would it mean this year?

"Five bucks for your thoughts," Clay said, as he stood and studied Zack as well as the tree.

"Not worth that," he said with a grimace.

"It must be difficult for you being back here after all this time."

The tree supported now, Zack stepped away from it. "Actually, each day's gotten easier. I guess part of me missed winter and the horses and memories I'd tried to bury."

"How are you and Silas?"

"Peaceful for the moment, but that might not last, especially when I tell him I'm leaving January second."

Clay didn't comment on that, but rather helped Zack gather trimmed tree boughs. Finally he said, "Parents understand more than you think. They want to protect us and keep us close. They just don't always know how to do that without interfering."

"You said you and your dad have gotten closer."

"Celeste had everything to do with that."

"Jenny believes my father is a changed man, and even though her own dad has disappointed her over and over, she keeps the door open for him."

"Maybe women are just more forgiving."

"Maybe."

"What's bothering you, Zack? Something's on your mind today. It's obvious."

Zack raked his hand through his hair and decided his long friendship with Clay was worth a lot. "After I left the Rocky D, Jenny found out she was pregnant. But then she had a miscarriage. I found out about it after Dad's heart attack."

Clay's eyes widened with surprise. "That had to feel like a sucker punch."

"It did. She didn't trust me enough to tell me. She didn't trust me enough to go with me, either, so maybe I shouldn't be so surprised."

"She was only eighteen."

Why couldn't he let go of it? Why couldn't he let go of Jenny?

Because nothing had changed. He'd be leaving, and she'd be staying despite chemistry and memories and connections.

Suddenly, Abby came running into the long living room like a miniature tornado. Stopping beside Clay, she looked up at the tree and clapped her hands. "It's up."

"Sure is," Zack said with a smile for Clay's almost-four-year-old daughter. "As soon as we wrap it with some lights, it's all yours."

The hairs on Zack's neck prickled as Jenny walked in. He was more aware of Jenny now than he'd ever been. Celeste followed her with steaming mugs of hot chocolate on a tray. Clay's wife was a quietly pretty woman with light brown hair and green eyes. At first a surrogate mother to Abby, now she was her real mother. Clay didn't talk about his ex-wife, Zoie—Celeste's twin sister—very much, but Zack knew Zoie was now in and out of Abby's life like a favorite aunt and they were all happy.

As soon as Celeste set the tray of hot chocolate mugs on a side table, Clay wrapped his arm around her. They did appear to be substantially happy.

Carrying an ivory china Christmas plate with painted poinsettias—Zack recognized it as one of his mom's favorites—Jenny offered him a cookie. While he and Clay wrestled with the tree, Celeste, Jenny and Abby had been baking and decorating cookies. He now could choose from pink angels with yellow wings to blue stars with lots of sprinkles to a reindeer with green icing and an almost-red nose.

"You've been busy."

Jenny's gaze met his and for an instant, just an instant, he saw the intimate knowledge there of a man and woman who'd slept together. In a blink, it was gone and Jenny was making conversation as if that knowledge was something she wanted to forget.

"Did you tell Clay about your new project?" she asked Zack with enthusiasm that seemed a little bit too robust.

"He did," Clay answered seriously. "I think our veterans need a documentary like that."

"Look what I found," Abby announced from across the room.

Cardboard boxes full of Christmas decorations were lined up against the sofa. Zack had carried them down this morning. One of the cartons was home for the Christmas lights, but the one Abby had opened held ornaments. She removed a porcelain ornament with a horse painted on it. When he spotted it, he wanted to snatch it from Abby and bury it in the box again. But he couldn't, of course.

Celeste was running to her daughter saying, "Oh, be careful, honey."

Zack rounded the other side of the box and crouched down beside Abby, sliding his large hand under the ornament. "That's a very old one."

"How old?" Abby asked.

"About sixteen years old. It was my Christmas present to my mom one year."

"Where *is* your mommy?" Abby asked with all the innocence most children possessed.

Suddenly, Jenny was beside Abby, too, hunkering

down beside Zack. When he seemed at a loss, she answered, "Zack's mom is in heaven."

"Where the angels are?" Abby asked.

"That's right," Celeste said gently. She pointed to the ornament to veer the conversation away from a sensitive topic. "And that was Zack's mom's favorite horse. One of his friends painted it for him so he could give it to her."

"Brenna," Jenny said remembering.

Zack remembered Brenna McDougall and the ornament and that Christmas that had seemed so special because he and Jenny had spent a lot of time together. His chest tightened and he concentrated on conversation that wasn't so touchy.

"Did anyone talk to Brenna at the reunion?" he asked. "I caught sight of her dancing with Riley and was surprised." There had been problems between the McDougalls and O'Rourkes and it had been an oddity to see Brenna and Riley together when they'd kept their distance in high school.

"I just talked to her for a little while," Jenny said. "She has put all of her artistic talent to good use. She designs bridal gowns now, and is quite famous in her own right."

Abby pointed to the ornament. "Can I hang this on the tree?"

Zack stepped in right away so no one else had to. "Sure you can. As soon as we get those lights attached. Just give us fifteen minutes and we'll be ready for you."

When Abby looked disappointed she couldn't do it right away, Jenny reminded her, "We have to go roll those peanut butter balls in the chocolate chips."

"Can I eat one?" Abby asked.

"Sounds like something we'll all want to eat," Clay said with a laugh.

"Jenny made the hot chocolate with real chocolate," Celeste told her husband, "so I think you'll like it. Don't let it get cold."

"I won't. Like Zack said, just give us fifteen minutes then we'll be ready to decorate the tree."

"Can we play carols?" Abby's gaze targeted Zack because he seemed to be the one in charge.

Right now, he didn't want to be the one in charge. This afternoon with Clay and Celeste and Abby was becoming more than he'd bargained for. Yet, he wouldn't let down this little girl for anything.

"Sure, we can. I'll bet Jenny has a stack of them somewhere."

"From Elvis to Jewel," Jenny assured Abby and crooked her finger at her. "Come on, I'll show you where they are."

Celeste followed Jenny and Abby out of the room and Zack found he was still holding the ornament.

"I'm sorry Abby got into the box," Clay apologized.

Zack settled the ornament on the coffee table. "That's what kids do—they explore. That will be just another ornament on the tree."

Clay gave him a level look, but Zack ignored it just as he ignored the heart-lancing memories that he'd kept under lock and key for all these years.

A half hour later, Jenny and Celeste brought in not only more cookies to sample, but what Celeste called healthy food, too. There were veggies and dip, whole wheat crackers and cheese, barbecued meat on tiny sandwich rolls.

"We just did this backward," Jenny said with a smile,

and Zack could have kissed her, right then and there. Yet, something stopped him. Those walls around his heart? Other people in the room? Or disconcerting emotions he'd been battling all day?

Abby hung ornaments with enthusiasm, her soft brown curls bobbing around her face, the tiny red bow in her hair swinging as she tilted her head first one way then the other until she picked a perfect branch for each ornament. Jenny had found a CD player and set it on a table. Strains of "Rocking Around the Christmas Tree" were a backdrop to their conversation.

"I'm really having a great time putting together a family history with Clay's mom," Celeste told Zack. "The history of the Sullivans is fascinating. Did you ever think of interviewing your dad and capturing his memories on videotape?"

"I never did," Zack admitted.

"Where *is* Silas?" Clay asked.

"He and Anna Conti went to dinner."

When Clay's eyebrows arched, Zack shrugged. "They're old friends."

While Zack's fingers fumbled with some of the oldest ornaments that reminded him of days gone by, Clay revealed the process he was going through to interview potential partners for his wilderness guiding service.

"It has to be just the right person, not too bookish and not too extreme, someone who really gets along with people."

"Would you consider a woman?" Jenny asked.

Clay shook his head. "I'd be more comfortable with a male partner." He raised a hand before the women could protest. "That's not just chauvinism. I don't want misunderstandings."

"Do you think I'd be jealous?" Celeste teased.

"Well, would you?" Clay joked back.

"That depends on what she looked like and how she acted around you."

"See what I mean?" he muttered. "Besides that, this town's too small to take any chances with gossip."

Just then, Abby brought the porcelain horse ornament over to Zack. "Up, Uncle Zack! I wanna hang it on top."

Uncle Zack. He liked the sound of that. "Okay, honey. Let's see how high we can go." He held her in his arms while Jenny looked on. He could see Jenny's eyes mist up and he could only imagine what she was thinking. Their son or daughter would have made Christmas special, too.

Suddenly, a deep voice said from the doorway, "We hang that on the tree every year. Find a really good spot for it."

Still holding Abby steady, Zack turned to see his father. Apparently, he remembered the ornament, too.

Everyone greeted Silas and then Abby asked, "Here?" as she tried the third branch in a row.

"Looks good," Silas agreed.

She let the ornament swing from the branch.

Zack lowered her to the floor, kissed her forehead and said, "Good job. Now why don't we see how everything looks all lit up?"

As "Have Yourself a Merry Little Christmas" played on the CD player, Zack plugged in the lights. White twinkles danced all around the evergreen and the expression on Abby's face was priceless. Her mouth rounded in a little O, and she just stared at the tree.

Finally, she looked at Clay. "Can we have one like this?"

"Maybe not quite as big as this, but I'll see what I can do."

Zack felt that tightness in his chest again. As his gaze met his dad's, he saw a look of longing on his father's face. What was that about? Regrets? He certainly had a trunkful of his own. Maybe the way he'd handled his father all these years was in that stack.

Crossing to him, Jenny asked in a low voice, "What do you think of Christmas now?"

Her soft brown eyes seemed to try to see into his very soul. He'd never felt closer to her or more distant from her and that was crazy.

"I think Christmas is what we make it. We can't expect too much of it or we'll be disappointed."

She looked disappointed in what he'd said and he suddenly wished he could take it back. Because the truth was—this afternoon maybe he'd understood the true meaning of Christmas. Yet, if he'd told her that, he'd feel too damn vulnerable. And that was the last thing he wanted to feel around Jenny right now.

Jenny made her rounds of the horses almost every night before she turned in. It was a ritual that was necessary not only for her peace of mind, but for Silas's, too. They both had their favorites and that last check of the night told them all was well. Hank, Tate and Ben were always on the alert for problems, though they usually had an apple or carrot stick in their pocket for a bit of conversation with their favorite horse, too. Jenny's walk through the barns was a labor of love that sometimes cut into her sleeping time.

Tonight, however, she had a lot on her mind. The day had been brimming with emotion, from making cookies with Abby, watching her hang Olivia's ornament on the Christmas tree, to seeing the lights go on and everyone's response to them. Silas had been super quiet after his return home. Zack had seemed not so much remote as just very far away. Still, whenever their eyes met or their fingers brushed, the smoking hot electricity between them didn't quit. For her, the idea of his leaving again created an even deeper hole in her heart than the one he'd left so many years ago. She loved him now with a woman's love and still wasn't sure what that meant. Should she grab every moment she could with him? Should she go with him to California and leave the Rocky D? How could Silas ever manage without her?

Letting herself into Songbird's stall, lowering herself to the fresh straw, she asked the horse, who was her closest friend in the stable, "What should I do, Songbird?"

In a corner of the stall, Songbird munched from her feedbox. Jenny could *really* use a little input. When her horse's soft brown eyes seemed to study her with old-soul wisdom, Jenny asked, "You think I should grab love when I can, don't you?"

Songbird gave a soft whinny.

"And just where would that leave you if I took off for the luxurious life?"

She remembered the premiere and the paparazzi, the lights and the questions, the designer gowns and the glittering jewels.

The barn's night creaks and rustlings were interrupted by the outside door opening and then closing.

She hoped it was Zack. She stayed put, knowing if he wanted to find her, he would.

But it wasn't Zack who peeked over the stall. It was Silas. "I thought I'd find you here."

She pushed herself up from the straw. "I came out here to think."

"Accomplishing anything?"

"Not much."

"I bet all your thoughts surround my son."

"Most of them," she admitted. "Can I ask you something?"

"You know you can."

"You knew us both back then. If I had gone with Zack, do you think we would have made it? Do you think we'd still be together?"

Silas unlatched the stall door so Jenny could step out, then he closed it again. "Olivia and I talked about the two of you."

At Jenny's raised brows, he said, "We didn't fight *all* the time, in spite of the way Zack remembers it."

"What if I had left with him? What if I had found out I was pregnant after I was gone when we were together out there? Would he still have been so hell-bent against marriage? Would he have tried to be a father? Could I have been a good mother?"

"Whoa," Silas said, holding up both hands. "Let's take a bit broader look. Zack was determined to succeed so he could wipe my face in it...so he could see his mother's approval. If you had gone with him, I believe he would have wanted you to be part of that, whether a baby was in the mix or not. So then the question becomes—what would have happened through the hard years? Personally, I think you're just as determined as he is. I think you would have stood by him and become the kind of woman who knows how to hold a family together. That's what I believe, Jenny. Both of you have grit and motivation. I've seen it. And let's face it, you had a lot of feelings that needed a place to grow."

"I'm the one who spoiled everything. If I had taken the risk and said yes, I might have the child and family I'd always wanted."

"How would you have felt if Zack hadn't wanted to marry you, even with a baby? Out there, propriety isn't what it is here."

"I don't know how I would have dealt with that. I really don't know. I guess it would have depended if we were the substance of his life, or on the periphery of it...if he was there to promote himself and his career and the life he wanted to make, or if he was really there to take us along with him."

"See? You don't have the answers and you never will. The only way you'll have answers is to do something and take the consequences, whatever they are, and work with them."

As Silas studied her, she felt self-conscious. "What?" she asked.

"I know what you're worrying about."

"I have so many worries you couldn't even begin to count them."

"You know what I mean," he chided. "You're worried about *me*. You can't worry about me. I'm doing better each day. You have to go after what you want, Jenny, or it will slip right through your fingers. Regrets mount up and you want as few as possible when you get to my age."

"You're still young," she said, believing it.

"I'm still young enough to have some years left to enjoy. But I'm also old enough to see the end of my life. That puts perspective on everything. Have you heard whether your dad will be here for Christmas?"

Jenny's heart squeezed a little at the mention of her dad. "I have no idea. I know he has to make money to live on and that's what he's doing with his rodeo technique courses. But just one Christmas I'd love it if he put me first. Selfish, isn't it?"

"You deserve to be selfish. I can't believe you aren't bitter like Zack."

She jumped in quickly. "I don't think he's bitter anymore."

"But he's still leaving."

"I know."

"He's out with Dusty if you want to go to him."

She'd had no idea Zack was with Dusty, but maybe he didn't want to return to the silence of *his* room, either.

After she gave Silas a quick hug, she headed out of the barn.

Jenny found Zack sitting on top of the fence, even though a breeze whipped across the corral. Olivia's jingle bells sounded in the distance. Dusty stood about ten feet from Zack, nosing a clump of grass sticking out from a patch of snow. Had Zack been talking to Dusty the same way she'd been talking to Songbird? He said he was happy with his life. He said Christmas was what he made it.

As quietly as she could, she stepped outside of the barn and walked along the inside perimeter of the fence. Dusty knew her now and shouldn't be spooked by her presence. He lifted his head and eyed her, then returned to munching.

"It's a little cold to be communing with nature," she advised, the night chill already nipping her nose.

Zack's sheepskin collar was turned up and his gloved hands were jammed into his pockets. His Stetson rode low over his brow. The outside barn light barely reached them and his face was in shadows. "Dusty doesn't seem to mind the cold and I thought—" he gave a half shrug "—the winter air would clear my head."

"What are you trying to clear it of?" Her breath made a white puff as she spoke.

When his answer was a swish of the pines and a dark silence, she asked, "Of memories?"

He glanced at her and she felt a warm stirring in her belly. The temperature might be dipping into the thirties but the heat between them never ceased.

"It's odd," he said, looking away again, back at Dusty. "All these years, I thought I remembered everything exactly the way it was. But then today, finding Mom's ornament—" He shook his head as if he still couldn't clear it, as if he still couldn't see straight. "I remember the day Dad gave Mom that horse. His name was Quicksilver, a beautiful Appaloosa. I was fourteen and I remember videotaping her riding him. I think all those tapes are packed in the crawl space on the second floor."

"Maybe you need to watch them, to get the real picture of what your life was."

"I was a kid whose parents fought over my dad's affairs and gambling."

"But not all the time."

"Jeez, Jen, you see the world through rose-colored glasses."

She felt hurt by his comment and tried not to be. She tried to keep her face a mask because Zack was too good at reading her.

He climbed down off the fence a little too quickly and Dusty took a turn around the corral. Pulling off his gloves, Zack stuffed them into his pocket, then took her face between his palms. They felt warm against her cold cheeks. They felt warm because this was Zack and she wanted him to touch her.

"I don't know how you squeeze the best out of everything," he wondered. "You should be bitter about your mom dying, your dad leaving you for weeks at a time, a neighbor who looked after you not caring if there was decent food on the table. You were close to my mother and you lost her, too, yet somehow you remember the good about that and you've left the sadness behind."

Zack thought her leaving the past came naturally without a price. But that wasn't true. "Maybe I remember the good because I accepted feelings as they came. I was lonely and knew it. I felt abandoned and cried through it. I lost my mom and your mom but I didn't deny the grief. Ever since I've known you, Zack, you close down when you're in a situation that makes you feel lonely or uncomfortable or sad. You pack it all away and pretend it doesn't matter. It *does* matter. It will come back to haunt you if you don't live in the moment with it."

"So that's your secret? To live in the moment?"

"I try."

Dusty trotted by them and clomped into the stall that would give him protection against the weather.

As if the moment had gotten too intense, Zack dropped his hands from her face. They both turned to watch the horse.

"I think he's been spending more time in there," Jenny said. "That means he's beginning to feel safe here."

"He's fine as long as no one closes that stall door. If it's closed, he feels trapped."

Was that why Zack couldn't seem to settle in one place? Because if he did, he would feel trapped?

All at once, she was overwhelmed by the love she felt for him. If he was leaving in January, so be it. They had now and didn't now matter?

Closing the distance between their bodies, she looked up at him, reached out and stroked his beard stubble, the cleft in his jaw. "Maybe *we* should go inside, too."

His gaze filled with the desire she'd seen there before. She could feel the pulse in his jawline thumping under her fingers.

"Inside the house or inside the barn?" he prompted.

"The house is awfully far away."

Swinging her up into his arms, he carried her over the uneven ground and strode through the barn's back door to one of the empty stalls strewn with clean hay. The wind whistled in eaves and she heard the swish of Dusty's hooves as he shuffled around his stall.

Zack moved away and came back with a blanket to lay on the straw and another to cover them. Without thinking, Jenny removed her down parka then kept her gaze on Zack as he removed his sheepskin jacket. Watching each other undress was a turn-on, much different from their wild desire on the beach in Malibu, their fast and furious lovemaking that had been more instinct than forethought.

When Zack lay down beside her, she didn't hurry to remove his sweater. Rather, she gazed into his eyes as she ran her hands over him.

He swallowed hard, then in a husky voice said, "You don't get to have all the fun."

His large hands mirrored what she was doing to him until his palms settled on her breasts, until he ran them over her nipples, until she wanted their clothes off as fast as they'd discarded them in his sunroom. But he'd taken his cue from her and Zack wasn't hurrying this time. No, apparently this time, his aim was optimal pleasure.

When he leaned in to kiss her, she was surrounded by the outdoor scent of pine and cold air, the earthy scent of Zack himself. His lips took a slow tour of hers and his tongue eased into her mouth. She clenched a fistful of his heavy sweater, the wool coarse against her palm. At first she thought about their tryst in the hayloft when they were only eighteen, but past memories soon gave way to new ones. Zack was a complicated man now. His passion aged and deepened by experience. Hers rippled under the surface until he kissed her or touched her and brought it hungrily to life.

When he broke away for a moment, she rubbed her nose into his neck and breathed in his scent. Everything about him was wondrously familiar yet different, too. Although he seemed to be in no hurry, she wanted him to need like she did, wanted him to feel restless and hot until their joining was necessary for him to live. She released her grip on his sweater and slid her hand below his waist. He was hard and huge and she rubbed her fingers against his fly until he groaned. He captured her mouth once again and ravished it with his desire. After that, he quickly unsnapped her jeans and she unbelted his. He shucked off his boots while she tugged off hers. They didn't speak because they had nothing to say. They'd gone over it all. They didn't want to debate or argue. They wanted to make love.

Have sex? a little voice asked her. But she ignored it. At this moment, both were one and the same. Maybe later… Later slid into the same place as doubts and worries and consequences. This time Zack protected her. This time she saw something in his eyes that gave her hope.

After he slid on the condom, he stretched out on his back and pulled her on top of him. "You ride," he said. "The straw can poke through the blanket. I don't want it to scratch you."

That had happened before. She'd had red streaks all over her back. He was protecting her and she loved that about him. Had he forgiven her for choosing a life here at the Rocky D? Had he forgiven her for not telling him about the baby?

She hoped so. Oh, how she hoped so.

They were both naked from the waist down. He slid his hands under her sweater and gripped her hips. She lowered herself onto him slowly, taking him in, closing her eyes, holding her breath. She began moving up and down and his hands caressed her as she did. They rocked together, their pace increasing as the heat built. Before, *ecstasy* had merely been a word in the dictionary. Now, it was a reality, wrapping itself around her, bringing a flush to her cheeks and a trembling to her limbs. Her climax was so sudden, blinding and earth-shaking that she felt her voice shatter as she called his name. He climaxed moments later and shuddered as she leaned forward to hold him. Clinging to each other, Jenny realized what living in the moment meant.

Living in the moment was wonderful until the moment passed. After the moment passed, she had to make a crucial decision about the rest of her life.

Chapter Twelve

Jenny had spent the night in Zack's room. It had been a wonderful night of being held...of being loved. At least that's the way she'd seen it. They hadn't talked. They'd just kissed and sighed and touched and groaned with the pleasure they could give each other. But the night had been about more than pleasure. She'd slipped out of bed before Zack to go down to the barn to do the overseeing that she did every morning, making sure the Rocky D was ready for the day. Then...

She'd felt the slight cramping. She'd taken a break, gone to the bathroom and found...her period. She had to tell Zack, but she needed to absorb the idea of not being pregnant first...had to tamp down her disappointment that should have been relief.

She couldn't keep the questions from running through her head. After their loving last night, would

Zack still leave after New Year's? Would he ask her to go with him? *Could* she leave the Rocky D? But the one that bothered her most was the one concerning Zack and how he felt about marriage. She'd always dreamed of marriage and a family. She wanted them both together. She wanted to do it right.

But if Zack couldn't commit to forever...

She and Hank were saddling up two of the horses to exercise them in the arena when Zack came into the barn, his expression worried.

What she'd love was a morning kiss and a hug. What she'd like was to put her arms around Zack and ask him what was wrong. But with Hank standing there, they couldn't seem to be free with each other.

"Can you come up to the house?" Zack asked.

"Problem?" she inquired, knowing there was even before the question popped out.

"Dad wants to talk to us."

Hank took the horse's reins from her hands. "I'll take care of Jiggs."

With a "thanks," she reluctantly let go of the reins, then followed Zack. Once outside the arena, she stole a glance at him as they walked. "Is your dad okay?" *Are you okay?* she wanted to add.

"I'm not sure. He has this look of grim determination on his face and we're meeting in his study, so this is formal."

"He seemed quiet yesterday."

"I know. I was going to spend some time with him last night but—" He cut off abruptly.

But they'd met in the barn. They'd made love in the barn, and then all night long. Did Silas know they were together? Is that what this meeting was about? She was so aware of Zack beside her, his brooding intensity, his sheer physical presence. He hadn't worn a jacket. His thick, navy sweater made her want to burrow into his chest. His quick strides made her want to shout, *Stop, let's talk about last night.* His black hair blowing in the wind made her want to run her hand through it, not just for today, but for tomorrow and all the tomorrows to come. But Zack's tomorrows, at least for the next few months, consisted of traveling and interviews and production meetings and a movie he wanted to make. Where could she possibly fit into that?

Maybe he was wondering the same thing. Because suddenly, he wasn't on the move. He was stopping, stepping closer, sliding his hand under her hair, bringing her to him for a kiss. It was a long, heated, deep kiss that reminded her of the closeness they'd had last night. But then he was leaning away and saying, "Let's go find out what this meeting's about."

Silas sat in his wood-paneled study, not looking as imposing as he once did behind the huge mahogany desk. With a no-nonsense business look on his face, he motioned to the two leather club chairs.

"Have a seat," he said. "There's something I need to say to the both of you."

Jenny couldn't tell from Silas's expression or the way he looked at her and Zack what this was about. Over the years she'd had hundreds of meetings with Silas in this room. But none of them were quite as formidable as this one seemed to be. A chill ran up her spine and she wanted to take Zack's hand for support. But he stood ramrod straight, waiting for her to be seated before he was. She sank down onto the chair, rather wishing she could stand. Zack seemed to be feeling the same way because it took him a few moments before he lowered himself into the chair.

Silas folded his hands on the desk blotter, as if he needed some kind of calming gesture, too. Then he cleared his throat. Finally he said, "I've received an offer for the Rocky D that I have to consider."

Jenny felt a gasp escape her lips, as if she'd been punched in the solar plexus. Zack had gone motionless, just staring at Silas in silence.

"A businessman from Houston wants to develop the land into a retirement village."

Silas's words hung in the air and Jenny couldn't seem to find a response.

But Zack did. His voice tight, he said, "I didn't think you'd ever want to sell."

"I don't see that I have a choice." Silas sounded weary and defeated as he went on, "I can't act like an owner anymore, driving to sales, keeping up with the latest breeding techniques, training yearlings myself."

"That's nonsense!" Zack protested. "You're recovering from your heart attack. You can do whatever you want to do. You're still young." He said it forcefully, as if his energy could somehow instill in Silas hope for the future.

"Maybe I'm just plain tired. The doc says I should reduce stress. Maybe I want to slow down. Maybe the dreams I have for the future have nothing to do with the Rocky D."

"What are those dreams?" Zack asked, as if he had the right to know.

"I want to spend more time with Anna. I don't want to worry if we've got red ink on the books. I don't want to worry if I'm overburdening Jenny, or taking advantage of the hands, or simply not doing everything I need to do. That heart attack made me see everything in a different light."

His gaze came to rest affectionately on Jenny. "I'm not going to leave you out in the cold. I would never do that." He lifted a piece of paper from his desk and slid it across to her. "Brock Winchester owns a place near Sedona. His foreman is retiring. I told him about you and he's interested in bringing you in. You'll have to interview with him, but I don't think there's any doubt that he'll like your résumé."

Her résumé. Leaving the Rocky D...like this. Retirement cottages or condos sitting on the land she loved.

"You can't sell the ranch as it is? Where will the horses go? Songbird and Tattoo and Dusty?" she asked with real fear in her voice.

"To sell this place as it is would take too long. I'd need somebody with money to burn. Somebody who didn't want to turn the ranch into a breeding factory rather than the place it is. I'd rather find good homes for all the horses, or give them away, than see that happen. And Songbird is yours, wherever you go."

She supposed she would like to see all the horses placed in good homes, too, with people who would love them. But still—

Suddenly, the door chime reverberated through the house.

Silas stood. "I know I've given you both a lot to think about. We'll talk about this again in a few days. Mr. Lowery is going to fly up here next week and he can answer all your questions. We're thinking about making the transaction final by the end of March." Silas targeted Zack. "But with you leaving, I wanted him here before Christmas."

Martha came to Silas's study door and peeked in. "I don't want to interrupt, but Jenny and Zack, you have visitors. The Larson family is here."

Silas motioned Jenny and Zack out of the den. "Go on," he said. "We're done here for now."

Jenny still felt shell-shocked when she and Zack entered the living room and found Stan, Helen, Tanya and Michael waiting. Helen had called to cancel their lesson on Saturday because they were driving to Phoenix. The two adults looked uncomfortable, but the kids wore smiles.

"We didn't mean to intrude," Stan said right away. "But we wanted to say goodbye."

"We're moving tomorrow!" Michael announced, re-adjusting his backpack on his shoulders and approaching Zack. "Tanya and I are gonna have our own rooms and everything."

Stan added, "After we got to Phoenix, your friend, Mr. Barrett, showed us a few places he thought would be suitable. Once we really get on our feet again we'll look for a house. But in the meantime, we found a townhouse that will be perfect."

Helen crossed to Jenny and gave her a hug. "Thank you so much for everything you've done."

"I'm going to miss you," Jenny said, her voice catching. She was going to miss them, but she was going to miss so much more, too, if Silas sold the Rocky D. This family was heading toward their future, something better for all of them. But she didn't know what was ahead for her, and as she took a glance at Zack there were no answers there.

Obviously putting aside what Silas had told them—maybe it was easier for him than for her—Zack said to Michael and Tanya, "Come with me. I want to show you that project I was working on."

The two kids exchanged a glance and then grinned. "I thought you forgot," Michael whispered to Zack in an aside that Jenny could hear.

"Not a chance."

The two kids ran down the hall after him.

Jenny found out more about where the Larsons would be living. They really did seem happy as Stan slipped his arm around his wife's waist. "Mr. Barrett told us he went to school with both you and Mr. Decker. He seems like a great guy. I mean, he owns this construction company, yet he acted like I was his equal."

"Dawson remembers where he came from."

They were talking about everything the kids would love about Phoenix when Zack, Michael and Tanya came back into the room, Michael swinging his backpack happily. They all wore smiles, though now Zack's seemed a bit forced.

Ten minutes later, the Larsons were gone and it was just Zack and Jenny standing in the living room. "You did a wonderful thing for them," Jenny said again.

Zack was sober. "Michael and Tanya told me they're going to miss their friends, but then Michael added his parents have stopped fighting. That's huge for a kid."

She knew how huge that would have been for Zack. How his ideas of marriage would have been so different if his parents had had a different relationship.

Zack checked his watch as if the conversation had gotten too uncomfortable, or as if he wanted to shut it down before it did. "I have to make a few calls."

"Zack, we have to talk."

"I think we should wait until what Dad told us sinks in."

"It's already sunk in. If he does this, the Rocky D will be no more."

Zack's jaw tightened and his shoulders squared. "Don't you think I realize that? I grew up here, Jenny. I learned to ride here. I gentled my first horse here. I shot my first video here."

He'd first kissed her here, too. "Then you do care if he sells the ranch?"

"I care. But I don't know if that means anything to him. I don't know if it changes anything for me. Are you going to try to convince him not to sell?"

"Only *you* can do that. You're the heir."

"The heir? I haven't thought of myself as that for years. You're more of a daughter to him than I've ever been a son. If you want to stay, then you need to convince him not to sell. Here, you're like a daughter. Somewhere else you'll be an employee."

"Do you want me to convince him so you don't lose the Rocky D?"

When Zack didn't answer, she just shook her head. "You say you love traveling. But I'm not so sure you like wandering any more than I do. If the sale of the Rocky D bothers you, have you asked yourself why?"

"Memories of my mother are here," he said gruffly. "Memories of you and our friends are here. I hate to think we'll lose who we once were to a retirement village."

"Are you telling yourself you wouldn't feel as bad if Silas were selling the Rocky D as is to someone who wanted to keep it going?"

"It wouldn't be destroyed."

"No, but it would be changed. No one will handle the Rocky D like your dad."

"Before this visit I might have said that was a good thing. Now, I'm not so sure."

Jenny couldn't wait any longer to tell him what she needed to tell him but didn't want to tell him. "I'm not pregnant. I got my period."

Again he kept silent and Jenny knew Zack did that when he wanted to withdraw, when he didn't want to show anyone his feelings. He was so good at not showing anyone his feelings.

Finally, he said, "That's for the best."

His calm and stoicism lit her anger. "For the best? For who? For you? So you don't have to think about ties and commitment and what you really feel?"

His voice gentled as he asked, "Jenny, would you really want to have a baby this way?"

"What way? You mean without marriage? Without vows? Without a white dress and a picket fence? Maybe I'll take a baby any way I can get one. Maybe I want your baby more than I want anything. But you're leaving after the New Year and you're going to treat *us* like an affair that never should have happened. I get it, Zack. You just don't want the strings. Or if you want any strings, you want them to be all on your terms."

She felt tears pushing against her eyes and she would *not* cry in front of him. She *would not*. The idea of losing Zack's baby and the Rocky D all in one day was just too much. "I have work to do in the barn." She started for the door.

"Jenny."

But she couldn't turn back. She couldn't look at him

and not ache so deep down in her heart. She didn't know if she'd ever be without the pain again.

"Go make your calls, Zack. I'm going to spend as much time with the horses as I can, *while* I can."

Then she was through the kitchen and out the back door before Zack could come after her. There would be no point in him coming after her…because he simply didn't love her the way she loved him.

Zack had never felt so unsettled in his life. The foundation of his world seemed to be breaking apart and he didn't understand it one bit. His life wasn't here anymore, at the Rocky D. He'd been happy in California before he'd come.

Hadn't he?

Or had a sense of restlessness nagged at him often the past couple of years? Had he buried himself in his work because the rest of his life was so barren? When Jenny had revealed she wasn't pregnant, why had he suddenly felt the same way he had the night she'd told him about her miscarriage? Shaken up, different, wondering what his purpose was in being on this earth.

His movies had always been his purpose. If they weren't enough anymore—

He rambled through the ranch house, memories from his life here floating back in every room. Maybe he needed to purge himself of them. That was all. Then his father's selling the Rocky D wouldn't mean anything.

The house was large. As he stepped into each room, he let movies play in his mind—his mother telling him stories and reading him books, her joy in arranging fresh roses in each room, her care in choosing furniture, decorations and the menu Martha would make. He even remembered times when she and his father had their heads together over a magazine, when they'd held hands walking to the barn, when they'd gone riding together on moonlit nights. They'd once loved each other deeply. Maybe his father just hadn't known how to express it, or hadn't felt worthy of it. Maybe as he grew older, he grew more desperate to reclaim his youth. Zack didn't know when he had forgiven his father for his weaknesses. Maybe when he'd seen him lying in that hospital bed. Maybe when Jenny had pointed out his mother had made her own decisions and poor choices. Maybe when Zack realized his own life wasn't what he wanted it to be. Jenny had seemed to understand that. She seemed to understand his ties to the Rocky D were stronger than he ever imagined.

Where *would* she go if his father sold the Rocky D? To a ranch in Sedona? Would she come to California with him? Yet he didn't want her doing that by default. Had he wanted her to choose him over his father and the land she loved? Had he wanted her to choose him without conditions? Rambling from room to room only made the churning in his chest more tumultuous.

Maybe he needed a session with Dusty. Maybe he just needed to escape the claustrophobic feeling that seemed to be hemming him in.

Jenny was in the mares' barn when she heard a noise—a noise that didn't belong. At first she thought it was the wind or the door banging, maybe a branch dislodged from a tree that had blown against one of the buildings. But then she heard it again...and a chill shivered up her spine. She'd been grooming one of the mares, trying to calm her turmoil, trying to make decisions with her head, along with her heart.

But nothing was clear. Nothing felt right. So she'd gotten into the rhythm of brushing and just concentrated on that. Now she slipped out of the stall, latched the door and ran to the side entrance.

The pounding was louder and she knew exactly where it was coming from—hooves against a stall door. Without a thought for anything but Dusty, she ran to the rescue barn, letting the wind whip around her, under her vest. She was barely mindful of the snow beginning to fall. The temperature was supposed to plummet tonight, and with the wind chill... She suspected exactly what had happened. One of the hands had thought he was being kind and instead he'd caused a disaster. Dusty needed his freedom as well as kindness. Maybe that's why he and Zack understood each other so well.

The banging became louder, more desperate. Jenny was afraid for Dusty...afraid he would do irreparable damage to himself. He'd been hurt so badly in the past. She couldn't bear to see him hurt again.

As snowflakes settled on the arms of her sweater, she didn't think. She just felt for the horse and the panic that had probably overtaken him. Since Dusty had been going into his stall more often, one of the hands must have thought they'd do him a kindness and close him in there for the night against the cold, against the wind, against the snow. But Dusty was afraid to be closed in, afraid someone would hurt him while he was there.

Running into the barn, Jenny called Dusty's name. He was kicking the outside stall door with all of his frantic desperation.

Jenny knew she had to get to that outside door and

open it. Her boots sliding on the icy walkway, she rushed to the outside entrance to the corral and pushed open the door. She reached Dusty's outside stall door and called to him again as her fingers fumbled on the latch.

Then it was open. But the force of wrenching it free made her slip on a patch of snow. She groped for something to hold on to. There was nothing there. Her legs went out from under her and she fell as Dusty reared up, his hooves hovering over her.

Zack heard the banging as soon as he'd stepped outside the house. Jogging to the corral, he climbed the fence in time to see Jenny unlatch Dusty's stall door. His heart jumped into his throat as she slipped and fell. He'd never been so afraid in his entire life, never felt so helpless or powerless, never realized his whole life was wrapped around one blonde woman who had held his heart since high school.

"Jenny, *roll!* Oh, my God, roll!"

At the sound of Zack's voice, Dusty rotated on his hind legs. Zack's body thrummed with adrenaline and his thoughts skidded around his head until only one was very clear—if anything ever happened to Jenny his world would collapse. He raced to her, ready to protect her however he could.

Dusty's hooves hit the ground about a foot from Jenny's shoulder. As he galloped past them, Zack wrapped his arms around her, breathing hard, holding her close, so grateful for a second chance to do what he should have done fifteen years ago.

Jenny had held his heart all this time and now he wanted to hold hers. He wanted to keep her by his side for the rest of his life. In that one terrifying, unforgettable moment when Dusty had reared up, he'd known he deeply loved Jenny Farber. And he'd never love anyone else. At that moment he'd known all of his excuses, all of his pride, were simply defenses against being vulnerable.

Now, he'd never felt so vulnerable.

He pulled away, only far enough away to ask, "Are you okay? Are you hurt?"

"No," she said as breathless as he was, and he wondered if she could read in his eyes what he was feeling. Since he didn't know if she could, he had to make it clear.

He kissed her. With snow swirling around, with the wind blowing, he held her tight and let his lips and tongue tell her everything he didn't know if he could put into words.

But she pulled away, looked up at him and said, "I'm okay, Zack, really."

She sounded confused, maybe by everything that had happened, maybe by his kiss.

"I love you, Jenny."

Her eyes widened and he thought he heard a small gasp.

"When I saw you fall, when I thought of you getting hurt. When I even entertained the possibility I could lose you, I knew then I was being a stupid fool. I came home for the reunion because you called...because you said you needed me. But when I saw you, I couldn't forget what had happened, couldn't forgive, couldn't understand."

"I should have gone with you," she said. "I should have trusted you."

"You'd had no experience trusting a man's word. We were young. We didn't know where life was going to lead. And I shouldn't have been so full of myself as to expect you to run off with me. Not after the childhood you'd had."

"Zack, I loved you. I really did. When I lost your baby I didn't know if I'd ever get over it. I tried so hard to forget you. I tried so hard to build a life here without you. But when you came back, I really had no defenses. It didn't take me long to realize I'd fallen in love with you all over again."

"This time everything's going to be different," he told her. "I'm going to move my editing studio here. I'm going to convince Dad not to sell the Rocky D and let the two of us run it. I *do* want to continue to make movies and I'll have to be on location. But you can come with me if you want and I will always come home. Although I've tried to deny it all these years, Miners Bluff *is* my home. More important, *you* are my home. If Dad's determined to sell, I'll buy the ranch."

"Zack, are you sure? Because if you want to live in California, I'll go with you. I love you. You are my home, too."

"We have a lot of talking to do. We'll work it out. But whatever we decide, we'll be together. And not just together." He took her face between his palms. "Jenny Farber, will you marry me?"

"You said…"

"I said a lot of things. But now I'm feeling a lot more. I understand what vows mean. I understand the type of commitment you need. I need it, too. I want you to be my wife and I want to be your husband. And then I want to have lots of kids."

She was crying now, and he felt his throat tightening up and his eyes burning. Not from the cold, either, but from the emotion he'd been trying to deny for so long. He buried his nose in her hair. "I have to get you inside before you turn into an icicle."

She laughed and wrapped her arms around his neck. "Not before I give you an answer. I *will* marry you, Zack Decker. And I will always be your home."

He kissed her again as the snow swirled around them, as Dusty took another run around the corral, as their love enveloped them and Christmas bells jingled on the barn door.

Epilogue

Zack paced in his father's study, checking his watch. "He said he'd be here."

"The weather's bad, son. He might be having trouble on these roads. He still has half an hour."

This Christmas Eve, when his father called him "son," Zack felt like one. Maybe because he'd found the love he'd always needed, the love he never thought he'd have. Now, with Jenny's help, he'd found a different perspective on his father and on his childhood. He and his dad finally seemed to understand each other. After much discussion, he and Jenny had decided to live at the Rocky D most of the year and use his house in Malibu as a getaway. Silas could keep his hand in the ranch if he wanted, but he could retire if he didn't. The upside for him was that he could still live in the house on the land he loved, the house and land they all loved.

"This is why I didn't tell Jenny I called him. I didn't want her to be disappointed," Zack said.

"You did what you could. The rest was up to him."

There was commotion in the hall. Friends and family were arriving and taking seats in the living room where their wedding ceremony would take place. Mikala, Celeste and Abby were down the hall with Jenny, helping her get dressed.

Clay peered in the door of the study. "I think someone's here to see you."

Charlie Farber walked in, his suit a bit mussed and wrinkled, but presentable. "I got here as soon as I could," he said breathlessly. "The road from Sedona to Flagstaff was closed and I had to take the long way around." He went over to Zack and extended his hand. "I know I congratulated you on the phone, but I want to do it again. And I want to thank you for calling me. I know Jenny didn't because she didn't want to ask me to come and then be disappointed."

"You're here," Silas assured Charlie. "That's what matters. I offered to walk your daughter down the aisle when she told me she and Zack were getting married. But she's independent. She assured me she'd be giving herself away."

"I have no right to play any part in this," Charlie muttered. "I'll just be grateful if she doesn't throw me out. Can I see her now?"

"This way," Zack directed, leaving Silas's study and going down the hall with Charlie following.

Jenny was getting dressed in one of the spare bedrooms. When he knocked on the door, Celeste opened it, all smiles. "Hey, Zack. She's almost ready." Then she saw Charlie. She nodded her approval to Zack and called to Jenny, "Someone's here to see you. We'll be down the hall waiting for you." Zack had alerted Jenny's friends that Charlie might be coming.

Mikala exited the room along with Abby and Celeste, and Charlie went in.

One minute Jenny's bridesmaids had been flitting all around her, then the next—

She was facing her father. Her hand went to her mouth. "Daddy!"

"Hi, baby," he said approaching her. "You look beautiful. I've never seen a prettier bride."

Jenny had felt so special as soon as she'd tried on this gown. It was satin and lace with long sleeves, and a ruffled lace hem that fell into a train. Her headpiece was a very feminine version of a Stetson with tulle, lace flowers and beading.

Her father said, "I'd give you a hug but I don't want to mess you up."

Seeing his hesitancy, she hugged him, tears brimming in her eyes. "I'm so glad you decided to spend Christmas with us. I'm so glad you're here."

"I can't take credit on my own. Zack called me. He found me and told me about the wedding. I assured him nothing would keep me away. I haven't been a very good father to you, Jenny, but from the first time I saw you with Zack I knew there was something special between you—something special like your mom and I had."

"Will you stay for Christmas?"

"Aren't you and Zack going on a honeymoon?"

"We're not leaving until New Year's Eve. Everything happened so fast. We decided to stay and spend the holidays with Silas and our friends and then go to

Zack's condo in Vail. We didn't want to go too far away in case Silas needs us. How long can you stay?"

"As long as you want me here."

"You don't have to be somewhere?"

"Just here, seeing my girl get hitched. Silas tells me you're going to walk yourself down the aisle."

"I am."

"Good for you. Now I'd better get out there so I get a good seat."

"Since Zack called you, I'm sure he reserved you a place in the front row. Oh, Daddy, thank you for coming." She hugged him again.

When he kissed her on the cheek, he murmured, "Be happy, baby." Then in a stronger voice, he added, "You deserve it." He opened the door and stepped into the hall.

She'd hardly had time to recover from her surprise when Zack came in. "Are you okay?"

She and Zack had already agreed that they would make their own traditions and that his seeing her before the wedding wouldn't bring them anything but good luck. "I'm more than okay." She flung her arms around his neck. "Thank you. Every girl wants her dad at her wedding. And you've made it happen for me."

"I want to make a lot of things happen for you…for us. I have something for you."

"I don't need anything but your love."

The night Zack had proposed to her had been the most wonderful night of her life. He'd told her exactly how he felt that night. He'd risked his pride and made himself vulnerable. After he'd kissed her senseless, they'd checked on Dusty, making sure he hadn't hurt himself in his desperate attempt to escape his stall. In between making plans to get married, telling Silas and calling their friends, they'd checked on him. By morning he'd sought the shelter of the stall again, but this time with the door wide open.

Jenny loved the diamond she and Zack picked out together and the beautiful band that went with it. She couldn't imagine what Zack was bringing her now. He'd removed something from his inside tuxedo pocket. It was a velvet box.

When he opened the box, her breath caught. She recognized the beautiful pearls with the diamond and sapphire clasp. They had belonged to his mother. Tonight when she'd put on the pearl earrings Olivia had given her, she could feel Zack's mother's presence.

"My mother would want you to have these," he said. "Turn around and I'll put them on you."

Jenny turned and faced the mirror over the dresser. The pearls were a special wedding keepsake and she'd treasure them forever. The necklace meant the world to her and her eyes filled with tears again.

"Don't cry," Zack murmured as he secured the necklace and turned her into his arms.

"They're happy tears," she assured him.

Zack tipped up her chin. "I want to make you happy for the rest of our lives."

"And I want to do the same for you."

Zack's kiss spun her into a passion-filled future where their dreams would all come true.

* * * * *

PROPOSAL AT THE LAZY S RANCH

PATRICIA THAYER

To Timothy Paul Brooks, Jr.

You were too young to leave us,
but you'll never be forgotten.

RIP Timmy.
March 19, 1990-February 26, 2013

CHAPTER ONE

SHE WAS A COWARD.

Josefina Slater jumped into her BMW and drove away from the Lazy S Ranch, her childhood home. Before she'd left California two days ago for Montana, she'd told herself she would be able to come back here and help with her father's recovery from a stroke. But when she'd arrived at the house and saw her older sister, Ana, she found she wasn't ready to face Colton Slater, or her past.

When Josie had arrived at the ranch house and was greeted by her older sister, Ana, she froze right there on the spot. She needed more time. She told her sister she wasn't ready and got back into her car and started driving. To where, she had no idea.

She'd grown up here on the ranch with a man who didn't want the daughters Lucia Slater left behind when she walked out. Outside of her siblings, her twin, Tori, and older sister, Ana, and younger sister, Marissa, there hadn't been much else to keep her here. This was Josie's first time back in nearly ten years.

About two miles down the road, she opened the window. The air was brisk, reminding her that winter was fast approaching. With the quiet hum of the engine mingled with soft music from the radio, she finally started to relax.

She glanced out the windshield at the rolling green pastures that seemed to go on for miles and was framed by the scenic Rocky Mountains. Tall pines covered the slopes as the majestic peaks reached upward to the incredible blue sky.

Quite a different landscape from her home in Los Angeles, or her life. Success in her career as an event planner came with a lot of hard work and little sleep. Except she'd been told if she didn't stop her hectic pace, her health could be in serious trouble. To help ease her stress, her doctor suggested she take time off. Tori, her twin sister and partner in Slater Style, had been the one who'd insisted she come back here to the ranch and try to relax.

Sure, returning here was going to ease her stress. Right. She couldn't even get through the front door.

Her grip tightened on the steering wheel. No. she wouldn't let Colt Slater turn her back into that insecure little girl. She shook her head. "Not again." She wouldn't let any man do that to her.

She continued to drive down the road until she could see part of the Big Hole River. Memories flooded her head, reminding her how she and her sisters used to sneak off and swim there. That brought a smile to her lips. It was also where Ana was building the new lodge along with some small fishing cabins. They'd hoped to add income to help the other problem, the Lazy S's struggling finances.

Curiosity had Josie turning off onto a dirt road and driving the half mile to where several trucks were parked. She pulled in next to a crew cab pickup that had GT Construction embossed on the side.

Why not check out the progress? Anything to delay her going back to the house. She climbed out, glad she'd worn her jeans and boots, and pulled her lined jacket closer to her body, shielding her from the late-October weather.

Feeling excitement for the project she'd helped create

with Ana, she headed across the grass toward the river to observe the progress of the two-story log cabin structure taking shape about thirty yards from the water's edge.

"Good job, Ana," she breathed into the cool autumn breeze.

Suddenly someone called out, but before she could turn around she felt something hit her in the back, sending her flying. Josie let out a cry as she hit the hard ground.

Garrett Temple felt pain shoot through his body as he cradled the small woman under him. It took a few breaths to get his lungs working from the impact, but at least he'd kept her from getting hit by the lumber truck. He managed to roll off her as his men started to gather around.

"I didn't see her, boss," Jerry said as he leaned over them. "You okay?"

Garrett nodded, but his attention was on the still woman facedown on the grass. He knelt beside the petite body and traced over her for any broken bones or visible injuries.

"You want me to call the paramedics?" someone asked.

"Give me a minute," Garrett said as he gently brushed back the long whiskey-colored hair from her face. He froze as recognition hit him. The olive skin, the delicate jawline, long dark lashes. He knew that underneath those closed lids were mesmerizing blue eyes. His heart began to pound even more rapidly. "Josie?"

She groaned, and he said her name again. "Josie. Can you hear me?"

With another groan, she started to raise her head. He stopped her, but caught a whiff of her familiar scent. Hell, how could he remember what she smelled like? He drew back, already feeling the familiar pull to this woman. It had been nearly ten years.

She rolled to one side.

"Take it easy," he told her. "Do you hurt anywhere?"

"My chest," she whispered. "Hard to breathe."

"You got the wind knocked out of you."

She blinked and finally opened her eyes, and he was hit with her rich blue gaze. She looked confused, and then said, "Garrett?"

He rose to his knees. "Hello, Josie."

Josie felt as if she were in a dream. Garrett Temple? It couldn't be... She blinked again, suddenly realizing it was reality. She pushed him away, sat up and groaned at the pounding in her head. "What are you doing here?"

He didn't look any happier to see her. "Trying to save your neck."

"Like I need your help for anything." She glanced up and saw several men peering at them. "I'm fine." She brushed off her sweater and jeans, trying to act as if nothing was wrong. "I just need a minute."

The crew didn't move away until Garrett stepped in. "Everyone, this is Ana Slater's sister Josie."

The guys mumbled a quick greeting, and then headed back to their jobs.

Once alone, Josie turned to the man she'd never expected to see again. The man who'd smashed all her dreams and the last person she needed to see right now.

"Do you hurt anywhere?" he asked again.

A broken heart. "No, I'm fine," she lied. Her ankle was suddenly killing her.

Garrett got to his feet and reached down to offer her some help. She got up under her own power, trying to ignore her light-headedness and her throbbing ankle.

"Still as stubborn as ever, I see."

She glared at the large man. He was well over six feet. Nothing had changed in the looks department, either. He was still handsome with all that black wavy hair, not a bald spot in view. Her attention went to his mouth to see that sexy grin, and her stomach tightened in awareness. Well, dang it. She wasn't going to let him get to her again.

She tested some weight on her tender ankle. Not good. "I know why I'm here," she began, "but…why are you?"

He folded his muscular arms over his wide chest. So he'd filled out from the thin boy she once knew in high school.

"I own GT Construction. Ana hired me."

No. Her sister wouldn't do that. Not when she knew how much Garrett had hurt and humiliated her. "We'll see about that." She started to walk off but her ankle couldn't hold her weight and she started to fall.

"Whoa." He caught her in his arms. Big strong arms. "You are hurt."

"No, I just twisted my ankle. I'll be fine when I get back to the ranch."

"You aren't going anywhere until I get you checked out."

"You're not doing anything—" She gasped as he swung her up into his arms as if she were a child. "Put me down," she demanded, but he only drew her closer and she had no choice but to slip her arm around his neck to keep her balance.

He carried her the short distance to his truck. One of the men rushed over and opened the passenger door. Garrett set her down in the seat.

"You can't kidnap me, Garrett." He was so close to her, she could inhale that so-familiar scent of the man she'd once loved more than anything. "Just take me home."

He shook his head. "You were hurt on my construction site, so I'm responsible for you. We're going to the E.R. first, then I'll take you back to the ranch."

She started to speak, but the door got shut in her face.

A few minutes later, he appeared in the driver's seat. He handed her purse to her. "You might want to call your sister and tell her where you're going."

"No. She'll get all worried and she has enough on her mind." She stole a glance at the man beside her, unable to stop studying his profile. Okay, so she was curious about him, darn it. "What about my car?"

"I'll have one of the men drive it back to the house."

She folded her arms over her chest.

Garrett started the engine and began to back up, then headed for the highway. "Josie...maybe this would be a good chance to talk."

She glared at him. "What could we possibly have to say to each other, Garrett? I got the message nine years ago when you said, 'Sorry Josie, I'm going to marry someone else.'" She hated that his words still hurt. "So don't waste any more words."

Josie managed to fight back tears. She had to concentrate on getting through this time with a man who broke her heart once. She wasn't going to let it happen again, so she decided to head back to Los Angeles as soon as possible.

An hour later at the emergency room in Dillon, Garrett sat with Josie while they waited for the doctor. Even in the silly gown they had her put on, she still looked good. There was no denying that seeing her again had affected him, more than he thought possible.

From the moment when he noticed Josie Slater in Royerton High School and saw her big blue eyes, he'd been a goner. They'd been a couple all through school, even after he graduated and went off to college. Josie finished high school and went to college locally two years later. Then one weekend he'd come home to tell her about his apprenticeship. They had a big fight about him being gone all summer, and they broke up. Josie refused to talk to him for months. Then he met Natalie....

Now all these years later, Josie was back here. Seeing her today had been harder than he could imagine. But her reaction toward him was a little hard to take. He didn't have to worry about her having any leftover feelings for him.

Garrett stood outside of the cubicle and the curtain was drawn as the doctor examined Josie.

"So, Ms. Slater," the doctor began, "you're getting a nasty bruise on your forehead." There was silence for a moment, and the middle-aged man continued, "You're lucky. It doesn't seem you have a concussion."

Grateful, Garrett sagged against the wall, knowing he shouldn't eavesdrop, but he still listened for more information.

"I want you to take it easy today," the doctor told her. "Your ankle is swollen, but the X-ray didn't show any broken bones. But you'll need to put ice on it." He paused. "Do you take any medications?"

Garrett heard Josie rattle off a few. He recognized one was for anxiety and the other for sleeping. What was wrong with her?

The doctor came out from behind the curtain. "She'll be fine, although she'll have some bruises."

"Thank you, Doctor."

He nodded. "Just make sure she rests today and have her stay off her feet."

"I will."

The doctor walked away, and Garrett called, "You decent?"

"Yes," she grumbled.

He went behind the curtain and found her sitting on

the bed, not looking happy. "I got a clean bill of health, so can we go home?"

He nodded, suddenly wishing she was home. But he had a feeling that Josie was headed back to California real soon, and he'd lose her for the second time.

It was another forty minutes before Garrett pulled up in front of the Slater home. Josie's pulse started racing once again as she looked up at the big two-story brown house with the white trim. It was a little faded and the porch needed some work. So a lot of things around the ranch hadn't been cared for in a while.

Garrett got out of the truck and walked around to her side. He pulled the crutches out of the back, but propped them against the side of the truck as he reached in and scooped her into his arms. Instead of setting her down on the ground, he carried her toward the house.

"Hey, I can do this myself."

"It's crazy to struggle with these steps when I can get you in the house faster."

She wasn't going to waste the effort to argue. Soon she'd be inside and he'd be gone.

Garrett paused at the heavy oak door with the cut-glass oval window. She drew a quiet breath and released it. It was bad enough that the man she'd once loved was carrying her around in his arms, but she still had to face the other man in her life. Her father.

"You okay?" Garrett asked.

"Yeah, I'm just peachy."

He stared at her, but didn't say a word. Wise man. He managed to turn the knob and open the door.

Inside, she glanced around. This had been part of the house she hadn't seen much as a child. Everyone used the back door off the kitchen. This was the formal part of the house.

Nothing much had changed over the years, she noted, as Garrett carried her across glossy honey-colored hardwood floors and past the sweeping staircase that led upstairs. He continued down the hall where the living room was closed off by large oak pocket doors. She tensed. Her father's new living quarters since coming home from the hospital.

They finally reached Colt's office. "She's home," Garrett announced as he carried her inside.

Ana Slater glanced up from the computer screen and froze. Her older sister was tall and slender with nearly black hair and blue eyes.

"Josie! Oh, God, what happened?"

"I had a little collision at the construction site."

Garrett set her down in the high-back chair across from the desk. "She'd gotten in the path of a truckload of lumber," he told her. "I pushed her out of the way. She landed funny."

"You mean, *you* landed on me."

Ana glanced back and forth between the two. "When you called me, you said nothing about being injured." She looked concerned. "But you're all right?"

"Yes!"

"No!" Garrett said. "The doctor wants her to rest."

"I need to stay off my ankle, but I have crutches to help get around."

"I'll go get them," Garrett said, and walked out of the room.

Josie turned to her big sister. "So when were you going to tell me that Garrett Temple was building the lodge? Or was it going to remain a secret?"

Ana tried to look innocent and failed. "Okay, how was I supposed to tell you?"

"By telling me the truth."

Josie glanced around the dark paneled room that had been Colt's sanctuary. They'd never been allowed in here, but that didn't seem to bother Ana these days. By the looks of it she'd taken over.

"I'm sorry, Josie. I thought since you said you weren't coming home, I didn't need to say anything."

Josie had trouble hiding her anger. "There have to be other contractors here in town you could have used."

"First of all, Garrett gave us the lowest bid, and some of our own ranch hands are working on the crew. Secondly, he's moved back here and now lives at the Temple Ranch to help out his father."

Josie closed her eyes. It was enough having to deal with her father but now, Garrett. "Then I'm going back to L.A."

"Josie, please. I need you to stay, at least for a little while. We can make it so that you and Garrett don't have any contact." She hesitated, then said, "And Colt, he definitely wants you here. He was so happy when I told him you came home."

Her father wanted her here? That didn't sound like the cold, distant man who'd raised her.

"We all need you here, sis." Ana continued her pitch. "I can't tell you how wonderful it is to have you here, even if it's only for a short time. So please, give it a few days. At least until your ankle is better."

The Lazy S had been her home, once. If Colt had changed like Ana said, she wanted to try and have some sort of relationship with the man. Was it crazy to hope? At the very least, she wanted to help Ana with the financial problems. It was no secret they needed outside income to survive.

Ana and her fiancé, Vance Rivers, the ranch foreman, had already opened the property on their section of the river to anglers. It brought in a nice profit. That was why they were expanding on the business.

Her sister spoke up. "The lodge was your idea to help with income for the ranch. Don't you want to stick around to see your vision come true?"

It had been Josie's idea to build housing to rent out. As an event planner she knew the large structure could be used for company retreats, family reunions and even small weddings. It was to bring in more revenue to help during lean years.

Maybe a little while here wouldn't be so bad. "How soon is this wedding of yours?"

"As soon as possible," came the answer from the doorway.

They both turned and saw Vance Rivers smiling at his future bride.

Ana's grin was just as goofy. "Oh, honey, I don't think I can pull it off that soon."

The sandy-haired man walked across the room dressed in his cowboy garb, including leather chaps. "I'm glad you're home, Josie," he told her. "Ana has missed her sisters."

Josie fought a smile and lost. "Seems to me my big sis has been too busy to miss anyone."

Ana came around the desk and slipped into Vance's arms. Josie couldn't miss the intimate look exchanged between the two. "Yeah, she's miserable all right."

That brought a smile from the handsome man. "A few weeks ago, she was ready to string me up and hang me out to dry."

Josie frowned as she looked at her older sister. "A misunderstanding," Ana said. "It was all resolved and we're all working hard to help the Lazy S and Dad."

"So that was why you hired Garrett?"

"At first I offered to be their partner."

Josie swung around to see Garrett standing in the doorway with her crutches. She stiffened, hating that he still got to her.

Josie didn't want to hear any more from Garrett Temple. "I don't think that will be necessary."

He walked into the room, and Ana and Vance walked out, leaving her alone with the man she once loved more than anything, until he betrayed her. Now, she didn't want to be around him.

With her bum ankle, she was stuck here. That didn't mean she would fall all over this man again.

"I was trying to help out a friend," Garrett said. "And I believe it's a good investment. A lot of ranches have to go into other business to help stay afloat."

"I might be stuck working with you, Temple, but I'm not the same girl who was falling all over you. I've grown up."

"Come on, Josie. What happened between us was years ago."

Eight years and eleven months, she silently corrected. She could still recall that awful day. She'd been so eager to see him when he returned home. It had been months since their argument. She'd finally agreed to see him, then he broke the devastating news.

He stared at her with those gray eyes, and she still felt the old pull. "I was hoping enough time has passed so…"

"So I'd do what? Forgive you? Forgive you for telling me you loved me, then going off and getting another woman pregnant?"

Later that afternoon in the parlor converted into a first-floor bedroom, Colt Slater sat in his chair in front of the picture window. He squeezed the rubber ball in his right hand. He knew his strength was coming back since the stroke. Just not fast enough to suit him. His therapist, Jay McNeal, kept telling him to have patience. He would get his strength back.

Right now, Colt's concern was for his daughter, Josie. He had watched her drive away from the house and prayed that she would come back, but he wouldn't have bet on it. Not that he could blame her; he hadn't been the best father in the world.

Then a truck pulled up about an hour ago. He held his breath and watched Garrett Temple get out, then lift Josie out of the passenger seat and carry her into the house. He heard the footsteps that went right past his room.

He tensed. What had happened? Had she been in an accident? Finally, Ana came in and explained about Josie's mishap at the construction site with Temple. He wasn't sure he was happy that those two were together again. That man had hurt Josie so badly. He'd wished he could have been there for her back then.

"Will you stop worrying? You're going to end up back in the hospital."

Colt glanced at his friend, Wade Dickson in the chair next to his. Dressed in his usual business suit with his gray hair cut and styled, his friend and lawyer knew all the family secrets.

"I can't stop worrying about Josie," Colt admitted.

"Hey, things worked out with Ana, so there's hope with Josie, too." Wade stood up. "I'll go see what's going on, then I need to get back to my office. Some of us have to work."

Colt nodded. "Thanks for everything, Wade."

"I love those girls, too. It's about time you realize what you have." He turned and walked out.

Alone again, Colt started having doubts again. Would Josie finally come to see him now?

He stood, grabbed the walker and made his way to the sideboard in the dining room. Now it was his exercise area, since he'd been released from the rehab center. He pulled open the drawer and dug under the stack of tablecloths until he found the old album.

Setting it on top, he turned the pages, trying to ignore the ones of his wife, Lucia. He should have burned those years ago, but something kept him from erasing all the past.

He made it to the picture of his four daughters together. The last one taken before their mother walked out the door. His hand moved over the photo. Josie was the one who was a miniature version of her mother, petite and curvy, although her hair was lighter and her eyes were definitely Slater blue.

He frowned, knowing he'd been unfair to his girls. He couldn't even use the excuse of being a single parent. Kathleen, the longtime housekeeper, handled most everything while he worked the ranch. He sighed, recalling those years. Since the day Lucia left, he'd closed up and couldn't show love to his four daughters.

He studied the photo. Analeigh was the oldest. Then came the twins, Josefina Isabel, followed five minutes later by Vittoria Irene. The memory of him standing next to his wife, and encouraging her as she gave birth to their beautiful daughters, Ana, Josie, Tori and Marissa.

He felt tears gathering in his eyes. Would he get the chance to fix the damage he'd done?

"Hello, Colt."

He turned and saw his beautiful Josie leaning against a crutch in the doorway. He'd just been given a second chance, and he wasn't about to throw it away.

CHAPTER TWO

JOSIE FELT STRANGE, not only being back in this house, but seeing her father after all these years.

"J...Josie. I'm gl...glad you're home."

Colt still stood straight and tall as he had before his stroke. Thirty years ago, he'd been a rodeo star, winning the World Saddle Bronc title before he retired when he married Lucia Delgado and brought her back to the Lazy S to make a life, raising cattle and a family.

Now in his mid-fifties, he was still a good-looking man, even with his weathered skin and graying hair. His blue eyes were the one thing she'd inherited from him. Her dark coloring was what she'd gotten from her Hispanic mother.

"This hasn't been my home for a long time." With the aid of her crutch, she bravely made her way into the room.

"You had an accident," Colt said.

"It seems I got in the way at the construction site." She nodded to her ankle. "In a few days I'll be as good as new. Looks like you're stuck with me for the duration anyway."

"Hap...happy to have you."

His words gave her a strange feeling, making her realize how badly she wanted to be here.

She began to examine the rehab equipment to hide her nervousness. "Looks like I don't need to go to a gym to exercise. You have everything right here."

"You're welcome to u...use it," he told her. "When you're able to."

She sat down on the weight bench and eyed the parallel bars, then Colt. Outside of some weight loss, he looked good. "Is all this helping you?"

He nodded. "Been working hard. I hope to get a lot better s...soon." He studied her. "Thank you for coming home."

That was a first. Her father actually thanked her. "Don't thank me yet. I'm not sure how much I can help, or how long I can stay."

Colt smiled.

Another first, Josie thought, not to mention he was actually carrying on a conversation with her. How many times had she tried to get some attention from this man? She felt tears gathering.

"Just glad you're here," he told her.

Suddenly her throat tightened so she nodded. "I should go and unpack." She got up, slipped the single crutch under her arms and headed for the door, but Colt's gravelly voice made her turn around.

"M...made a lot of mistakes, Josie. I would like a s...second chance."

His words about threw her over the edge. She raised a hand. "I can't deal with any more right now. We'll talk later."

She managed to get out the door and headed toward the staircase. She hopped up the steps on her good leg until she got to the second floor. Using her crutch, she made her way down the familiar hall to the third door on the left that had been her and Tori's bedroom. She stepped inside and froze. It looked the same as it did when she'd left here.

The walls were still pale lavender and the twin beds had floral print comforters with matching dust ruffles.

She walked to her bed against the far wall and sank down onto the mattress. Taking a toss pillow from the headboard, she hugged it close against the burning acid in the pit of her stomach.

Great, this trip was supposed to help relax her. This time when tears welled in her eyes she didn't stop them. Colt wanted to rebuild their relationship. What relationship? They'd never had a father/daughter relationship.

Memories of the lonely times welled in her chest. She'd been grateful for her sisters, especially Tori. When something wonderful happened to them, they'd been each others cheerleaders, along with Kathleen, the housekeeper and their surrogate mom, replacing the mother who'd disappeared from her kids' life when Josie had been only three years old. It had been pretty clear that neither parent wanted their children.

Josie wiped a tear from her cheek. Dang it. She thought she'd gotten over all this. Leaving here and the pain behind, she'd gone off to L.A. and worked hard on a career, building a successful business, Slater Style.

She got up and hobbled to the window and looked out at the ranch compound. From this room, she had a great view of the glossy white barn with the attached corral. There were many outbuildings, some old, plus some new ones that had been added over the years. Her attention turned to the horses grazing in the pasture. There were mares with their foals, frolicking around in the open field.

Smiling, she pressed her hand against the cool glass, knowing cold weather was coming, along with unpredictable Montana snows. Surprisingly, that had been what she'd missed since moving to L.A.

She caught sight of her car coming down the road and watched as it pulled up in front of the house. Good, she had her vehicle back.

Then she caught sight of two men stepping off the porch below her, Vance and Garrett. She felt a sudden jolt as she got the chance to observe the man she had once called her boyfriend. Both men were about the same height, and drop-dead handsome.

Josie hadn't been surprised at all when she learned Ana and Vance had fallen in love and planned to marry soon. The guy had been crazy about Ana for years, since he'd come to live at the Lazy S when he was a teenager.

She smiled, happy for her sister.

Josie looked back at Garrett. She couldn't help but take notice of the man. He'd filled out since college, and he still had those incredible eyes and sexy smile. And she hated the fact that just seeing him again still had an effect on her. She released a breath, recalling how it felt when he carried her in his arms.

After Vance shook hands with Garrett, her future brother-in-law headed off toward the barn. Garrett went to her car and spoke to the driver, one of the men on his crew.

Then as if Garrett could sense her, he looked up. Their eyes locked, and suddenly she felt her heart pounding in her chest. She finally moved out of his sight and went to lie down on the bed.

What was she doing? She didn't need to rehash her past. All there was here were the memories of the pain and heartache over her father. Now she also had to deal with Garrett. It had taken her a lot of time to get over him. She'd only been back a few hours and he was already involved in her life again.

Why, after all these years? Normally she never let men distract her, mainly because she hadn't met anyone who could stir her interest. She hadn't met anyone in L.A. she wanted to have a relationship with. She thought about the times she'd tried to find a man. Problem was she'd compared them all to Garrett Temple.

She thought back to the kind and considerate man who'd showed her in so many ways how much he loved her. How Garrett had told her they were going to marry and build a life together after they'd graduated college. Then all too quickly she learned that all those promises were lies when it all came crashing down around them that day....

There was a knock on the door.

She wiped away tears as she rolled over on the bed. "Come in," she called, thinking it was Ana.

The door opened and Garrett stepped inside, carrying her suitcases. "I figured you might need these."

Her heart leaped into her throat. She sat up. "You didn't need to bring my things up."

He set the bags over by the closet. "I told Vance I would. He needed to check on one of his horses."

She nodded. She wasn't sure she believed him. "Thank you."

"How are you feeling?" he asked as he crossed the room.

"I'm fine."

Garrett paused, his gaze searching her face. "I'm sorry I pushed you so hard. I was only trying to get you out of the way." He frowned. "I was worried the truck would hit you."

She nodded. "I should have been paying attention. But I'm fine now, so you can stop feeling guilty."

He still didn't leave. "Some habits are hard to break."

She knew what he was talking about, but their past was the last thing she wanted to rehash. "Well, stop it. I'm a big girl."

He studied her for what seemed to be forever. "Since you're still angry, maybe it's time to clear the air."

"I don't think anything you have to say will change a thing."

He was big and strong, and he seemed to take up a lot of space in the room. "Josie, I don't blame you for not wanting to see me again."

She raised a hand, praying he would just disappear. "I don't want to talk about this, Garrett."

"Well, if you want me to leave then you're going to have to hear me out first."

His gray gaze met hers, causing her pulse to race through her body. Darn the man. "Okay, talk."

"First, I'm sorrier than I can say for what happened all those years ago. I regret that I hurt you. But we broke up, Josie. We hadn't been together all summer, and you wouldn't even talk to me."

Just as it had been all those years ago, Garrett's words were like a knife slicing into her heart. "Feel better now?"

He released a breath. "Although I have many regrets about how things happened between us, what I'll never regret is my son. He's the most important thing in my life."

A son. She had to remember the innocent child. "I'm glad, Garrett. I'm glad you're happy."

He gave a nod. "I just want us to be able to work together on this project."

She wasn't even sure she could stay here. "Is that all?"

He nodded, then turned to leave, but for some reason she needed to know. "Was she worth it?"

Garrett paused and glanced over his shoulder. "I take it you're talking about my wife."

Another pain shot through Josie. "Yes."

"Natalie was my son's mother, so yes, the choice was worth it." She saw the pain flash through his eyes. "But our marriage didn't survive."

* * *

The next day at the Temple Ranch, Garrett forced himself out of bed after a sleepless night. Josie Slater was back. He knew he couldn't let her mess with his head, or his heart. Not again.

Why was he even worrying? There was no room for her in his life. So for both their sakes, he hoped she was headed back to California soon.

He walked down the stairs of his father's home. Now, not only had it been Garrett's for the past year, it was Brody's, too. And this morning he'd taken off work from the construction site to spend time with his son. Soon the boy would be starting a new school, so today was going to be just for them. With Brody's recent move to Royerton, he knew it was going to take some time to make the adjustment. And for Garrett to win his son's trust.

Since the divorce two years ago, it had been difficult on his child. Then his ex-wife's recent death in a car accident had struck Brody yet another blow. Garrett hoped that a stable home at the ranch would help the eight-year-old. As his father, he was going to spend as much time as possible with his son now that he was the sole parent.

Garrett finished tucking in his shirt as he walked into the kitchen. He found Brody sitting at the counter, eating a bowl of his favorite cereal.

"Good morning, Brody."

He was rewarded with a big smile. "Morning," his son murmured.

Garrett smiled at the boy who was his image at the same age.

Brody was tall and lanky, with a headful of unruly dark curls and big green eyes. The thing that tore at Garrett's heart was knowing that his son would have struggles without having a mother around. As Brody's father he'd vowed from the day he'd been born that he'd always be there for him.

He walked to the counter and took the mug of coffee from the housekeeper, Della Carlton.

"Thanks, Della." He took a sip. "Sorry I wasn't down earlier, but I needed to phone my crew foreman. How has Brody been this morning?"

"A sweetheart. He does need his routine, though."

Garrett nodded. "Change is hard for all of us."

The short stocky woman had gray hair pulled up into a ponytail. "It's so wonderful you brought him here. It's been good for your father, too."

Garrett glanced around. "Speaking of Nolan, where is he?"

"Jack Richardson came by and took him to a horse auction."

He frowned, thinking about his father's arthritis. "Dad was up to it?"

Della nodded as they watched Brody carry his bowl to the sink. "The new medication seems to be helping him a lot."

The main reason Garrett had moved back to the ranch was to help out his father. Relocating his construction company took longer, but business was picking up, and with his foreman, Jerry, they could still put in bids on long-distance projects. And now, Brody would be raised here, too.

"Can we go get my horse now?" Brody asked.

Garrett smiled. "Give me a minute."

"Okay. I'm going outside to wait." The boy took off toward the back door.

Garrett glanced at Della. The Temple men were lucky to have her here to help fill in with Brody. "We should be back from the Lazy S by lunch. If plans change I'll call you."

The middle-aged widow nodded. "You just have a good time today."

Garrett knew today Brody would be meeting new people. He'd been so withdrawn since his mother's death. "You think he's ready for his own horse?"

Della smiled. "I'm not an expert, but it seems to me this is the first thing I'd seen the boy get excited about since he's come here to live. I'd say that's a good sign, and isn't horseback riding therapeutic?"

"Dad!" Brody's voice rang out.

"Okay, I'm coming."

"You're doing the right thing by the boy," Della said. "You're a good man, Garrett Temple."

Garrett felt a sudden rush of emotion, but managed a nod. He caught up with his son and headed toward his truck. They were going to see Vance to get a suitable mount.

They climbed in the vehicle, and after buckling up, Garrett drove off toward their closest neighbor.

Since Nolan Temple's health had deteriorated most of the barn stock had been sold off. One of the jobs Garrett had taken on was to get the operation up and going again. Thanks to the ranch foreman, Charlie Bowers, and neighbor Vance Rivers, they now had a herd that was twice the size as last year's, along with an alfalfa crop for the spring.

Even his dad was feeling good enough to want to participate in the operation. Garrett enjoyed it, too, and he hoped the same for his son. He wanted a place where his boy would feel safe and secure again. He wanted that for himself, too.

He glanced at the boy sitting next to him. "Vance has three horses for you to see, but that doesn't mean you have to pick one of them. We can keep looking if you don't find what you want."

Brody shrugged, looking down at his hands. "Okay."

Garrett was eager to get his son something to distract him from the loss of his mother. There had also been some big changes in his life. He just wanted Brody to know that he was his top priority. Not even work was going to distract him from rebuilding a life with his son.

Then he'd seen Josie yesterday.

All these years and she was back here. Seeing her again had been harder than he could imagine. But by her reaction toward him, he didn't have to worry about her being interested in him. Besides, she was probably headed back to California really soon.

Josie had slept in until eight o'clock. After she'd tested the tenderness of her ankle, she managed to shower and rewrapped it. She dressed and was even able to put on a pair of canvas sneakers. Making her way downstairs, she went to the kitchen and was greeted by Kathleen's big smile and hug.

"Where is everyone?"

"Your father is with his therapist, Jay McNeal." The fiftysomething housekeeper glanced at the kitchen clock. "It'll be about another hour. Afterward, Jay helps him shower and get dressed."

"How is Colt really doing? I mean, Ana hadn't given a lot of details." Maybe Josie just hadn't been eager to listen. "Only that he's improving."

"He is improving and very quickly. We're all happy about that." Kathleen sat down across from her. "But your sister still wants your help. She won't ask you to, but she needs you to stay as long as you can spare the time."

Josie felt bad, knowing how much her older sister had taken on by herself. "I should have come sooner."

"Under the circumstances, I can't blame you all for not

wanting to come home," she told her. "But I'm sure glad you're here now. Please tell me you're staying awhile." The older woman squeezed her hand. "I missed you, Josie."

"Ah, Kathleen, I've missed you, too." But two weeks was about all she could handle with Garrett. "I said two weeks. After that…" She hesitated. "Remember, Tori is handling my end of the business while I'm here."

"Maybe she'll decide to come back, too."

Josie smiled. "As soon as I get back there, she can come home."

"So you still think of the Lazy S as home?"

Josie shook her head. "Don't start, Kathleen. Let's just take this slow. I've been away a long time." She finished her coffee. "Where's Ana?"

"She went out to the barn with Vance. They have someone coming to look at some horses this morning." Kathleen checked the clock. "Then she had to go to work at the high school."

Josie nodded, knowing the reason she came home was because of Ana's job as high school counselor.

She stood and tested her ankle. "Maybe I'll walk down to have a look around, then come back to see Colt." This was all so new to her. She was actually going to see her dad.

Josie kissed Kathleen's cheek. Grabbing her coat, she headed out the door and slowly made her way down the same path she used to take as a kid. Not that she'd been invited into the barn much. Colt had pretty much kept his daughters out of any ranch business. Even when they got older, he didn't want them around. It had been some of the ranch hands who taught them to rope and ride. When Colt learned of it, he made sure they learned to muck out stalls, too.

She stepped inside the large structure, where the scent

of straw and animals hit her. She smiled, thinking a few days here might not be so bad. She looked down the rows of stalls where several horses were housed. She liked this. Walking down the center aisle, she passed the stall that had the name Blondie on the gate. *Ana's buckskin,* Josie thought as she walked up and began to stroke the animal. Then she went to another stall with a big chestnut, Rusty.

"Well, aren't you a good-looking fella."

"That's Vance's horse."

Josie swung around when she heard a child's voice. She found a boy who was about eight or nine. He must be the buyer's son. "And I bet he's fun to ride, too," she said.

The child didn't make eye contact with her, but he wandered toward her. "Vance says he can chase down calves, too. That's what he's best at."

"We all have to be good at something." Who was this child? "I'm Josie, Ana's sister. And you are?"

"Brody. Vance said my horse can be like Rusty if I train him."

Where was her future brother-in-law? "You have your own horse, Brody?"

Josie watched the child nod, wondering why he looked so familiar. He nodded. "My dad's buying me one. He's brown with a black tail and mane. That means he's a bay. His name is Sky Rocket."

"Cool name."

The child nodded, causing his cowboy hat to tip back. "I'm going to teach him to run really fast."

Josie smiled. "That sounds like a lot of fun."

She was about to say something to the boy when she heard another voice calling out from the other side of the barn. "Brody!"

Josie looked at the boy. "Seems someone is looking for you."

The boy jerked around just as Garrett and Vance came walking down the aisle. "Brody Temple."

Temple. This was Garrett's child. Oh, God, she needed to leave. The last thing she wanted was to see the man again.

"Oh, no," Brody said as he stepped closer to Josie. "My dad is mad."

Suddenly Garrett and Vance came up to them, and she knew she couldn't ditch the boy.

"Brody, you were told not to wander off," his father said. "You're too young to be around horses without someone older."

Suddenly, the kid threw her under the bus. "It's okay. I was with Josie."

CHAPTER THREE

GARRETT WAS BOTH relieved and surprised to find Brody standing beside Josie. His son didn't usually approach strangers.

He looked down at the boy. "Son, you know you can't leave like that."

Brody stiffened. "I was careful," he said defensively, but that changed when Vance walked up to the group. "You sure have a lot of horses here."

"We hope to have a lot more in the spring," Vance said. "So we can keep selling them to other kids." He looked at Josie. "Josie. What brings you out here?"

"I came to find Ana." She looked at the boy and managed to smile. "And found Brody instead."

That smile quickly died when she turned to Garrett. "Seems you spend a lot of time at the Lazy S. I thought you were busy building a lodge."

So she was going to stay angry at him. "I am. My foreman has everything under control." He placed his hands on Brody's shoulders. "I was taking the morning off to spend with my son. We're picking out his first horse."

"I know. We were talking about Sky Rocket." She sighed. "Look, I should get back to the house to check on Colt. It was nice to meet you, Brody."

Vance stepped in. "Don't go yet, Josie, I was going to show Brody the new foal."

"Yeah, go with us," Brody pleaded.

Garrett knew it was inevitable he'd see Josie, but today he wanted to focus on his son, not his ex-girlfriend.

He could see her indecision, but she finally relented. "I can stay a few minutes."

Brody looked at Vance. "Where is it?"

Grinning, Vance pushed his hat back. "Down a few stalls." They all began walking. Garrett stayed back and let Brody and Josie take the lead, but once they got to the oversize stall, the boy waited, a big grin on his face, until the adults arrived before he got too close. He saw happiness in his child that he hadn't seen in a long time.

Garrett looked over the railing to find a dark chestnut mare. Close by was her pretty brown filly with four white socks just like her mama.

"Oh, she's so little," Brody said as he looked through the stall railings. "How old is she?"

Vance walked up and began to stroke the mare's nose. "Just two weeks."

Josie asked Vance, "Do you think the mama will let us pet her?"

Garrett enjoyed seeing the light in her eyes, the excitement in her voice. It had been a long time since he'd seen this carefree side of Josie.

"Sure. Sugar Plum is a sweetheart." He opened the gate, went inside and nudged the mare back and stood in front of her so the group could see the long-legged filly.

"So what do you think of her, Brody?" Vance asked.

Garrett knelt down away from the new mother, then reached out a hand to coax the filly, turning to Brody. "Come here, son."

The boy walked inside the stall and mimicked his dad. "She's so little."

His son seemed to have no fear of animals as he reached out his hand to the foal. Surprisingly, the horse sniffed it and allowed the boy to touch her. Brody grinned. "She likes me. Josie, she likes me."

Josie moved in next to Brody. "Animals are trusting as long as you don't hurt them."

Garrett couldn't take his eyes off the exchange between his son and the foal, also between Josie and Brody. He felt a tightening in his chest. Josie always had an easy way, a knack to make people feel comfortable.

Josie stood up and let Brody interact with the foal. There was a bond growing already. She glanced at Garrett, seeing the love and protectiveness he had for his child. She felt tears welling in her eyes as she thought about past regrets. What could have been if only… She quickly blinked them away.

"Hey, Brody," Vance said. "Can you think of a name for our filly?"

The child shrugged. "I don't know any names for a horse."

Josie saw the boy begin to withdraw. "Maybe," she suggested, "'cause her mom's name is Sugar Plum, you can call her 'Sweet' something." She shrugged. "You know, like Sweet Pea. Sweet Georgia Brown. Sweet Caroline. Sweetheart. Sweet Potato."

"Sweet potato?" Brody giggled. "That's a silly name."

"Well, come up with something better," she told him.

The child continued to stroke the animal. "How about Sweet as Sugar," he said. "My mom used to say that to me when I was little." His voice faded out. "Before she died."

Oh, God. Josie's heart nearly stopped as she shot a look

at Garrett. He didn't make eye contact with her. His gaze stayed on his child as he went to the boy. "I think your mom would really like that name."

Vance spoke up. "I think that's a perfect name. It's got her mother's name in it, too. We'll call her Sweetie for short. How do you like that, Sugar?" The horse whinnied and bobbed her head.

Brody flashed a big grin and his green eyes sparkled.

Josie felt a tug at her heart. "Yeah. That's a good name. Sweetie."

Vance patted the mare's neck as he winked at Josie. "Thank you. Good idea."

"Anytime, soon-to-be brother-in-law." She smiled and glanced at Garrett. He was watching her, and she felt the familiar feelings, that warm shiver as his gaze locked on hers. She hated that he still had an effect on her, but she refused to let him see it. "I should get back to the house and Colt."

"We all need to leave," Garrett said. "The mama has been patient long enough with her visitors."

Brody stood up. "Bye, Sweetie. Bye, Sugar."

After the stall gate closed, Josie turned to the child. "It was nice to meet you, Brody."

"Nice meeting you, Josie," the boy said, then when she started to walk out, he asked shyly, "Will I see you again?"

She was caught off guard. "Oh, probably. We're neighbors. And your dad is building a lodge for us."

"I know. My dad builds a lot of stuff."

She smiled, trying desperately to get away. "Enjoy your new horse." She stole a look at Garrett. "Goodbye." She tried not to run out of the barn, not that her sore ankle would allow it anyway.

Twenty-four hours home, and this man had been everywhere she turned. She knew one thing. She needed to get out of Montana as soon as possible.

She didn't need Garrett Temple messing up her life... again.

An hour later, Josie sat at the desk in her father's office talking on the phone with Tori. "How did the meeting go with Reed Corp?" she asked her sister, who'd pretty much taken over Josie's event business while she was here.

"It went well. They were disappointed that you weren't at the presentation. I think Jason Reed has a thing for you."

Josie shook her head. "He also has a wife and two kids." The short, balding fortysomething man liked all women. "I don't share well, remember?"

She glanced around Colt's private domain as she listened to her sister. The den walls were done in a dark wood paneling, and against one of those walls was a floor-to-ceiling bookcase filled with books, old rodeo buckles and trophies along with blue ribbons for Lazy S's award-winning cattle and horses.

The furniture was worn leather and the carpet needed to be replaced. How long had the ranch finances been bad?

Tori's laughter came over the speakerphone. "That's right, you were pretty stingy when we were growing up, not sharing your dolls or your boyfriend. Speaking of which, how is Garrett?"

Josie froze. Why did everything come back to that man? "How would I know?"

"Because Ana said you've been spending time with him."

"That's not by choice."

"So how does he look? Please tell me he's gotten fat and gone bald."

Josie had only confided in her twin what really happened the day Garrett confessed that he'd planned to marry another woman. Later she'd learned he'd gotten her pregnant. "No, he pretty much looks the same."

"Ana also told me that he's moved back to the Temple Ranch with his son." Tori paused. "If you want, Josie, you can come back to L.A., and I'll take your place."

"No, I can't keep running away from my past. We both decided that we'd help Ana and Vance. Besides, I want to find out if Colt's new attitude toward his daughters is for real."

"You have doubts?"

Josie wasn't sure, still leery of the man's sudden change of heart. "He's nothing like the man we remember, Tori. He actually talked to me this morning at breakfast. Since the man had pretty much ignored us when we were growing up, I'm not sure how to handle the new Colt Slater."

Tori joined in. "Like I said, we can change places if you want to come back here."

Josie was a little worried. Why was Tori so eager to come to Montana? "Is there something you're not telling me?"

"No, I've just been working a lot of hours."

"You're being careful, aren't you? Have you heard from Dane again?"

"No."

Tori's ex-boyfriend, Dane Buckley, had abused her. Josie shivered, recalling the night her sister had showed up on her doorstep with the bruises and busted lip. When she wanted to call the police, Tori begged her not to, not wanting anyone to know. They'd settled on getting a restraining order.

"You need to call Detective Brandon if Dane comes anywhere near you."

She heard the hesitation. "What aren't you telling me?"

"It's just a feeling... Dane's around. I saw a car like his down the street by the town house."

Josie leaned her arms on the deck, fighting her anger. "Then tell that to the detective. He can check around to make sure you're safe. That's their job."

"Okay, I will."

"No, I mean it, Tori. You don't want to take any chances with that jerk."

Josie looked up and saw Garrett standing in the doorway. She quickly picked up the receiver, taking the phone off speaker. "Just listen to me about this. Please, promise me."

She heard the exaggerated sigh. "I said I would. Right after I hang up I'll call Detective Brandon."

"Good. I better go, but could you send your samples for the lodge's website design?"

"Sure. Bye, Josie."

"Bye, Tori." She hung up the phone and looked across the room at the man who seemed to be everywhere she was. "Is there a problem, Garrett?"

"I was about to ask you the same thing," he said. "Is Tori all right?"

Josie shrugged. "She's fine."

Garrett walked to the desk. "Look, Josie, if someone is stalking your sister, it's serious. Maybe I can help."

Josie didn't want to talk to Garrett about this, or anything else. "Thank you, but we have it under control."

Garrett watched for a moment, and then finally nodded. "Okay, but the offer stands."

"Fine. So what brings you here?"

"I just got a call from my foreman from the lodge. He has questions about the bathroom locations."

Josie shook her head. "I have nothing to do with that. You need to ask Ana."

"I would, but Ana's not available. She's tied up in meetings all day and can't get away. If you want to keep this project on schedule, the rough plumbing problems need to get resolved before any walls go up."

"Fine. The last thing I want is any delays." She stood. She found she was excited about getting involved in the project. She'd always been a natural-born organizer. She just didn't want to spend any time with Garrett. "How soon do you need me there?"

"Right now. I can drive you out, but Brody will be going with us. Then I can come back here to trailer his horse."

Josie hated the idea, but what choice did she have? "Okay." She grabbed her jacket off the back of the chair. She headed out, but Garrett's voice stopped her.

"Brody's in the kitchen. Kathleen is feeding him some lunch."

Josie felt her own stomach protest from lack of food. "That's not a bad idea. I could use some nourishment."

They walked down the hall to the bright kitchen and heard laughter. At the big table sat Brody and her father. Kathleen was at the stove stirring a pot of soup. "Sit down, you two," the housekeeper said. "And I'll fix you something to eat."

Colt looked up at them, as did the boy. Both smiled mischievously.

"Hey, Dad, did you know that Colt used to be a World Saddle Bronc champion?"

Garrett nodded. Who would have thought, gruff, strictly business Colton Slater could make his son smile?

"I might have heard it somewhere." He nodded at the older man across from his son. "Hello, Colt. How are you doing these days?"

Colt looked at Josie. "Not bad. T...two of my daughters are home."

"Colt's learning to talk again," Brody explained. "'Cause he had a stroke. But he's getting better."

Garrett sat down at the table. "That's good news." He looked at Colt. "Did Brody tell you we just bought one of your horses?"

"Yeah, Sky Rocket," Brody said. "I'm going to learn to ride him really fast."

Colt frowned. "I'm s…sure you are. But f…first you have to learn to take care of your animal so he'll trust you."

A confused Brody looked at his dad.

"It means when you get an animal you have to take responsibility for it. You need to feed and clean up after Rocket."

He glanced back at Colt, his green eyes worried. "But I'm just a kid."

Kathleen brought two more bowls of potato soup to the table. Josie reluctantly took her seat beside her father.

"You'll learn some now, and as you get older you'll do more," Garrett told him. "You live on a ranch now. That means everyone does their share."

Brody took a hearty spoonful of soup, then said, "If I do all that stuff, will you teach me how to ride a bucking bronc?"

Colt watched out the window as the threesome drove off to the lodge site. He had to admit that he'd enjoyed sharing lunch with them.

"See, that wasn't so bad, was it?" Kathleen said. "Too bad you didn't get cozier with your kids a lot sooner."

Colt turned and made his way back to the kitchen table, but didn't say anything. Nothing to say. He'd messed up big-time when it came to his girls.

Kathleen placed two mugs filled with coffee on the table, then sat down across from him. "Looks like you're getting another chance at being their dad. I hope you realize how lucky you are."

Colt hated that it had taken him so many years to learn that. He thought about his girls. Why had it taken him so long to realize what they meant to him? Josie was home, but so was Garrett Temple. How was she handling seeing him again? He recalled how badly she'd been hurt by their breakup. Now Garrett had returned and brought his son with him. He could see being around the man bothered Josie, in more ways than he knew his daughter would ever admit.

"Did you see Josie with Garrett?"

Kathleen set down her mug. "That girl has a lot of you in her. If Garrett comes sniffing around again, I doubt she's going to make it easy for him." She shook her head. "Of course that little boy has to come first. From what I hear from Della, Brody's had a rough few years with the divorce and lately with his mother's death."

Colt nodded. "A horse would be good for him."

Kathleen smiled. "And maybe some time with you. He sure didn't have any trouble talking with you."

Colt would always regret that he never took time to console his own daughters. He couldn't get past his own anger. "Sometimes it's easier with strangers."

Thirty minutes later, Josie sat in the front seat as Garrett pulled his truck into his makeshift parking area at the site. He pulled his hard hat off the dashboard, then reached in the back and found one for Brody, then another for Josie.

"Keep these on for your safety," he told them both.

"Good idea," Josie said and put it on. "Let's go check out this place." She climbed out as Garrett opened the back door and helped Brody out.

Even though the circumstances weren't ideal, she was

eager to see the lodge. She pulled her coat together against the chill and waited for Brody and Garrett to catch up to her.

Together, they walked across the wet ground to the sheets of plywood covering the mud caused by last night's rain.

They reached the front door. Well, it was where the door was going to be. This was still a two-story log cabin shell. The outside logs were up, along with the roof, but not much more. She inhaled the scent of fresh-cut wood as they walked through the wide doorway into what would be the main meeting room. More like an open area with high ceilings of tongue-and-groove oak.

Josie glanced around at the huge picture windows that overlooked the river. Drawn to the beautiful scenery, she walked over. This was a perfect spot. In her head, she was already figuring out different events that could be held here.

The first was the Slater/Rivers wedding right in front of these windows. She began to visualize the number of chairs that the room could handle, leaving room for an aisle. She turned to the men working on the floor-to-ceiling fireplace made out of river rock. It took her breath away.

"How do you like it so far?"

She swung around to see Garrett and Brody. She couldn't help but smile. "It's really nice. In fact, it's better than I thought possible. There's a lot we can do with this space. Are the floors going to be hardwood?"

When Garrett nodded, she looked toward the roughed-in stairs to the second floor. It was going to be left open, a mezzanine level for the bedrooms upstairs. She hated that anglers would be using it. She could really promote this for high-dollar functions.

"Okay, I see your mind working," Garrett said. "Tell me what it is."

Josie turned toward him. "It would be nice if we didn't have to use it for anglers."

Garrett arched an eyebrow. "Before we open to the public there's going to be a wedding here."

She tensed, recalling when she was planning her own wedding, until her groom betrayed her.

She wiped the picture from her mind. "I know. I'll go over those details with Ana." She released a breath. "Okay, where are these bathrooms that need my attention?"

He glanced around. "I need to find Jerry."

When Garrett went off to find the foreman, Josie realized she had to find a way to get over her resentment toward him. It would be the only way this project would get completed.

Her cell phone rang and she reached inside her purse to answer it. "Hello."

"Josie, it's Ana."

"Hey, Ana. Are you planning to come out to the site?"

"No. I'm at the house, but we need to discuss the lodge."

"What about it?" she asked, and walked away from the group.

"I found out today that I'm going to a teacher's conference in Helena," Ana told her. "The school principal is sick and he asked me to take his place. I have to go out of town for three days."

Three days. She looked at Garrett talking with the foreman. "You're leaving me here alone?"

Ana paused. "I'm not doing this on purpose, Josie. It's only for a few days. Since you helped with the building plans, I figured this should be easy."

Josie glanced across the room. She was going to have

to spend more time with Garrett. Hadn't she already been doing that over the past twenty-four hours?

"Come on, I've seen you organize and delegate," Ana said. "This will be easy."

What could she say? "Okay, have a safe trip. But expect a lot of phone calls, because I'm still going to need your help."

"You've got Garrett."

That was what she was afraid of. Already her stomach began to hurt. She said goodbye and hung up as Garrett walked over.

"Is there something wrong?" he asked.

"Ana has to go out of town. Looks like you're stuck working with me."

A smile twitched at the corners of his mouth. "I can handle it, but can you?"

She wanted to wipe that smile off his face. "This is business. I can handle it with ease." Garrett Temple, the man, she wasn't so sure.

CHAPTER FOUR

GARRETT COULD SEE how hard Josie worked to hold her temper, but the frown lines between her eyes, and her clenched hands gave her away.

"Hey, don't be angry at me. I didn't send Ana out of town."

"I didn't say you did. I'm just saying, I'm not that sure about what's going on here at the site."

He glanced around at the work going on. "I don't believe that. Wasn't this lodge your idea?"

"A general idea is far from making decisions on the design," she argued. "Shouldn't you be doing that?"

"I could, but in order to save money on this project, your sister was going to handle that."

Before she could say anything, Brody walked toward him.

"Hey, Dad, Jerry said if it's all right with you he'll take me to look at the bulldozer. Can I go, please?"

Garrett glanced at his foreman to see him give the thumbs-up. Since Jerry had three of his own kids, he knew that his son would be taken care of.

"Sure. Just do what Jerry says." He tapped his son's head. "And keep your hard hat on."

"Okay," the boy yelled as he shot off toward Jerry.

Garrett turned back to Josie. She still wasn't happy.

"Come on, let's go upstairs so we can discuss this in private." He grabbed her hand, surprised that she didn't fight to get it back.

He led her through the crew working on the inside walls, then up the makeshift steps to the second story.

"Be careful," he told her. Once on the plywood floor upstairs, he still didn't let go of her small hand. Even with the flood of memories that reminded him how easily he could get mixed up with Josie Slater again, he held on tight to her hand.

Once safely on solid ground, he released her hand and went over to his plumber, Pete Saunders. "Hey, Pete, how's it going?"

The stocky-built man turned around, and seeing Josie, he smiled. "Hey, Garrett."

"Pete, this is Ana's sister Josie Slater. Josie, Pete."

She nodded. "Hi, Pete. I hear you have some problems."

"Well, not exactly problems, but more or less, a design issue. I'd rather get it right the first time than have to redo any work. It saves time and money."

"A man after my own heart." Josie smiled at him, and the plumber smiled back. "So, Pete, what do you need from me?"

"Well, there are four bedrooms upstairs. Each has its own bath." Pete walked her through a framed room and into a smaller area. "This is one of the bath spaces." He pushed his hard hat back. "My question is, do we put in bathtubs with showers, or a tub with a separate shower stall? I know that most fishermen could care less about a tub, but you want this lodge to be multifunctional. So I thought you should be the one to choose."

Garrett watched Josie, and without missing a beat, she said, "We definitely are going for the bigger clientele base here. They'll want a retreat." She glanced at Garrett. "I know we're trying to save on the budget, but since we're hoping to add on to the structure later on, I feel the upgrades would be a good investment now."

Garrett gave her a nod, agreeing, too.

Josie turned back to Pete then pointed to where everything was going. "So, a spa tub here, then a separate double shower with several sprays, here and here. Can you get in a vanity with two sinks?"

Garrett didn't hear anything else after double shower, big enough for two people—lovers. He glanced at Josie in her slim jeans and turtleneck sweater that showed off her curves. The picture quickly reminded him that he hadn't been with a woman in a long time. He'd been divorced for two years. His dating life had been virtually nonexistent because he wanted to spend as much time as possible with his son.

Now he'd been thrown together with the one woman who could cause him to regret what he'd been missing.

"Garrett, what do you think?" Josie asked. "Is there money in the budget for what I want?"

Get your head back on business. "What? Oh, I think so. If you shop for some good bargains on the fixtures and cabinets, the budget can handle it."

Josie looked thoughtful. He could see her mind working. She was no doubt planning out her strategy to get the job done. It seemed she wasn't thinking about going back to California just yet. Great. Just what he needed—another complication in his life right now.

Two hours later, after a complete tour of the lodge, and going over the progress and building details, Garrett drove Josie back to the house. Was it her, or did it seem easier to talk to him? At least when the subject was business. She only hoped that she didn't physically need to be by the man's side to make more decisions.

Garrett pulled up and stopped in front of the house. Josie reached for the door handle and paused to say, "If you'll point me in the direction of the wholesale plumbing house I'll go see what I can find."

"I'll come up with a list of places. We have some time before they're needed."

With a nod, Josie looked in the backseat at Brody. "Have fun with Sky Rocket, Brody."

The boy didn't look happy. "I can't because I have to start school."

Josie smiled. "Oh, that's good. You'll make all kinds of new friends there. It's a nice school."

"Is that where you knew my dad?"

Josie felt the heat move up her neck. "Yes, we were friends, but it was a long time ago."

Brody looked at his dad. "Was that before you knew Mom?"

Josie's breath caught as she glanced at Garrett. She could see he was uncomfortable with the question. Good.

"Yes, I knew Josie in high school." He rested his hand on the steering wheel. "I played football and she was a cheerleader. When we got older we used to go out with other friends, too." Garrett grinned. "If my memory serves me, Josie used to like to dance and sing karaoke."

She gasped. How could he remember that? "That was one time," she told him. "And as I recall, I did it on a dare."

He continued to smile, knowing he'd been the culprit.

She glanced at Brody again. "Give me some time and I'll tell you stories about your dad that will make you laugh your head off."

She got a smile from the kid. "Oh, boy," he said.

"I've got to go now." Josie waved. "Bye, Brody and Garrett." She opened the door and climbed out, knowing she couldn't get chummy with Garrett Temple and his son. No matter how cute, or how charming. It would lead nowhere.

She headed up the steps, opened the front door and walked inside to see her father coming out of his downstairs bedroom. He was using a cane today.

"Well, look at you. You seem to be getting around like a pro."

He stopped and waited for her. "It's all the great nursing."

They started a slow walk toward the kitchen. She was surprised he was doing so well. "It's good that you're recovering so fast."

"And th…thank you for coming home to help." He paused. "I gave you plenty of reasons never to come back here. I'm sorry."

Whoa. This was too much to handle. "Is the apology for bringing me here now, or for all the years you ignored your daughters?"

"F…for all the above. I know there isn't anything I can do to change the past, but if p…possible, I want to try and change how things are between us now."

Josie tried to speak, but emotions swamped her.

"It's okay." Colt put his hand on her arm. "I don't expect an answer, or your trust. I just want a chance to get to know you while you're here."

Josie nodded and went into the kitchen. Kathleen was preparing supper. "Hey, you two, what are you up to?"

"Just talkin'," Colt said.

Josie walked to the large bay window that overlooked the barn, where Garrett's truck was hooked to the horse trailer. She eyed the man as he led Sky Rocket to the ramp and up into the trailer. Brody stood by and watched as his father latched the gate, then he placed his hand on his son's shoulder and helped him into the truck.

"Nice boy."

Josie didn't turn when she heard her father.

"He's had a rough time," Josie said.

"Seems they both have," Colt answered.

Josie gave her father a sideways glance. "He brought on his troubles himself."

"I know. He hurt you badly. I wish I could have protected you all those years ago."

It surprised her that her father had known what happened. "I wish you'd have been there, too," she admitted.

She'd hurt more than she could tell anyone. More than she ever wanted to remember. But Garrett hadn't been the only man in her life to hurt her.

Monday morning Garrett drove Brody to school. He wanted to take his son on his first day. He glanced down at his solemn-looking eight-year-old. Six months ago when Natalie was killed in the automobile accident, he let his ex-in-laws keep the boy while he finished his move from Butte to Royerton. Although he'd visited Brody as much as possible, he knew that the move would be difficult for the boy. His son had to leave his home, friends and grandparents to move to a new place. That was tough for a kid, especially a kid who'd recently lost his mother.

"Look, Brody, being the new kid in school is never easy, but Royerton is your home now. It's a new start for both of us."

"But I liked my old school."

"I know, but I couldn't stay there. Grandpa Nolan needs us here to help with the ranch."

He pulled into the parking lot and they got out and walked toward the large complex that housed the community's school-aged children from kindergarten through eighth grade. The other building was the high school.

Standing in front of the elementary building was Brody's new teacher, Miss Lisa Kennedy. She looked about eighteen. Garrett had met with her last week, and was confident that she would do everything possible to help his son adjust to his new school.

"Mr. Temple," she said with a smile as she looked at Brody. "Good morning, Brody. I'm so happy that you'll be joining my class."

"Morning, Miss Kennedy," he murmured.

She kept eye contact with Brody. "I know it's tough starting a new school, so Royerton Elementary started the buddy system. And I have someone who's been anxious to meet you." The teacher looked toward the playground and motioned to someone. A small, redheaded boy about eight years old came running to them. "Brody, this is Adam Graves. Adam, meet Brody."

"Hi, Brody," Adam said. "You're going to be in my class." The freckled-faced boy smiled. "I was new last year, so I wanted to be the buddy this year."

Brody didn't say anything.

The boy looked at his teacher and when he got a nod, he said, "I hear you got a new horse."

The question got his son's attention. "Yeah, Sky Rocket. Do you have a horse?"

Adam shook his head. "Not anymore because we moved into town. But when my dad was around, I used to have a pony, Jodie."

Brody studied the boy. "Hey, maybe…you can come out to my house and see Sky Rocket sometime." He glanced up at his father. "Can he, Dad?"

Garrett felt a weight lift on seeing his child's enthusiasm. "Sure. Maybe after I talk with Adam's mother." He wanted to make sure he followed the right protocol for playdates. "Right now I think Miss Kennedy wants you to go to class."

The pretty teacher nodded as the bell rang. "Adam, why don't you take Brody to the classroom and show him where his desk is?"

"Okay, Miss Kennedy. Come on, Brody."

"Bye, Dad." Brody took off with his new friend.

"Bye, son. Have a good day," he called, but knew Brody wasn't hearing him. That was a good thing, right?

"He's going to be fine, Mr. Temple."

He nodded. "I know, but it's been a rough few months." It had been for him, too. He hadn't known how to handle his son's sadness.

"I'll call you if there are any problems."

"Thank you." Garrett walked off toward his truck and grabbed the lodge plans off the seat. Since he was here, he could catch Ana up on the progress and see if he could steal her for a few hours to help him with some design decisions.

He walked across the same school yard that a dozen years ago he once attended, and memories flooded back. He'd liked school. He had friends and was a good student. The girls liked him, too. But on that first day of his junior year when he walked though the front doors and literally ran into the new freshman, Josefina Slater, he was a goner.

He'd known the Slater sisters all his life, but that summer something changed with her. Josie's eyes were a richer blue, her face was prettier, and her body... Oh, God, her body.

He shivered, recalling how beautiful she looked. If only she still didn't have that effect on him.

He pulled open the door to the high school, and was quickly brought back to the present when he was nearly knocked over by a rush of teenagers.

Garrett removed his cowboy hat and headed to the office as his thoughts returned to Josie. He had to stop thinking about her because nothing could start up between them.

Not that she wanted anything to do with him. What they once had, had to stay a fond memory. He needed to concentrate on the future. Brody needed him full-time and so did his dad.

He opened the door and smiled at the receptionist, Clare Stewart. He remembered her from school. Of course, in a town of six thousand people, everyone knew most of the citizens.

"Hey, Garrett, it's been a few years."

He shook her hand. "Hello, Clare. It's good to see you again."

"So what brings you to the principal's office?"

"I'm not here to see the principal, but Ana Slater. Is she in her office?"

The pretty blonde shook her head. "No, she's in there." She pointed to the door that read Principal.

"Is she in a meeting?"

"No, she's with her sister, Josie." Clare raised an eyebrow. "You remember Josie, don't you?"

Garrett didn't answer. Everyone in school pretty much knew that they'd been a couple. With Josie's return home, no doubt there would be gossip around town. He knocked on the door and opened it to find the two Slater sisters in a heated discussion.

Josie swung around and glared at him. "What are you doing here?"

So much for getting along, he thought. He ignored her and closed the door behind him. "I came to see Ana, but good, I got both of you."

The last person Josie wanted in on this discussion was Garrett. She wanted to walk out, but she knew it wasn't the professional thing to do. She counted to ten to calm her racing pulse, then asked, "Did you need something?"

"Yeah, a project manager." He looked from Ana to her. "There needs to be someone around to make the decisions."

Ana turned to Josie. *Oh, no, this wasn't going to land in her lap.* "I thought I answered your questions Friday," she told Garrett.

"There are still more decisions to make. If either of you could stop by the site daily so there aren't any holdups that would be nice. When I have to chase down someone, it causes delays and costs money."

Josie turned to her sister. "Well, Ana?"

Her older sister shook her head. "Josie, I explained to you already." She then turned to Garrett. "My principal is in the hospital with pneumonia. I've been asked to take his place for the next few weeks. I've already taken so much time off as it is, and with my wedding coming…"

Ana sighed. "I'm sorry, Garrett. I never planned for this to happen. Like I was trying to tell Josie, I need her to take my place on the project."

"And I've told you, I'm not going to be in town that long," Josie shot back.

Josie could see Garrett was losing patience. "Seems that's been your tune since you've arrived here. Fine, you want me to have all the control? I can make the decisions and the hell with you wanting your corporate retreat."

He turned and started for the door. Curse that man. "Hold up there, Temple."

Garrett stopped and waited for her to speak.

"Are you headed out there now?" she asked.

Garrett nodded. "Yeah, I just dropped Brody off at school."

Josie walked toward him. "Okay, but I don't have my

car. I needed to get my brakes fixed. I'll have to ride out with you, but that also means you'll have to drop me off at the ranch." She'd get one of the men to bring her back to town later to get her car from Al's Garage.

After saying goodbye to Ana, Josie hurried to get outside. The air was downright cold today. She pulled her sweater coat tighter.

"You're going to need a warmer coat if you stay around much longer. My dad's predicting an early winter."

At the mention of Nolan Temple, Josie got all soft inside. "How is your Dad?"

"He's been doing better on this new medication, but his arthritis gets worse in the colder weather."

They reached his truck, and Garrett opened the passenger door, but he knew better than to help her in. A flash of memory took him back to how he used to swing the teenage Josie up in his arms and set her down on the seat. He used to be rewarded with a kiss.

A sudden ache constricted his chest as he watched her climb into the pickup. She did just fine without him, like she had for all these years. Maybe that had been their problem, her stubborn independence.

After he shut the door, he hurried around to the other side and got in behind the wheel. He immediately started up the engine and turned on the heat. The soft sounds of country-Western music filled the cab. He caught a whiff of her scent. It was the same perfume she'd worn years ago.

He needed a distraction. "Are you up for a drive into Butte?"

She looked at him, her eyes leery. "Why?"

"I thought we could pick out the bathroom and kitchen tiles along with the sinks and tubs. We can get it out of the way now...before you have to go back to California."

He checked his watch. "I have until three o'clock when I pick up Brody from school."

She hesitated as their gazes locked. It seemed to be a battle of wills. Even years ago, Josie liked to be in control. "Sure."

Hiding his surprise, Garrett put the truck in gear and pulled out onto Main Street and headed for the highway out of town. "You know this working together would be so much easier if you weren't always ready to fight me all the time."

She didn't say anything.

"Josie, what happened between us was a long time ago. I'm not saying you have to like me, but can't we put what happened aside? We were kids. It's time to move on."

"You're right, Temple. I need to think about the River's Edge project and nothing else." She glared at him as he turned onto the highway. "But that doesn't mean we can be friends."

Her words hurt him more than he wanted to admit. At one time, Josie Slater had been his best friend and his girl. They shared everything, but then that summer everything changed and not for the good.

"I'm sorry to hear that, Josie."

By noon, Josie was enjoying herself. They'd gone to a builders supply house and looked over cabinets and sinks for the kitchen and baths. She also realized that Garrett had good taste when it came to colors for tiles and flooring. The store's designer, Diana, was more than willing to help them. The way she looked at Garrett, Josie suspected the two had more than a business relationship. She hated that the other woman's attention toward Garrett bothered her.

After the order had been placed and a delivery date set, they walked back out to the truck.

"You seem to be well-known around here," she said.

"I built my construction company in this area. It's a good idea to be nice to everyone because most of my work is from word of mouth. I worked years to build a good reputation and I've done most of my trade here."

They climbed in the truck. "So why did you move everything back to Royerton?"

"Dad. He can't handle the ranch on his own." He released a breath. "And since my divorce and only getting to see Brody twice a week, I could spend more time at the ranch."

Josie didn't want to talk about his marriage. It wouldn't matter anyway. Garrett had given up on her years ago.

"How is the business since moving to Royerton?"

Garrett stopped at the light and glanced at her. "Not bad. I'm lucky that my foreman is willing to bid on jobs here in Butte. My crew is pretty mobile and they'll go almost anywhere for work."

Garrett drove down the street, then pulled his truck into the parking lot of the local café and shut off the engine. "Come on, I'll buy you some lunch."

He got out before she could argue. Since she was hungry, she didn't put up a fight. She hurried to catch up with him. Okay, so he was treating her like one of the guys. Wasn't that what she wanted him to do?

He stopped at the entrance and held open the door. She went inside first and glanced around the mom-and-pop place, with ruffled curtains and floral wallpaper.

"They've got the best food around." He smiled as an older woman came over. "Hi, Dolly."

The fortysomething woman looked at him and smiled. "Well, well, if it isn't Garrett Temple. Where is that sweet boy of yours?"

Garrett removed his cowboy hat. "He's in school in Royerton."

She moved across the café, her blond ponytail swinging back and forth. "So you got him settled in?"

"I'm trying. He's still a little sad about the move."

"He's lucky to have you." The woman turned to Josie. "Hi, I'm Dolly Madison." She raised a hand. "I've heard every joke there is. And if that guy cooking in the kitchen there wasn't about perfect, I wouldn't have married him and put up with the headache."

Josie smiled. "Nice to meet you, Dolly. I'm Josie Slater."

"Welcome to Dolly's Place." She grabbed two menus and led them to a table in the corner. Once they were seated, Dolly brought over two mugs of coffee, and the busboy filled their water glasses. After they ordered a club sandwich and a hamburger, Dolly left them alone.

Josie looked at him. She hated that she was so curious about Garrett's past. "You seem to have a nice life here."

His gray eyes were distant. "It's funny how looks can be deceiving."

Later that night, Colt had retired to his room, but he couldn't sleep. He thought about Josie and how quiet she'd been at supper. She had started to open up, to talk to him, but tonight she was quiet again. He knew she'd spent the day with Garrett. Had something happened between them?

He fought to keep from phoning the Temple Ranch and having a word with the man. Colt stood and went to the window and looked out into the night. The security lights were on, so he could see all the way to the barn and into the empty corral.

It was all quiet.

Problem was he wanted to be the one who did the last walk through the barn to check on the horses.

So many things had changed in the past few months. Two daughters had come home, one was engaged to marry. He smiled at the thought of Vance officially becoming a part of the family. Vance Rivers was a good man.

Colt sobered. If he wasn't careful, he could lose another daughter. Josie just might head back to California if she decided she couldn't deal with her past.

He knew everything about dealing with his past. He still couldn't let go of their mother. Lucia had nearly destroyed him. He walked slowly back to his bed and sat down. He worked the buttons on his Western-cut shirt and then pulled it off. He kicked off slippers, and couldn't wait until he was sure-footed enough to put on his well-broken-in Justin boots again. He stood and stripped down his jeans. He managed it all without Jay's help. He might not get to cowboy much these days, but he still liked to dress like one.

He turned off the bedside light, pulled back the blanket and got in. He laid his head against the pillow and stared at the outside lights making a pattern on the ceiling.

He shut his eyes as the familiar loneliness washed over him. He'd had the same feelings for a lot of years, but hard work helped him fight off the worst times. He closed his eyes, hoping sleep would take it away.

He must have dozed off when he heard the pocket door to his room open. It was probably one of the girls checking on him. When the figure moved to the bed, he caught a whiff of her fragrance. His eyes opened and his breath caught. "Lucia..."

"Yes, *mi amor*. I am here," she said, her voice soft and throaty. Her hand reached out and touched his face. Colt shivered as he looked at the woman he'd given his heart to so many years ago. Her face was in the shadows, but he saw the silhouette, the delicate features and the black hair that caressed her shoulders.

He knew it was her. His Lucia.

He blinked several times to get a better look, but his eyes grew heavy and he couldn't keep them open any longer. He didn't fight it, not wanting to disturb this wonderful dream.

CHAPTER FIVE

It was about six the next morning when Josie awoke to the sound of voices outside her bedroom. She got up, realized how cold it was and pulled her sweatshirt over her head then went to the door.

Outside in the hall were Ana and Vance. "Hey, what's going on?" She rubbed the sleep from her eyes. "Is there a fire or something?"

The twosome didn't smile.

"Sorry to disturb you, sis," Ana began, "but Vance needs to move the herd in from the north pasture."

"There's a blizzard headed our way," Vance added. "And we're going to need every willing body we can get our hands on to help." He glanced over her pajama-clad body. "Think you're able to ride with us?"

Ana gasped. "Vance, no. Josie hasn't been on a horse in years. And it's cold out there."

Vance grinned. "So our California girl can't take the Montana cold?"

The two were talking and leaving her out. "Hey, I can speak for myself."

They both looked at her. "I remember how to ride, and if someone loans me a pair of long johns and a heavy coat, sure I'll join you."

"No, Josie. It's not safe."

"Ana, you'd be riding out if you weren't needed at the school."

Ana started to argue, then said, "You're right, but if this storm is as bad as they say, the high school will be shut down tomorrow. So I need to go in today. But I want you to take Blondie. She's a good mount and knows how to work cattle." She glanced at her soon-to-be husband. "You better take care of her, or you'll be moving back into the barn."

Josie left the couple to finish the argument and went into the shower. When she got back to her bedroom, she found thermal underwear, a winter coat, scarf and gloves on the bed and fur-lined boots next to the chair.

Josie dressed quickly, then went down to the kitchen, where she found Colt and Kathleen at the table.

"Hey, I hear there's a storm coming," she said as she poured some coffee.

Her father turned to her. "I wish you didn't have to go out in it. I sh…should go."

She sat down and began to eat the plate of eggs Kathleen put in front of her. "You will. Just keep getting better, and the next blizzard is yours."

She watched as a smile appeared on his face. Her chest grew tight and her eyes filled. Colt Slater smiling?

"That's a deal, but I'd like you to ride with me."

This was killing her. "If you get back on a horse, then I'll go with you." Why did it matter so much that her dad wanted to go riding with her? "Deal?"

Colt's blue gaze met hers as she stuck out her hand. "Deal."

They finished breakfast in silence, and she put on her coat, wrapped the scarf around her neck and chin and hurried out to the barn. She found Vance had finished loading four horses into a trailer.

Once finished, he gave her a hat, and she climbed into

the passenger side of the pickup as two more men got in the backseat. "We're meeting the other men at the pasture gate." The ride was slow over the dirt road and across Slater land as snow flurries blew, and she looked up at the dull gray sky with concern.

They finally made it to the gate and saw the other trucks. One stood out. Garrett's pickup. Of course he would be here to help a neighbor.

She could deal with him for the sake of the cattle. The men unloaded the already-saddled horses. Josie went to Blondie and waited for Vance to give out the orders.

"It's a precaution, but I don't want anyone riding by themselves," he said. "We'll work in teams. When visibility gets bad, we quit and go back to the house."

Everyone climbed on their mounts and Garrett headed toward her. "Looks like we're a team."

Garrett knew that Josie wasn't happy, but he didn't care. He wanted to finish this and get back to his house and Brody. He was thankful he'd moved his herd yesterday.

"We'll take it slow," he told her as he directed his roan, Pirate, through the gate behind her. At first, she looked a little awkward on her horse, but soon found her stride.

"I can keep up with you," she told him.

She proved she was a woman of her word as she quickly rode behind the herd and managed to do her part.

It was slow going over the next few hours as the mamas and calves resisted going along with the move and kept trying to run off, but the worst part was the size of the snowflakes, and the snow was sticking, even with the wind.

Garrett kept thinking about a warm fire, some hot coffee and... He glanced at Josie. Why couldn't he stop thinking about her? He spotted a stray calf and got him back to the herd. He hated that she'd been distracting him ever since she'd showed up in Montana.

He pulled his scarf over his nose as the cold burned his skin. He turned to Josie and called out to her, "You okay?"

She nodded. "Just cold."

When suddenly another calf shot off, Josie kicked into Blondie's sides and went after it. Garrett waited about five minutes, but Josie didn't return.

"Dammit." With a call to Vance to let him know where he was going, he tugged Pirate's reins and headed in the direction she'd gone.

It wasn't long before the visibility turned bad. Dammit, he knew this wasn't good. He knew where he was, but did Josie?

He cupped his hand around his mouth. "Josie!"

With his heart pounding, he waited for some answer, but heard the roar of the wind. "Josie."

Finally, he heard his phone and pulled it out of his pocket. "Josie?"

"Hey, I might be lost," she said.

"Can you see any landmarks?"

"I'm next to a big tree. I passed over the creek a ways back."

"Stay there, I'm coming for you. Listen for my voice."

He adjusted his direction and kept calling out to her. He walked his horse through the snow building on the ground. Worry took over, and he knew he had to find her fast.

After a few minutes he was about to call for Vance when he yelled out her name again. This time he got an answer.

"Keep talking," he told her, and he finally found her. She had roped a small calf. "What the hell?" He climbed down and reached for her. "Are you crazy?"

"I thought I was doing my job."

"Well, going after one small calf isn't worth losing your life, or mine." He glanced around, knowing they had to get out of the weather. "Come on, I know where we are."

He helped her back on her horse, then he climbed back on Pirate and pulled out his compass again.

"Think you can make it about a quarter of a mile to find shelter?"

She nodded and wrapped the rope attached to her calf and followed Garrett. He took out his phone and let Vance know that he'd found Josie and they were headed for the homestead cabin.

Garrett prayed they were headed in the right direction. There wasn't much visibility left as the storm intensified, but finally he saw the black stovepipe peeking out of the cabin's roof.

He stopped in front of the porch and lifted her down from the horse, and began to carry her inside.

"Hey, I can walk," she argued.

"This is easier," he told her as he opened the door to the dark cabin and sat her down in a chair.

"I'll be right back as soon as I take care of the animals."

Shivering, she nodded. "I'm okay."

Garrett went back out and got the horses in the lean-to along with the calf. They were out of the weather, so he got some feed from the bin and pumped some water into the trough. He hurried back inside and found Josie had lit the lantern on the table and was putting wood into the stove. "Here let me do that."

She relented and sat back down in the chair. "I'm never going to hear the end of this, am I?"

He kept working. "Probably not." Once the fire caught, he turned back to her and took hold of her hands. "How are your hands, fingers?"

"They're fine."

"What about your feet. Do you still feel them?"

"Yes, they're fine. And no, I don't feel sleepy. I'm feeling great." She pulled her hands away. "So you can quit playing doctor."

"I didn't realize I needed to play keeper."

"Hey, that could have happened to anyone. The storm decided at that moment to get worse."

Just then, Garrett's cell phone rang. "Hey, Vance. Yes, we made it to the cabin."

"Then stay put," the foreman told him. "We barely made it back to the truck with the men."

"How'd the herd survive?" Garrett asked, knowing Josie wasn't going to be happy.

"They're safe as possible in these conditions."

"Well, count one more calf because we have him up here with us."

That got a laugh. "Stay warm. We'll come dig you out tomorrow."

Garrett hung up the phone and looked at Josie.

"So are they coming to get us?"

He shook his head. "Not until morning if the storm stops."

"What do you mean, tomorrow?"

"Josie, you were out in it. You saw that the visibility was close to zero. Do you really want to risk someone's life to come and get you because you can't stand to be anywhere near me?"

The small room was finally getting warm, but Josie was still miserable. Not because of the cold, but for the trouble she'd caused Vance and the men. She shouldn't have been so set on going after the calf.

"I'm sorry. I had no idea the storm was so bad, or how far the calf led me."

"Not a problem. I found you. Besides, this is a freak

storm." The wind roared. "We have enough wood to keep us warm until someone comes for us."

That wasn't Josie's biggest problem. They were going to spend the night here. Together.

She sighed and looked around the rustic cabin that her great-grandparents built when George Slater brought his bride, Sarah Colton, here from Wyoming. There was the double bed against the wall with a nice quilt covering it. There was a small table and two chairs and a lantern in the center, also some personal items, candles, dishes and an assortment of canned food on the shelves. She had no doubt that someone had taken advantage of the cabin as their personal retreat. Ana and Vance?

Josie got up, went to the one window over the sink in the cabin and pulled back the curtains. A little more light came into the space. But there was nothing to see but blowing snow. She glanced across the room to find Garrett watching her.

"It's a good thing that Ana and Vance have made this place livable."

She folded her arms and nodded. "It doesn't look too bad. And there's some food. Some canned stew and soup."

"And coffee," Garrett added. "But sorry, no inside facilities."

His words nearly made her laugh except she could really use a bathroom right now. "How far away is it?"

He did smile, and her heart took a little tumble. "Just a few feet around back behind the lean-to." He buttoned his sheepskin-lined coat and waited for her to do the same.

Once bundled up, he said, "Earlier, I strung a rope from the porch railing to the lean-to. We'll string another line to the outhouse."

Suddenly the seriousness of the storm hit her. She paused. "You can't see that far?"

"I'm not taking any chances if the storm gets worse. Call it a safety net."

She gave him a nod, and he opened the door to a gust of wind. Once outside, he took her by the arm and escorted her to the edge of the porch and the lead rope. Together they made their way to the lean-to. After checking the animals, they trudged on, fighting the strong winds and biting temperature as they found the small structure. They finished their business quickly, then headed back to the cabin.

He opened the door, and she practically tumbled into the warm room. "Oh, man, it's crazy out there," she breathed, feeling the cold burning her lungs. "How much worse is it going to get?"

"I can't answer that. We're safe here, though. Vance knows where we are, and we have enough firewood and food to keep us for a few days."

She went to the stove to warm up. "A few days? We're going to be here that long?"

Garrett pulled off his gloves and put his hat on the table, but left the hood to his thermal up. He was chilled to the bone. He walked to the heat.

"I can't say, Josie. This is a big storm front moving through. It's the reason we were moving the herd. And since we don't have a radio, I'm not wasting the charge on my phone to find out." He stood next to her. "In fact, you should shut off your phone, too."

She took it from her coat pocket. Her hands were shaking, so he took it from her and pressed the button. "Thanks."

He saw the fear in her eyes. "It's going to be okay, Josie. I'm just glad I found you."

She didn't look convinced. "If I hadn't taken off on my own, you'd be safely home in a warm bed."

"We can't change that. Besides, there's a bed here, and we'll be warm."

In the shadows of the fire, he could see her eyes narrow. "You're crazy, Temple, if you think I'm sharing a bed with you."

He knew ten years ago she'd have been eager to steal time away with him. He shook off the memory. "Why don't we find something to eat?" He went to the group of shelves and found a large can of stew. He also found some bowls and flatware. "Looks like Vance and Ana have all the conveniences of home."

Josie glanced around. "I recognize her touches."

"The old homestead looks good."

He worked the can opener. "They're going to build a house not far from here."

"Let me guess—you're going to build it for them."

He smiled. "We're working on some of the details. But not until the lodge is finished, and revenue starts coming in, then they'll break ground. I'd say late spring."

"That will be nice." Josie glanced at her watch. Two o'clock. It seemed later. She went to the window and looked out, but there wasn't anything to see through the blowing snow.

"Are you returning for their wedding?" he asked.

"Of course. Ana's my sister."

He dumped the contents of the stew in the pan, then took it to the cast-iron stove and placed it on top. "It shouldn't take too long."

He wasn't sure if that was a true statement. Being alone with Josie Slater wasn't a good idea, not the way she still made him feel.

He released a long sigh. It was going to be a long night.

Later, with a mug of coffee in hand, and only the sounds of the wind and the crackling fire, Josie was still uncomfortable. She knew that she had to start up a conversation just to save her sanity.

"How long ago did your wife die?" Wonderful. Why not get personal, she thought.

He turned from the stove, where he'd just added wood. He walked to the shelves, looked inside and pulled out a bottle of wine. "Natalie died six months ago in a car accident, but she hadn't been my wife for two years."

"I'm sorry. I'm sorry that Brody lost his mother."

He went through the silverware bin and took out a corkscrew. "It's been tough on him, especially with our move here," he said. "Brody had been living with Natalie's parents since the divorce, so when I wanted to bring him here, I got a lot of resistance."

"It's tough for them to lose their daughter and now, their grandson moving away."

He opened the bottle and poured two glasses of wine. Setting them on the table, he returned to stir the stew. "It didn't help the situation when they tried to fight me for custody of my own son."

She felt a tugging on her heart as she retrieved some bowls and brought them to the table along with spoons. "I'm sorry, Garrett. I can see how much you love Brody."

He nodded and filled the bowls. He put the pan in the sink and came back to the table and sat down across from her. "Dig in."

She took a bite and realized she was really hungry. "This isn't bad." She took another bite.

He was eating, too. "Anything would taste good at this point." He sat back and took a sip of wine. "Now, this is good." He looked across the table at her. "What about you, Josie? Is there anyone special in your life?"

Whoa. She needed the wine now, and took a drink. "What is this? Secret confessions in a blizzard?"

"No, just curious how your life's going. We were a couple for a long time."

"Back when we were kids." She glanced away, then back at him. "What do you want me to say, Garrett? That there hasn't been anyone since you? Well, there have been, several, in fact."

Garrett didn't doubt that. Josie Slater was a beautiful woman. He could lie all he wanted, but truth was he'd never gotten over her. "You're too special to settle, Josie."

She glared at him. "Funny you'd be the one to tell me that. You didn't have any trouble walking away and finding someone else."

He leaned forward. "Your remembrance of that time seems to be a little different than mine. We broke up. Correction, you broke up with me."

"Because you weren't coming home for the summer," she argued. "We had plans."

"And as I explained back then, I was offered an apprenticeship with a large construction company. It was too good an opportunity to turn down."

She took a drink from her glass. "You didn't even discuss it with me."

"I tried. You weren't willing to listen to anything I had to say."

"So you went off, found someone and slept with her."

He froze at her words, but he quickly recovered. "Let's get that story straight, too. You broke up with me in May, saying we were finished for good if I took the job. Those were your exact words. When I tried to call you, you refused to talk to me. I met Natalie in July."

He was right. "Then why did you call me in September and tell me you loved me?"

Garrett remembered that night. It had been the night

Natalie had told him she was pregnant. He stood and walked to the window. "I was drunk."

He heard her intake of breath. "That makes me feel so much better."

Hours later, neither one of them were talking much. Garrett had gone out again to check the horses. He'd asked her if she needed the facilities again. She went, but only to break up the boredom.

Once they returned, Josie looked around for something to read, but there was nothing, not even a magazine. Why would her sister need reading material with Vance around? No, she didn't want to think about how the two were lovers.

She went to the cupboard, thinking she could open another bottle of wine, but that wouldn't help. She didn't need to add to her problems. Somehow she had to get through this night and keep away from Garrett. And not just tonight but at the site, too. Maybe she could handle all the business with the job foreman, Jerry. Then Garrett wouldn't have to put up with her, either.

Garrett finished adding wood to the stove and the room was nice and warm. He went to the bed and drew back the quilt and blanket. Then he sat down and started pulling off his boots.

"What are you doing?" she asked.

"I'm going to bed."

She stared at him. "But—"

"We're going to share, Josie. Sorry, but I'm not sleeping on the floor." He lay back against the pillow and pulled the blanket up over his large body. "Oh, this feels good," he said, patting the spot next to him. "Join me. I promise to behave."

She was either too tired, or too mellow from the wine, to care. She walked over and sat down on the other side.

Pulling off her coat and boots, she slipped under the blankets. It did feel good.

Garrett sat up and pulled the quilt over them. "It's going to get a lot colder later."

Not from where she was. Garrett's body was throwing off some serious heat. She had to resist curling into him.

"I'm sorry, Josie," he whispered into the darkness. "I shouldn't have said those things to you. We were kids back then, and I didn't always think clearly about all my choices."

The cabin was dim. Only the lantern on the table shed any light. Maybe that was what made her brave. "We were both wrong," she admitted. "You needed that apprenticeship. I just didn't want you to leave me. But you did anyway," she whispered. "You found someone else."

He turned toward her, his eyes serious. "There was never anyone except you, Josie. But things didn't work out for us." He paused. "When I married Natalie, I wanted my son to have a family, and I did everything possible to make that happen."

She started to speak, but he stopped her.

"Right now, Brody is my life. My focus is on his future. Also my dad needs me."

"You're a good father, Garrett," she told him, wishing she could turn back the clock for them.

His gaze met hers. He was too close and too tempting. "I've made a lot of mistakes, Josie, but I can't with Brody."

This was hard. They were supposed to have children together. "Of course he's got to be your first concern."

He leaned closer; she could feel his breath against her cheek. "I lied to you earlier."

She swallowed hard. "About what?"

"I did remember calling you that night. I missed you so much back then." He inched closer. "I didn't realize how much until I saw you again." Then his head lowered to hers, capturing her mouth in a kiss, so tender, so sweet that Josie was afraid to move.

She'd dreamed about this for so long. Slowly, her arms went around his neck, and she parted her lips. Garrett slipped his tongue into her mouth, and she couldn't help but groan as her desire for the man took over. It had been so long, but the familiarity was still there.

He pulled her closer against his body, and her need intensified. He released her, but rained kisses over her face. "Josie, you feel so good. This is such a bad idea, but I don't care." His mouth took hers again, and he showed her how much he wanted her.

She was gasping for a breath by the time he broke off the kiss again. "Garrett," she whispered against his mouth, wanting more and more.

He finally released her. "God, Josie. I'm sorry."

She tried to push away, but he held her close. "Gosh, woman, I'm not sorry I'm kissing you. I'm sorry that I'm taking advantage."

"I'm a big girl, Garrett. I'll let you know if you're taking advantage."

He grinned and she saw his straight white teeth. "Maybe the best idea is to try and get some sleep." He turned her on her side and spooned her backside. "But we need to share body heat."

She didn't care what kept them close. She just loved the feeling and sharing the intimacy with this man. Maybe she wasn't truly over him.

CHAPTER SIX

JOSIE FELT A strong body pressing into hers, cocooning her in warmth. It felt so good. She was too comfortable, too relaxed to move, and she snuggled in deeper.

That was when she heard voices. "I really hate to wake them. They look so...cozy."

Recognizing the man's voice, Josie struggled to open her eyes and blinked at the two figures. Finally, she managed to focus on Ana and Vance standing next to the bed.

Bed? "Oh, Ana. Vance."

She tried to sit up and quickly realized that she was pinned down by a strong arm. She glanced over her shoulder to find Garrett. Oh, God, a stream of memories flooded back. The snowstorm, the wine, Garrett's kiss... She felt the blush rise to her cheeks. Okay, this didn't look good.

"Garrett, wake up." She fought to separate them. "We've been rescued."

He refused to let her go. "Too cold to get up." He tightened his grip and snuggled against her.

Vance grinned. "We can come back if you need more time."

Ana swatted at her husband-to-be. "Stop it." She looked back at her sister. "Josie, are you okay?"

Josie managed to untangle herself from Garrett and sat up. "Yes, even better since you're here." She looked around and saw the sunlight coming through the window. "What time is it?"

"It's about eleven."

"Eleven in the morning?"

Her sister nodded. "The storm finally died out about 5:00 a.m. I was so worried about you two, I convinced Vance we should come and look for you." Ana eyed Garrett. "I'm just glad you found shelter when you got caught in the storm yesterday."

"It's a good thing we fixed up this place so you could enjoy the amenities," Vance said as Garrett finally sat up. "Hey, buddy, I see you survived." He glanced at Josie. "I'd say you two must have called a truce."

Josie practically jumped out of the bed. "We were only trying to keep warm." She tried not to make eye contact with Garrett, but she lost the battle. He, too, was remembering what had happened during the storm. "Unless you wanted us to freeze to death."

Garrett knew they'd been far from freezing last night. They'd gotten pretty heated up. "I had to wrestle her down to get her to cooperate. And her claws are sharp."

Ana went to the table and held up the empty wine bottle. "Looks like you had some help."

Garrett grinned and caught Josie's blush. "We ate in candlelight so...why not some wine?"

Ana started to reply when Vance said, "We better get you all back to the ranch. There's more snow coming."

Garrett pulled on his coat and followed Vance out to give the women a chance to straighten up the cabin while they got the horses ready. On the porch Garrett was greeted with a beautiful winter wonderland scene.

"This is quite a view." He nodded toward the mountains. "It's no wonder you want to build your house here."

Vance glanced at his friend. "There's not a prettier piece

of land. So you better come up with a house design to do it justice."

Garrett placed his hat on his head. He'd already had some ideas. "I'll do my best."

They trudged through the snow to the lean-to and found the horses along with the calf had survived the storm just fine.

"So this is the little guy who caused all the trouble?" Vance asked as he knelt down to see the baby red Angus and looked for an ear tag or brand. "He must have been dropped late and missed the last roundup." The calf bawled in answer. "Okay, guy, we'll get you back home and get you something to eat."

They readied the horses, and Garrett led them to the front of the cabin as Ana and Josie came outside. Vance was carrying the calf.

Josie smiled, and Garrett felt the familiar stirring. "Oh, good, Storm's okay."

Vance looked at Josie. "Since when did you start naming livestock?"

She petted the calf. "He's had a rough time, and I doubt we'll find his mama."

"So does that mean you'll bottle-feed him?" Vance asked her.

Josie nodded. "I can."

"What about when you go back to California?"

Josie shrugged. "Maybe one of the ranch hands can take over."

Garrett swung up into the saddle and reached for the small animal as Vance lifted him up and helped lay the calf across Garrett's lap. He watched as Josie climbed on her horse, and for a second there he regretted having to return to reality instead of staying here with her. He wouldn't mind at all continuing those sweet, heated kisses and close out the rest of the world and make love all night.

Vance rode up beside him. "Something wrong?"

He shook his head. "No. Just thinking about what I need to do." First on the list was to stop thinking about Josie Slater. "I just want to get home."

"Then let's go."

They walked the horses through the deep snow for about a mile until they reached the road where a four-wheel-drive pickup with a horse trailer was waiting for them. Although the road had been plowed, it was still slow going back to the Lazy S especially with a bawling calf in the truck bed.

The backseat was tight, making Garrett very aware of the woman next to him. It was hard not to think about how her body was pressed against his all night. It had been a long while since he'd shared time or a bed with a woman. Not just any woman; someone who'd once been the love of his life. He'd quickly discovered there were still sparks between them.

They finally arrived back at the ranch, and Vance pulled up in front of the barn. When they got out of the truck, Garrett heard, "Dad! Dad!"

He turned toward the house and saw Brody running down the steps and across the yard, struggling to get through the high snow.

Garrett hurried toward him and as soon as he got close enough, his son launched himself into his arms. "Dad, you're okay." Those small arms wrapped around his neck, and he caught his son's sob against his ear.

"Hey, Brody, I'm fine. Didn't Vance tell you that?"

The boy raised his head, wiped his eyes and nodded. "But the storm was so bad, and if you got really cold you could freeze to death."

Garrett swallowed back his emotions, seeing his son's

fear of being left again. "Hey, I didn't. We were in a warm cabin that belonged to Ana and Josie's great-grandfather. We had a wood-burning stove and…" He started to say *bed,* but he saw his own father walking toward him. "And plenty of food."

"I'm glad. I thought you might never come home."

Garrett shook his head. "No, son, I was going to do everything to get back to you." He tried to lighten the mood. "It's you and me."

Brody smiled. "And Grandpa Nolan."

"And Grandpa Nolan," Garrett agreed, and set his son down on the plowed driveway as the man in question appeared and pulled him into a big hug.

"It's good you're safe," Nolan said.

"Yeah, it is." He searched his father's worried look. "Is everything okay? How did we fare at home?"

"Not too bad, but we lost electricity during the night, and service hasn't been restored yet, so there isn't any heat. Charlie and two of the hands took out some feed for the herd. They got a generator in the bunkhouse to keep them warm."

"We came here to wait for you," Brody said. "Mr. Colt invited us to stay here to stay warm. We sat in front of a big fire, ate popcorn and watched some movies."

Josie listened to the conversation, surprised that Colt would invite anyone into his house. She walked back to the truck bed while the ranch hands unloaded the horses from the trailer and took them into the barn for a well-deserved feed and brush down.

Vance got her calf down, and Brody came up to her and said, "Wow, is he yours?"

"I guess he is since he lost his mama. We'll have to feed him with a bottle."

Those so-like-his-father's green eyes lit up. "Can I help?"

Josie didn't want to do anything to keep Garrett here any longer, but how could she turn down this boy? "Sure, just check with your father."

She handed the calf's rope to Brody so she could greet the elder Temple. "Hello, Mr. Temple."

A big smile appeared on the man's weathered face. "Well, aren't you a sight for these old eyes." He grabbed her in a tight bear hug. "It's so good to see you, Josie."

"It's nice to see you again, too."

He released her. "It's about time you came back home. Although, I'm betting right now, you'd like some of the warm California weather."

"It would be nice right about now." She shivered. "But I have missed the snow, just not this much of it."

"And not getting lost in a blizzard." He sobered. "So glad that Garrett found you."

"Ah, I would have found my own way home eventually."

They laughed and heard someone calling to them. She looked up to the porch to see her dad waving at her.

"Come up to the house where it's warm."

She waved back. "Okay. As soon as we get the calf settled in."

Brody came up to them. "Dad, can I help Josie feed him?"

Ana spoke up. "I'm going to have to put my foot down. Everyone up to the house," she ordered, then turned to Vance. "Could Jake handle the calf until Josie gets something to eat and a warm shower?"

Okay, so she could use a shower. Josie realized she must look a mess. She turned to Brody. "It seems the boss has spoken. Maybe after we eat, I'll bring you down a little later."

The boy smiled. "Okay. I helped Kathleen make cookies and hot chocolate."

"Why didn't you say so earlier?" Josie smiled. "Come on." They headed to the porch where her father stood. "Dad, it's too cold for you out here."

"I can handle it." His blue eyes showed his concern. "I was w...worried about you." He reached for her hand and pulled her close and whispered, "I'm glad you're safe."

She closed her eyes and let the unfamiliar feeling wash over her. "I'm glad, too, Dad. I'm glad, too." She pulled back and smiled. "Now, I could use some coffee." She took his hand and together they walked into the house. It was good to be home.

An hour later, Josie was refreshed from a shower and feeling like a new person. Dressed in clean jeans and a sweater, she came downstairs to find Garrett and the rest of the Temple men sitting around the kitchen table with her father and Vance. She had no idea where Ana was.

She noticed that Garrett had on different clothes and looked like he'd showered and shaved. She couldn't help but think about last night. The feel of Garrett's body pressed against her, holding her during the long night.

"Josie." Brody spotted her first. He got up and came to her. "Are you going to go feed the calf now?"

"Brody," Garrett called as he stood. "Let Josie eat something first."

"I'm fine," she told him, then looked down at the boy. "How about we go in about an hour?" She had no doubt that the guests would still be here, so she might as well get used to it. "I'm sure Storm will be ready for another bottle by then."

Brody looked back at his father and got a nod. "Okay.

Do you want something to eat? Kathleen left a plate in the refrigerator."

She didn't have an appetite right now. "I think coffee and maybe a few cookies would tide me over for a while."

Brody went to the cupboard and got her a mug and set it in front of the coffeemaker. "I can't pour it yet, not until I'm nine. My birthday isn't until May. May 19."

Josie didn't want to think about the child's conception, but she couldn't stop the addition. The boy was conceived sometime in August. She poured her coffee, trying not to let her hand shake. She and Garrett had been broken up nearly three months.

She shook away the thought and took a sip. "Are you going to have a party?" she asked.

Brody shrugged. "I don't know. I don't have any friends here, 'cept Adam. He's in my class."

She could feel for the child. She always had her twin sister to be her best friend. "Well, you've only been in school a few days. And you still have six months to make more."

His eyes brightened and then he grinned at her. "Will you be my friend and come to my party?"

He was killing her. "I would love to be your friend, Brody. And thank you for the invitation, but I live in California. I don't know if I'm going to be here then."

Suddenly the smile disappeared. "Oh."

Great, she was breaking the boy's heart. "We'll see." She glanced at the table to see that she had an audience. Her gaze went from her father to Garrett. She wasn't going to answer any more questions from this group.

"Hey, Brody, I think feeding Storm might be a good idea."

"Now?" His eyes brightened once again.

With her nod, he went to his dad. "Dad, can I go and feed the calf?"

Garrett's gaze locked on Josie. "Sure. In fact, I'll go with you."

She didn't need this. She wanted to get away from the man. "Sure, the more the merrier." She walked off to get her coat.

Garrett got his son bundled up and put on his own jacket as Josie met them at the back door and they all left together.

Colt watched the threesome walk out together, then he turned back to Nolan. Over the years they hadn't exactly been friends. Of course, over the years, Colt Slater hadn't been friends with too many people.

Nolan and he had a falling-out years ago, but when Colt had called him to tell him about Garrett and learned about his lack of heat, he invited him to the house to wait out the storm. They'd managed to bury any bad feelings.

"Do you think there's any chance for them?" Nolan asked.

Colt picked up his mug and took a sip. "If the way they're looking at each other is any indication, I'd say yes. Only problem is, my daughter is pretty stubborn."

"As is Garrett," Nolan said. "He's been burned once." The man shrugged. "Of course, in my opinion he picked the wrong girl to start with. He's always belonged with Josie."

Colt nodded in agreement, but he also knew that loving someone didn't mean you could keep them. He glanced at Nolan. He'd been happily married to Peggy for thirty years before she died from cancer a few years back.

Colt hadn't been as lucky to have that many years with Lucia. Only about a half dozen, and he'd thought they'd been happy ones, then she'd left him. Now he had his daughters—that was, if he could convince them to give him another chance.

He sighed. "Okay, what are we going to do to nudge them along?"

Nolan gave him a slow smile. "Well, I'd say this blizzard is helping the cause. I wonder if my son was smart enough to take advantage of last night." The man raised his hand. "Sorry, I didn't mean it like that."

"No offence taken. Josie has been an adult for a while, and I can't interfere in her business. But I heard from Vance that some wine was consumed and that they'd shared a bed—to keep warm of course."

Nolan shook his head. "And they think we're too old not to remember what it's like to be with someone you care about."

Colt remembered far too much. "So what do we do to help them?"

Out in the warm barn, Josie stood outside the corner stall as Garrett helped show Brody how to feed the calf.

"Keep the bottle tilted up," Garrett instructed the boy.

Brody giggled as he struggled to hold on to the bottle of formula. "He's wiggling too much."

"That's because he's hungry. You were like that, too. You couldn't get enough to eat."

"Did I drink a bottle like this?"

Garrett grinned. "Not this big, but yes, you drank from a bottle sometimes."

Josie had trouble thinking about Garrett sharing that experience with another woman. A woman who had his child, a child that she was supposed to have. *Stop it,* she told herself. That was another lifetime. She didn't get the guy or a child.

Brody looked at her. "You want a turn, Josie? It's fun."

"Sure." She took the bottle and immediately felt the strong tug. "Hey, this guy is a wrestler."

"Maybe you should rename him Hulk Hogan," Garrett said.

Josie couldn't help but laugh, recalling how Garrett used to watch wrestling on television. "Hey, Brody, did you know that your dad loves wrestling? He was a big Hulk Hogan fan."

The boy frowned. "Who's Hulk Hogan?"

She stared at Garrett. "You haven't taught your son the finer points of the WWF?"

"What's the WWF, Dad?"

Garret was shocked that Josie remembered that about the past. "The World Wrestling Federation. I'll tell you about it later." He leaned closer to Josie. "You enjoyed watching as much as I did."

She rolled those big blue eyes that had haunted him for years. "I was a teenage girl. I would enjoy just about anything my boyfriend liked."

She'd done that for him. She'd cared that much about him. It also surprised and saddened him that she'd pushed him out of her life. "So it wasn't Hogan's muscles?"

Josie's calf gave another long pull, this time throwing her off balance. He grabbed for her, but lost his balance, too, and all three went down in the fresh straw.

Brody began to giggle, then Garrett caught on and soon Josie joined the laughter. The white-faced calf cocked his head as if to say they were all crazy.

Garrett looked at Josie and mouthed a thank-you. He loved to see his son laugh as he tried to adjust to the move here. "Well, Brody, we better head for home." Garrett climbed to his feet and offered a hand to Josie and helped her up. "There's more snow coming."

The boy stood. "But our house is cold. We gotta keep Grandpa warm. You said it's not good for his arthritis."

"The electricity should be back on by now." Brody

didn't look too happy as they walked out of the stall and went outside the barn to see more gray clouds and snow flurries in the air. His son ran ahead toward the house as Garrett walked beside Josie.

"Well, we've managed to survive the past twenty-four hours without killing each other." If he ever got a hand on her again, it definitely wouldn't be to harm her.

"Speak for yourself, Temple. I've had a few wayward thoughts."

He stopped. "I can't believe you remembered about Hulk Hogan."

She opened her mouth, and all he could think about was kissing her. Instead, he placed a gloved finger over it. "Too late to deny it."

"Okay, you got me." She blinked those incredible eyes at him. "Thank you again for finding me in the storm yesterday."

He shrugged. "Anytime, especially when we find accommodations as nice as the cabin." With a big bed, he added silently. "About those kisses…"

She froze, then quickly shook her head. "Hey, so we got a little nostalgic."

"Yeah, nostalgic," he mimicked, but all he could think about was capturing her lips once again. Bad idea.

Suddenly, they broke apart, hearing Brody calling to them. "Hey, Dad, guess what?"

"What, son?"

"Grandpa Nolan said we have to stay here tonight. The electricity still isn't fixed." A big grin appeared. "We're going to have so much fun."

Garrett looked at Josie. "Yeah. Fun."

CHAPTER SEVEN

THE DAY WAS a long one. Having to stay inside with the blizzard raging across the area made it worse. Everyone was uneasy as they stayed glued to the television news channel telling of the destruction.

Josie watched her dad and Vance either pace around, or call down to the barn to check on the men and the animals. Garrett held his cell phone to his ear, talking with his foreman at the Temple Ranch. She saw the concern on his creased brow.

This storm was deadly serious. Herds could be wiped out. That had been the reason they'd moved the cattle closer to the house so they could at least get feed to them.

She went to Garrett. "Is everything okay?"

He shrugged and put his phone back into his pocket. "We won't know until the storm is over. My men are okay, though. They have generators running in the bunkhouse and the barn. I don't know why the one for the house isn't working." He nodded to Nolan. "I'm just glad Dad thought to bring Brody here."

Once again, she hated that she caused this problem. Garrett could have been home taking care of things if she hadn't gotten lost. "I'm sorry I caused all these problems for you."

He frowned. "You didn't cause the storm."

"But I was foolish enough to get lost. You would have been home dealing with your ranch."

He gave her that slow, sexy smile she remembered from so long ago. "And miss being with you last night?"

She gasped. "Stop making it sound improper. We didn't do anything."

He took a step closer. "You ever wonder what might have happened if Ana and Vance hadn't showed up? If we could finally have our night together?"

Only for the past eight years, she thought, then quickly shook off any memories. "Well, we're back here now, with family. There's plenty of room here, and because of Kathleen, we won't go hungry."

He looked at her, his eyes locked on hers. "Seems the elements are bent on throwing us together."

She glanced away. "It's a storm, Garrett, nothing more."

"Hey, Dad," Brody called.

Garrett started off, but stopped. "Maybe we should continue this discussion later."

She shook her head. "We can't look back, Garrett. Your son needs you."

He didn't move for a second or two, then he finally went to see what Brody wanted from him. She released a breath, glad he didn't push the issue. After last night, it would be easy to give in to her feelings. Wait. Wasn't that what got her hurt all those years ago?

The morning turned into a glum afternoon as the snow continued to fall. Josie tried to stay busy catching up with her work and went off to the den for some privacy.

About ten minutes later a young visitor showed up. Brody. The cute, inquisitive boy was polite and talked her into playing hooky. That was when she learned he was also a cutthroat video game player, beating her at everything.

"I give up," she cried. "You win."

The eight-year-old pumped his fist in the air. "I'll teach you to play better if you want." Those big green eyes sparkled in delight. "You can be good, too, Josie."

The boy was a charmer like his father. Watch out, all females, another Temple was coming soon. "And what happens when I get hooked on games and I spend all my days playing instead of working?"

Garrett stood outside the office door, listening to the conversation between his son and Josie. He was surprised at Brody. The boy hadn't been outgoing, especially with strangers, and it got worse since his mother's death. But something was happening between Brody and Josie.

Join the group, son. She's a real heartbreaker. He thought back all the years ago to that summer. He'd loved Josie, but he hated being so far away at college, and only getting to see her every few months. Getting married was the only solution, and that meant a job and working all summer to make enough money. When he'd gotten the apprenticeship with Kirkwood Construction it was so he could afford a wife and also get his college credits. Before he had a chance to propose marriage, Josie broke up with him.

Then that summer Garrett met Joe Kirkwood's daughter, Natalie. Four months later she was pregnant and they were married. He closed his eyes and thought how he should have worked harder on their marriage. He'd always regret that. Natalie might have wanted the divorce, but only because she knew that there was someone else who had his heart.

He closed his eyes. Did Josie still have his heart? He thought back to last night and how she felt in his arms. The familiar feelings…that he'd buried so far down that he didn't think they could ever surface, until last night when he'd held Josie again.

The sound of laughter brought him back to the present. His son's laughter. He pushed away from the wall and walked inside. He found Brody sitting across from Josie. They were playing some kind of card game.

Brody looked up. "Hey, Dad, Josie is teaching me to play War."

His gaze connected with Josie's. "Come on, Temple, join us. Unless you're afraid a girl will beat you."

Her eyes danced with mischief. He smiled. "That will be the day. Deal me in."

By afternoon, the daylight faded into darkness. Once again Garrett would be staying over, and although she hated to admit it, his presence made her restless.

She kept replaying their time together at the cabin. The kisses they'd shared. How his body felt against her. How secure she'd felt with him as the wind howled outside. She'd been far too eager to fall right back into Garrett Temple's arms. Storm or no storm, not a good idea.

She sighed and stole a glance across the room when Garrett got up from the sofa and walked through the wide doorway to the kitchen and the coffeemaker. After filling his mug, he leaned his hips against the counter and crossed his booted feet at the ankle then took a sip of coffee. Oh, yeah. The man was hard to resist.

Her gaze ate him up. He was tall with wide shoulders and a torso that narrowed to his waist and flat stomach. He was just long and lean. There wasn't anything about the man that she could complain about. And he still took her breath away.

Against her better judgment, Josie stood and walked

into the kitchen. She told herself she wanted coffee, but mostly she wanted the man standing beside it.

"You don't have to spend your entire evening entertaining my son," he told her.

She poured a cup of coffee. "Brody's not a problem. You've done a fine job with him, Garrett."

"Thank you." His eyes met hers. "I wasn't always there for him like I should have been. I was busy building my business. I made money, but I think I lost the connection to my family." His sad gaze caught hers. "Sometimes you can't get that back. That's why Brody is so important to me. He deserves the best father I can be."

Unable to stop herself, she touched his arm. "I can see how much you love him. And he loves you, too."

This time she saw the emotion in his eyes. "Sometimes we're lucky enough to get a second chance."

She didn't know how to answer that, but was grateful she didn't have to. A belly laugh escaped Brody as he rolled on the carpeted floor watching a cartoon video. She couldn't help but smile, too. Yet, she knew this child was a strong reminder of why she needed to keep her distance.

That little boy needed his father, and someone who could take over as a mother. That dream flew out the window a long time ago when the man she'd loved chose another woman over her.

Garrett's marriage to Natalie had broken her heart, and when she learned about the baby that nearly killed her. She shook away the sudden sadness. Another dream that had died was her hope of a life with Garrett. She turned to her career instead, and Slater Style had become her life. End of story.

After supper that evening, Josie decided to give up trying to work, but she still couldn't sit around, trying to avoid

Garrett. So she went back to her Dad's office and found Ana there.

Her sister glanced up from the computer. "Hey, I'll be done in a few minutes."

Josie shook her head. "It's okay, take your time." With her tablet cradled in her arms, she sat down in the big leather chair across from the desk.

"Okay, I'm done," Ana announced, and turned away from the screen. "I emailed all the parents about tomorrow's school closures." She smiled. "Although, I think they can figure that out without me telling them."

"So you're staying home tomorrow?"

Ana raised an eyebrow. "I know you've lived in sunny California for a long time, but yeah, this storm will keep everyone indoors, but hopefully not for very long."

"Hope so, too," Josie said, not realizing she spoke out loud.

Her sister studied her. "Did you come in here because of our guests?"

Josie frowned. "Of course not. Besides, we can't send them home in this storm and without heat in their house."

Ana smiled and leaned back in her chair. "Of course there's always body heat. That seemed to work for you last night."

Don't blush, Josie told herself. It didn't work as she felt her cheeks heat up. "We didn't have much of a choice."

"I can't help but be curious about what happened between you two last night."

"Nothing," Josie denied and stood up. "I was stupid enough to get lost yesterday, and Garrett rode after me. He knew where the cabin was, thank God. We stayed there until you came by this morning. End of story."

Ana stood up, too. "Hey, I know you're having a rough time with Garrett being here, but I'm grateful he was there when you got lost. As for the rest of what happened at the cabin, it's none of my business," her sister said, then grinned. "And if sharing a bottle of wine helped make the night more bearable, more power to you."

There was no way she was ready to admit anything to Ana, nor did she want to analyze what happened between her and Garrett.

Time to get off this subject. "Since you'll be home tomorrow, maybe we can look at wedding dresses on the internet. It's only about six weeks until the big day."

Ana got all dreamy-eyed. "We're not planning anything too elaborate with the financial problems and all." She smiled. "Besides, I already found this incredible dress. It's at a consignment shop in Dillon. It's slim fitted and done all in creamy satin, covered with antique lace. The owner, Carrie Norcott, promised to hold it for me a few weeks."

A consignment shop? "This is your big day, Ana. It's my job to make it special, and on a budget. We can afford to get you a new dress."

"I know. Vance said the same thing, but wait until you see this one. It came out of an estate sale from Billings. It looks like something out of the 1930s and it's perfect for me. Besides, we don't have time to order a new dress and get it here in time."

Josie knew she wouldn't win this. "If it's what you want then that's one more thing off our list. Since we have the location locked down, the rest will be aisle runners, seating and decor."

Ana frowned. "Now with this early storm, I'm worried that the lodge won't be finished in time."

Josie hoped that Garrett wouldn't let them down, either. "All we need completed is the main room, one bathroom and the kitchen. We can do that. And as for decorations, it will be Christmastime. How do you feel about a Winter

Wonderland theme? We place several pine trees on either side of the big picture window and add some poinsettias for color. An archway where that good-looking guy of yours can stand in his Western-cut tux. He'll have a perfect view of his bride coming down the aisle."

"Oh, Josie, it's perfect." Ana's eyes filled as she nodded, then pulled her sister into a big hug. "Thank you for coming home. You'll never know how much it means to me."

Josie pulled away, fighting her own tears. "I wouldn't miss it for anything."

Ana grew serious. "Then would you consider being my maid of honor?"

Josie felt tears welling in her eyes. "Oh, Ana. I'd love to." She hugged her sister.

Josie pulled back, wiping away tears, when she saw Vance and Garrett; both were bundled up in their coats. It was obvious they'd been outside.

"Oh, Vance. Josie was talking about the wedding. She's going to be my maid of honor." She went to her future husband. "And it's going to be a Christmas theme."

He kissed her. "Just tell me it's going to be this Christmas and I'm a happy man."

Ana laughed, and Josie turned her attention to Garrett. Once their eyes locked, she felt the pull. She couldn't help but think about being stranded in the cabin with the man's arms wrapped around her.

Josie heard her name. "What?"

"I wondered if you'd like some hot chocolate?" her sister asked.

"Sure, but I need to get some work done."

"I'll bring it to you here." She started out and stopped. "Oh, and Vance asked Garrett to be his best man." The couple walked out, but Garrett stayed.

Great. The last thing she wanted or needed was more time with this man. "Do you need something?"

"You don't want to talk about our duties as maid of honor and best man?"

She glared at him.

"Okay, how about we talk about the lodge. I was thinking when this weather clears we should get back to work on it. If the electrical is roughed in, then we can get the heat on and begin to drywall the inside."

She frowned. "I thought when the electrical was finished, your job was done and we take over."

Garrett shrugged. "I don't mind helping out so the wedding will come off on schedule. I'd hate to have them move the ceremony to the courthouse."

Josie shook her head. "I won't let that happen, but there isn't much extra money right now for the work."

Garrett walked toward her, and she had to fight to stand her ground. "I didn't say I would charge. I'll be doing the work myself, not my men."

"You?"

"Hey, I can still hang Sheetrock, even tape and mud the seams. And my carpenter skills are pretty good, too." She watched his delicious mouth twitch at the corners. "I still have a tool belt."

Oh, God. She didn't need to picture Garrett in a tool belt. "What about the time? Surely you have other jobs to do."

"With this weather there isn't much work right now, just a few small residential jobs that Jerry can handle. What do you say, Josie? You want to be my helper?"

No! She didn't need to spend any more time with this man, but the sooner the job got done the better. First the wedding, then the lodge could open for paying customers. Then she could go back to California and forget all about Garrett Temple. "Apprentice. I like that title better."

About midnight, Colt sat by the fire in the family room and watched the flames dance, holding a glass of whiskey in his hand. He was probably breaking all the rules drinking alcohol, but right now he didn't give a damn. Sometimes a man needed a stiff drink. He was tired of his solitary bedroom and more dreams about Lucia.

The house was quiet even though there were three guests. Ana and Vance had gone off to the foreman's house across the compound to spend the night. They'd given up their bedroom upstairs to Garrett and Brody. Nolan had been assigned to his youngest daughter, Marissa's, bedroom. He smiled, hoping his neighbor liked pink.

Josie had gone upstairs to her room hours ago. He had no doubt that had been to keep the distance between her and Garrett. The two had spent most of the day trying to stay out of each other's way. But there were sparks flying everywhere.

"Mind if I join you?"

Colt looked up and saw Nolan standing in the doorway. He still wore his jeans and the shirt he had on earlier, but the boots had been replaced with a pair of moccasins.

"Not at all. Come in and pour yourself a drink."

That got a smile from the sixtysomething neighbor. "Don't mind if I do." Nolan walked to the bar, took down a glass from the shelf and poured a splash of bourbon. He made his way to the other overstuffed chair across from Colt.

Nolan's dark gaze met his. "Couldn't sleep?" he asked.

"Seems that's all I do these days," Colt murmured. "I hate it." He smacked the cane beside his chair. "Can't wait until I lose this, too."

"Hey, you might be losing one, but I'll probably be taking up one soon with this dang arthritis." He ran a hand over his thinning gray hair. "But I can't say I'm unhappy that my son and grandson moved back home. He's doing a great job of running the operation." He smiled. "I have to say that my grandson really lights up that old house."

Colt knew his neighbor had been lonely since his wife, Peggy, died. Colt was ashamed he hadn't stayed in touch with his neighbor. "I love having Ana back, and now Josie's home." But soon Ana would marry Vance and Josie would go back to L.A.

Nolan took a drink and nodded. "I've sure enjoyed spending time with that sweet Josie of yours. I've noticed that Garrett liked it, too." He sighed. "I wish I could have helped those two out years ago. Maybe if I'd stepped in, things would have turned out different."

Colt sighed. "Did any of us listen to common sense when we were young? We had all the answers. Maybe they'll find a way to get together this time around."

Nolan nodded. "Got any more ideas?"

"Well, since this storm is expected to move out tomorrow, you can't use that excuse any longer to stay here."

"We might not have to," Nolan said. "Garrett told me that Josie is going to work with him on the lodge."

"Well, dang. That's not going to help much with the crew around."

Nolan shook his head. "No, the men won't be there. They have another job. They both decided this was going to be a wedding gift for Vance and Ana. They want to make sure the lodge is finished in time for the wedding."

Colt nodded. "That's a lot of time together. If your boy doesn't take advantage, there's no hope."

Garrett lay on the bed until he heard Brody's soft snores. The kid had been hyped up most of the day. Of course, he'd gotten a lot of attention. He'd even let his son go out to bottle-feed the calf.

Garrett stood and slipped on his jeans and shirt, but didn't bother with the buttons. He grabbed his shaving kit that his dad had brought over to the Slaters earlier and went down the hall to the bathroom. He quickly went through his nightly routine. Once he'd brushed his teeth, he put everything back, but left the small leather bag on the counter next to Josie's things.

He paused a moment to inhale the scent of her shampoo and soap that were so her. He wasn't going to get much sleep tonight. He stepped out into the hall and nearly ran into a petite body—Josie. He reached for her as she gasped.

"Sorry, I didn't know anyone was in here," she whispered.

"I just finished up." He watched as her tongue began to lick her lips. The memories of last night flooded his head. Josie in his arms, his mouth covering hers, hearing her soft moans.

"It's all yours," he finally managed to say, but he didn't move. He glanced down at her flannel pajamas and thought how sexy she looked.

As if she could read his mind, she said, "They keep me warm."

"Last night, I kept you warm."

She frowned, but he saw the blush. "That was an emergency."

"So is this." He gripped her arms and walked her backward into her bedroom, then his mouth covered hers.

It was heaven. Oh, God, he couldn't get enough of her as he drew her close, loving the feeling of her lush body sinking into his. Last night he'd been a fool to turn her away. He broke off the kiss, only to trail kisses down her jaw.

"Garrett..."

He pulled back, hearing her plea, but desire overtook him. His mouth returned to hers; he angled her face and deepened the kiss.

"I'd wanted to do this all day," he breathed against her lips in between teasing nibbles.

Then reality quickly intervened with the sound of someone out in the hall. He broke off the kiss and pulled her close.

They waited in the dark bedroom until the bathroom door opened and closed. He looked down at her, still feeling her heavy breathing. Then she pulled away and hugged herself. He suddenly realized what might have happened if they hadn't been interrupted. Not wise.

This wasn't the time to continue this. "I should get back to my room. Good night, Josie."

He left her, knowing there wasn't any future in starting up something with Josie or any woman right now, especially a woman who had a home and career in California. Over a thousand miles away.

So now he had to figure a way to keep his distance for another few weeks. He should be able to do that. So why had he asked her to work with him? Was he crazy? He groaned. Yeah, he was crazy about Josie Slater.

It took two days for the ranch to get back to operating as usual. The storm had taken its toll with downed fences and lost cattle. Not too bad, considering the intensity of the blizzard's destruction, Josie thought as she pulled up to the construction site.

She'd spent the past forty-eight hours trying not to second-guess her decision to help Garrett with the inside of the lodge. She thought back to the other night and the breathtaking, toe-curling kiss. What frightened her more was what might have happened if Brody hadn't gotten up.

Would things have gone further than just a kiss? No! She couldn't let the man back into her life. There was no future with Garrett Temple.

Josie parked Colt's four-wheel-drive pickup next to Garrett's truck. She stepped out onto the still-frozen ground, wrapped her scarf around her neck and made her way down the plowed path to the lodge. She smiled at the two-story rough-log structure with the green metal roof. The chimney stacks were covered in river rock and the wraparound porch also had rough-log railings, adding to the rustic look.

"You do good work, Garrett Temple."

She walked up the steps to the double doors with the cut-glass insert that read River's End Lodge. That one extravagance was well worth it. She ran her fingers over the etched letters.

She felt her excitement build as she opened the door and stepped inside. It was hard to take it all in. So many things drew her attention as she glanced around the nearly finished main room. The dark-stain hammered hardwood floors, partly covered for protection in the traffic areas were well-done. She moved on to the huge river rock fireplace. The raised hearth had room for a dozen people to sit down and warm themselves.

She walked past the staircase, arching up toward the second-floor landing, a wrought-iron railing with the Lazy S brand symbol twisted in the design. Okay, another splurge. Her gaze continued to move around the room, seeing special touches that made this place more cozy and comfortable. It could almost be someone's home. At the wall of windows, she looked at the river and the mountain range. Amazing view. Okay, she was definitely going to push this place for weddings.

She heard a noise upstairs, then a loud curse. Garrett.

Hurrying to the steps, she made her way to the second floor and went on to search room to room. She started to call out his name when she spotted him and froze.

His back was to her and what a sight. A tool belt was strapped low on his waist and he wore faded jeans that hugged his slim hips and long legs. Her gaze moved to his dark T-shirt emphasizing his wide shoulders and muscular arms.

He was balancing a sheet of wallboard and trying to reach for a tool. Then he glanced at her. "Well, are you going to stand there or help me? Hand me that screw gun."

Josie shot across the large bedroom and reached for the electrical tool he'd pointed at. Once he had it in his hand, he said, "Here, hold this up." He nodded to the large sheet of wallboard. Once she pressed against it, he began to work on adding screws into the edges. "There, that does it." He looked at her. "So you finally decided to come to work."

"You said I could come when I had time. I need to check in with my office, and there's a few hours' difference between here and Los Angeles. If you wanted me here at 7:00 a.m., you should have told me."

Garrett hated that he'd snapped at Josie. He'd almost called her and told her not to come at all. After the other night and that kiss, he didn't need to spend any more time with her. He should have gotten one of his men. No matter what it cost.

"Sorry. I'm an early riser and just take it for granted everyone else is."

"I am, too. But I'm trying to run my business long-distance. There's a big wedding I'm coordinating a few weeks from now. My assistant is doing a great job, but she still has to run everything by me."

He walked over to the drywall compound and seam tape. "Sounds like your business is doing very well."

She shrugged. "I do well enough, but long-distance is hard, especially since I'm not able to do bids on jobs."

He nodded, loving the look of her in her jeans and sweatshirt. He liked her better in her pj's. *Don't go there,* he warned. "Okay, you ready to go to work?"

"Sure, what can I do?"

He handed her a long, narrow pan partly filled with a white compound and a putty knife. "We need to fill all these screw holes."

She glanced around the room. He knew that she was silently counting the thousands of screw heads. "Okay. I'm not sure how good I'll be."

"You'll be great."

He gave her a quick lesson, put her in front of one wall, and he went to the other end.

It wasn't long before they met in the middle. He was surprised at the progress they'd made. But it was only one room.

"Garrett," she began. "Not to complain, but how many rooms do we have to do?"

"Actually, all the rooms have been drywalled."

She turned to him, and he could see spots of compound on her cheek. "Wait, I thought you said that wasn't in our contract with GT Construction."

He shrugged. "It wasn't that much more in cost. Besides it was going to be a lot more work for us. It was easier to have one of my men do the hanging."

"Then I want to pay for half," she argued.

"Josie, that's not necessary."

She glared at him. "You can't take all the cost. I want to pay, too."

"Why are you being so stubborn about this?"

Her eyes widened. "Because you asked me to help with

this project and we agreed to work together." She paused. "If I were a man, you'd gladly take my money."

"If you were a man, I wouldn't be thinking what I'm thinking right now."

Josie worked hard to keep her composure. She couldn't let Garrett know how his words affected her, but she didn't want to deal with this all the time. She put down her mudding pan, grabbed her coat off the sawhorse and headed for the door. She never got there because Garrett grabbed her by the arm and turned her around.

"You want me to apologize for kissing you the other night? Why, Josie? You didn't stop me then." His gaze was heated. "Are you going to stop me now?" He leaned toward her and his mouth closed over hers.

Josie was ready to push him away, but the second his lips touched hers everything changed. She moaned and her arms wrapped around his neck, holding him there, afraid he would stop. Then he drew her against him, and she could feel his desire, his need for her.

He broke off the kiss. "God, Josie... What you do to me. What you've always done to me."

She hated how he made her feel vulnerable again. "I guess this isn't getting much work done. Besides, your tool belt is digging into me."

Grinning, he released her. "I can take it off."

Keep it light. "Thanks for the offer, but we need to get to work. We have a wedding in a month."

She caught his look, but ignored the pain she'd felt remembering their own wedding plans so long ago. She'd learned the hard way they were foolish dreams.

CHAPTER EIGHT

OVER THE NEXT five days Josie worked long, hard hours at the lodge with Garrett, then spent evenings with Ana, Vance and her father. Exhausted, she slept very well at night. She valued those hours of slumber, but it didn't look like she was going to get many tonight.

It was her duty as maid of honor to do a bachelorette party for the bride. So on Friday afternoon, the celebration began. She'd gone with Ana to see her sister's wedding dress in Dillon. Josie fell in love with the gown and agreed it was the perfect choice.

Once finished with shopping they stayed in town, and the plan was to meet some of Ana's friends for dinner. The three women—Sara Clarkson, a longtime friend; Clare Stewart, another school friend; and Josie—all convinced Ana to go into the Open Range Bar and Grill.

If they were going to misbehave tonight they wanted it to be away from their small community. The surprise was they were headed off to a honky-tonk for a few drinks to celebrate the upcoming wedding. Josie hadn't expected her commonsense older sister, Analeigh, to be so eager to go.

Inside the bar, Josie looked around the rustic-looking room that was a little raunchier than she liked. Although, it didn't seem to bother anyone else but her. It was crowded with people, and a country-Western song was blaring from the DJ booth. The dance floor was filled with couples two-stepping to the latest Tim McGraw song. This wasn't Josie's kind of fun, but seeing the look on Ana's face was priceless.

Her sister leaned toward her and cupped her mouth. "I've heard about this bar—I can't believe I'm really here."

"Every girl needs a send-off," Josie said, and glanced at the bartender, Tony. She'd spoken to him earlier, and he'd been happy to help out. "Come on, let's go find a table."

She took her sister's hand and pulled her through the crowd until she spotted a table that had a sign on the top. Reserved for Slater Sisters.

"Oh, look." Ana sighed. "Did you do this?" she asked Josie.

Josie smiled. "A phone call," she yelled over the music.

They sat down just as the music ended, and Clare said, "Oh, my, look at all the guys."

"I'm not looking. I've already found mine," Ana said.

"You are so lucky to have Vance, Ana," her friend Sara told her.

Her sister got that dreamy look again. "I know. And he's been right under my nose for years."

Josie recalled the runaway boy, Vance Rivers, that their father had taken in. Of course, back then she and her sister were jealous because Colt had paid more attention to Vance than his own daughters. Josie realized now that it wasn't Vance's fault.

The young waitress dressed in a little T-shirt, a pair of jeans and boots took their drink order, margaritas all around.

Clare drew their attention. "You know who else is a really good-looking man? Garrett Temple." The blonde looked at Josie. "Do you still lay claim on the man, or do the rest of us get a chance with him?"

Josie stiffened as all eyes turned to her. She found she wanted to ward them off, but she hadn't the right to. "It's been years since Garrett and I were a couple. Besides, I'm headed back to L.A. soon."

The music started up again, and the waitress brought over their drinks. Josie handed over her credit card for the first round as Sara and Clare got up to go to the dance floor with two guys.

Ana leaned over and said, "Sorry, I don't want Clare to bring up bad memories."

Josie shook her head and took a drink and tasted the salt along the rim. "It's okay, Ana. Everyone here remembers Garrett and I together. I can handle that."

"Good." They drank and caught up on local news the past years. Soon the music turned to a fast-paced song, and everyone got up to do a popular line dance. Ana grabbed Josie's hand. "Come on, I want to dance."

Lined up on the floor next to Ana, Josie began to do the steps. She laughed as she messed up, but then finally caught on and got the rhythm. Maybe this night would be fun after all.

It was nearly eleven o'clock. This wasn't how Garrett wanted to spend his Friday evening as he walked into the Open Range Bar behind his friend Vance. He could smell sweat and liquor.

Vance had called him earlier and said his friend the bartender, Tony, had phoned him about a party with the Slater sisters and was worried about them driving home.

Garrett glanced around the crowded room and the couples dancing, or cuddled up together at tables. There were still guys lined up three deep at the bar looking hopeful they'd find that special girl, at least for tonight.

He'd never been the type to hang out in places like this.

He'd been married and had a child when he was barely the legal age to drink alcohol.

"You sure they're still here?" He wasn't too upset that he'd get a chance to see Josie. Would she be happy to see him? Would she be with another guy? She'd been keeping her distance at the lodge, making sure she worked in another area.

"Yes. Tony called and he's been watching the party for the past few hours. It seems they've been drinking tequila shots. He wanted to make sure they got home safely. Thanks for helping out, friend. I wasn't sure if I could handle all four of them."

"Not a problem." Garrett was more worried that Josie would be angry that he came to break up the party.

Vance pointed toward the table. "Hey, there they are." He started in that direction, and Garrett followed him.

When the girls spotted him they cheered, and Ana jumped up and threw herself into her future husband's arms. "Vance, you came to my party."

He kissed her. "I hope you don't mind. Garrett and I wanted to make sure you ladies got home all right. It's a long drive back."

"Oh, that's so sweet," Ana said. "But first you have to dance with me." She tugged Vance's hand, leading him onto the floor. Soon Ana was plastered against her man.

Garrett couldn't help but look around for Josie. He soon discovered her on the dance floor with some guy. He stiffened, seeing the man's hand moving lower on her hip. He immediately walked through the crowd. "Excuse me, but would you mind letting go of my...girlfriend?"

The shorter man with the wide-rim Stetson glared back.

Garrett stole a glance at Josie, then back at the guy. "Look, we had a big fight and she left. I went out looking for her to tell her how sorry I was." His gaze locked on hers again. "I'm sorry, darlin'. Will you forgive me for being such a jerk?"

Josie opened her mouth to speak, but instead, Garrett reached for her and planted a kiss on her lips to convince her dance partner of his intentions. When he'd released her—not that he cared—the stranger had disappeared.

"I guess he's gone," he told her, but he couldn't get himself to release her. She felt too good in his arms.

"What are you doing here?" she asked.

The music started up again with the Miranda Lambert song, "Over You." Garrett pulled Josie close and began to move to the slow ballad. The feel of her body against him had him groan in frustration. "Dancing with you."

"No, really, what are you doing here?" she whispered against his ear.

He wondered the same thing himself. "The bartender is a friend of Vance's. So we came to drive you ladies home," he told her as he led her around the dance floor to a secluded corner.

"I can manage getting everyone home," she told him. "And I can handle groping men."

He pulled back and looked in her eyes. "I guess I didn't need to kiss you to get rid of the guy."

"No, you didn't need to do that," she answered weakly, but he saw the desire in those cobalt-blue depths.

"What a shame, that was my favorite part." He placed another sweet kiss against her lips.

She swallowed hard, wanting more. "Garrett…"

Before she could finish, Ana and Vance danced toward them, and Ana said, "Oh, Josie, I'm having so much fun. This is the best bachelorette party I've ever been to."

Vance frowned at Ana. "Since when have you been to any other ones?"

Ana giggled. "I haven't, but this is still the best because

it's mine." She wrapped her arms around Vance's neck. "And you're going to be my husband. Oh, I love you so much." She planted a kiss on her groom.

Vance finally pulled back. "Hey, honey. Why don't I take you home?" He leaned in and whispered something in her ear that had her smiling.

Ana turned to Josie. "We're going home now." She wrapped her arms around her sister. "Thank you so much for the party. It was fun to spend time with you."

"You're very welcome," Josie said. "Don't worry, I'll make sure Clare and Sara get home."

She looked at Garrett. "You can go, too."

He shook his head. "Not on your life, darlin'. I'm you and your ladies' designated driver tonight. You got a problem with that?"

God help her. Josie shook her head and handed him her keys. "Not a single one."

The next morning, Josie slept in later than usual, but felt she'd earned the extra hour. After all, it was Saturday. She went down to the kitchen and had a quiet breakfast while Colt joined her with coffee, but there wasn't any sign of Ana or Vance.

She thought about Garrett and last night. He'd insisted that he drive her car, and then made sure that Sara and Clare had gotten home. During the ride back to the ranch, Josie realized she'd had more to drink than was safe to drive. Although she wouldn't admit it to Garrett, she liked that he'd taken care of her. She just couldn't let herself get too used to having him around, not when their futures were headed in different directions.

She only had to hold on a few more weeks. She needed to make it through Thanksgiving, then soon came the wedding.

Refilling her mug, she headed to the office to work. She knew the safe way to avoid temptation was to avoid Garrett altogether. She might just have a solution to the problem.

Josie walked in, sat down at the desk and dialed Tori for an update on upcoming events.

"Slater Style," her twin answered.

"So we're still in business?"

Tori groaned. "It's crazy here. Do know how many parties are scheduled for the holidays?"

Josie smiled. "Yes, I've been following the bookings Megan sent me, and we've gone over things."

Megan Buckner had been her assistant for over two years. The woman had really stepped up and taken over two jobs. Of course, Josie hadn't planned on being gone from L.A. this long.

"We need more help," Tori said. "I'm not sure I can do these parties myself."

Josie knew she'd put a lot on her sister's shoulders, but she figured there was something else on her mind.

"Tori, Megan has the list of regular employees we hire for big parties. What's really wrong, sis? Did something happen?"

She heard the long sigh. "No, it's not the business. It's just…"

"What? Is it Dane? Is he bothering you?"

There was a long silence.

This wasn't like her twin. "Tori, tell me."

"I have no proof it's him, Josie. I know he's watching me, but as far as I know, he hasn't violated the restraining order. And yes, I called Detective Brandon like you suggested. He said the police's hands are tied, too."

Josie closed her eyes. "I'm sorry, Tori. I shouldn't have left you alone. I called to tell you that I'm getting the next flight to L.A. At least I can take some of the business pressure off you."

There was a pause, then Tori said, "It's great you're coming back, but I don't want you to get involved with my trouble. Dane will just get angrier."

Josie was frustrated. "Fine, but we need to handle this situation, Tori."

"I know. Please, can we talk about something else? I'm worried about the wedding in Santa Barbara. Will you be here in time for that?"

Josie knew how important the Collins/Brimley wedding was to her. Both affluent families, they could bring her future business, or give her a bad name, and Slater Style would be finished. "Yes, I'll be there Friday."

Josie asked to speak with Megan. When her assistant came on the line, it wasn't long before Josie knew everything was under control, but the wedding party's families were concerned about Josie's absence. "Thanks for all your work, Megan. Will you put Tori back on the phone?"

"What do you need, sis?" Tori said.

Josie went over the flight time, then added, "I want you to be careful, Tori. Dane has already proved he can be violent. So don't go out alone at night and set the alarm in the house."

With Tori's promise, Josie said her goodbyes and hung up the phone. That was when she caught Garrett's large figure in the doorway. His sheepskin jacket was open, revealing a fitted Western-cut shirt and jeans over his slim hips and long legs. His cowboy hat in hand.

She ignored her racing pulse. "Garrett, is there something wrong?"

He held up her keys as he walked across the room, his gait slow and deliberate. He'd driven her car home last night, then used the vehicle to get himself back to his place. "And I stopped in to see how you were feeling this morning."

She shook her head, barely able to meet the man's gaze. "You don't have to babysit me." Then she quickly added, "I appreciate you taking me home last night. Thank you."

He smiled and it did things to her. "You're welcome," he told her, but didn't leave.

"Is there something else you need?"

"Just some input on the lodge. I have some countertop samples I need you to look at. Charlie's brought my truck, and the samples are inside."

"What happened with the ones we picked out two weeks ago?"

"They didn't have enough granite slabs to do the entire lodge."

"Okay." She glanced back at the computer screen. "Give me a few minutes. I need to book a flight to L.A. first."

He frowned. "You're leaving?"

She nodded. "Just for the weekend." She continued to scan through the flights. "I've been contracted to do a large wedding, and I need to be there."

Garrett already knew from the conversation it was more. "Is that the only reason?" He sat down on the edge of the large desk. "Is an ex-boyfriend bothering her?"

Josie hesitated, then nodded. "Dane hasn't broken any laws yet, but I'm worried about Tori's peace of mind. It's getting to her."

"My offer is still good. I can call my friend." Why did he keep getting mixed up in her life? "He's a private investigator and might be able to help."

"I appreciate your offer, Garrett, but when I go to L.A. I plan to bring Tori back here. She can work her web design business from here and help me with Ana's wedding." Her fingers worked the keyboard on the webpage.

Just leave, Garrett told himself. *She doesn't want your help.* "Book me a seat, too."

She jerked her head around to look at him. "You? You can't go."

He shrugged. "Why not? Someone's got to watch out for you two."

Her eyes widened. "For one thing, Tori and I have handled things on our own for a long time. Secondly, we're not your problem."

"I'm Vance's friend, and you're his family. Besides, there's a jerk out there who's making your sister's life miserable. What would Ana do if she knew?"

Josie shook her head. "She doesn't need this worry. I can take care of Tori."

His stomach tightened at the thought of some jerk possibly hurting her or her twin. "Josie, I can't just stand by and let someone hurt either you or your sister. What if I'm a deterrent for this guy? Wouldn't my presence help keep him away? Although I wouldn't mind taking a few jabs at him."

He watched her fight with his reasoning. "Okay, say it does, it still doesn't solve the problem."

"Let's just see the situation, then go from there."

"Wait, what about Brody? You can't leave him."

"Brody will be in Bozeman at his grandparents' house. It's a three-day weekend from school. So I'm all yours."

She didn't look convinced.

"This is your sister we're talking about, Josie. We wouldn't want to take any chances with her safety. We'll just tell Tori that I'm helping you with the event."

Those blue eyes bored into his. "This still isn't a good idea."

Hell, he already knew that, but it was too late to stop. He wanted to be with Josie.

* * *

Friday afternoon Josie found herself seated next to Garrett on an early-morning flight to Los Angeles. She'd been grateful he hadn't said much and she was able to get some work done. He'd slept.

When they'd landed at LAX, Garrett got a rental car, and knowing that Tori would be working at home, they drove straight to the town house that she shared with her twin.

Garrett pulled into her parking spot, but Josie hesitated before going inside. "I don't want you grilling Tori. She's been very secretive about her relationship with Dane, and when things turned abusive it made her more ashamed."

"It's not my place to tell her what to do. I only want to help her."

"She probably isn't going to want to share much of her personal life."

Garrett glanced away from the road. "Then you're going to let her think that you trust me, that we're friends again. More than friends."

She glared at him. "Garrett, I don't want to trick Tori into thinking anything like that."

He shook his head. "Look, Josie. This Dane guy seems like a loose cannon. He's already hit Tori, and now he seems to still be hanging around."

Josie knew what he said was true. This could be a dangerous game. "Okay, let's go inside and see how things are, but please don't mention anything about a private investigator."

He nodded. "Okay."

She didn't let go of his arm. "Have I told you how glad I am that you're here?"

He smiled. "You just did."

They got out of the car in an area off Los Feliz Ave.

This was old Los Angeles, where some structures were built in the 1930s. Their home was once an apartment that had been converted into town houses.

The Spanish-style building had original tile and archways, and that had been what drew Josie to the place. And nearly a year ago, Tori moved in with her after her breakup with Dane. She could still see her sister's battered face after he'd used her for a punching bag.

Josie used her key in the door, then immediately called out to Tori.

"Hey, is anyone home?"

In a few seconds, a petite woman came down the hall. Vittoria had glossy black chin-length hair and midnight eyes. Her twin had inherited their mother's Hispanic skin tone.

"Josie!" She picked up speed and soon the sisters were locked into a big embrace. "I'm so glad you're here."

Josie pulled back. "Why? Has something else happened?"

Tori quickly shook her head. "No, I'm fine. I just missed you these last few weeks." Her gaze shifted to Garrett, and she frowned. "Well, I'm surprised to see you here. Hello, Garrett."

"Hello, Tori. It's good to see you again."

Tori didn't smile. "Do you have business in L.A.?"

He glanced at Josie. "No, I just came to help your sister." He put their suitcase down on the tiled floor. "I hear there's a big wedding in Santa Barbara."

Tori placed her hands on her hips. "Okay, someone tell me what's going on here."

Garrett wasn't sure how much he should say. So the truth might be a good start. "Okay, truth is, I wanted to spend some time with Josie. At the ranch everyone has been watching us, and the same in town." He reached out and drew Josie to his side. "So when Josie needed to be in L.A. I offered to come along and help out. We thought if we came here we wouldn't have that pressure."

He felt Josie tense. "I think what Garrett left out is the fact that we aren't officially a couple." She turned those blue eyes toward him, and he suddenly wished for what he couldn't have.

"We're taking things slow," she added, not liking their made-up story.

Tori's dark eyes went back and forth between the two of them. "Yeah, like I believe that. Come on into the kitchen."

Garrett followed but took the chance to look around. The main living space was painted dark beige and had a sectional sofa in crimson. They passed a staircase that led to the second floor. The hall was tiled, but the rest of the floors were a dark hardwood. They walked through an archway into a big kitchen and family room area. The cupboards were painted a glossy cream color with colorful tiled counters.

"Wow, I really like your home. There's so much character."

Josie went straight to the large worktable in the family room with French doors leading to a patio. "That's the reason I bought the place, and it was a good investment at the time. It's been a lot of work." She smiled proudly. "Now that I know how to tape and mud drywall, I can do more remodeling."

"Or you can call your favorite handyman," he told her, and felt the heat spark between them.

"Hey, you two," Tori called.

They turned to Tori. "In case you've forgotten we've got a wedding to put together in two days. Isn't that the reason you came back?"

CHAPTER NINE

EARLY THE NEXT MORNING, there was little traffic on the 101 Freeway, so it had been a pleasant drive up from Los Angeles to Santa Barbara, especially with the springlike temperatures.

Occasionally, Garrett glanced at Josie, seated next to him in the car, but the conversation had been all but nil because she was either on her cell phone or working on her notes for the wedding later today.

Last night they hadn't talked much, either. They'd ordered pizza for dinner and discussed the details of the Santa Barbara wedding trip. Then Josie went up to her room, and Garrett went for a walk. Although the street was busy with traffic, he liked the older neighborhood. It seemed safe enough, but that could be the perfect cover for the ex-boyfriend, Dane. He still didn't feel good about leaving the two sisters alone with a crazy on the loose.

He thought about what Josie said to him a few days ago. "We're not your problem." What if he wanted her to be?

He glanced across the car at Josie. This could all end up badly if he got his heart involved...again.

Garrett shifted in the driver's seat and concentrated on following the white cargo van with Slater Style embossed on the sides as they made their way through the coastal town into the hills and the Collins Family Rose Farm.

It was 7:00 a.m. when they drove up the steep road through the rose-covered hillsides toward a huge white-washed barn. Standing in front was a group of workers, probably waiting for the next set of instructions.

"Good, the crew's here," Josie said more to herself than anyone else. "Looks like the tables and chairs have been delivered. And Mrs. Collins is here, too."

Practically before the car stopped, Josie grabbed her clipboard, was out the door and giving instructions to the crew. Then she took off again toward the older woman.

Garrett had trouble keeping up as he followed her toward the huge barn. He stood in awe of the hundred-year-old two-story structure as Josie talked to the mother of the bride. Using soothing hand motions, Josie assured the woman that nothing would go wrong on her daughter's special day.

"I assure you, Mrs. Collins, we'll have everything set up and ready hours before the first guests arrive for the ceremony."

The attractive older woman shook her head. "We could have had the wedding at a five-star hotel, but no, my daughter had to have it in a barn."

Josie's voice remained calm. "The renovations on this structure came out beautifully. Wait until you see it when I finish decorating the inside."

The mother of the bride didn't look convinced. "Nearly a hundred thousand dollars won't change the fact it's still a barn." She walked away and climbed into a golf cart and rode off toward the large house on the hill.

Garrett offered her an encouraging smile. "She's just nervous about the wedding."

Josie released a long sigh. "Welcome to my world."

He followed Josie inside the barn, but paused and looked around the huge open space. Along with a new concrete floor, a few horse stalls had been rebuilt along one side that would probably never see an animal. The beams overhead were massive and stained a rich walnut color.

Josie gave him a quick rundown on the Collins family history. The rose farm had been owned by them for over a hundred years. And great-granddaughter, Allison, wanted to be married in the barn her great-grandfather had built. "Of course after the renovations, it's perfect for what she wants."

"I think it's a great idea," Garrett said.

Before Josie could answer, her cell phone rang, and she quickly attached her Bluetooth to her ear and listened to her first crisis.

The portable bar collapsed, while workmen scurried around. Garrett got busy using his carpenter skills to get it fixed, then he went to look for Josie to get his next assignment. She directed him to stacks of chairs.

When that task was completed, he walked through the chaos to find Josie with Tori, and they were directing the florist about wrapping the greenery around the trellis that was placed in front of the open barn doors. It was where the ceremony would take place in the late afternoon.

Assured that Josie got her point across, she sent Tori off for another job, then made a call to the bride to remind her of the time for prewedding pictures. And that Megan would be there to help her.

Then she snagged Garrett to help dress the several round tables, adding burnt-orange-colored runners over the white linen. All the chairs had to be covered, too. By the time Garrett tied his last bow, he needed a break and grabbed two bottles of water and handed her one.

He stood next to Josie as they surveyed the area. The tables were now adorned with centerpieces of roses. Greenery had been draped over every stall, and baskets of multicolored flowers were everywhere. There was the sound of crystal and china being set out on long banquet tables. He was amazed how this production was all coming together.

"That was quite a workout," he admitted.

Josie was dressed in jeans and a sweatshirt, and her ponytail was askew. She took a hearty drink. He eyed her long slender neck as her throat worked to swallow. He felt the same familiar stirring he'd always had for her.

Her voice brought him back to the present. "It's the best workout, and you don't even need a gym membership." She glanced at her watch. "We need to get cleaned up. We have a wedding to go to."

Josie had to admit, Garrett had put in a hard morning without any complaint. She hadn't even had time to think about whether his coming this weekend was a good idea or not. She was just glad he'd been here to help out.

Back in the car, Josie directed Garrett to one of the guesthouses on the property that Mrs. Collins had supplied the Slater Style crew. It was more convenient, so they didn't have to keep running up and down the hill to a hotel, especially to shower and change for the event. Catch was, she had to share it with Garrett.

About two hundred yards away from the Collins home and the barn, they found the small house nestled in a group of trees. They parked in the gravel driveway, and Josie used the key as Garrett and Tori brought in the bags.

"Oh, this is nice," Tori said.

Inside, the main room was surprisingly large with an open kitchen that had all the luxuries of home. There were two bedrooms, each with their own bath. Josie and Tori chose the larger of the bedrooms. "Garrett, you can use this one," she said, avoiding any eye contact with him. If things were different maybe… No, she couldn't go back there.

With a nod, he carried his bag into the first room with two single beds.

Tori stared at her twin. "I thought you said you two were a couple?"

"I said we're going slow, too. Besides, this isn't a get-away weekend. I'm working, so today is for my bride." Josie tossed her bag on the bed, hoping she convinced her sister. "Now, do you want to shower first?"

Tori watched her for a moment, as if she would argue the point, but said, "Sure." She picked up her things and walked into the bathroom.

Josie sank down onto the king-size bed. Her sister could read her better than anyone, so she had to know that she and Garrett weren't a couple. She had no idea what they were. Old high school sweethearts? Friends?

Josie shook her head. *The wedding. Think about the wedding.* She wished now she'd changed places with Megan and taken the first bride duty.

Once she heard the shower turn on, she headed to the kitchen, wishing she could have a glass of wine, but that would have to wait until after the festivities.

She passed the living area and stopped short when she saw Garrett. He was bending down, getting something from the refrigerator, giving her a close-up view of his backside, slim hips and taut thighs. Then he stood, and she discovered he was shirtless.

She gasped and he quickly turned around. Oh, boy. His chest was impressive, too. Wide and well-developed and his arms...

"Is something wrong?" he asked.

"No. You...you just startled me. I didn't expect you... to be out here." *Stop rambling,* she told herself. "We don't have much time to get ready."

His gray eyes locked on hers. "Loosen up, Josie. We

have time." He reached out and touched her cheek. "It's going to be perfect. You've done a great job. You have to be proud of this, and the business you've created."

She tried to speak, but her throat grew tight and she swallowed hard to clear it. It didn't help.

"I am proud of you. But I always knew you'd be a success at anything you attempted," he breathed as his head descended toward hers.

Even knowing what was about to happen wasn't wise, she couldn't move away as his mouth brushed over hers. She sucked in needed air, but before she could protest, he pulled back and gave her a smile.

"I should get back to my room before I get us both into trouble." He stepped around her and headed down the hall.

She sagged against the counter and watched the man walk away. The way her thoughts were going, she was already in trouble. Big trouble.

It was midnight, so Josie's job was officially over. The wedding ceremony had gone off with only minor mishaps, including a five-year-old ring bearer who suddenly refused to participate. No amount of bribing would make the boy go down that aisle.

The best man's toast revealed a little too much about the groom's past, and the bride got a little too much cake on her face. Josie leaned against the stall gate next to the dance floor and watched the happy couple grooving to a fast-paced song, and smiled. Okay, she'd done a good job of putting this together, from the bride's spark of an idea to have her wedding on her family's estate.

She thought back to the project at the lodge. Could she put together a few wedding packages to help make it a successful venue and bring in money for the ranch?

"Looks like you can use this," a familiar voice said.

She looked over her shoulder and found Garrett holding two glasses of champagne. She accepted the crystal flute and took a sip of the Napa Valley vintage. Heavenly. She closed her eyes and savored the warm feeling the bubbly liquid gave her.

"You're a lifesaver."

She took a sip as she examined Garrett, dressed in his dark tailored slacks and wine-colored shirt with a dark print tie. Her heart went all aflutter gazing at the handsome man.

"At your service, ma'am."

Garrett leaned against the post on the stall and studied the beautiful woman in a basic black dress. Except there wasn't anything basic about Josie Slater. The knit material draped over her body, subtly showing off her curves. Her hair was swept up on top of her head, revealing her long graceful neck. Diamond studs adorned her sexy earlobes.

"I should have come to your rescue sooner, except I couldn't seem to catch up to you. I don't think anyone could."

"There's always a lot to do at these events. I'm actually off now, but until the bride and groom leave, anything can happen." She checked her watch. "I'm hoping that will be in the next thirty minutes."

The band ended one song and applause broke out in the crowd, then quickly died down when a ballad began, Al Green's "Let's Stay Together." Garrett didn't hesitate as he took the glass from Josie's hand and set it on the railing, then reached for her.

"I can't... I shouldn't, Garrett."

He shook his head as he drew her into his arms. "No one will even see us," he told her as they began to move to the music inside the privacy of the stall.

When he pulled her close, she didn't fight him. He bit

back a groan, feeling her body pressed against him. He could barely move, afraid to disturb the moment. The familiarity of her scent, her touch, churned up so many emotions, emotions he thought had died long ago. He was wrong. So wrong. He'd never gotten over her.

When his thigh brushed Josie's, she drew a breath. He tightened his hold, knowing this moment in time was fleeting for both of them. He knew he shouldn't want this so much. It couldn't last. Soon they had to go back to reality and their different lives. Just seeing her in action today proved that.

Slowly the music faded, but he didn't release her. He closed his eyes, feeling her softness molded to him. They were a perfect fit. Hearing people approach, Josie pulled back, her eyes dark and filled with desire.

"I need to get back to work."

When she started to leave, he reached for her. "Josie..."

She stopped but didn't look at him. "This isn't a good idea, Garrett."

"It felt pretty good a few seconds ago."

Before she could speak, someone called to her. "I can't do this right now, Garrett. I need to get back to work." She pulled away and hurried off.

Garrett walked to the edge of the stall. "This isn't over, Josie."

It was after one in the morning before the caterers finished cleaning up and left the premises. The band had packed up their equipment and driven off thirty minutes earlier.

The newlyweds had a formal send-off just after midnight, and the party finally began to wind down and the rest of the Collins/Brimley families went home, too. Josie pulled the sweater coat tighter around her shoulders to ward off the night's chill. She caught up with Tori and Megan while they finished packing up the Slater Style van.

"Thank you so much," she said and hugged them both. "Everything turned out wonderful."

"Wait until you get my bill," Tori teased, fighting a yawn.

"Then let's go to the cottage so we can get some sleep. Mrs. Collins said we can stay as late tomorrow as we want."

Tori shook her head. "I'm not staying. I'm going back with Megan."

"But the traffic," Josie said, trying to change her decision. She wasn't sure if she could handle Garrett as close as the next bedroom. "And what about Dane?"

"I'm not driving. And I haven't seen Dane in over a week. Besides, I'm going to spend the night with Megan."

"No need to stay with Megan, I'll go back, too. Give me fifteen minutes to pack up." She glanced around for Garrett. "I'm sure Garrett would be willing to drive back."

Tori took her sister's hand. "No, Josie. You stay here." She paused and pulled her away from the others for some privacy. "I've been watching you and Garrett dance around each other all day and this evening in the stall."

Josie released a breath. "That wasn't very smart of me."

"You need some time alone to figure out where to go with those feelings."

Josie knew that was the last thing she needed. Garrett could hurt her again. "I can't get involved with him again."

Tori hugged her. "Dear sister, that's the problem. You've never gotten uninvolved with the man. And if you look closely, he still has feelings for you. Maybe you should find out where it goes."

Josie shook her head. "This isn't a good idea. I can't let him hurt me again."

"How do you know that will happen? It's been nearly ten years. Maybe there's something there to build on, but at the very least you need closure." She kissed her, then started walking toward the van. "I'll see you tomorrow."

Josie watched Tori climb in, and soon they drove off. Her heart pounded in her chest as Garrett walked toward her. Did she really want to get involved with Garrett again?

"It seems we have this knack for getting stranded together." He reached out and cupped her cheek, then leaned down and brushed a kiss over her mouth. She shivered at his touch. Oh, God, she ached for him.

He pulled back. His dark gaze said so much. "Do you want me to take you back to L.A., too?"

Darn the man, he was leaving this up to her. "No, I want to stay here tonight. With you."

Garrett's hand was shaking as he took Josie's and they made their way along the path that led to the small cottage with a single light on the porch. The rush of excitement from being with her was even stronger than all those years ago when he'd first met her. He still cared about her.

He took out the key and inserted it into the lock, then pushed open the door, allowing her to go inside first.

He followed then closed the door, but quickly found himself pushed up against the raised panels with Josie's hands wrapped around his neck. She pulled his head down to meet her hungry mouth and didn't stop there. She went to work on seducing him with her lips, hands and her body.

He broke off the kiss. "I take it you're glad we're staying."

"Don't get cocky, Temple, or I won't let you get to first base, let alone make all your dreams come true tonight."

Well, well! He couldn't help but grin, remembering that first base had been as far as he'd gotten while they'd dated in school. He quickly sobered, and leaned down to whisper in her ear, "I want to make your dreams come true."

His mouth brushed over hers, so gently, so softly she nearly groaned in frustration. She told herself this was crazy, but it felt too good. It always felt good with Garrett.

Josie shivered at his words. "Oh, Garrett," she breathed.

His lips found hers again, and he angled her mouth to deepen the kiss, letting her know how much he wanted her. When he released her, they were both breathing hard. "Let's continue this somewhere we'll be more comfortable." He swung her up in his arms and carried her down the hall into her room.

"Good idea." She kicked off her shoes as they went to her bedroom.

It was dark, only the light from the hall illuminated the room, helping to direct him to the king-size bed. He set her down and kissed her again and again. "I thought you'd appreciate the bigger bed, since my room has singles."

Josie looked around the room. Her sister had straightened up the mess they'd left earlier with the rush to leave for the wedding. She looked back up at the man she'd wanted since the first day she'd met him in high school.

He leaned down and pressed his lips against her ear. "I want you, Josie Slater. More than you could ever imagine, but if you're having second thoughts…"

More like third and fourth, yet she reached out with shaky fingers to unbutton his dress shirt. With her heart beating wildly, she parted the material, and her hands came in contact with his chest. He sucked in a breath. "Only if you want to stop—"

His mouth came down hard on hers. This time slow and deeper, giving her his tongue and feasting on her until she was clinging to him. Her fingers tangled in his hair, holding him close. It left her no doubt what he wanted. The sensations that he created had her pressing against him as his hands worked the zipper at the back of her dress. Soon the soft fabric landed in a heap on the floor. Her pulse danced.

This time he sucked in a breath. "You are gorgeous." He dipped his head and kissed her. No man's touch had ever affected her like this.

"My turn," she said bravely. She pushed his shirt off those wide shoulders, then hungrily ran her fingers through the mat of dark hair that covered his beautiful chest. Next she used her lips to place kisses along his heated skin, causing him to tense.

"I'm not sure how much I can stand." He cupped her face and leaned down and kissed her. "I want you so much, Josie."

She looked into his eyes, seeing his need, his desire for her. "I want you, too, Garrett."

His mouth came down on hers, and true to his promise...he began to make her dreams come true.

CHAPTER TEN

It wasn't even dawn yet, but Garrett was wide-awake. It might have something to do with the woman lying next to him. Last night had been incredible. Loving Josie had been only a dream, and now that dream had become a reality.

He wasn't naive enough to think she would wake up and want to continue what they'd started last night. But he had all morning to try and convince her. Even he wasn't sure how they could solve many of their problems. She had a life here, and she'd told him so many times that she didn't want to give it up. How could she give up a thriving business? He had a business, too, and so much more. There was his ailing father and a son to raise. Brody had to come first.

Josie moved beside him, then she rolled toward him, throwing her arm across his chest. He tensed, feeling her warm flesh against his, stirring him once again. He wanted her even more than he had all those years ago. He made the mistake then of giving up on her. There was no way he would do that again, not easily. Not when he knew Josie still had feelings for him.

He felt her cheek against his shoulder, her breast brushed his chest. Her legs tangled with his, inciting him further. Then her eyelashes fluttered and she finally opened them.

He froze and offered her a smile. "Hi, there."

She smiled back. "Hi, yourself."

She looked a little unsure and started to turn away. He wouldn't let her. Then he leaned down and opening his mouth against her throat, he kissed her, causing her to shiver. He wanted her to understand that whatever was happening, he wanted more than one night.

He raised his head and looked at her. "No hiding, Josie. Not after last night. You have to realize that there's still something between us."

She didn't say anything.

"Can you at least admit to that?"

"Okay, so you rocked my world. That doesn't mean it goes further than last night."

She was so stubborn. "It's not even up for discussion?"

"I thought we agreed that we had separate worlds, and there's no possible way we can combine them."

He felt the constriction in his chest. There had to be a way for them to be together. "I don't want you to walk away again."

She hesitated. Wasn't that a good sign? "Garrett, we talked about this. Our lives are so different…"

"The hell with our lives, what about what we feel?" He placed her hand against his bare chest. "Feel my heart pound, Josie. Only you can make that happen."

Josie had tears in her eyes as she moved his hand and put it against her chest so he could also feel the rapid rhythm. "Ditto."

Garrett rolled her onto her back and captured her mouth in a hungry kiss. He felt her palm against his chest starting to push him away, but not for long. Her arms wrapped around his neck and brought him closer. When her mouth opened on a groan, he pushed his tongue inside, stroking and teasing her. Soon, his hands moved over her body, caressing her warm skin.

"Garrett…"

He looked at her as the morning sun began to slowly illuminate the bedroom. He could see the desire in her eyes and he touched her cheek. He'd never felt such closeness with anyone, only with Josie.

"I love it when you say my name, especially when I'm doing something to please you." He felt like a teenager again. "Tell me what you want, Josie Slater."

She arched her back as his hand cupped her breast. "You. I want you."

"You've always had me, Josie," he said as his mouth captured hers just as a cell phone began to ring. It was Josie's.

She sat up, holding the sheet against her, and reached for her purse on the table next to her side of the bed. She checked the caller ID.

"It's Tori." She punched the button. "Tori, what's wrong?" Garrett watched her expression change to panic. "Get out of there and call the police." Josie nodded as she listened. "Okay, we'll be home as soon as possible." She hung up and looked at Garrett. "Someone broke into my house and trashed the place."

The trip back from Santa Barbara was fast. Josie didn't argue with Garrett about his speed, knowing she only wanted to get to her sister. By the time they pulled up in front of her condo, Josie was out and running to her sister, who was standing on the small lawn.

Josie grabbed Tori close and felt her trembling. "Oh, Tori, I'm so glad you're safe." She shivered. "Thank God you were staying with Megan and not here."

Tori nodded at Garrett then back to her. "I'm so sorry about your house, Josie."

"Why are you sorry? You didn't do any of this."

She saw the tormented look in her twin's eyes. "If I'd only pressed charges against him before…"

"No! That's in the past, Tori. Dane's not going to get off free this time." She glanced around. "Where's Detective Brandon?"

"He's inside," Tori said. "But he wants us to wait out here."

"Too bad." Josie marched up the two steps and through the doorway.

She bit her bottom lip, trying to hold back the emotion as she glanced around the entry. All the work she'd put into her home and some crazy had broken in and destroyed it.

She couldn't hold back a gasp as her gaze roamed toward the living room, where furniture had been turned over, cushions were sliced with a knife and stuffing was scattered all around. Pictures had been destroyed and thrown to the floor. In their place on the walls were spray painted messages. Horrible words.

Garrett cursed. "They'd better have this creep and bully in custody," he said.

Teary-eyed, Tori shook her head. "Detective Brandon said until they find proof that Dane did this, they have to treat it like a random break-in. We're not to touch anything."

Just then Josie saw a uniformed officer coming down the hall. He had on a pair of rubber gloves and was carrying a plastic bag. She fought back her anger that someone was going through her personal things.

"It's going to be okay," she told Tori, but wasn't sure she believed it.

"How can you say that? Look at this place," Tori said, barely holding it together.

Garrett stepped forward. "These are just things, Tori. It's you we're worried about." When Tori nodded, he hugged her. "We'll get to the bottom of this," he promised her.

He turned to Josie and pulled her close, too. She stiffened, hating that she wanted his comforting embrace. In a few weeks Garrett Temple wouldn't be around for her to lean on. He'd be back in Montana and she'd be here. And once again, she'd have to learn to live without him.

Their moment of quiet was interrupted when a middle-aged man dressed in dark slacks and a white shirt and a tie under a nylon jacket that read LAPD walked into the room.

"Miss Slater." Detective Brandon nodded in greeting. "I'm sorry we have to meet again under these circumstances."

She was working to hold on to her composure. "Sorry, doesn't cut it, Detective. You know Dane Buckley is behind this. A random thief doesn't leave personal messages," she told him, and pointed to the wall.

The detective nodded in agreement. "But until we have proof who did this, I can't arrest him or anyone. We are bringing him in for questioning. We're also talking to your neighbors. Maybe they saw him around." He frowned. "We should be finished with photos and fingerprints by the end of the day, so you can call your insurance company and make arrangements to clean and paint the place."

Josie knew that new paint and furniture wouldn't erase this memory. How could she ever feel safe here again?

After exchanging goodbyes, the detective walked out the door, and Garrett followed him, but it was difficult to stay calm.

"Detective, tell me you aren't going to just push this case aside and wait for Buckley to strike again."

He saw the frustration in the man's eyes. "Like I said, we find some proof, and I'll do everything I can to get this predator off the street. If you want to help, I suggest you get both sisters away from here. This guy's message is clear. He wants revenge."

Garrett already knew that. "How would you feel if I bring in some outside help?"

The cop watched him. "As long as you don't interfere with the investigation or do anything illegal, I don't have a problem."

Garrett shook the officer's hand before he walked away. He took out his cell phone, not intending to stand by and let anything happen to Josie or Tori.

He needed someone he could trust. Brad Richards had helped him out before when someone hacked into his business computer system. He punched in the number and after the third ring it was answered. "McNeely Investigations."

"Hey, Brad, it's Garrett Temple."

There was a pause, then the ex-Special Forces soldier said, "What can I do for you, Garrett?"

"I need you to look into someone's past. Someone who preys on women."

"When and where do you need me?"

Two days later, after contacting the insurance company and scheduling the cleanup, Garrett had finally managed to get Tori and Josie on a noon flight back to Montana.

Josie had put on a brave front, but he knew she'd been frightened by this lunatic. He'd hoped that she would lean on him. Instead, she'd done everything she could to avoid coming near him.

She had stayed busy dealing with all the mess, trying to gather up their things to take back to Montana. He'd at least gotten them to move into a hotel, and then their agreement to come back to the ranch until Ana's wedding. There was no way he was going to leave them behind.

He was just happy Josie was returning with him, but his

true wish was that they were still in Santa Barbara. Before her world had suddenly been turned upside down. Before reality invaded and threw yet another obstacle at them. Before she pulled away from him once again.

He drove under the archway to the Lazy S Ranch. The pastures were covered in layers of snow, but the roads had been cleared from the recent snowstorm. "We're almost home," he told them.

"This isn't my home," Tori murmured.

Garrett glanced in the rearview mirror. Tori was looking out the window.

It might not be her home any longer, but as long as Dane was on the loose they were in danger. He prayed both Tori and Josie would stay here for as long as it took for them to be safe again.

"It will be for the next few weeks."

He heard Tori's sigh. "As long as you don't tell anyone what happened, I'll stay."

He didn't like that deal. Everyone needed to be vigilant if a stranger showed up.

"Deal," he said, and looked at Josie. That meant she'd be going back, too. He honestly didn't want her to go. Would she even think about staying in Montana to give them a second chance? By the look of her body language, he had no chance at all.

Garrett pulled into the driveway and saw his dad's truck. He parked, then the front door opened and Brody came running out. He couldn't get out of the car fast enough. The bitter cold air stung his face, but he only saw his son.

"Dad!" The boy launched himself into his waiting arms. "You're home."

"I'm glad I'm back, too." He set his son down and pulled his jacket together to ward off the cold. "Did you have fun with Grandpa and Grandma Kirkwood?"

He nodded. "But I missed you."

Those were wonderful words to hear. "I've missed you, too, son."

Brody's attention went to the passengers. "Josie! You came back, too." He ran to her side of the car and hugged her. "Colt was afraid you might stay in California."

She ruffled the boy's hair. "No, I had to come back so I can get a video game rematch. You promised to teach me how to get to the next level." She directed him to the other side of the car. "Brody, this is my sister, Tori. She's going to be staying for a while."

"Hi, Tori. I can teach you how to play video games if you want."

"Great to meet you, Brody."

Garrett got the suitcases out of the trunk and urged the group toward the house. "Hey, let's take this conversation inside where it's warm."

Brody ran up ahead calling back to the sisters, "Yeah, Kathleen baked a cake."

Josie stopped on the porch and waited as Tori stepped across the threshold and into the entry. She was pretty sure she knew what was going through her sister's head. It was hard not to think about the past years here along with the father who'd ignored them. It had been a cold existence for the four girls growing up here.

Josie looked down the hall and saw Colt walking toward them. His gait was slow and maybe not as steady as it should be, but there'd been improvement since Josie had first come home over three weeks ago.

She watched her sister's reaction. Would she accept the changes in this man? Even Josie had been leery that maybe the cold, distant man would return. Over the past weeks, she'd seen changes in Colt. She was willing to give him a chance to be the father he'd said he wanted to be, but Tori had to make her own decision.

"Vittoria." He came to her and without hesitation reached out and took her hand in his. "I'm so glad you're home."

"Hello, Colt. I'm glad to see you're doing well."

Josie could see how hard it was for her sister to hold back the tears.

"It gets better each time one of my daughters comes home," Colt told her.

She shook her head. "I'm only staying until Ana's wedding." She glanced around. "Speaking of Ana, where is my big sister?"

"She's working at the high school," a familiar male voice answered.

They turned to see Vance coming toward them. "She'll be home soon. Hi, Tori. It's good to see you again."

Tori smiled. "Good to see you, too, Vance. How are you surviving the wedding plans?"

He grinned. "Anything Ana wants. I just hope it happens soon before she realizes I'm not such a great catch."

"Oh, I think Ana knows what a good man you are." Tears welled in her eyes. "And you've always treated her well."

"I love her and wouldn't intentionally do anything to hurt her."

Tori nodded. "Good." She stepped back as another woman hurried in.

"Kathleen," Tori cried as the older woman took her into her welcoming arms.

"Another of my babies came home." She wiped her eyes. "Praise the Lord."

Tori grinned and looked at the older woman. "I can't tell you how much I've missed you."

"I know, child. I always enjoyed your cards and presents." Those kind hazel eyes searched Tori's face. "Your heart is sad. I'm glad you came home."

Even Josie had to wipe away tears.

Tori nodded. "Would anyone mind if I went upstairs and rested?"

"Of course not," everyone chimed in. Tori looked toward the staircase. "Which room?"

"I put your suitcase in your old bedroom," Garrett told her.

Josie felt her cheeks redden and rushed on to explain. "Garrett and Brody stayed during the blizzard two weeks ago."

Tori gave her a knowing smile and walked off with Kathleen.

Josie looked across the entry at Garrett. He turned his gray gaze on her, and she felt that familiar jolt. He was a hard man to resist. She'd already let her defenses drop, but she couldn't let it happen again. She was L.A. bound.

At eleven o'clock the house was quiet, and everyone had settled in for the night. In his room, Colt stood in the darkness by the window. If there was one thing he enjoyed about having to move his bedroom downstairs, it was the view. He could see the entire compound, the corral, the barn. He could keep an eye on the operation.

He looked out at the foreman's cottage and saw the lights go off. He smiled to himself. Ana and Vance were probably heading to bed. His oldest daughter had no qualms about staying with the man she planned to marry. Colt didn't, either. Life was too short to waste; love was too fleeting.

Regrets. Colt closed his eyes against the memories. He had too many regrets to count. The biggest mistake had been turning away from his daughters when they needed him the most. No more.

Three of his four daughters were home now. Not for long, and somehow he needed to prove to them that he was worth the risk. Okay, Ana was happy with Vance, and they would be living close. Josie was a different story. He'd been watching the sparks fly between her and Garrett. He doubted that his girl was going to give the man a second chance easily. But he had hopes that they would work things out.

Then there was Tori. Something bad had happened to her in California. He didn't know what it was, and she didn't trust him enough to tell him. He hated to see the pain in her beautiful dark eyes. He had to help her.

Suddenly, fatigue hit him hard, and Colt closed the window shades and walked to his bed. When would he get his energy back? When would he get his life back? He opened the buttons on his shirt and stripped it off his shoulders and tossed it on the chair. He liked that his arm had regained strength. His therapy with Jay was tough, but it was paying off. He had good muscle tone.

He went for the button fly on his jeans when he caught a familiar scent. Roses. He glanced toward the door and saw a small figure standing there. He blinked once, then again.

"Who is it?" he asked, afraid to know. "Who are you?"

"Colt..." a woman's voice said.

He froze. No. It couldn't be. He felt his heart hammering in his chest as the figure stepped into the dim lamplight. The slender figure was dressed in black. Her hair was long, reaching her shoulders. Although her face was in the shadows, he knew her eyes were almond-shaped and as black as midnight. He forced himself to take a breath. "Lucia..."

CHAPTER ELEVEN

AFTER A RESTLESS NIGHT, Josie slept in later than usual. Tori was already up and gone from the room. Not surprising, since she'd heard her sister tossing around in the other bed most of the night. Not that she'd blamed her for feeling uneasy after the break-in. For now, they were both safe here. But how long could they hide out at the ranch when their lives were in California?

Of course, Montana had Garrett Temple. And now, after his visit to L.A., she knew firsthand how he would never fit into her life, any more than she'd fit into his. No matter how incredible their night together had been, it had to be a onetime thing.

Not that he would ever ask her for more. He had a child to think about. She smiled. Brody was a sweet boy, but his home was here, too.

She sighed. No more dreams about Garrett. She needed to focus on Ana's wedding, and enjoy her remaining time here with her family. She thought about Colt. She'd been surprised how much she liked spending time with him. He'd even taken an interest in her life and her work. The Colt Slater she'd remembered never had time for his daughters.

Could her father change that much?

After showering and dressing, Josie went downstairs to find Ana, Tori and Colt waiting for her in the kitchen.

"Good, you're finally awake," Ana said. "We want to drive out to the lodge. Garrett and Vance are already there finishing up any last-minute details. Also, Colt and Tori haven't seen the place."

"Do you think I have time for some coffee and toast?"

"Of course you do," Kathleen said, filling her cup.

As much as Josie wanted to delay the inevitable, she had to go. After her quick breakfast, they jumped into Colt's pickup and headed out to the river.

Ana chattered most of the way about wedding details. Josie took notes and asked even more questions, trying to concentrate on her job rather than on seeing Garrett again. When Ana pulled up to the construction site, Vance and Garrett's trucks were there, and her heart began to race.

"Good, the guys are already here. I can't wait to see all the finishing touches to the place." She turned to Colt. "Oh, wait until you see it, Tori, Dad. It's beautiful."

They climbed out and helped Colt while he used his cane to get over the plywood walkway toward the wide porch. Josie made more notes about some minor landscaping needs.

Colt stopped and gazed at the two-story log structure. "Land sakes, she's a beauty." He looked overwhelmed. "I'm glad Ana didn't listen to an old man's rantings and got this place built."

Ana grinned. "Actually, the lodge was Josie's idea."

"Well, I give you all the credit for coming up with ideas to help out. I'm so grateful."

They finally reached the front door, and Ana paused and brushed her ebony hair off her shoulders. "It's been a while since I've been here. Vance said he didn't want me to see it until it was completed. Dad, welcome to River's Edge Lodge." She swung open the doors, and the group walked across the threshold.

Ana let out a gasp as her gaze moved around the large open room with the massive floor-to-ceiling river rock fireplace. There were honey-oak hardwood floors and the far wall was all windows, overlooking the river and mountain range.

Tears came to Ana's eyes. "Oh, it's perfect."

"That's good to hear," a familiar man's voice said.

Josie swung around to find Vance and Garrett were right behind her. The handsome men wore tool belts to let the others know they'd been working this morning.

Ana ran to her man. Josie stood in her place, hating the fact she wished she could go to Garrett. Whoa. *He isn't yours to run to.*

"It's perfect," Ana said.

"Then it's worth all the work we put in." Vance looked at Colt. "How do you like it?"

Her father shook his head. "What's not to like?" He glanced at Garrett. "Thank you for all you've done."

"You're welcome, but your future son-in-law and Josie put in a lot of work, too."

Vance turned to Ana. "I know Josie worked really hard, and Garrett also logged in time he didn't bill us for. These two put in a long few weeks to make sure it was finished for our wedding."

Ana looked at her and mouthed, "T+hank you."

Josie didn't want any praise. "Hey, I'm the maid of honor, and besides, we need to get this place rented to start making some money."

"Well, then, let's start booking the place," Ana said.

Tori jumped in. "We'll need to take a few pictures for the website and then we can begin to advertise River's Edge Lodge." She turned to Colt. "Do we have your approval?"

Josie could see the emotion on her father's face. "My approval? But I didn't put in a lick of the work."

Ana stepped forward. "The Lazy S is your ranch, Dad. Vance and I had power of attorney while you were recovering, but you're still the head of this family, and we make decisions together."

Colt nodded as tears filled his eyes. "Let's have a wedding, and then start taking reservations."

Ana clasped her hands together. "I have another question to ask you, Dad." Ana paused a moment. "Would you give me away?"

The room grew silent. Josie glanced at Garrett. He caught her gaze, and she couldn't seem to look away until her father answered, "Oh, Analeigh, I'd be honored." He took her hand. "But I hate to give you away since I just found you."

"I think Vance would be willing to share me with you. And we'll be living practically outside your door in the foreman's house." She glanced at Vance and smiled. "Until we get our new home built this spring."

Colt tapped his cane. "I wish I could do more to contribute to the operation."

Vance patted him on the back. "Come spring, Colt, I have no doubt you'll be back on a horse. Until then we'll help each other because that's what families do."

Colt nodded.

Vance tugged on Ana's arm. "Come on, we want to show you the rest of the place."

Vance and Ana took Tori and Colt up the stairs.

Garrett stayed back watching Josie taking some notes for the wedding beside the big window. She'd been doing her best to keep her distance ever since they returned to Montana. They'd spent four days together while in California, and then yesterday they'd gone their separate ways. He'd found he'd missed her. Lying in bed last night, he couldn't sleep as memories of her flooded his head. He knew these feelings he had for her complicated his life. It would be disastrous if let himself fall in love with her again.

He wasn't listening to common sense when he walked up to her. "How'd you sleep last night?"

She swung around, looking startled. "Oh, fine. I was pretty tired after the flight."

He reached out and touched her cheek. "I miss you, Josie. Being with you in Santa Barbara was incredible."

He watched her eyes darken and knew she'd been just as affected by what happened between them as he was.

She closed her eyes a moment. "It was, but we can't go back there again."

He knew that. He heard the voices upstairs. "Maybe we could go somewhere and talk about that."

Josie shook her head. "Garrett, we had our night. A night that we should have had as teenagers, but we aren't those kids anymore."

Years ago, they'd planned to wait until they were married to have sex. He forced a smile. "We still have feelings for each other."

"I think we always will." She sighed and glanced away. "We have different lives now. I'm going back to L.A., and you're staying here because it's where you belong...with your son."

He felt tightness in his chest as his heart lodged in his throat. He was losing her again. He should be used to her rejection, but it still hurt like hell. "You're right. Brody has to be my main focus." Wanting her had made him forget that. "Then I guess there's nothing more to say."

Josie avoided his gaze. "I guess not." She finally looked at him. "If things were different—"

He raised his hand to stop from hearing her regrets. The familiar ache brought him back to all those years ago. He felt the pain again. "There's no need to explain. It's been over for a lot of years. It's best we stop now before—"

All at once the rest of the group appeared above them along the open staircase and started down the steps.

"We're all going to lunch at the Big Sky Café," Vance announced. "You two want to join us?"

"Sure," Josie said, lacking enthusiasm.

Garrett couldn't be with Josie and keep pretending. He looked at his watch. "I'll have to pass. I need to check on another job in Dillon."

After another round of thanks to him, the Slaters started out the door. Josie was the last to leave. She turned and looked at him. "This is for the best, Garrett. You'll see."

He nodded and she left. "Yeah, we'll always have Santa Barbara." Why wasn't that enough?

It was Thanksgiving morning, and Garrett had to start the celebration by breaking the bad news to his son. They weren't going to the Slaters' today.

"But we were invited," Brody said. "Why can't we go?" The child was close to tears.

"There's been a change in plans, son. They have family home from California and they should spend time together."

Brody jumped up from the kitchen table. "It's not fair. I wanted to be with Josie and Tori. We were going to play video games."

"I'll play games with you."

"I don't want to play with you." The boy glared at him. "What did you do to make Josie mad?"

He was taken aback by Brody's comment. "I didn't do anything."

"Yes, you did. You always made Mom mad."

Whoa, where did that come from? "It wasn't intentional, son. People argue sometimes."

The child didn't look convinced, so Garrett went on to say, "We're not Josie's family, and Josie, Tori and Ana need time with their dad."

"I don't believe you," the boy shouted before he ran from the room.

Garrett started to go after him, but walked to the kitchen window and looked out. They both needed to cool off. It was obvious he and his son had more to work through. Worse, Brody was getting too attached to Josie. When she went back to L.A., he knew his son would be hurt.

"You okay, Garrett?"

He turned to see his father and nodded.

Nolan Temple walked over to him. "Kids say things because they're hurt and disappointed."

"Maybe he's right," he began. "I wasn't the best husband."

"But you were always the best father to that boy," Nolan countered. "He had a rough time with the divorce, then his mother's passing not even a year ago, and the move here. Give him time."

"What if I do it all wrong?"

"Just keep loving that boy." His dad nodded. "But don't let your marriage to Natalie keep you from moving on."

Garrett sighed. He didn't want to think about his ex-wife or their bad years together. "I wasn't the man she needed. As you saw with Brody's attitude, I caused a lot of damage."

"Don't be too quick to take all the blame, son. It takes

two to make a marriage work." Nolan shook his head. "I'm sorry. I won't speak ill of the dead."

His father changed the subject. "When Josie showed up, I was kind of hoping you two would find each other again. You kind of gave Colt and I some hope when you went off to L.A. together."

He'd given himself some hope. Garrett shrugged, not wanting to rehash this. He hoped he'd been able to accept the fact that once again she'd leave and he'd stay here. "And she's returning to L.A."

His father nodded. "Have you asked her to stay?"

Garrett thought back to the wedding in Santa Barbara. He'd seen Josie at work. "She has her business there. I have my work here. We have the ranch and our home, and there's Brody."

"I guess you've thought this out."

"Look, Dad, I'm not that boy she left behind years ago. I have to think of my son. I'm not going to chase after someone who doesn't want me."

"Who said she doesn't want you?"

"She did, okay," he answered a little too loud. "Sorry."

His father reached out and placed a hand on his arm. "It's hard to give you advice, son. From the minute I saw your mother, I fell in love." His father's gaze settled on him. "I don't have any regrets except I didn't have enough time with her. Twenty-five years seems like a lifetime, but it's not. I miss her every day. I wake up missing her, and I go to bed every night missing her."

Garrett had always envied his parents and the affection they showed each other. He smiled. "You two were so loving."

"Josie and her sisters haven't been as lucky with their parents. Colt might be seeing the error of his ways since his stroke, but those girls never had a mother and father who were there for them growing up. It makes trust hard."

Garrett didn't say anything. He knew, outside of Kathleen, Josie and her sisters had been on their own growing up. He recalled the teenage Josie who was afraid of the passion they shared. Then he'd gone away to college and left her behind.

Garrett shook his head. No, he needed to move away from the past. How could he do that when all he wanted was in his past?

Josie never remembered having a Thanksgiving like this. The kitchen was filled with her sisters helping Kathleen prepare the large turkey. Laughing and joking went on all the while they worked on the food prep. It was almost the best Thanksgiving ever. Then she thought about Garrett, knowing he wasn't coming today because of her. It was for the best. In the long run, he would thank her.

Ana walked into the room carrying a large leather album.

"Did you find the silverware?" Josie asked.

Ana held up the book. "No, but look what I found."

Josie and Tori went to the table where Ana laid out the book. Ana sat down, and the twins looked over her shoulder. Her sister gasped as she turned to the first page that showed a young Ana. "That's me!"

Josie smiled as she looked at the toddler in her little cowgirl outfit and bright red boots and hat. "Oh, weren't you cute."

Ana turned to the next page and saw the twins, side by side wrapped in pink blankets. "Gosh, we look so much alike," Tori said. "I don't know who is who."

Ana pointed at the photo. "This is you, Josie, and this one is you, Tori."

They both stared at their older sister. "What? I was there so I know this. Our mother always put Tori on the left side because you, Josie, would fuss if she didn't."

"You always liked being the boss, even back then," Tori said.

Ana turned to the next page and they all froze. There was a large picture of Lucia and Colton Slater staring back at them. "Oh, my, I didn't think Colt kept any of her."

"We can't even say her name?" Tori asked. "It's Lucia."

Josie studied the beautiful woman in the portrait, their mother. She could barely remember the woman with the long black hair that smelled like flowers. She and Tori had only been three years old, and Marissa had been a year old when their mother left the family.

In the picture Ana was standing next to Colt, and the twins were in between them and Lucia held a toddler in her arms. "That's Marissa."

"There are so few baby pictures of her," Ana said.

"Maybe that's the reason she became a photographer," Tori said.

Ana looked at Josie. "Have you talked to her recently?"

"No, I tried before we left L.A. I wanted her to know we'd be out of town. Have you spoken to her?"

"Just once," Ana admitted. "I wanted to make sure she's coming to the wedding, and I hoped she'd come early for Thanksgiving."

Josie thought about all the times she'd called Marissa. San Diego was less than three hours away, but somehow they couldn't seem to get together. "What was her excuse this time?"

"That she has to photograph a big magazine layout. I asked her if she'd do the pictures for my wedding. She's going to try to make it. That's all I can ask." Ana got another dreamy look. "My sisters home. That would be a perfect day."

Not so perfect for Josie, not with having to spend the entire day with Garrett. All she had to do was get through the rehearsal dinner and the wedding before she could cut her ties with Garrett for good. She'd done it before; she could do it again. She just couldn't come back, knowing he'd be here, reminding her of what she couldn't have.

At least she didn't have to see him today, but found she was disappointed that he and Brody weren't coming to Thanksgiving dinner.

There was a knock on the kitchen door, and Ana went to answer it. "Garrett. Oh, good, you've changed your mind about dinner."

He looked upset. "No, but I was hoping I'd find Brody here."

Josie felt a sudden panic. "No, he hasn't been here."

He removed his hat and ran his fingers through his hair. "He was upset with me for changing our dinner plans. He went to his room, but I discovered he took off on his bike. I was hoping he came here."

Josie gasped. "Garrett, we're over two miles from your house."

He shook his head. "Not if you take the shortcut along the river. Since the weather is so mild that road is pretty clear. It's the way I think he'd go." He started off the back stoop and grabbed his horse's reins. "I've got to go find him."

Dear God. Josie began to shake. "Then let's all go looking for him," she said.

Ana picked up the phone and dialed. "Vance is in the barn. I'll have him saddle up some horses."

"Have him saddle a mount for me, too," Josie said. "I'm

going." This man came after her when she'd gotten lost. She had to help him find his son.

Dinner forgotten, the sisters grabbed warm coats and hats, then headed down to the barn. Ana's Blondie was saddled along with Vance's Rusty. Jake had a gentle mare, Molly, ready for Josie.

They had daylight in their favor, but still nightfall came fast in November. They had to find the child because a freeze warning was predicted for tonight.

Temple and Slater land bordered each other, but that left a lot of land to cover.

"My three men are fanned out along the bank on our side," Garrett said. "I thought Brody might show up here since this was where he wanted to come today."

"Is there anywhere else he might go, a special place?" Vance asked.

"I've talked to him about the river and the old cabin. I thought I explained we'd have to wait to go there until spring."

The riders were all given an area to search, and equipped with cell phones. Josie was going with Garrett, whether he wanted her to or not. "We're going to find him, Garrett."

He didn't say anything.

"He's a smart boy," she told him, praying that she was right, realizing how much she cared about the child.

Josie saw the pain on Garrett's face. She wished she could comfort him.

"Too smart for his own good," he blurted out. "Wait until I get..." He didn't finish the thought, just kicked his heels into Pirate's sides and took off.

She rode after him, knowing nothing else mattered but getting the child and his father back together.

An hour had passed, and the homestead cabin had been checked, but was found empty. Garrett was about to go out of his mind. "Dear God, where would he go?"

The wind had picked up, and the daylight was growing dim as clouds moved in.

Garrett looked ahead and side to side, knowing he had to phone the sheriff and get help in the air. Then he saw a shiny object flash in the sunlight. He rode closer and saw Brody's chrome bike just a few yards from the river. "It's his bike."

Josie climbed off her horse and reached for her cell phone to call Vance. "We found the bike, but no Brody." She gave her location as she led her horse along the rocky bank of the wide river behind Garrett.

"He's close by, Garrett. I just know it."

They walked about a quarter mile calling Brody's name. That was when she heard the sound. She stopped Garrett. "I heard him."

Again the sound of Brody's voice. She dropped the horse's reins and took off toward the big tree and found the boy sitting against it. "Brody!" she cried and hurried to him.

Garrett passed her and got to the boy's side and reached for him. "Son, it's okay. We're here."

"It hurts, Dad." The boy was fighting tears. "Really bad. I slipped on that big rock by the river. I couldn't ride my bike home."

Garrett quickly examined his arm, then his shoulder. "It's going to be all right, son. Just hang in there for a few minutes and we'll get you some help."

Josie took Garrett's place next to Brody and took the boy's hand. "It's okay, Brody. Your dad's here. He'll take care of you."

Garrett pulled out his phone and called to have some-

one bring a truck. He looked at Josie, raw emotion showing on his face.

She looked up at him with those big eyes. "He's safe
now, Garrett." She let her own tears fall. "Brody is safe."

CHAPTER TWELVE

THEY LEFT THE emergency room two hours later, after the doctor's diagnosis.

Brody had a hairline clavicle fracture. It wasn't a complete break, so the healing time would be shorter with less chance of losing any movement in his arm. Garrett breathed a sigh of relief.

After his son's arm had been put into a sling to keep his shoulder immobile, they headed back to the Slater house to drop off Josie and get Nolan.

It had been at Brody's insistence that she go along with him. And he was glad she'd been there to calm his son.

It was dark by the time Garrett pulled up, but before anyone got out of the truck, family filed out of the house. Brody was out of the vehicle before he could stop him.

After hugs all round, Ana coaxed them. "Come on, Josie, Garrett. We have Thanksgiving to celebrate."

Josie saw that Garrett wasn't happy as everyone went inside ahead of them. "I know you're still upset about what happened to Brody, but now is not the time."

Garrett shook his head and started to speak, then stopped. He walked back to the truck and turned around. "I could have lost him today. What if we hadn't found him?"

Josie went to him, feeling his pain. "Oh, Garrett, there are so many what-ifs, but what really happened today is your son made a mistake in judgment. But he's safe now, and he's going to be sitting down to Thanksgiving dinner with you."

He turned to her. Even in the darkness, she could see his tears. "This is hard. I'm so angry with him, but all I want to do is hold him close and protect him from all harm. I didn't do that today."

Josie tried to stay back, but she, too, had been terrified of losing Brody. She felt her own tears. "I'm not an expert, but I think you did everything right. You're a wonderful dad, Garrett." She went into his arms and hugged him close. It seemed the most natural thing to do.

Thanksgiving dinner was a joyous event, something that Josie had never experienced in the Slater house. Everyone was seated at the large dining room table, her father at the head and Kathleen at the opposite end. Having the Temple family here added so much more to this day, more than she should allow herself to dream about. Although Nolan, Garrett and Brody had become a part of her life, it wouldn't be for much longer.

She glanced at the eight-year-old boy. Brody didn't seem to mind the discomfort in his shoulder. He was going to have a great story when he returned to class on Monday.

She turned her attention to Garrett, seated across from her. He looked tired, and there were still worry lines on his forehead. Again, she wanted to comfort him, and that was a mistake. Only days ago, they'd decided it was best to stay away from each other. Now look at them—they were acting like one big happy family.

Brody's laughter filled the room. "This is the best Thanksgiving ever," he said.

Garrett disagreed. "You might not think so when you receive your punishment for your stunt today."

The boy looked embarrassed as he glanced around the table. "I'm sorry that I caused so much trouble and spoiled everybody's Thanksgiving." He glanced at his father. "Did I say it right, Dad?"

Josie saw Garrett's pride. "You did it perfect, son. I'm proud of you for taking responsibility."

The boy perked up. "Do I get less punishment now?"

Everyone laughed, and Kathleen stood. "You better come with me, young man, and help me cut some pies. You can put on the whipped cream."

Colt called to the housekeeper. "Kathleen, could you hold off on dessert for about fifteen minutes?"

She nodded and took the boy's hand, and they walked into the kitchen.

Colt looked around the table. "I need to say a little something." He cleared his throat. "First of all, I'm very thankful that my daughters are here, also Vance and my friends—some old." He nodded to Wade. "Some new." He saluted Nolan and Garrett. "I'm not going to sugarcoat how bad things were through those years. If I apologize every day for the rest of my life, it still wouldn't make up for the hurt my daughters have lived through. I'm not going to make excuses... I am just going to say I'm sorry. I love you all, and I hope in time you girls can forgive me."

Josie felt the tears start. She glanced at her twin and saw the same. Vance put his arm around Ana and pulled her close.

"I made a vow when I was in the hospital that if I was given a second chance, I'd do whatever it takes to try and make it up to you girls." He sighed and pulled out an envelope from his pocket. "I need to start with some honesty. This here is a twenty-five-year-old letter...from your mother."

Ana gasped. Josie froze, not wanting to feel anything. She glanced at Tori.

"It was sent along with the divorce papers. At first I was so angry, I nearly threw it away. Then I decided to save it until you girls got older. I honestly forgot about it and just found it the other day."

"Why even tell us about it?" Tori threw out. "Bring up memories about a woman who abandoned us? I don't want to hear anything she had to say."

Garrett felt uncomfortable and started to get up and leave the room, but Colt asked him to stay.

"You'll understand in a minute," Colt told him.

"I opened it because I wanted to protect you all." He glanced at Ana. "The last thing I want is for your mother to hurt you any more than she already has."

Josie didn't want to feel anything for a woman she barely knew. She didn't even care enough about her own children to stick around. "We don't need her letter now. Her leaving us says it all."

Ana gripped Vance's hand. "Do you want us to read the letter? Open all those wounds again?"

Colt glanced around the table. "I blame myself for not showing this to you before. My main reason is, as I told you, I wanted to be honest with you girls. So I'm leaving the decision up to you."

"I don't want to hear her tell us stuff just to ease her conscience," Tori said.

Colt sighed. "Look, I still have no idea why she left. For years I was selfish enough to think it was all about me. I think I was wrong…. So maybe you should read the letter and judge for yourself."

Garrett followed Colt, Vance and the family lawyer, Wade Dickson, into the office. His dad took charge of Brody, and they were watching a video in the Slaters' family room. The sisters disappeared upstairs to discuss the mysterious letter.

Garrett needed to be home with his son tucked into his bed, but he couldn't help thinking about Josie and the letter she had to deal with.

After shutting the door, Colt made his way to the desk chair. "Honestly, I had forgotten about that letter."

"Maybe it should have stayed forgotten," Vance said. "None of the girls need to be reminded their mother left them."

"I know, but let me explain something first." He looked at Vance, then to Garrett. "I trust you two not to say anything to them just yet."

"You're asking a lot," Vance said. "I'm marrying your daughter in less than two weeks. I don't keep anything from her."

Garrett had no idea why he was here. "All we can promise is we'll hear you out, and then decide." He didn't want Josie hurt, either.

Colt nodded. "At first I thought it was the medication." He looked at Vance. "At the hospital after my stroke, someone came into my room late one night. She looked like Lucia."

"It probably was the meds," Vance told him. "They wanted you to rest and heal."

"I thought the same thing," Colt said. "But it happened again when I went into the rehab facility." He hesitated. "And then again when I returned home."

Garrett leaned forward. "Are you saying Lucia was here in this house?"

He nodded. "I'm as sure as I can be that the woman was in my room two nights ago."

"You talked to her?" Vance asked, looking skeptical.

"No, but she spoke to me. She said my name."

"What did you say to her?"

"When I said her name, she smiled. It made me angry, and I told her to get out. I turned around but when I looked again, she was gone."

Garrett wasn't sure what to think. "Do you think she's come back because she wants something? Money? Her daughters?"

Colt shook his head and looked at his friend, Wade. "I don't know. And it wasn't until I started looking at old pictures that I remembered the letter." He shook his head. "I knew I couldn't keep it from the girls. I want to be completely honest with them."

Vance began to pace then asked, "How could she get onto the ranch with no one knowing?"

Colt looked tired. "Hell, I don't know. And since I'm the only one who's seen her, I'm probably just going crazy." He waved a hand. "Maybe you should forget I said anything."

"No," Garrett said. "I think we need to check into it." He turned to Colt. "Do you know where Lucia went all those years ago?"

Colt shook his head. "Even though she was estranged from her family, I assumed she went back to Mexico." He got up and went to the wall safe and used the combination to open it. He pulled out a manila envelope and brought it back and tossed it on the desk. "Here are the divorce papers and the last correspondence we had through our lawyers."

He looked at Garrett. "Do you think your friend the P.I. can find out where Lucia is now?"

Vance put his hand on the papers. "Whoa, we aren't going to spoil Ana's wedding. She deserves her day."

Colt nodded. "Of course she does, and so do you. We can hold off with this until after the holidays."

Garrett nodded. Once again, he was getting involved in Josie's life. "I think the girls should decide if they want to find their mother."

Upstairs, the three sisters sat in Ana's room on the big bed with the letter. It was still in the envelope because a decision couldn't be made about what to do.

"What can she do to us now?" Josie asked. "The woman hasn't been in our lives for years." She glanced at Tori. "Besides, we barely remember her."

"I remember her," Ana said. "I loved her so much, I wanted to die after she left." Her voice was a hoarse whisper. "I never understood why she left and never even said goodbye." She took the letter. "Yes, I want to know what she wrote us. What we did that made her walk away from her family."

Ana got up from the bed and took out a single piece of paper from the yellowing envelope. She took a breath and released it, then read,

"'To my *bambinas,* Analeigh, Josefina, Vittoria and Marissa.

It is so hard to have to say these words to you, but I must. I cannot stay and be your mother any longer. It's not because I don't love you all, it's because I do. So I must leave you for a while. I'm needed back in Mexico to be with my family.

Please, know that I will think about you every day and pray that someday I will be able to return to you. For now, take care of your papa, and never forget me.

I vow, no matter how, I will find my way back to my *niñas.*

Love, Mama'"

Ana swallowed hard. "Oh, God. It sounds as if she didn't want to leave."

Josie wasn't so sure. "What else could she say? And where has she been all these years? Surely, if she wanted to come back, she would have been here before now. I don't want to do this." She got up from the bed and started to walk away.

"Wait, Josie," Ana called.

Josie turned around. "What?"

"Do you want to pursue this?"

"No! I don't know. Can we just wait a little while? I can't face this right now."

Ana nodded and said, "We'll decide after the wedding and the holidays."

All the sisters agreed, and Josie walked out of the room, her emotions in turmoil. She didn't need another rejection. Then a thought struck her. What if she wasn't even alive? Dear, God. What if Lucia Slater had died and she couldn't come back to them?

Trembling, she sank down on the top step, unable to stop the tears. She hated being weak. Her mother never mattered before. Why now? She'd never had her in her life. Why did she want her so badly now?

"Josie…"

She looked up from her perch on the step and saw Garrett. She saw the compassion in his eyes and knew she couldn't hold it together any longer.

"Oh, Garrett," she cried and went into his open arms. "She said she loved us. But she left anyway."

Garrett cupped the back of Josie's head and held her against his shoulder. She was heartbroken, and he couldn't help her. He couldn't stop her pain. "I'm here, Josie. I'll help you through this."

Suddenly, she pulled back and wiped at her tears. "I'm fine."

Garrett felt her pull away, both physically and emotionally. "There's nothing wrong with leaning on someone, Josie. I want to be there for you."

She shook her head. "You'll go away. Everybody always goes away." She got up and hurried down the hall to her bedroom.

Garrett started to go after her, but knew she wasn't ready to listen. "I'm not going anywhere, Josie. Not this time."

He was going to figure out a way for them to be together. He wouldn't lose her again.

Another week had gone by, and Colt had filled his days with his therapy routine so he could be strong enough to walk Ana down the aisle at her wedding.

He felt fatigued as he looked out the window of his room. Had that been the reason for his confusion, for imagining the mystery woman in his room last week?

Was this part of the brain damage from his stroke? All he wanted to do was rebuild a relationship with his daughters, and so far he'd caused more problems. Vance was right. He should have waited until after the ceremony to dredge up the past.

Colt closed his eyes. He hated remembering back to that time. The years of misery without the woman he loved, but there had been years of joy with her, too.

"Oh, Lucia. What have you done? If you were to come back, do you realize the problems you'd create?" Dear God, for a long time after Lucia had left, he would have sold his soul to have her back in his life again.

"I was hoping you'd let me explain," a familiar voice said.

He sucked in a breath and turned around. There was a

small figure standing in the shadow of the doorway. His heart was pounding in his chest.

"Then step out of the dark and tell me who you are and what you want here."

He held his breath as he prayed, but he didn't know what he was praying for until she came into the light.

She moved forward, and the dim light shone on the small, slender woman with inky-black hair as he remembered. Her face... She was still beautiful, with her perfect olive skin and high cheekbones. It was those eyes, ebony in color and so piercing.

He swallowed back the dryness in his throat. "Lucia?" Was she a dream?

"Yes, it's me, Colt. I came back as soon as I could get here."

He blinked several times, but she was still there. Suddenly, he felt his anger build, years' worth of anger. "Well, you're too late," he lied. "Too many years late."

The next week had been a blur of activities preparing for the wedding. When the day finally arrived, Garrett helped his son with his tie. They were both in the wedding party.

They'd spent the past two days decorating the lodge for the wedding, and the rehearsal dinner last night had him already exhausted. Today was going to be the end of it. Would it also be the end of his seeing Josie?

"Dad, do you want to get married again?"

Whoa, where did that come from? "I think I'm going to wait awhile for that, son. I have you and Grandpa, and that's enough for me now."

Brody wrinkled his nose. "But Grandpa says that it's really good to have someone to share stuff with. You know, like when you come home from work and she kisses you and makes supper."

"What are you getting at, son?"

The boy shrugged. "I was just thinking maybe it would be nice to have someone to live with us. Someone who gives hugs and kisses at bedtime. I mean, I know I'm almost too big for that, but having a mom again might be nice."

"But your mother…"

"I miss her, and Grandpa says I always will, but he says there's always more room in our hearts to love people. So can we love Josie?"

Boy, could he. He knelt down in front of his son. "If it were that easy, son, I would have figured out a way by now. Josie lives in California."

"Can't she live here?"

"She does weddings and other special parties. She needs a place like this lodge, but bigger."

Brody's green eyes searched Garrett's face. "Well, that's easy. Can't you build her a really big place for all her parties closer to our house?"

CHAPTER THIRTEEN

THE WINTER WONDERLAND scene was perfect for a December wedding.

At seven o'clock the music cued the wedding party to begin the procession down the River's Edge Lodge's staircase. Fresh garlands intertwined with white ribbon had been strung along the banister. Downstairs in front of the picture window were four pine trees decorated with twinkling lights and at the white arch stood pots of bright red poinsettias.

Josie glanced at Ana, dressed in her beautiful antique-white satin gown. The long veil was the perfect touch to highlight the bride's dark hair, pulled away from her pretty face.

Tori and Josie were dressed in dark green ankle-length dresses. Bridesmaid Tori started her descent down the staircase. The only one missing was their youngest sister, Marissa, who couldn't make it that day.

Josie handed Ana a bouquet of blush-colored roses, then blew a kiss before she made her way down. Immediately, she looked toward the front of the main area where the groom and the best man stood at attention. She smiled at the small group of friends seated on either side of the aisle, but she couldn't take her eyes off Garrett. He looked so handsome in his tux. His dark hair had been cut and styled. Their gazes locked, and she felt a warm tingle all the way to her open-toed heels.

Just make it through today and tomorrow, she thought, knowing she already had her flight booked to leave in two days. And then she could put this all behind her.

Josie arrived at her spot at the end of the aisle. She broke her eye contact with Garrett and smiled at Brody, standing beside his father, then went to her place next to Tori. She stole another glance at Garrett and found him staring at her. The pull was so strong she had to fight to look away. Leaving was getting harder and harder.

The music changed, and Ana appeared at the top of the staircase and walked down alone, then Dad met the bride at the bottom.

Colt Slater drew his eldest daughter into his arms and held her close. Seconds ticked off as the big man blinked away tears and he whispered something to Ana. Finally, he kissed her cheek then offered his arm to her, and together they made their way up the aisle toward her soon-to-be husband.

Once they began to exchange vows, Josie's gaze kept wandering back to Garrett. He was watching her, too. She looked away but felt the heat of his gaze.

Finally, the ceremony was over, and the bride and groom came down the aisle arm in arm. The wedding party was next. Garrett offered Josie his arm and they walked out.

Before he released her, he said, "It was a nice ceremony. You look beautiful, Josie."

"Thank you, but you should be telling the bride that." She loved hearing the words, but it didn't change anything. She was in love with a man she couldn't be with.

Brody rushed up to them. "You look so pretty, Josie. Doesn't she, Dad?"

He winked at her. "Yes, son, she does."

Josie smiled. "Okay, you two flirts, I need to supervise the reception. So I'm off." She headed toward the banquet room past the fireplace. Round tables had been set up, decorated with white linen and multicolored floral centerpieces. At the head of the room was the long bridal party table. She'd be seated with Garrett. She had to blink away the tears. For the last time.

An hour later, the reception was in full swing. Garrett watched as Vance took Ana in his arms and began to move around the small dance floor. Envy tore at him. His friend went after what he wanted, and he'd found the woman of his dreams.

He watched as Vance kissed Ana, then released her as Colt made his way out to the floor. "Father and daughter dance," the DJ announced. Colt took his oldest daughter in his arms and began to move to the song. It was touching to see how far the man had come to repair the relationship with his daughters.

Then the DJ called for the wedding party to join them. Garrett didn't hesitate and escorted Josie onto the floor. He closed his eyes and drew her against him and prayed he'd be able to find the words to keep her with him. He swayed to the soft ballad, then placed a soft kiss against her forehead.

He danced her off to a corner. "Josie...I need to talk to you."

She shook her head. "I can't, Garrett."

He held her close. "Can't you give me five minutes so I can tell you how I feel?"

"Please, Garrett. We've gone over this so many times."

"Then hear me out once more."

Just then the DJ came up to them. "It's time for the maid of honor and best man's toasts."

Josie took off, but Garrett was stopped by his son. "Dad, did you ask her yet?"

His son looked hopeful. "Look, Brody, I don't think this is going to work. Josie is set on going back to L.A."

"You can't let her. Tell her we love her. A lot. And we want to her stay." The boy squeezed his hand. "Don't be afraid, Dad, 'cause she loves us, too. I know she does."

Garrett nodded and watched as Josie took the microphone and began with a childhood story and then talked about how Vance came to the ranch. Josie also spoke about how much she loved her sister and how lucky Vance was to have her in his life.

After the applause, it was Garrett's turn, and he walked to the front of the room. He looked at Vance and Ana and smiled.

"I can't be any happier for the two of you. Of course, there were times, Ana, that this man was going half-crazy because you wouldn't give him the time of day." Everyone laughed. "I told him to be patient because you were worth it." Garrett sighed. "I hope you two know how lucky you are to find each other."

He turned and looked at Josie. "I know because it's hard to find that special person to love." His gaze met hers, and he was determined to make her hear this. "If you do find her, tell her how much you love her. Tell her how your life is so empty without her in it. Because you might not get another chance." He realized the guests were silent.

He raised his glass as Josie left the room. "To Vance and Ana, may your life together be a long and happy one." He took a drink of champagne, and then hugged the bride, then Vance.

"Go after her, Garrett," his friend said. "Don't let her get away this time."

* * *

Josie rushed upstairs into the bedroom they'd used as a dressing room. She paced in front of the window. She couldn't keep doing this. Garrett wanted her. Okay, she wanted him, too, but that didn't mean it would happen.

There was a knock on the door, and Colt peered inside. "If you'd rather be alone, I'll leave."

She fought tears and motioned for him to enter. Without a word she walked into his open arms and let the tears fall.

After a few minutes, he pulled back. "I hate seeing you hurting."

"Some things can't be helped."

"Do you love Garrett?"

"Yes, Dad, I love him. I don't think I ever stopped loving him, but when he found someone else and had a child… It hurt me."

Colt looked serious. "I'm new at this giving advice stuff, and you might not like what I have to say, but here goes. If my memory is correct, about ten years ago you sent Garrett away. And as for finding someone else, I believe that was months later, after Garrett made several attempts to talk to you." Her father's eyes grew tender. "And the man did the right thing and married the mother of his child. Now he's raising his son alone. Brody is a great kid." Colt tipped her chin up. "I take blame in this, too. I made you girls afraid to trust a man to be there because I was never there for you. I'm so sorry, Josie."

She nodded and wiped her tears.

"Just don't let what I did cloud your judgment toward Garrett. He's a good man and he loves you. You know those second chances are pretty sweet. At least give him that chance to tell you what he wants."

She wrapped her arms around this man. It felt so good. "I love you, Dad."

"I love you, too, Josie," he said in a gruff voice. "Now, go find your guy and put him out of his misery."

Could there be a chance for them? She had to find Garrett. Smiling, she opened the door and there stood Brody.

"Josie, please don't leave. Dad and I want you to stay here with us. He can build you a big building and you can do weddings and parties so you don't have to go back to California."

She pulled the boy into a hug, overwhelmed by a rush of feelings. "Oh, Brody, it's going to be okay. I just need to talk to your father."

Her wish came true, and Garrett appeared in the doorway. "I'm right here."

Her heart stopped then began to race. "Garrett…"

Colt slipped out behind her and took Brody's hand. "How about we let Josie and your dad work things out?" The two walked away, and Josie's fear almost had her running after them.

Garrett wasn't sure he could handle another rejection from her, but at least he wasn't going to do it in public. He guided Josie back into the room and closed the door. "I'm going to give it one more shot, then if you don't like what I have to say, I promise I won't bother you again." He prayed he could find the right words. "Josie, from the second I saw you in high school, you had me. We were both young back then, too young to know what we wanted. No, that's not true. I wanted you. I've always wanted you."

Her eyes were big and so blue. He had to glance away so he could concentrate.

"Ten years ago, when I took that job, I'd planned to make enough money that summer to buy you an engagement ring. I'd hoped we could be married and I'd take you back to college with me. I couldn't stand being without you."

A tear slid down her face, and he brushed it away. "I'm sorry." She raised a trembling hand to her mouth.

"When you refused to talk to me I nearly quit work and school to come home, but I needed the job for college credit. Natalie Kirkwood was my boss's daughter, so she was around a lot. The first time I went out with her it was to try and forget you." He glanced away again. "I was hurting so much…it just happened between us. But I'll never regret having Brody. My son is the best of me, and I love him."

"He's a wonderful boy," she whispered.

"I'll always care about Natalie because she's Brody's mom. But our marriage was doomed from the start because I still had feelings for you. I want another chance for us."

She blinked back more tears. "Maybe I should be asking for a second chance. I was the one who pushed you away." She shrugged. "I was afraid, Garrett. I knew you wanted to get married, and I panicked."

"Why didn't you tell me?"

Again she shrugged. "I thought you'd leave me." She gave a tiny laugh. "You left me anyway."

He brushed away the moisture from her cheek. "Like I said, you always had me, Josie." He felt the trembling, but didn't know if it was her or him. "How about we forgive ourselves for the past and start a clean slate?" He took her in his arms. "I love you, Josie Slater. I always have and always will."

"Oh, Garrett, I love you, too."

"I love hearing you say those words again." He dipped his head and covered her mouth in a soft kiss, making him only want more. He took several nibbles, then had to stop. There was so much that needed to be settled between them.

He drew back. "Now we have to find a way to be together. And I don't want a long-distance relationship."

She raised an eyebrow. "Brody said something about you wanting to build a place for my weddings and parties."

He couldn't help but smile. "So my son's been playing my pitchman. I had to talk to him about the future, Josie. We are a package deal."

Josie realized that she wanted Brody in her life as much as his father. "You are so lucky to have that boy. I'm already crazy about him."

Garrett hesitated, then finally said, "I'm asking a lot of you, Josie, to take on an eight-year-old child, my father and me. And if it was just us two, I'd follow you back to L.A. But I can't leave. So I'm offering to help you build a business here. I know Royerton might not be able to handle enough work for an event planner. Maybe Butte, or Bozeman, and I'll build you another lodge, a wedding chapel, a retreat. You name whatever you want, and I'll do what I can to get it for you."

She couldn't believe he was doing all this for her. "You. I want you...and Brody and Nolan in my life."

"God, I love you." He picked her up and swung her around, then finally put her down.

She raised a hand. "I'll still need to travel back and forth to L.A. until I finish out the contracts I've already signed. But I'm ready now to be with the man I love."

"That's music to my ears," he told her, then covered her mouth with his. He nudged her lips with his tongue, and she opened eagerly to welcome him. He finally broke off the kiss. "You are one big distraction."

She was too dazed to react to what happened next. He drew back and lowered to one knee.

"I hadn't planned to do this here, but I'm not about to let you get away again. Josie Slater, I love you with all my heart. Would you do me the honor of being my wife and the mother to my son and all the other children we may have together?"

Tears flowed again. "Oh, Garrett. Yes! Yes, I'll marry you."

He kissed her tenderly, and she melted into his arms, nearly forgetting where they were. That's when she heard the commotion downstairs.

"Oh, gosh, the wedding. We've got to get back."

Josie opened the door and, almost giddy, they rushed along the open railing to the top of the staircase. Looking down, she found the wedding party and guests in front of the picture window. Ana was standing alone with a line of ladies about twenty feet away. "Oh, she's going to toss the bouquet," Josie said.

Ana looked up and spotted them. "Josie you're just in time. Come on down, I'm going to throw my bouquet."

Josie looked at Garrett.

He grinned at her, then he addressed the crowd. "Josie Slater isn't going to be single for very much longer. She's just agreed to marry me."

The crowd cheered as Ana walked to the staircase. "Then this is rightfully yours." Her sister tossed the bouquet toward the balcony. Josie leaned forward and snatched it out of the air.

She blushed as everyone applauded and Garrett pulled her into his arms. "It's too late to back out now."

"No way. I have everything I've always wanted."

She touched her lips to his. She knew she didn't have to give up anything, because this man was what she'd always wanted and so much more.

EPILOGUE

THREE DAYS AFTER Ana and Vance's wedding, Colt was alone for the first time since his stroke. The newlyweds were off on their honeymoon, and Josie and Garrett had flown to L.A. to deal with her business and the town house cleanup. Tori had gone off to visit an old school friend in town, and it was Kathleen's day off.

It was all set. Colt was free to go to his meeting without any questions. Only his friend and lawyer, Wade, knew what had been going on. He had to confide in someone.

"Are you sure you want to do this?" Wade asked as he glanced away from the road leading to Dillon.

"Hell, no, I'm not sure of anything, except I have to see her." He looked at his friend. "I need to hear her reason for why she left."

"What about the girls?" Wade asked.

He felt a little traitorous for not telling his daughters. "I'm not going to tell 'em, yet. Not until Lucia convinces me she doesn't want to claim something that isn't hers."

"I think maybe you should wait until the P.I. has finished checking things out."

Colt sighed. That would be the wise thing, but when it came to Lucia Delgado, he hadn't always acted wisely. "All I'm doing is listening to what she has to say."

Wade stayed silent as they pulled into the chain hotel

parking lot. Colt and Wade got out of the car and walked through the double doors. He looked into the restaurant/ lounge to see it was nearly empty except for a woman seated at a corner booth.

Colt squared his shoulders as his stomach took a tumble. She looked across the room, then stood up. His breath caught. She was dressed in a leather jacket and a black turtleneck sweater with a bright scarf around her slender neck. Even though she was wearing jeans, there was no way this woman wouldn't turn heads.

"Damn..." Wade breathed from behind him. "It's like time has stood still. I'll be at the bar if you need me."

Colt started across the room, careful his steps were sure and true. The last thing he wanted was to fall on his face. He had some pride. He made his way through the empty tables until he stood in front of his ex-wife.

"Lucia." Even at the age of fifty-two, he was slammed in his gut by her beauty.

"Hello, Colt."

Even though he'd expected her, he couldn't believe she was really here. "We should get this over with." He motioned for her to sit, then he slid into the booth across from her.

Although it was dim in the room, he stared into those incredible dark eyes. "It's been a long time, Lucia."

Not counting the night she'd come into his room. Then she'd called him yesterday and asked to meet with him.

"Yes, it has." Her voice was soft and throaty.

He felt as shaky as a teenager. "Okay, I agreed to talk to you, so we should get started." The waitress appeared and he ordered some coffee. He wanted something stronger, but knew that wasn't wise. He needed a clear head.

The waitress came back with two coffee cups and a

cream pitcher. Lucia looked surprised when he pushed the creamer toward her.

"You remember how I like my coffee." The words came out in a soft voice.

"I remember a lot of things. The sound of your voice as you read stories to our babies. How you cuddled them in your arms, how you loved them."

He drew a breath and worked hard to release it. "I also remember the way it felt to make love to you, to hear your gasps of pleasure." He watched her eyes widen, her face flush. "I also remember you saying you loved me, that you loved the girls. Then the next day you disappeared from our lives."

She stayed silent for a long time, and then said, "I had no choice, Colton."

"There's always a choice, Lucia. You chose to leave your family...your *bambinas,* your *marido.*" *Husband.*

She shook her head. "You have to believe me, *mi amor.*"

"No! You can't call me your love. The woman I married, the woman I loved would never leave me. I don't know who you are."

Lucia stiffened and pulled back. So she still had a temper. "I never wanted to leave my family, *mi corazon.*" *My heart.* There was a fierce look in her ebony eyes, and his body betrayed him as he reacted to her.

"And you were my heart, too, Lucia. I gave you everything, but you left anyway."

"You don't understand," she insisted. "I gave up my *familia* to keep you from harm."

He frowned. "You're saying that someone wanted to harm us?"

He saw her hands shake as she nodded.

"Who was this person?"

"Vicente Santoya... My husband."

Her declaration was like a knife to his heart. Of course, she'd been with other men. Was Santoya the reason she'd left him?

"I don't want to hear about your lovers." He was unable to keep the anger out of his voice. "I've made a life without you. So you can just go back to him." Hell, he didn't need this. He'd learned to live without her before—he could do it again. He started to get out of the booth. Then she placed her hand on his and stopped him.

"*Por favor,* Colt! I can't go back there. It took me too long to get out. Vicente is dead. So I've broken most of my ties there. So I can safely come back…to you."

He didn't want to hear about her marriage. "What about your father?" Cesar Delgado never wanted his only child to marry an American, especially a broken-down, ex-rodeo cowboy. How did he feel about her return to Montana?

Lucia straightened and looked him in the eye. "My parents are gone. My ties and loyalty are only to this country. So please, I ask that you hear what I have to say before you send me away."

He wasn't going to be fooled again. Lucia had made a life for herself without him. "I don't see how anything that you have to say will change my mind."

She looked nervous, almost panicky. "What if it concerns your sons?"

He shook his head. "I don't have sons."

Lucia nodded. "Yes, you do. I was pregnant with twin boys when I left you."

Five days later, a happy Garrett and Josie arrived back in Montana. The only reason she'd wanted to stay in L.A. a little longer was because Josie had liked having her man all to herself. Still, she knew they needed to get back. She had a wedding to plan.

She was also able to start her life in Montana because she had a great assistant. That was why she'd offered Megan Buckner a partnership in the business. Megan had eagerly accepted the deal. So Josie would be able to wean herself from her L.A. projects and not cancel a single event.

Garrett reached across the seat and took her hand as he drove down the road. "Would you mind if we made a quick stop in town first?"

"Not a problem, but I want to be at the house so we can meet Brody's bus."

"I thought we could pick him up at school after I show you something."

She smiled. "I like that idea better." She was so anxious to see the child. She couldn't believe how easily she'd fallen in love with the eight-year-old boy. Of course all the Temple men were very appealing.

At the end of Main Street, Garrett turned into the driveway of a three-story Victorian house. The huge structure showed years of neglect with faded and peeling paint, and the wraparound porch needed a railing at the very least.

"Isn't this Mrs. Anderson's house?"

Garrett put the truck into Park and shut off the engine. "Yes, but she died last year and her daughter inherited it. She wants to sell the place." He rubbed his hand along the back of his neck. "I thought with a little rehab and TLC it would make a great office for Slater Style and maybe even a place to hold some small events. The large backyard could be landscaped for weddings."

Josie was suddenly excited. "I want to go see it." She jumped out of the car and rushed to the door. She tried the knob but it was locked.

"Hold on." Garrett came after her, put a key into the lock and got it open. "Now, don't get too excited," he warned. "It needs some work."

She kissed him. "I'm going to love it, but not as much as I love you for doing this," she said as she walked inside.

The entry was huge, with a crystal chandelier hanging from the high ceiling. The staircase was a work of art, with a hand-carved banister that ran up to the second floor, and stained-glass windows above the landing.

There were raised-panel pocket doors that could close off the three large rooms downstairs. The hardwood floors needed refinishing, but there would soon be a contractor in the family.

She was a little giddy as she walked down the hall to a kitchen that was in really bad condition.

Garrett came up behind her. "This needs a gut job, honey. But we can make it look like the era of the home. Anything you want."

"You're spoiling me."

"Get used to it." He turned her around and lowered his mouth to hers for a kiss that was slow and easy. The result had her breathless.

"I plan to make sure you're happy working here."

"I have you and Brody in my life, and that makes everything just about perfect."

She brushed another kiss on his tempting mouth, then went to check every nook and cranny of the area, which included a large pantry and sunroom off the kitchen. Then she opened the back door into a yard that seemed to go on forever. A high fence circled the property and there was a gazebo toward the back.

"Oh, Garrett, it's lovely."

Garrett came up behind her and wrapped his arms around her to ward off the winter cold. "I'm glad you like it. You've had to make all the sacrifices, Josie. So I wanted you to have this house." He loved her so much. "Your career is important."

She smiled at him, and his heart raced. "Being with you and Brody doesn't feel like a sacrifice to me. And I get to be around my family, too. Ana and Dad." She shook her head. "Can you believe I'm calling Colt, Dad?"

"You have to give him credit, Josie. He's trying hard with you girls."

"I know." She shook her head. "Now, if I can convince Tori to stay around for a while." She frowned. "At least until we're sure that Dane is out of her life."

"Richards is working on that. Until then, I promise I'll do everything possible to keep her here and keep her safe."

She smiled. "I love you so much, Garrett Temple. I can't wait to start our life together."

He pulled her into his arms. He wanted that to happen very soon. "About that. I was wondering when that special day is going to take place. I'm not happy about you still living in your dad's house."

They'd both decided because Brody was at an impressionable age, that they wouldn't live together until after the wedding.

"How soon can you get the renovations done here?" she asked.

"That depends on what you want done."

"The downstairs. The floors refinished and some new paint."

"A few weeks, maybe a month with a new kitchen. The crew can start renovations right after Christmas."

She sighed. "Christmas is only ten days away. I've always hated the holiday…." She glanced up at him. "Until now. Now, I get you, Brody and my family."

"I'm gonna make it special for you," he told her. "We'll start some good memories."

Josie held up her hand to inspect the diamond solitaire engagement ring he'd bought her in Los Angeles. "Oh, I do believe you've already made everything very special." She glanced back at the yard. "So how do you feel about having the wedding right here?"

Garrett arched an eyebrow. "Outside?"

"Oh, I'd love that. A garden wedding, but even I don't want to wait that long. How about Valentine's Day in the front parlor?"

"If that's what you want, I'll work day and night to get this place ready." He grinned. "And it will be great advertising for future weddings at Slater Manor."

Josie had trouble holding on to her emotions. "Slater Manor..." She repeated the name over in her head. "I like that, but how about Temple Manor?"

He shook his head. "No, Josie. You've worked hard to build a name with Slater Style. Slater Manor makes good business sense." He smiled. "I still want you to take my name for everything else."

"I've waited a long time for you, Garrett Temple. So only in business will I use Slater." She swallowed hard. She bravely went on, hoping he wanted the same thing. "And while you're doing the renovations, could you make a nursery upstairs?"

This time she watched him swallow hard. "A nursery? A baby nursery?"

She nodded. "So I can work and keep our babies with me."

"I would love that. But not as much as making a child with you," he whispered as he placed kisses along her jaw to her ear, finally reaching her mouth. The kiss was hungry, letting her know he desired her. When he released her, she could see he'd been as affected as she was.

"God, we're so lucky, Josie. We got a second chance." He cupped her face. "There's never been anyone I've loved as much as you. There's no one else I want to spend the rest of my life with."

She smiled. "Then it's a good thing you don't have to, because I'm not leaving you ever again."

"And this time, I'd just follow you, because you are my heart." He kissed her again, holding her close.

Josie held on, too. She'd stopped running away. She'd found everything right here. She would never feel alone again.

* * * * *

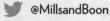

MILLS & BOON

THE HEART OF ROMANCE

A ROMANCE FOR EVERY KIND OF READER

MODERN

Prepare to be swept off your feet by sophisticated, sexy and seductive heroes, in some of the world's most glamourous and romantic locations, where power and passion collide.
8 stories per month.

HISTORICAL

Escape with historical heroes from time gone by. Whether your passion is for wicked Regency Rakes, muscled Vikings or rugged Highlanders, awaken the romance of the past.
6 stories per month.

MEDICAL

Set your pulse racing with dedicated, delectable doctors in the high-pressure world of medicine, where emotions run high and passion, comfort and love are the best medicine.
6 stories per month.

True Love

Celebrate true love with tender stories of heartfelt romance, fro the rush of falling in love to the joy a new baby can bring, and a focus on the emotional heart of a relationship.
8 stories per month.

Desire

Indulge in secrets and scandal, intense drama and plenty of sizz hot action with powerful and passionate heroes who have it all: wealth, status, good looks…everything but the right woman.
6 stories per month.

HEROES

Experience all the excitement of a gripping thriller, with an inte romance at its heart. Resourceful, true-to-life women and strong fearless men face danger and desire - a killer combination!
8 stories per month.

DARE

Sensual love stories featuring smart, sassy heroines you'd want as best friend, and compelling intense heroes who are worthy of th
4 stories per month.

To see which titles are coming soon, please visit

millsandboon.co.uk/nextmonth

JOIN US ON SOCIAL MEDIA!

Stay up to date with our latest releases, author news and gossip, special offers and discounts, and all the behind-the-scenes action from Mills & Boon...

 millsandboon

 millsandboonuk

 millsandboon

It might just be true love...